BONE
ON BONE

BONE
ON BONE

JULIA KELLER

MINOTAUR BOOKS ✳ NEW YORK

BONE ON BONE. Copyright © 2018 by Julia Keller. All rights reserved. Printed in the United States of America. For information, address St. Martin's Press, 175 Fifth Avenue, New York, N.Y. 10010.

www.minotaurbooks.com

Designed by Omar Chapa

The Library of Congress Cataloging-in-Publication Data is available upon request.

ISBN 978-1-250-19092-5 (hardcover)
ISBN 978-1-250-19094-9 (ebook)

Our books may be purchased in bulk for promotional, educational, or business use. Please contact your local bookseller or the Macmillan Corporate and Premium Sales Department at 1-800-221-7945, extension 5442, or by email at MacmillanSpecialMarkets@macmillan.com.

First Edition: August 2018

10 9 8 7 6 5 4 3 2 1

To Carolyn Focht

Acknowledgments

I am passionately and everlastingly grateful to the friends and family members who have been along for the ride, across seven Bell Elkins novels and innumerable conversations about crime, punishment, life, death, human destiny, and the mysterious allure of the sour cream doughnut: Susan Phillips, Catherine Dougherty, Lisa Keller, Colleen Sosa, Marja Mills, Patrick Reardon, Joseph Hallinan, Holly Bryant, Ron Rhoden, Jean Thompson, and Edward Crawford Keller.

A special nod of thanks is owed to Brenda Kilianski for the trip to Fort Lauderdale to track down the ghost of the great John D. MacDonald. And a warm shout-out goes to Linda Kass, owner of Gramercy Books, as well as to the coaches at OTF who keep me (reasonably) sane and (to stretch a point as well as a hamstring) somewhat fit, despite my foolhardy affinity for the aforementioned doughnut: Martha, Lamara, Brei, Eugene, and Claire.

Once again, I am indebted to Kelley Ragland for her fine editorial hand, and to Lisa Gallagher for her patience, guidance, and friendship.

Do you ever think how death may be? I do. I think of it as dusky and cool, a room with a door open to the outside, and a soft wind coming in as cool as if it blew off the stars. In the doorway, which faces away—in these visions I am never looking back—may at any moment appear the faces that one has wholly loved, and the dear voices that one remembers will be saying softly, like a blessing, We love you, we forgive you.

—WALLACE STEGNER, *Angle of Repose*

BONE
ON BONE

PART ONE

Chapter One

"'Belfa.' Is that right? Unusual name."

Bell nodded. She'd been fielding that inquiry or a version thereof her entire life. It used to rile her when she was a kid—*Yeah, granted, it's not Jane or Sue or Mary, but maybe you could just shut up about it*—because, really, why should she give a damn what anybody else thought about her name?

She'd let go of that anger a long time ago. After all, it *was* unusual. People often mistook it for "Belva." Or, if a new teacher back in Acker's Gap High School had been calling the roll and thought it was a typo, she'd ask Bell how to spell it.

B-E-L-F-A.

B-E-L-F-A? With an F?

Yeah. B-E-L-F-A. With an F. F as in—

Bell would stop herself just in time. Good way to get expelled.

So, yes. Her name was a hassle. No wonder her sister Shirley had started calling her Bell when she was barely two years old.

She shoved the thought of Shirley out of her head. She didn't have time for that today. Her life was about to change—again—in a very big way, and she needed to focus.

"Some kinda family name?" the man asked. Unwilling to let it go.

Bell nodded again, even though she didn't really know. There was nobody to ask. Her mother had died when she was an infant and her father . . . well, he wasn't the kind of man you questioned. About anything. Unless you wanted a punch in the face.

The state official shrugged. His eyes dropped back to the document, which he was filling out with a blue Bic pen. He was right-handed. With his other hand, he anchored the paper to the desk while he wrote. His desk faced the wall.

Other than the man's breathing, the only sound in the room was the occasional swish of paper-shuffling when he shifted from one page to another page, checking something, and then returned to the original page.

His name was Clifford A. Spalding. Bell knew that not because he'd introduced himself—he hadn't—but because he had signed it on the required line at the bottom of each page.

She sat in a gray metal chair next to the left side of the desk. Her hands were folded in her lap. During a previous visit to this office last week—she was meeting with another bureaucrat that time, not this man—she had automatically perched her left forearm along the edge of the desktop, the same as anyone might do when a chair was angled sideways to a desk.

Instantly, the woman had told her to take her arm off the desk.

Bell, startled, had tried to explain that she wasn't trying to—

"Right now."

Okay, so she wouldn't be making *that* mistake again. She kept her arm off the desk today. Feet flat on the floor. She would only speak when spoken to.

The office was bland, cramped, and beige, slapped together with cheap paneling and thin carpet and shoddy furniture. The drop ceiling was marked with yellow-brown stains; in certain spots, mysterious, pimple-like bulges hinted of backed-up water from roof leaks. There was a stubborn smell of warm plastic and old aftershave, with a yeasty tang of secret mold.

It was depressingly similar to all of the other state offices to which Bell had been summoned over the past month, as her community service neared its end and the amount of pre-release paperwork escalated.

Freedom was now within sight. Yet the prospect of that freedom didn't make her excited or relieved or even especially happy.

It made her edgy. Apprehensive.

Spalding moved in his chair. He was a middle-aged, skinny-legged man with a soccer-ball paunch and a bald head that looked like a greasy peeled egg under the too-bright fluorescent lights. The skin on his fore-arms—he wore a short-sleeved, blue-plaid shirt—was the color of marga-rine, and included a string of tan blotches that would, Bell surmised, warm the heart of a dermatologist who'd been pricing sailboats.

He kept his eyes mostly on the form. But when he did look at her, there was, she thought, little to cause his gaze to linger. She was a forty-nine-year-old woman with gray, hooded eyes' and an expressionless face. Her brownish-blond hair was long, falling well past her shoulders; it was longer, in fact, than it had been since she was a teenager. She'd had nowhere to get a decent haircut and so she just let it grow. She was heavier, too, than she had ever been before in her life, owing to the food in the prison cafeteria, the preponderance of starchy carbs. If she never saw a potato again, it would be too soon.

Even now that she was living in her own home again, as she fin-ished up the community-service portion of her sentence, she still hadn't gotten back into a routine of healthy eating. Hard to make herself care.

"You'll be getting a packet with the basic information you need to know," Spalding said. "There'll be a phone number. And a website. Any questions, anything you're not clear about, you call that number. Or go to the website. Always have your ID number handy. Okay?"

"Okay."

"Good." He checked another box on the form.

He was treating her with the indifference that she had come to ex-pect from all state officials over the past three years, from guards to cooks to custodians to employment counselors. She was a number, not a person.

That didn't bother her. In fact, it was a comfort. Being treated as special was not a kindness. It always carried a price tag. Anonymity was armor.

"Okay," Spalding said. "So you're almost done with your commu-nity service. Says here you've got five more days at Evening Street Clinic."

"Nights."

"What?"

"Five more nights. I work the night shift."

That got a reaction. He lifted his eyes from the paper and looked at her. He didn't like to be corrected. "Nights. Whatever." Back to the document. "The point is, I need to inform you that you're eligible for employment assistance from the state if you qualify and if you fill out the—"

"I'm fine. I have tons of support from lots of family members." That part wasn't true. "And financial means." That part was. She had always lived frugally, and her ex-husband had kept an eye on her mutual fund and her 401(k) while she was away. She wasn't wealthy, but compared to most women leaving prison, she was, Bell knew, practically Oprah-rich.

"Okay, fine," Spalding said. Still looking at the paper. "Moving on. I know you've already heard all this, but it says here that I've got to go over it again and then have you sign a form that says you acknowledge that you received the information. Okay?"

"Okay."

"You'll be required to check in with your parole officer at a time and place designated by the PO. You're responsible for your own transportation to and from said meetings. You won't be reimbursed—so don't ask. If you're caught with a firearm you're subject to immediate arrest. And you can count on random drug tests, okay? Not that drugs had anything to do with your offense—it's just policy."

"Okay. I'm not complaining."

When he looked at her this time, it wasn't out of annoyance. It was curiosity. She saw it in his eyes: the hunger to know more. His mouth twitched.

"You don't do that, do you?" he asked. The pen hovered over the paper, and he moved it in a small clockwise circle. "There's nothing in here about any sort of complaint. You didn't bitch about anything. In three years. That's pretty rare."

She shrugged. "Just wanted to get along. Let the time pass." She was keenly regretting the fact that she had said anything beyond "Okay." She'd interrupted his rhythm, causing him to give her an extra bit of scrutiny.

He was looking at the document again, but she wasn't off the hook and she knew it. This time, his eyes didn't automatically sweep over the long paragraph in the middle of the second page, the single-spaced summary of her life—her offense, her sentence, her background. Her story was unusual. Unusual got you noticed. She didn't want to be noticed.

Dammit.

Had she kept her mouth shut, he'd probably be finished with his spiel by now and would be signing the bottom of the last page of the form, crafting the letters that spelled *Clifford A. Spalding* and doing it with the same bold, dramatic flourish she'd spotted on previous pages. A lot of bureaucrats—this was her pet theory—channeled all of their thwarted individuality and their tamped-down creativity into the way they signed their names. The signatures on the various forms that defined her life now were a veritable art show, a one-dimensional aerobatic circus of loops and swirls and spirals.

Too late. She wasn't just a number anymore to Clifford A. Spalding. She watched his face as he read—*really* read this time, not just skimmed—her file. There it was again: the mouth twitch. He was intrigued.

Intrigued wasn't good. Intrigued meant hassle.

"Says here you used to be a county prosecutor," he said.

"Yeah."

He offered her a small, tidy smile. It might have been a smirk. She didn't know Clifford A. Spalding well enough to know if he was the smirking type. "Not something we see every day around here," he said.

She shook her head. "No. I guess not."

At first, of course, she'd expected to be recognized everywhere. By everyone. She thought the whole world knew her story. She had braced herself for celebrity, for a bobbing knot of reporters outside the courthouse and at the entrance to the prison. Video cameras. Shouted questions.

And initially, right after her sentencing, there *had* been a brief squall of press coverage. She had refused comment but that was irrelevant. In a two-paragraph story, a *USA Today* writer referred to her ten-year-old self as a "pint-sized patricide." A snippet in a news roundup in *The Washington Post* included a quote from one of her classmates from Georgetown Law. It was a neutral observation, something about how quiet Bell Elkins had been back then, quiet and smart, but still she wished her classmate had kept his mouth shut. She barely remembered him. She was convinced he didn't really remember her, either. Just wanted his name in the paper. MSNBC made her the lead story on a thirty-second newsbreak. They'd dug up a photo from her undergraduate days, a black-and-white headshot from the West Virginia Wesleyan yearbook. She had forgotten how long her hair was back then. Almost as long as it was now.

But that was the extent of the ripple she'd made. The world, it turned out, didn't much care about Belfa Elkins, no matter how terrible her crime. Or how unusual the circumstances.

Three years ago, she had resigned from her job as prosecuting attorney of Raythune County, West Virginia, and pleaded guilty to murder. Bell declared that it was her, and not her older sister, Shirley, who had killed their father, Donnie Dolan, thirty-nine years ago. She had rejected every mitigating circumstance offered to her by the court—her age at the time of the crime; her sister's claim that Bell had blocked out any recollection of cutting their father's throat while he slept; the fact that Donnie Dolan was abusing them repeatedly, physically and emotionally.

Bell had been adamant with the judge: She deserved punishment. It wasn't just the murder, she argued. Because she didn't remember what she'd done, she had let her sister take the blame. She had let her sister spend the majority of her adult life in prison.

Deliberate or not, Bell had taken Shirley's place in the world. That was her point. She had flourished, prospered, while Shirley sat in a prison cell.

The judge reluctantly went along with her request. Bell served her time in the women's minimum-security prison in Alderson, West Virginia. She had been released eight weeks ago to do her community service at Evening Street Clinic.

Now that, too, was coming to an end.

By Friday she'd be a free woman.

"Because you're almost done," Spalding was saying, "we've had some media requests to interview you. I'm obligated to pass 'em along."

"Do I have to respond?"

"Nope."

"Then put down 'No response.' I'm not interested."

"Gotcha." Spalding checked a box on the third page of the document. "We don't give out any information on your whereabouts, so if somebody finds you, that's not on us," he added. He licked an index finger and riffled twice through all four pages—one, two, three, four—to make sure he had signed and dated each page.

He looked up at her. "Mind a question?" he asked.

Here it comes. She knew what he was going to ask. It was the same question everyone asked.

She shrugged. Of course she minded. But "no" was a luxury she couldn't afford right now. He still had power over her.

"What're you gonna do?" he asked. "You can't be a prosecutor again, am I right? Or practice law?"

A nice surprise. Not the question she'd anticipated.

"Correct." Her conviction had triggered mandatory disbarment. "Honestly, I haven't thought that far down the road."

Not true. She knew what she was going to do, at least initially. She'd figured it out during those endless nights in Alderson, when she read every news report she could get her hands on.

But that was none of Clifford A. Spalding's business.

He didn't say anything, and so she started to stand up. Surely their session was over now.

Wishful thinking.

"Also," he said, "I wondered about something else, too."

Her heart sank. She'd almost gotten away clean.

"I don't get it," he went on. "Based on what it says here, why'd you serve time? Jesus—you were ten years old when you did it. Sure, you let your sister take the blame. But that wasn't your fault. She wanted to, according to the statement. She told you she'd done it and you believed her. And besides, your old man was messing with you, right? The both of you? In my book, that made it pretty darn justifiable. So—why?"

And there it was. The question she had expected to be asked. The one she knew she'd face over and over again, slung her way by just about everybody. Once she was out, once she was fully back in the world, the question would clang as reliably as a church bell on Sunday mornings:

Why?

She'd been auditioning answers in her mind for months now, as her final release date approached. Trying them out to see how they felt when she said them. "None of your damned business" was her first instinct, but she'd rejected that one as maybe a little too combative. "It's complicated" was a possibility, but that sounded coy, as if she were inviting speculation, daring people to keep on guessing.

Finally she had settled on the answer she offered right now to Clifford A. Spalding. She knew it was a lie, she knew it was lame and weak, she realized she'd have to come up with a better one—without, of course, ever revealing the truth—and she would have to do that soon.

But for now, as a short-term solution, as something that would get her out of this place and on the road toward what might pass for a life, it would have to do:

"I don't know."

Chapter Two

This room belongs to me, Ellie thought.

It was hers. All hers.

There was no lock on the door. No KEEP OUT—OR ELSE sign like the one her brother Henry had taped to his bedroom door when they were kids, complete with a crudely drawn skull and crooked crossbones.

No, there was nothing like that.

So nothing really stopped anyone in the house from climbing the steep wooden steps from the second-floor hallway and opening the door and coming into the attic room when Ellie wasn't here. But why would they do that?

It was the very lack of locks or warnings that probably kept the room safe. Ordinariness, not a crackerjack security system, did the trick. After all, it was just a middle-aged woman's sitting room, a modest place filled with sunlight and trifles: books, chair, table, teacup.

It was harmless. Benign.

That, of course, was a lie.

It was not harmless. It was not benign.

The walls had sopped up too much suppressed rage for that. The carpet and ceiling had absorbed too much of her pain, too great a measure of her tightly furled fury. Despite how this room looked to the uninformed eye—soothing, serene, pleasant—in truth it seethed with emotion and chaos. With hatred and pain. Invisible things, but things that caused other things to happen.

Momentous things. Things that, once set into motion, couldn't be undone.

This room is like me.

That is what she told herself.

I'm the same way. You look at me and you think you know what's right there in front of you—but you don't.

People saw a toned, polished, well-dressed woman, with a striking smile and an abundance of expensively maintained blond hair. They saw Ellie Topping, the forty-six-year-old wife of Brett Topping, vice president of Mountaineer Community Bank in Acker's Gap, West Virginia. They saw a person who lived in a nice house and drove a nice car. They saw a fortunate fate, especially when considered in context, juxtaposed with the gritty, hard-luck lives that surrounded her in this tattered and run-down town.

They saw a calm optimism and a cheerful demeanor.

They saw an illusion.

But as long as she had this room to retreat to, she could keep the illusion intact. Keep everything under control. The room was her protector. It enclosed her. Enfolded her. And henceforth, it would keep her secret.

When she left it later today, when she closed the door behind her, she would seal off the room and what it knew. She'd leave it to reckon with what she had revealed this morning in the dire spiral of her thinking.

She had arrived here five minutes ago. It was just before 7:30.

Her husband had left the house at 7:15 on the dot, like always, hoisting himself up and into his beloved black Escalade with a grunt, backing out of the garage and down the long driveway, waving at her when he reached the street. Ellie, watching from the vast living room window, a pretty smile fixed on her face, waved back.

Again, like always.

And Tyler—where was Tyler? She didn't know. Their son hadn't come home last night, slinking out after the fight in the kitchen. That was nothing new; there were many nights when he didn't come home.

But Ellie didn't worry about him anymore. Not like she had in the early days, back when they didn't know what was happening to their sweet, sweet boy. Or what kind of devil had taken over his soul.

What she worried about now was her husband. And herself, too.

She stood in the center of the snug little attic room, arms crossed, head bowed, eyes closed. She needed to settle herself. Slow down her racing heart. Get her breathing back under control. Because she was terrified.

The threat didn't come from some stranger lurking outside the house.

It came from the idea lurking inside her brain.

Maybe if she tried to be quiet for a few minutes—she would never have called this practice anything pretentious like "meditation"—she might be restored to the person she was, the decent, moral, upstanding woman she had always been.

She took a deep, slow breath. Her shoulders rose. She let out the breath. Her shoulders dropped.

She did it again. And again.

Good. It was working. She could almost feel the room's sympathy and understanding as it drew itself up around her like a blanket, softly, consolingly. No wonder she loved it so.

It wasn't fancy, this room in a corner of the attic. It consisted of two simple, flimsy walls put up to make a compact square, a room-within-a-room. Particleboard shelves climbed three of the walls.

The doll room.

That's what the previous owner of this house, a ninety-six-year-old woman named Harriet Kinsolving whose children had finally intervened and shoved her into a nursing home, had called it. The old lady had kept her doll collection up here. The day Ellie and Brett saw the house for the first time and Ellie decided it was perfect for them, almost twenty years ago now, Ellie had called dibs on this tiny slice of the attic with the cheap shelving and the white-trimmed window, watched over by dozens and dozens of dolls. Brett had grinned. "All yours, honey," he'd said, later confessing that he'd found the dolls to be a little . . . well, *creepy.*

Not that it mattered: The dolls were long gone by the time the Toppings moved in. Harriet's children had bundled them up and hustled them away. Probably dumped them on eBay, Ellie suspected, and doubtless the kids regretted not having the same option with mom. Nowadays there was no sign any dolls had ever been in this room at all, lined up in their lacy pink or white or orange or lime dresses—sherbet colors—and their shiny black Mary Janes, each face locked into a mandatory smile.

Exactly the same kind of smile, Ellie thought, *I put on every morning when I stand at the living room window and wave good-bye to Brett.*

A year after they'd bought this house, Ellie was pregnant with Tyler. Her happiness was pure, complete, uncomplicated.

And for sixteen years, it had stayed that way. Oh, there were setbacks—a miscarriage, a year and a half after Tyler was born; Henry's death; the death of another of Ellie's siblings, her sister Lillian; and Brett's health issues, plus their worry over the steady economic downturn in the region. The usual stresses and strains.

All in all, though, Ellie had felt blessed.

Blessed.

Looking back, remembering that golden feeling, remembering the kind of woozy happiness that was her default state then, she was half-ashamed of her reckless complacency. Her willful blindness.

And her stupidity.

Because she had never dreamed how quickly it could all come crashing down, how life could go from placid to catastrophic in such a short period of time, and how things that had once been unimaginable—blue-jacketed EMTs on their knees in the living room, jamming vials of Narcan up Tyler's nose after his latest overdose, plus ambulances and squad cars parked every which way on the broad lawn in the middle of the night, and curious neighbors peering out through parted blinds—could now seem routine.

The doll room was the place Ellie came when it was all too much. When her desperation surged, overwhelming the sweetness and joviality she had shown the world for most of her life, including the period just after her brother Henry's death from cancer that was—until now—the greatest emotional and spiritual crisis she had ever faced. Worse, even, than the death of her mother when she was eight. Worse than the miscarriage.

So hard to believe Henry was gone.

Ellie came from a large family but Henry was her favorite, no question. She had loved everything about him, but the thing she remembered best was his laugh. He was a genial, good-natured man and he had a scoop-you-up kind of laugh, merry and unfettered.

There was another laugh she knew well, too. An entirely different kind of laugh. Her son's laugh was more of a cackle. It had no mirth in it, no joy. It was not about amusement. It was a weapon. Tyler laughed to show them he didn't give a damn.

He'd laughed that way last night.

Brett had caught him pawing through her purse. She'd left it on the kitchen counter. She *knew* better. But it was only for a moment; she had just come in from the grocery store and she needed to pee. Brett had recently arrived home, too, from . . . wherever. She hadn't yet had a chance to ask him where he'd been.

From the bathroom, Ellie had heard her husband's voice, shaky with outrage: "You're a thief. Nothing but a damned thief, you know that? Your mother and I work hard for our money. It's ours. Not yours."

Then she heard Tyler's cackle. Their son was nineteen, and his voice had changed years ago, but when he laughed his voice went back to a sort of fluted falsetto. A boy's voice. A naughty, naughty boy.

"Screw you, old man." That was Tyler's reply to his father. And then the cackle came again, barbed this time, threaded with menace despite the childish pitch. Edged with hysteria. Was he high?

Of course he's high, Ellie had said to herself, yanking up her slacks and fumbling with the button, trying to finish in the bathroom so she could intervene, keep the crisis from escalating. *When is he* not *high? High or stoned or whatever the hell they're calling it these days.*

"Put down that purse." Brett's voice was low and ominous.

Tyler laughed again. "Like I said. Screw you, Pops."

Ellie was in too much of a hurry to flush. She came running out of the bathroom. She saw exactly what she had expected to see: Her husband and her son, confronting each other across the butcher-block island in the center of the kitchen. Tyler had snatched up her purse from the white-tiled countertop over by the stove. By now he had her billfold out; it hung open like a trout's mouth, gaping and slack. He had dropped the purse. He was focused exclusively on the billfold. He had already grabbed the twenties and he was digging an index finger into the change compartment. He wanted it all, even the pennies.

"Stop," Ellie said. Her voice was weak. She hated her weakness. "Both of you—just stop."

Neither of them looked at her. They were focused only on each other, gazes locked like rams' horns. There was, she sensed, something primal and unprecedented in this standoff, something that made it different from the dozens of previous standoffs on other nights in this same kitchen, since the moment when they'd first lost their boy.

Or maybe not.

Maybe it was exactly the same as all the others. And maybe it would always be like this: brief, furious confrontations when Tyler didn't even try to be subtle about his stealing, then a lull, then another standoff. This could go on for years. Years and years.

Brett was panting, pulling the labored breaths in and out of his mouth. His forehead was buttered with sweat. He was at least thirty pounds overweight and his heart staggered under the strain; this kind of tension was the last thing in the world he needed.

Did Tyler care about that?

No. He didn't. He only cared about one thing: drugs.

Well, Ellie had instantly corrected herself, *two things, really: drugs—and the money to buy them with.*

Tyler's eyes were shiny-black. His curly dark hair—oh, he'd been a beautiful little boy, with a soft fumble of ringlets always trailing across his forehead, ringlets he would push aside impatiently on his way to go play ball with his best friend Alex—was yanked back and tied with a rubber band, making a thick knob of frizz that perched on his neck like a weird growth, like some fuzzy tumor that she was always tempted to whack off with a pair of scissors.

Her son looked terrible: skinny, brittle, his skin a color that Ellie could only describe as tombstone gray. His T-shirt was ripped and stained. The stains were the kind that smelled oniony and gross even if you weren't within smelling range of them; you could sense by looking just how bad they smelled. You could feel the stink. His jeans slouched languidly off his nonexistent hips.

He had been living with them again for the last four months—it was his counselor's idea, an attempt to give Tyler stability after his latest stay in rehab, the proverbial second chance, except that it was more like the seventh or eighth or ninth or tenth chance, she'd lost count—and he still didn't let her do his laundry, which meant his laundry didn't get done. He wore the same clothes for weeks at a time.

And he hadn't changed his behavior at all. Rehab or no rehab, he was still what he'd become.

Her son, the chipper, earnest little boy who had loved baseball and bikes and fireworks and Harry Potter and hot dogs and judo class—reeked. He wouldn't wash his clothes and he wouldn't take a shower. He cursed at her when she brought it up. Not always, though; sometimes he smiled. The smile was infuriating. She wasn't even worth getting mad at. He'd moved on. She and Brett were tools to him now, things to exploit.

Because Tyler was an addict. And addicts always did what addicts always do. No exceptions.

Ellie didn't have much education beyond high school. Not like Brett with his MBA, his grad work in finance and economics. But she'd loved her single semester in community college, all those years ago. She took a philosophy class. They were assigned to read an essay by a man named Camus—you didn't say the *S* out loud, which she discovered when she pronounced it wrong during the class discussion and the instructor corrected her, but not in a mean way—and she learned about Sisyphus, doomed to push a rock up a hill. The rock rolls right back down the hill. Over and over again. So over and over again, Sisyphus has to push and watch. Push and watch. Forever.

Hey, there, Sisyphus, Ellie had thought, as the extent of Tyler's transformation became clear to them and they tried first one thing and then another thing and nothing worked. *I'm Ellie. I think we have a lot in common*. But it was confusing, because at other times, she realized that Tyler himself was Sisyphus; he was the one with the rock and the compulsion, he was the one who couldn't stop what he was doing, he was the one whose life was now officially hopeless.

Last night's confrontation in the kitchen had ended without drama. Just like that, Brett gave up.

Ellie, frankly, had expected it. They didn't have the stomach any-more to sustain a fight with Tyler. She and Brett had been fighting with him for two years. Going on three. And what had it gotten them? Noth-ing. Brett usually tried, for the first few minutes of every skirmish, to hold the line, to implore Tyler to treat them decently and respectfully—and to stop *stealing* from them, for God's sake—but then her husband would relent. Let go.

What was the point?

"Take the money," Brett had said wearily. "Just go ahead and take it."

The crisis was over. Total capitulation had worked. Always did. The tension in the room instantly dropped to zero. Tyler nodded and smiled, as if they'd finally come to their senses and he was glad about it, but he was too nice to gloat, wasn't he? Yes, he was. Winning settled him down. He had made a clicking sound in his mouth as he stuffed the bills and the change in his back pocket. He side-armed his mother's billfold onto the counter. It skidded and hit the copper canister labeled FLOUR.

"Gonna pay you back," Tyler said. He gave his mother a quick wink. "One of these days."

It would never happen, of course, but to call him out on his lies was to court trouble again; any criticism could set him off. Nobody wanted that. When Tyler was around, she and Brett carefully planned conver-sational routes that would keep them well clear of their son's temper, the way you arrange a car trip to avoid road construction.

Once Tyler had cleared the back door, Ellie went over to her hus-band. His breathing was still noisy and strained, with a rasp. She reached up and put her arms around his thick neck and turned her head to the side, so that she could press an ear to his wide chest. He embraced her. His shirt was damp with sweat. She could hear his heart flailing away, the heart that needed care. That did not need stress. That did not need *this*.

Things that would have seemed outlandish and unfathomable at the start of the ordeal—a child stealing from his mother, a child breaking into houses *on their very own street*, the homes of their friends, and ran-sacking medicine cabinets looking for drugs, then jail sentences and rehab and promises, promises, promises, never-kept promises—were accepted now, commonplace, part of their daily reality.

"Next time," her husband muttered between his heavy-duty breaths, "don't leave your purse in plain sight. Asking for trouble."

She nodded, slowly moving her head up and down against the soft cotton of his shirtfront, still listening to his heart.

Remembering all of that as she stood in the doll room this morning, Ellie trembled. She opened her eyes. She reached for the chair, turning it around so that it faced the window. The window was set into the east side of the house; as the sun rose, it filled the room to the brim with a soft lemon-yellow light.

She needed that light. Desperately. She needed a scrap of abstract beauty in her life, something lovely, something lilting and innocent, a counterweight to the heaviness of her constant sorrow. Today, right now, she needed it more than ever. Because she had made her decision.

She was going to kill her son.

Chapter Three

Mornings were the worst. Nights were bad, too, when Jake Oakes waited, hour after hour, for sleep to do its damned job, when he thought too long and too hard and too clearly about his situation.

But mornings—morning were unbearable.

They were terrible because they sometimes included hope. Having no hope was one thing, but having it—and then watching hope leak away throughout the day—was excruciating.

Some days, there was a second or so just after he woke up in the hot, dark box of a bedroom when he didn't remember. His mind was blank. That was the place where the hope flooded in, filling the empty cavity. He thought he was still whole. Still fully functional.

He forgot about the shooting.

He forgot about that terrible moment of shock when he saw the kid's hand rising behind the counter and it dawned on him—*Omigod*—that the greasy black thing in that shaky hand was a gun.

Danny. Danny Lukens. That was the kid's name.

Jake had been told so many times about what happened next that those accounts, based on the eyewitness testimony of Sheriff Harrison and the forensic findings, had merged with his own fragile flake of recollection and before he knew it, he could see the whole thing unfolding in his mind's eye, every color, every nuance, every detail, including things he couldn't possibly have seen or truly recalled:

The store's front door whips open. Distracted, he turns, and so when the bullet comes it hits him not in the heart, the way the kid intended it to, but in his side, closer to his back than his front.

His big body pleats and folds. He accordions to the floor.

From behind him, Sheriff Harrison yells at the kid, "Drop it! Drop it NOW! *Drop your fucking weap*—" and then, when the kid doesn't comply, there is a second and a third gunshot. They smash into Danny's chest, slamming him back against the honeycombed rack of cigarette cartons. Dozens of cartons are knocked out of their slots. The kid slumps, hits the floor. His chest opens up like a precious red flower.

He's dead. And Jake is dead, too, or might as well be, because he can't speak and he can't move and somehow he knows, with a conviction that has already lodged in his soul the same way the bullet has lodged in his spine, that his life is now an entirely different thing from what it was just a moment beforehand, that the world—his world—has been ripped out its orbit and is now corkscrewing through the universe, crazy, random, uncontrolled, and he is lost, lost.

And yet some mornings, for a minute or so after he first opened his eyes, he forgot.

He'd go back to being himself again: Jake Oakes, deputy sheriff, Raythune County Sheriff's Department, based in Acker's Gap, West Virginia. Everything was the way it was, the way it was supposed to be.

Then he would try to move his legs, and it all rushed in on him again, the eternal present tense:

The gunshot. The spasm of panic and confusion and fear, followed by . . . more fear. The memory of that fear shamed him, then and now, even though he told no one about it. Not even Molly.

A knock at the front door.

Jake heard it and he scowled. He'd been sitting in the living room, looking at the worn-out, mashed-down places in the thin, cheap-ass carpet made by the wheels of his chair.

"Yeah, in a minute," he yelled, knowing his words were audible through the front door. The door was as flimsy as cardboard, but then again, so was the house.

It was all he could afford. The rambling old Victorian he had owned before the shooting was unsuitable; it had three floors, and the only bathroom was on the second floor. He had been forced to sell it, and everybody knows what happens when you are forced to sell, and sell fast: Buyers have the upper hand. They take advantage.

Toss in the definitely relevant fact that the house was located in Acker's Gap—not among the most desirable locations on God's green earth, it was only fair to point out—and you had all the ingredients for the current situation in which he found himself: stuck in a one-story dump with a couple of postage stamp–sized bedrooms and the won't-go-away smell of moldy damp. The topper: The house was wrapped up in a revolting peach shade of vinyl siding.

Steve Brinksneader, his buddy, still a deputy in the department, had come by one Saturday right after Jake moved in and built a ramp for him. It descended in choppy switchback segments from the dinky front porch to the driveway. Ugly but necessary.

The knock came again. Harder this time.

"Yeah, yeah," Jake muttered, lowering instead of raising his voice. Probably Steve, he guessed. Or that neighbor of his, Stan Howell. Retired coal miner. Liked to come over and shoot the shit.

He had a moment of surprise when he opened the door. He hadn't seen or spoken to Sheriff Harrison in—what was it now? Six months? Seven? Something like that.

She'd been attentive in the first year or so, stopping by often, just as you would expect from someone who had been your boss and who had probably saved your life to boot. Because if Pam Harrison hadn't arrived at that store when she did, and if she hadn't shot the asshole punk who had sent a bullet ripping into Jake's spine, the aforesaid asshole punk would surely have gotten off a second round and finished the job.

But then her visits tapered off. Predictable, Jake had thought, but it was still tough to swallow. She was busy. Everybody was busy. Who had time to stop by and watch him push himself in a chair around his crappy little house, while *The Price Is Right* shrieked and brayed from the big-screen TV?

"Hey," he said.

"Can I come in?" Harrison glanced down at his lap, which he'd turned into a handy staging area for his next Rolling Rock. He hadn't yet opened the green glass bottle. He had been saving that familiar plea-sure for a few minutes from now.

Harrison didn't comment on the Rolling Rock, but Jake could feel the heat of her disapproval.

Screw you, he thought.

"Sure," he said out loud.

He turned the chair around and guided it back toward the couch. Tough going on the raggedy-assed carpet, but he powered through. He assumed she was following him. On his way, he picked up the remote from the coffee table and clicked off the set.

Instant silence. He half-wished he'd left the TV on, forcing her to speak over the squeals and the gusts of applause and the bright, punchy music.

She took a seat on one end of the couch, back straight, hands clasped, feet together. Formal as hell.

Jake looked her up and down. That was one advantage of his cur-rent state: He could stare at anybody, anytime, and they had to take it. He wasn't sure why, but people were afraid to call him out on the star-ing thing; maybe it was because they were aware of their own desire to stare at him, and felt guilty about it. So they let him slide.

She wore, like always, her brown polyester uniform. Black boots, shiny black belt. No hat. She must've left it in the county-issued Chevy Blazer that she had parked out front, not in the driveway. He had seen it when he opened the door and he understood: The driveway that went with this runt-of-the-litter house was too narrow for the bull-necked SUV.

Harrison had always looked younger than her age but now, in her mid-thirties, she looked older. She was heavier; the shirt fit tighter around her midsection. The skin around her eyes was crinkled like a used paper sack. A few flecks of gray had infiltrated her eyebrows and her solid cap of dark straight hair; more gray was on the way, Jake thought uncharitably, and soon. Mainly, though, what he perceived was an all-over, nonspecific fatigue that had left its blurry stamp on her. He knew that kind of fatigue, from back when he was on the job.

Back when he had a life.

"How's it going?" she said.

"Well." He smacked his palms against the tops of the wheels. "I reckon you can pretty much guess how it's going," he added, and then he grinned at her to leaven the negativity, the bitterness. Good old Jake. Kidding around, like always. "What can I do for you, Pam?"

He could read the relief on her face. Okay, then: We're getting to the point. She wasn't being forced to engage in polite chitchat.

"Got a proposition," she said.

All at once he realized—with an oversized hope that flared up so suddenly that it was there before he had time to beat it back again, like a fire that starts on the stove—that she was here to ask for his help on a case. Maybe somebody he had arrested years ago was out on the streets, and she needed to know how they should approach. Maybe one of the two deputies she'd hired to replace him—Dave Previtt and Sawyer Simmons—needed to spend some time with him, a sort of refresher course. Taking advantage of his expertise.

He had been waiting for this moment. He didn't know that that was what he'd been doing—but he had. And now the moment was here.

"What's going on?" he said.

He kept his voice level. He was trying to sound casual. But he was already lining up his requirements: He wanted to wear the brown uniform again. If they wouldn't let him—well, that was a deal-breaker. Oh, and he'd need a new one. Yeah, he still had the old one, but it would be too big for him now, especially in the arms and chest. He'd lost a lot of muscle tone.

"We're getting slammed," the sheriff said. "The regular stuff—overdoses, of course, but also burglaries, car theft, shoplifting, domestics, DUIs. And some big-time stuff, too. Armed assaults. It's been relentless. That's why I wanted to stop by."

So here it was. She was getting ready to ask him to come back. To rejoin the sheriff's department. Christ, it had taken two people to replace him. That said something. That told you all you needed to know, didn't it, about how valuable he was? About the kind of lawman he'd been? Sure, he'd been easygoing, like any other good-ole-boy deputy—but you could tell what was in his core. What he was made of. It showed through. Couldn't hide it.

"Yeah," he said. "Heard things've been rough." That wasn't true. He'd heard nothing. He didn't hang out with anybody in the department anymore. After building the ramp, Steve had backed off. Kept his distance. And Jake's best friend, retired deputy Charlie Mathers, was dead.

But he wanted the sheriff to believe he was up to speed. And he would be—just as soon as he was back on the job. He was a quick study. You could ask anybody. *That Jake Oakes, he's got a good head on his shoulders.* Anybody. Just ask.

"On top of all that," Harrison went on, "the prosecutor's still feeling her way through, after three years. Lovejoy tries her best—but she's no Bell Elkins."

That brought another grin from him. "Nobody is."

The former prosecutor, Belfa Elkins, had resigned shortly after the night Jake was injured. The reason why had shocked Raythune County. It shocked Jake, too, when the heavy fog of the painkillers had finally dissipated and he'd heard the story, sitting up in his hospital bed, listening to the particulars from a woman named Molly Drucker as she fed him lime Jell-O—or tried to, bumping the tip of the metal spoon against his lower lip to get him to open up. *Come on, Jake, you gotta eat.* In the special election for a new prosecutor, Rhonda Lovejoy ran unopposed.

But getting the job—and doing the job—were two separate and very different things. Same as it was for a deputy sheriff.

"And so," Harrison continued, "I'm hoping you can help us out here, Jake."

He shouldn't act too eager. He'd already decided that. When she asked him to come back to work on the hardest cases, he would hesitate. Let his gaze linger for a long time at the drab carpet. And then maybe he'd let that same gaze travel with exquisite slowness up, up, up, until finally it met her eyes again. He would shrug and release a long column of air, and then he'd say, okay, yeah. Maybe he *could* see his way clear to returning.

Sure. He'd be happy to work with Dave and Sawyer. And Steve. And Rhonda Lovejoy, too. It was the least he could do, right? As a good citizen? As somebody who understood the challenges of law enforcement in a place like this better than—

"I need somebody to answer phones," Harrison said. "Spell the dispatcher. Beverly's eight months pregnant. Might have to leave on a moment's notice. I'd like you to take calls. All you'd have to do is sit there. You could bring a book to read. Whatever."

He felt as if he'd been punched in the face.

Answer phones.

Because that was all he was good for, right? Sitting on his butt and clicking onto the next call. Listening to liquored-up hillbillies bitch about their noisy neighbors or some beagle that won't quit barking or some kid who keeps riding an ATV across the damned yard. Wrecking the flower bed.

She was still talking.

"It's just part-time. Shift only goes to midnight. After that, the calls get switched over to the regional call center in Blythesburg."

He wanted to yell at her: *You think I don't* know *that? You think I don't remember what time the dispatch gets switched over to Blythesburg? Christ Almighty. I was a deputy in your department, I was the best you ever had, I worked there for five friggin' years, you—*

None of that anger showed up in his face, though, or in his voice when he replied to her. He hoarded the anger inside himself. He had done that from the beginning, to keep the counselors off his back, first in the hospital and later during his rehab. He rarely showed his anger. It belonged to him. Not them. It was all he had left.

He wondered sometimes if the stored-up fury had pooled in a certain corner of his body, and if the toxicity was leeching slowly into his system. Could be. He didn't care.

"Okay," he said. "Tell you what. I'll think about it." He smiled at her. He didn't want to tip his hand about how disappointed he was.

"Look, Jake. I know it's not what you wanted. I remember the talk we had. Back in the hospital, when you were starting your PT. But I checked with the commissioners. You're on full disability. I can't use you in the sheriff's department. Not as a deputy, that is." She read the question off his face. "The dispatcher's job is listed as clerical. The county has a special provision for hiring the handicapped. I can bring you back for that."

Clerical.

Handicapped.

The anger was rising in him again. He forced it back in its lair. The effort took everything he had.

He needed a few seconds to be able to speak. He forced himself to sound amiable. Neighborly. A reasonable man.

"No problem, Pam. I said I'd think about it."

"You could lose your benefits. If I hired you back as a deputy, I mean. And then if it turned out you couldn't do the job—you'd be screwed. You'd be out of work and you wouldn't have your disability, either."

I can do the job. I can still do the damned job.

He shrugged. His palms were stationed on the tops of the wheels, his thumbs hooked over the thin rubber ridge, fingers strumming the spokes.

"Promise I'll think it over," he said. A forced smile that he hoped didn't look forced.

"You'd be helping us out."

"Got it. I'll call. Day or so, maybe."

"Tell you the truth, we could use you before the week's out. Beverly's not feeling well. I'd like to know we've got it covered."

He wanted to work—God knows he wanted to be useful and not just sit on his ass all day long. But he wasn't sure what it would feel like to be back in the courthouse again—and not as a deputy this time, not as somebody in a brown uniform with a big hat and a gun on his hip, somebody with important work to do, difficult and dangerous work . . . but as somebody in a chair.

Answering the phone.

"Said I'd let you know." Another smile. Slightly less neighborly, maybe.

"Okay, then." She stood up. "Hope you'll see your way clear to do this. You know the county as well as anybody. You'd do a good job." Her voice was flat. That, he knew, was her way; she had grown up with a hard, silent father, and the lesson took.

"Like I said—I'll be in touch," he said. "Nice of you to come by in person." He didn't mean it, and he knew she'd pick up on it. That gave him a small bit of satisfaction. "Hey. Been wondering. You hear anything from Bell Elkins these days?"

"Nope," she said. "I think Rhonda Lovejoy keeps in touch with her. From time to time. Much as anybody can. You know Bell. Never had much to stay beyond courthouse business. And after all that's happened—" Harrison cut off her own sentence and shrugged. "Don't know about any plans she might have, once she's done with her community service."

"That's gotta be happening soon."

"I guess." Harrison crossed the short strip of carpet between the couch and the front door. He followed behind her the way a host is supposed to, so that he could close the door after she left. "You think about that job, okay, Jake?"

"You bet."

The sheriff dipped her head, acknowledging his pledge. And then she walked out the front door without looking back. Even if she had, there would have been little to see. You don't expect much movement in any case from a man in a wheelchair but Jake's stillness went well beyond that; his stillness was intensely reflective. It was the kind of careful waiting that might have many different meanings, depending on who was doing the watching, and who was doing the waiting.

He continued to sit motionless for a few minutes, gazing at the shut door. His umbrage at the sheriff's job offer was temporarily mitigated by curiosity at his own behavior: What had made him ask her about Bell Elkins? He had his own problems.

The truth was that he and Bell had never really gotten along back in the days when they worked together. She thought he was a show-off, a fundamentally unserious person doing a deadly serious job, and the disparity between what he was (a jokey charmer) and what he ought to be (a dedicated public servant) offended her.

Well, she'd gotten him wrong from the start. Not that he'd gotten *her* especially right; he had dismissed her on the first day they met as a tight-assed, sanctimonious know-it-all. It took him months—okay, a full year—to see what he'd missed about her.

And then it didn't matter anymore, their respective assessments of each other. Far more important things had intervened. The opioid addiction crisis had exploded in their faces.

Everything came crashing down three years ago on That Night, at the tail end of a rocky twenty-four-hour period during which a record number of drug overdoses had repeatedly bludgeoned their small, poor, done-in county. During the weeks that followed, before the town had even been able to catch its breath, Bell Elkii

cuting attorney—the reason for which, when

everyone in one black swoop of news, like

eclipse—and Deputy Jake Oakes was learning

use of the lower half of his body.

And through all of the changes ("changes" be

tame and oh-so-polite word to describe what he ҫ

total bullshit fate that had befallen him), Jake had ⸺ ⸺ ⸺ me to

understand the truth about Bell Elkins.

He discovered more about her in her absence, that is, than he ever had in her presence.

His original opinion of her hadn't been wrong, just incomplete. She *was* sanctimonious. She *was* a tight-assed know-it-all. And that's what had made her valuable. She was everything the county needed—a hard, steady presence, a counterbalance against the sponginess of surrender to sorry-about-your-luck circumstances. She had standards. Expectations. For herself. And for Acker's Gap.

She had proved that by the manner of, and motive for, her resignation. Jake didn't understand it. He didn't agree with it. He hadn't understood it or agreed with it from the first moment he was made aware of it, and time hadn't changed his view that it was maybe the dumbest damned thing he'd ever heard of anybody doing.

But it fit. For her, it fit.

He and Bell had spoken only twice in the three years since the night of his injury. Their brief exchanges occurred in public, in the high-ceilinged, cold-floored corridor of the Raythune County Courthouse. Bell had been accompanied by a corrections officer; she was serving her own sentence by then, a two-and-a-half-year term in a minimum-security facility, to be followed by eight weeks of supervised probation and community service.

One of their interactions came during a break at the inquest for the fatal shooting of Danny Lukens. The second occurred just before the commencement of the civil suit for wrongful death brought against the county by Danny's grandmother. On both occasions, Jake's exchange with Bell was formal, stilted, and short. The first time, she looked into his eyes, looked down at his wheelchair, and then looked in his eyes again.

Oh, Jake." He replied, "Yeah." That was it. The second as similar: Her "How're you doing?" was followed by his "Well can be expected, I guess." They'd always had their own system of communication—shrugs and sighs, mostly, and upraised eyebrows— and that system still adhered. They both sometimes found words to be impediments to true communication. They'd never discussed that— discussing it in words would have made them hypocrites, wouldn't it?—but sensed it in each other. *Words are superfluous and irrelevant,* is how Bell would've put it. *Words suck*, would've been Jake's way of expressing the same sentiment.

This morning, with the sheriff's job offer still filling the air like a skunk's how-do-you-do, Jake had found himself suddenly wanting to talk to Bell. Which was ironic, given the fact that their conversations had never been long or especially intimate.

And furthermore—talk about what? He didn't know. He simply hoped she was planning to stay in Acker's Gap now that she had the option to leave.

Was it, he wondered, just the desire of one wounded animal for the company of another? The solidarity of the damned?

He shook his head. *Get over yourself, Oakes.* The thought was too fancy. Too grandiose. There was an excellent chance he'd hardly ever see Bell Elkins even if she did stick around, as infrequently as he left this cracker box of a house.

He opened the Rolling Rock he'd been cradling in his lap. Drained it. It was too warm—the sheriff had overstayed—but that was okay. He felt better already.

Then he backed up his chair with a quarter-revolution of the wheels and executed a tight three-point turn—the only kind it was possible to make in here, the space was so small—and pushed himself into the kitchen to fetch another. He'd have to make up his mind about Harrison's offer, such as it was, and weigh the pros and cons. He liked to say that his favorite consulting psychiatrist was Dr. Rolling Rock, who never charged extra for house calls.

Chapter Four

The phone rang and Ellie almost dropped her teacup. The ring startled her. Her mind had been drifting again.

She looked around the dark living room. Night had slipped up on her, startling her almost as much as the sound of the phone. Where had the day gone?

She'd spent most of it up in the doll room. That much, she remembered. But when the sun went down she had returned to the first floor and then she had . . . what? How had she spent her time?

Well, hold on. Surely she could remember.

Let's see, she said to herself. She'd made a cup of tea, and then another and maybe another still—she'd lost count, the way she was losing track of a lot of things lately. She was preoccupied. She had so much to think about now that she'd decided, calmly and rationally, to do the worst thing in the world:

Kill her own child.

All at once, she remembered. After she'd made the second cup of tea she had left the kitchen for a minute. To find the gun in the garage. She'd taken it upstairs to the doll room. Settled on a good hiding spot. By the time she got back down to the first floor, her tea was tepid. She poured it out and made another cup. And then, somehow, hours had gone by. In the blink of an eye.

The phone. It was still ringing. Whoever it was, they were persistent.

She considered ignoring the call, but no. It might be Brett. He was out late again.

"Hello?"

"Ellie—hey. It's Sandy."

A neighbor. Across the street and four doors down.

Damn. Ellie didn't want to talk to anybody.

Why hadn't she checked the caller ID? She'd been in too much of a hurry to hear Brett's voice, that's why. She was so certain it was him. Calling from the bank. Another board meeting had run long, perhaps. Or something else. Some other duty. He belonged to a lot of local civic organizations—it came with the territory, with being vice president of a community bank. Rotary, Lions Club, Optimists Club. She always got mixed up about which meetings happened on which nights. He'd told her where he was going tonight—surely he'd done that, right?—but it hadn't registered.

"Hi, Sandy."

"Sorry to call so late. I hope I didn't—"

"Not a problem. I was up."

"Oh, good." Sandy hesitated. "How're you doing, hon?"

"Fine. And you and Rex?"

"We're great. Busy. You know."

"Of course."

Once, a lifetime ago or so it seemed, they'd been very close, she and Sandy. They had so much in common. They were married to busy, successful men and they lived in the best neighborhood in Acker's Gap. There had even been, long ago, some shared vacations: Myrtle Beach, Colonial Williamsburg, Disney World. Sandy's son, Alex, had been a friend of Tyler's in grade school and middle school. By the time they reached Acker's Gap High School, though, drugs divided them, the brightest of bright lines.

Alex was a No; Tyler was a Yes. A big, enthusiastic Yes.

In the spring, Alex would finish up his sophomore year at West Virginia University. Ellie knew all about Alex's academic progress not because Sandy had told her—that would be cruel, wouldn't it, to hold up the example of her own perfect child as a contrast to Ellie's sad loser of a son?—but because the whole neighborhood knew. Everyone took

note when Alex came home, skimming his way into the Banville driveway in his red Jetta with the blue-and-gold WVU decal in the lower
right corner of the back window. Ellie hadn't seen the Jetta there in a
while; Alex must be spending all of his weekends in Morgantown now.
No more trips home in the middle of the semester. Too much to do. A
bright, high-achieving kid.

Sandy was speaking again. Ellie forced herself to focus on the
words.

"Listen, hon. We saw Tyler last night. After dark." A pause. *How to
go on?* Sandy's pause said. "He'd just left your house and he was running
down the street. Well—maybe not running. But walking pretty fast. He
looked—agitated, I guess I'd call it. Kind of upset, to be honest with
you. I know he's back home with you all again. And that's great. Really
great. But is everything all—"

"Everything's fine."

Ellie confided in nobody because confiding was pointless. It changed
nothing. No one could possibly understand. She considered it a miracle
that Brett was able to do his job at the bank. Or that she kept the house
going. Or that either of them could behave normally anymore.

"Well," Sandy said, "I've mentioned this before, hon, but you
know—I *hope* you know—that Rex and I are here for you. And the kids
are here for you, too. I know Alex feels just terrible about Tyler, about
the struggles he's had. And Sara—she cares a lot about Tyler. She told
me so." Sara was their sixteen-year-old daughter. "If there's ever anything we can do, you just have to—"

"There's not. But thanks. Really."

She ended the call. Just like that. Sandy wouldn't get mad at being,
in effect, hung up on. She couldn't get mad. That was the only upside
to living in the midst of a lurid, long-running family crisis that everybody knew about because you lived in a small town: People had to cut
you a lot of slack when you behaved oddly. They knew your story and
they would always forgive you—because they pitied you.

They knew as well as you did that there was no solution. No rem-
edy for the tragedy.

But that's not true, Ellie corrected herself. *There is.*

And she had figured it out.

•   •   •

The doll room was different at night. Without sunlight, it seemed bland and ordinary. It didn't enfold her. Wouldn't take care of her.

It was just a room.

Ellie turned on the lamp by her chair—there wasn't an overhead light—and stood in front of the bookshelf. She reached out to the row of books at shoulder-level. She had to make sure, one more time, that she had what she needed.

After hanging up on Sandy Banville she had climbed the stairs to the second floor, and then the next set of stairs to the attic. And entered the doll room.

She pulled a small object from behind the copy of *My Side of the Mountain*. The book had been Tyler's favorite when he was a boy. She'd read it to him—how many times? Four, five times at least. Then, when he was old enough, Tyler had read it by himself. It was about a boy who runs away and lives in the woods.

She sat down in the chair and held the gun in her lap.

She reviewed the evidence one more time, just to be sure. Just to be really, *really* sure.

Life with Tyler was impossible. The shouting, the screaming, the fights, the daily duty of inventorying what their son had stolen from them most recently. So far, the list included their KitchenAid food processor, Brett's new raincoat, his golf clubs, her jade necklace. And money—of course. As much as Tyler could find, as much as he could stuff in his pockets when they weren't looking—or sometimes when they were. Small things, big things. Things he could sell. Things that weren't missed right away or things that *were* missed right away—but what of it? Because by now he'd picked up on the fact that they didn't like confrontations. He'd brazen his way through their attempts to make him acknowledge his thefts.

And so on it went: her earrings. Brett's Montblanc pen. The Keurig coffeemaker. Assorted sheets and towels. "What the hell does he do with *towels*?" Brett had asked her last week. Her husband—an intelligent and capable man, a success in business, a man people respected in this town—had sounded as baffled and helpless as a child lost in the woods.

"Who'd want to buy used towels? And *sheets*, for God's sake. What does he do with *sheets*?" She didn't answer.

Her private theory: It didn't matter what it was. Or what he got for them. Even a few dollars was more than he'd started with. Any money he got, he could use to buy drugs.

At first they had asked him about the missing items, which only made things worse. Instantly he would go from drowsy and amiable to angry. Volcanically angry. The words exploding out of him: "Right. *Right*. So you can't find some piece of shit and automatically it's *my* fault, right? *I'm* the bad guy. Gotta be me. It couldn't be that you just *misplaced* it, right? No. Fuck, no. Gotta be Tyler. Tyler's to blame. For *everything,* right? Oh, yeah." Alternately yelling and muttering, waving his arms, he'd march around the living room. His stealing was so obvious that the whole scene—every time—was like a bad play, Ellie thought, like an over-the-top melodrama in which the actors were deliberately hamming it up for their own pleasure.

Did she and Brett ask for help? Of course they did. Constantly.

When the counselor had first proposed Tyler's return to their home four months ago, after his latest stint at the rehab place in Florida, Ellie said, "Okay, but we need some resources this time. Strategies—in case it all falls apart again."

Promises. Oh, there were many, *many* promises. Promises from the counselor, and promises from Tyler. Their son was the absolute king of the enthusiastic pronouncement, the sincere pledge that begged to be accompanied by a flourish of trumpets or, at the very least, a flyover by the Blue Angels: "Mom—Dad—it's gonna be different this time, okay? It really is. Find me a bible. I'll swear on it. Find a whole stack of 'em. Gonna take things one day at a time. Let go and let God. I love you two, you know that? I really, really love you guys."

He promised to attend a Narcotics Anonymous meeting every day. Every day! Sometimes twice a day. Twice!

And do chores.

And keep his room clean.

And get a job.

It was all crap.

Ellie knew it was crap—this time, every time—even as she listened to her son saying it. Still she found herself strangely fascinated by how he could declare all those things yet again, the homilies, the platitudes, the histrionic pledges, the things he'd said four, five, six times before— or was it ten or twelve or thirteen?—without stumbling or hesitating or breaking out in giggles.

This time, it took less than a week. Four days after he'd moved back in with them he was the Same Old Tyler—or at least the Tyler of the last few years. He stopped showering. Stopped shaving.

Combing his hair? What a laugh.

And then the mysterious phone calls had started up again, coming at all hours, whenever he was home. At first he didn't have a cell—he needed to earn the privilege, the counselor told Ellie and Brett, advising them not to buy him one—but that meant he was dependent on their home phone. Before the initial ring had finished he'd grab it and punch the button, mutter a few words and then punch it off again, and then he'd be gone. They were supposed to let the counselor know about things like that—but why bother? Nothing was ever going to change.

If Ellie and Brett had refused, if they'd said he couldn't live here this time, if they'd said, *No, you've had too many chances already and you always screw up*, if they'd said, *We're not bad people, we're not selfish people, but we have the right to have a peaceful life again, don't we?*—then Tyler would have been sent back to the rehab facility in Florida. Their insurance company had finally agreed to pay for it, even though the price had made Ellie blink and go back over that section of the brochure, certain that she'd read it wrong the first time, certain that they'd added an extra comma. No—she'd read it right. The total cost of a two-week stay, she realized, could buy you a house in Acker's Gap.

Or maybe he'd be sent to jail, if he'd been breaking into houses and cars again to get his money and/or his drugs.

And once he was finished with rehab or jail, Tyler would be right back here on their doorstep, anyway, because he had nowhere else to go.

It was all a big circle. An endless loop. Unless and until they were willing to throw him out for good—some parents, Ellie knew, had done just that—they were chained to the wheel.

*   *   *

She felt her hands growing colder. It wasn't just the temperature, she decided. It was on account of what she held in her lap: a Ruger LCP.

Brett had bought the handgun a few years ago, after an epidemic of burglaries in this area of town had put everyone on high alert. Then the burglaries tapered off. Brett stowed the gun in a dark-green tackle box in the garage, and sequestered the tackle box on the top section of the gray metal shelving.

He hadn't touched the gun in months. By now, he might have even forgotten where he'd put it.

She had not forgotten.

She could handle a gun. Her father, Big Dave Combs, had been a hunter, and he taught all his kids how to shoot. It was a rite of passage. The five boys went first. And then Ellie and her sisters, Theresa and Lillian, took turns stepping up to the backyard range. Big Dave handed out little buttons of orange foam for them to plug in their ears. The noise could hurt. At first their hands trembled. After a few rounds though, they didn't tremble anymore. Their hands were steady.

But all of that was a long, long time ago. Ellie knew she needed to hold the Ruger for a while, to accustom herself once again to its weight. It wasn't heavy—in fact it was surprisingly light, for what it was—but there was a somberness to this object.

If fate were a thing you could hold in your hands, she thought, it would feel just like this: dense, ponderous but not heavy, a crucial accumulation. She needed to renew her acquaintance with the odd, thrilling experience of being in charge of a weapon.

It would be self-defense. No question. A jury would not, could not, see it any other way.

She had thought this through to its conclusion—she pictured herself in the immediate aftermath, calling 911, speaking calmly and clearly, handing the Ruger to the EMTs when they arrived, explaining what she'd done and why she'd done it—and she knew the ruling would be self-defense. There might not even be a trial. She had read somewhere that it sometimes happens that way: The authorities don't even make an arrest, the court system doesn't want to bother with it. Everybody just calls it a day and goes home. Because everybody agrees that the act was justified.

And that's what would happen here. Because once they understood the circumstances, they would nod, and the gentle light of pity would come into their eyes, and they would talk softly to her.

We understand, they would say, and someone would put a hand on her shoulder and add, *God knows you've been through enough already.*

Yes. God knew. Probably. Truth was, she didn't think much about God. Never did. Big Dave had made them all go to church, lining them up on Sunday mornings and checking their necks to see if they'd washed properly, especially her brothers, but church was just something you did. The idea of God was always superficial in her family, it never reached all the way down to her bones. If God existed, then yes, He would see what she did, and approve, and forgive her, although that part was entirely up to Him, and she didn't really care one way or another.

Self-defense. Perfect word for this situation. She had a right to defend herself, and a right to defend Brett, too. Because Tyler was killing them. And he was killing her husband even faster than he was killing her: Brett's blood pressure was frighteningly high, his diabetes was out of control, he ate too much, he drank too much, the stress was horrific, all the numbers on the little devices that defined his life were going haywire. Going headlong in the wrong direction.

Dr. Salvatore had been blunt with her last week: *I'm not trying to be an alarmist here, Mrs. Topping. But unless something changes—by which I mean making a pretty drastic change in your husband's lifestyle—it doesn't look good for the long run. I know you love him and that's why I'm saying these things.*

Dr. Salvatore didn't know it, but he'd told her what to do. How to help.

And now she was ready.

When Tyler returned from wherever it was that he'd gone this time, she would do it. She would do it before she had time to think about it or change her mind.

She would do it, that is, the very next time she saw him.

She heard a noise from the first floor: a click, a rasp. She felt a faint shimmy in the walls as the vibration was transferred up the framework, moving from floor to floor. She knew what that meant. It was the heavy front door, opening and closing.

Tyler was home.

Chapter Five

A few miles away, across a town now bathed in a faint blue wash of moonlight—or at least that share of moonlight able to slip in between the mountains—a woman stood at a sink in the far back corner of a busy room.

The sink was bolted to the wall, which meant that her back was to the room. The room was filled with expensive-looking medical equipment, most of it arranged between three rows of cribs.

Each crib bristled with IV lines, and with wires attached to tall stacks of monitors. The monitors featured jagged scribbles of green and orange and yellow that traveled across black backgrounds.

Lights had been turned low. The only regularly occurring sounds were the beeps and chirps and hums of the monitors, and the carefully muted footfalls of nurses as they moved between the rows, bending over to attend to the infants nestled in the cribs.

Other sounds flared up irregularly: brief, sharp cries from a fitful child, and then another and another, before they were soothed and quieted by the nurses, or, if the nurses' efforts were unsuccessful, finally by fatigue.

Bell finished rinsing out the bucket. She set it upside-down in the other side of the sink to dry. She'd rinsed out the mop first, twisting the strings one way and then the other way, squeezing out the excess water with steady pressure from her joined fists. Then she had propped it next to the sink and tackled the bucket.

By now her hands were red and cold, her knuckles swollen. She'd forgotten—again—until just this minute about the yellow rubber gloves back in the storage room.

Well, next time. And she was sure there'd be a next time. The night was shaping up to be a long one, filled with lots of messes and repeated cleanups.

"Hey, Bell."

She turned.

It was Glenna Stavros, the night nursing supervisor. The chunky woman looked uncomfortable in the blue scrubs that fit too tightly across her butt and belly. She was easily six feet tall—Bell had never asked for the specific measurement, figuring that Glenna had been answering that question for most of her adult life—with a froth of reddish hair that wafted from her scalp like strawberry meringue. She had a round, open face, a face that would have been mildly pretty had it not borne the cuneiform marks of ancient acne.

"Hate to ask," Glenna went on, frowning to prove her displeasure at being the bearer of this news, "but we've got another spill. You mind?"

"No problem."

"You sure? You just cleaned that mop."

"'Course not." *It's my job,* Bell would have added, except that it would've sounded sassy, petulant. Which wasn't how she meant it.

"Okay." Glenna still frowned. She'd thought she was well past her discomfort at ordering Bell around. Tonight, though, after all these weeks, Glenna was backsliding. Maybe because the clock was winding down on Bell's last few days.

Yes, cleaning up spills was definitely part of her required duties. So was swabbing the toilets and washing the windows. And yes, Glenna was technically her supervisor.

But sometimes, well . . .

"Really," Bell said, still trying to put her at ease. "I don't mind."

"Thanks. But I just don't feel right about it. I mean . . ." Glenna hesitated. "It's just . . ." She shrugged, letting her big shoulders hover up around her ears for a good long time before dropping them again. "You're totally sure it's okay?"

"Yeah." Bell, bucket in one hand, mop in the other, started to move past her. "Excuse me."

"Sorry." The nurse took a step sideways. Bell went by her, conscious of Glenna's eyes on her back. She could pretty much guess the nurse's thoughts. She knew Glenna was struck by the simple, telltale symbols of a situation she still occasionally found incongruous: the baggy sea foam–green jumpsuit Bell was required to wear, the clunky, skid-proof shoes. The hairnet. The mop and bucket.

As Glenna had explained to Bell on her first day of working here, she was uncomfortable telling her when to show up, when to take her break, when she needed to gather the soiled, stinking linens and put them in the bin.

You were a prosecutor, Glenna had added. *You have a law degree from Georgetown. And I'm telling you to bundle up the shitty sheets?*

Bell's reply had come swiftly and forcefully: *Get over it. Or I can't do my community service here.*

And so Glenna did get over it—mostly. She had to, because there was always something to clean up. The clinic was suffused with chaos. It was a low-level, everyday chaos, but it was chaos all the same, and it could not be otherwise. Too few staff members were charged with taking care of too many desperately ill infants in a too-small facility. The result was a constant churn of crises alternating with—mercifully—some random, compensatory minutes of fragile-as-glass calm.

At the center of everything were the rows of cribs. In them, babies born to drug-addicted mothers flailed and thrashed, their tiny bodies wracked by the spasms of withdrawal.

This was the Evening Street Clinic, named for the dusty, run-down side street in downtown Acker's Gap where it was located, in a former tobacco warehouse donated by a good-hearted local businessman who had watched the steady uptick in the number of afflicted infants and thought, *Oh my Lord.* Back when Bell was still prosecuting attorney, she had volunteered at the clinic. She'd arrive here after a long day of work filled with many frustrations and find, in the midst of ostensible hopelessness, a different kind of hope—a flinty, battle-tested, hard-won optimism. She'd hold an infant against her chest while she rocked gently back and forth, back and forth, in one of the big oak rockers, humming and cooing to the tiny, white-capped person in her arms.

When it came time for the community service portion of her sentence, Bell asked to be sent to Evening Street. The judge agreed, but stipulated that her service would be the same kind assigned to any other felon under court supervision. No special treatment. Her job would not involve rocking and cooing.

No. She would dust and sweep. She would scrub and rinse. She would dump trash cans and bundle up medical waste for secure disposal. She would replace lightbulbs and wipe down countertops and disinfect sinks. Bell had nodded at the judge, with no comment. She would do precisely as she was told to do by the court, for precisely as long as she'd been told to do it, because this was the fate she had chosen.

She had not shared her reasons for so doing with another living soul.

"What's next?"

Hearing the words, Glenna looked up from the paperwork on the chest-high rolling cart that served as her desk. Her pen hovered over a thick tablet of printouts of lab reports. The pages were crowded with boldface numbers and ruled lines and polysyllabic words typed in neat rows.

"What?" she said.

"Finished mopping. What do you need me to do now?"

"Oh. Well—let me think about it. Just relax for a bit."

"Okay," Bell said. She made it three steps away from the cart.

"Hey."

She turned back.

"It's getting close, right?" Glenna said. "Your last day, I mean."

Bell nodded. "End of the week."

"Wow. Went by fast." Glenna shook her head. "What am I saying? It probably didn't feel that way to you. I bet it seemed like forever."

"Sometimes the shift goes by really quickly. Other times—not so much."

Glenna waited expectantly, clearly hoping she would say more. Bell knew how much the nurse wanted to have a personal conversation with her. She could sense that Glenna was fascinated by her, by her dark past and by the height from which she had fallen. Glenna knew only bits and pieces about what had happened to bring Bell to this highly unlikely point in her life—the same basic information that everyone else in Acker's Gap knew—but it was enough to make her yearn for more.

"The work you do here," Bell said, filling in the gap because she knew Glenna wanted her to say something else, "is so important. I'm glad I could help. Even in such a small way."

"It's not small."

"You know what I mean. You're what these kids need. You and the other nurses."

"Sure. Us—plus a freakin' miracle." Glenna let her pen drop so that she could rub the back of her broad neck. She was tired and she was frustrated, and she didn't mind if it showed. "We all know what's going to happen to these kids. And it's not a pretty picture. Their lives are compromised from the start. All the health problems—respiratory, cardiac, neurological—and we send them home to families that can't or won't care for them in the ways they need. But what can we do? The foster system's overwhelmed. It's a mess. Sometimes I think about these children and all they're going to need and I just . . ." Glenna shook her head. This was not where she'd wanted one of her last conversations with Bell to go. "Anyway," she said, recalibrating, "I really just wanted to say thanks. This can't have been an easy thing for you. Being here, I mean. Doing menial labor. You handled yourself with a lot of dignity."

"Wasn't too bad. But thanks."

"And I wanted to say good-bye."

"Say it on Friday. I still have a few more days to go."

Glenna picked up her pen. "I'm off until next week. Took some vacation time. My granddaughter's in a beauty pageant up in Parkersburg. I gotta be there, too, because I do her hair. She likes the way I put in the sparkly barrettes. So—this is it. Next time I'm here, you'll be gone."

"Oh. Right." It occurred to Bell that she knew nothing at all about Glenna's personal life. Granddaughter? Grandchildren? Other people's lives were a hazy blur. The thing about catastrophe—the kind Bell had gone through, with everything familiar being ripped up and tossed away—was that it made you selfish. Or self-centered, maybe: That was a better word for it. It wasn't that you valued yourself above others; you just didn't think much about others, period.

There was you and your pain. And little else.

"Right," Bell repeated. "Well, then—yeah. It's been nice getting to know you." They both knew that wasn't true—they hadn't gotten to know each other—but it seemed like the right thing to say, and so Bell said it.

"Same here," Glenna said. "Absolutely." And then, emboldened by the fact that these were likely the last few minutes they would ever have for a private conversation, Glenna added, "Any idea where you'll be living? Or what kind of job you'll get?"

"My house needs a lot of work—it sat empty for two and a half years. But it's okay for now. So that's where I'll stay."

The answer to Glenna's second question—the one about what sort of work she'd do—was more complicated and so she ignored it.

"Okay," the nurse said. "Well—good luck."

Glenna was disappointed. Bell could feel it in the neutral sound of her words, see it in the slump of her shoulders. But she couldn't do anything about that. She couldn't make Glenna feel better. No more rescues. Her days of taking care of other people were over.

That duty had ended some three years ago, when her sister Shirley died.

"Before I forget," Glenna said. She reached into the front pocket of her uniform. "I want you to have this." She drew out a business card. "It's got the clinic's number. My number's on there, too. My cell. Maybe we can grab a cup of coffee one day."

"Thanks," Bell said. "Maybe we can." She looked around. "Thought I might step outside for a minute or two. Get some air. That okay?"

"Of course. You don't need to ask my permission."

Bell looked directly into her eyes.

"Yes. I do."

She was right, and Glenna knew it, and the reminder caused a flush to spread slowly up the side of the nurse's pale doughy face. It was easy to forget the line that separated them. A custodian didn't have the same privileges that a nurse or a doctor would have. Or the freedom that a prosecutor, here to volunteer to rock babies to sleep, would have.

"Okay, well—fine," Glenna said. "Just be careful. It's late. And cold." She had more to say, and she couldn't resist saying it. "Look, I—I hope you end up staying in Acker's Gap, okay? And that we actually have that cup of coffee one day. But I know—well, I can guess—that after all you've been through, you might want to get away from here. For good, I mean." A weary smile. "And I get it. I really do. West Virginia in your rearview mirror—that might be the goal."

It was, Bell thought.

And then one day—it wasn't anymore.

Chapter Six

Ellie listened.

It wasn't like Tyler to come all the way up to the doll room but he was doing just that. She could tell.

She knew the house so well that she could follow his progress, based on the volume and rhythm of his footsteps.

Maybe he'd come home to demand more money from her. Sometimes he even threatened her with violence. The drugs messed with his brain, turned him into someone he wasn't. *God help me—that's not Tyler anymore,* she had said once to Brett, after an especially terrible encounter. *That's not my little boy. That's somebody else. A stranger.*

Tyler broke her heart, over and over again.

Listening, she held her breath as long as she could. She took a brief sip of air and then held her breath again, the better to hear, to track, his movements. To visualize his ascent.

So that she'd be ready. *Forewarned is forearmed,* she reminded herself. And she was armed. Her hands weren't shaking at all. She was resolute.

There was a brief hesitation in his steps—maybe he had stopped to refashion his grip on the handrail, or to listen to a noise from somewhere else in the house—but then the steps continued.

Steadily.

Relentlessly.

She could tell that he'd just arrived at the landing between the first and second floors. Now he embarked on the second half of that staircase, the one that ended up on the second floor.

Now he was on the second floor.

She heard him moving across the hall toward the steps to the attic. It was a not a long hall, and it took him no time at all. She heard the hinges sing out as he opened the door, the one leading to the attic staircase. It wasn't the dreaded, drawn-out *crea-eeeeeeek* you heard in horror films, or anything silly like that; it was just the ordinary sound of an ordinary door being opened in an ordinary way. Not slow, not fast. Just opening.

She waited.

In seconds he would be at the door at the top of that steep staircase. At the threshold of her special place. For an instant she felt intensely vulnerable—there was no lock on the door, so Tyler could just twist the knob and enter—but then she reminded herself that she had the upper hand.

Because she had the gun.

He was blundering into an ambush and he didn't know it. It wouldn't even occur to him that she might fight back. He trusted her to be the same old weak, ineffectual person she'd always been with him, the pushover, the easy mark.

Good old Mom.

Her first instinct had to be right, she told herself: He was coming up here for money. He needed more of it. Always.

He'd spent what he had taken from her purse last night and once again he was tapped out, and she was his best chance. They would dance the same dance they always danced: He'd ask, she'd say no; he'd beg, she'd say no; he'd wheedle pathetically, she'd say no; he'd insult her and berate her and curse at her and then he'd switch tactics and moan, *You never loved me, that's why I'm the way I am, it's your fault, YOUR FAULT, you're a cold heartless bitch and you know it,* and she'd say:

Yes. Here, take it. Take all of it.

Funny. He didn't really have to steal from them, because she always ended up giving in, anyway, and handing him the money, and he knew that, but stealing was always his first impulse. Steal first, beg second.

Was it pride? That must be why he had to sneak around at the outset, pocketing what he could, before he finally broke down and just said: *Gimme.*

Yes, it must be pride. Some small particle of pride remained, perhaps, even in the midst of the ruins of his soul.

All of that was going to be irrelevant, however. In minutes it would be over.

Her mind had quieted down. At first, when she'd heard the front door open and realized it was Tyler, she was overwhelmed by panic. She was, in fact, quite dizzy from it. She was sick to her stomach. She felt a heave and a clench in her bowels. Something black moved in front of her eyes.

Was she actually capable of this? Could she really do it?

Yes, she could.

Because she had to.

The steps stopped. He was right outside the door.

Ellie's heart was pounding so wildly that she feared it might tear itself right out of her chest, leaving the arteries and veins dangling and sparking like downed power lines.

She was standing now, facing the door. The gun was raised and aimed, secured with both hands, her arms slightly bent, the way her daddy had taught her.

Would her daddy approve of *this*? Family, he believed, was sacred. You protected your loved ones. But Daddy had died when Tyler was ten. Still cute and earnest and loveable. Daddy never had a chance to meet the New Tyler.

And if he had, he would've shot the boy himself.

She was ready.

The knob turned.

The door swung open.

"Ellie? Honey? You up here?"

Her husband's big body filled the doorway, like something jammed in a box too small for it.

Brett Topping's eyes instantly went to the gun. He flinched, shocked by what he saw.

"Ellie—*for God's sake*—what in the name of . . ."

She let her wrists drop. The muzzle now pointed at the floor. She was breathing so hard and so fast that her shoulders juddered up and down. Her breath kept catching in her throat. She was crying now. Silently, but passionately. They were tears of relief, of course, tears of desperate gratitude that she had not mistakenly shot her husband, the love of her life—but she was feeling another kind of relief, too.

A secret one.

Relief that the necessary thing—killing her own son—had been postponed for just a little while longer.

"I—I was scared," she said, her voice hoarse and shaky, barely audible. She couldn't look at him and keep up the lie, so she looked away. "I heard a noise—I thought—it's just that—you're never home anymore. At night—at night I get so scared. I didn't know—I was afraid—I—"

While she was babbling he crossed the short space. He took the gun from her hands—gently, gently—and he set it on the small table by her chair. Now he held her, letting her weep into his chest.

She couldn't tell him about her plan. There was no reason to involve him. None.

"Sweetheart," he murmured, "I'm here, okay? It's all right. You're safe. You're safe now. I'm here." He stroked her hair. "I'm sorry I wasn't here. I had a meeting at the bank. Another one. It ran long. Like the others." He was breathing through his nose, a slow, deliberate kind of breathing, filled with solemn regret. "I wish I'd known how frightened you were."

"I don't like to bother you. It's just that with Tyler living here again—I mean, I haven't seen him since last night, but there's always the chance that—I keep thinking that somebody might come after—I mean, the people he hangs around these days, they're not—"

"I know, I know." He stroked and he stroked. He made a sound in his throat, an *mmmmm* sound that he intended, Ellie knew, to be soothing. "So he hasn't come home."

"No."

"Well, he's got some cash." Brett's voice was bitter, knowing. "Which means he won't be back for a while. That's for damned sure." A thought occurred to him. "Do you think we ought to call his probation officer? Tell him what happened?"

"We're supposed to."

"I know. But will it do any good? It never does. Nothing does. *Nothing*." Another deep breath. "Dammit. Look what he's done to you. Made you so scared that you had to bring a gun up here to defend yourself and—oh, God, Ellie. I'm sorry. I'm sorry about my meetings and I'm sorry about—everything. I'm so sorry."

Standing there in the doll room, her eyes drawn to a pale shaft of moonlight on the wooden floor, encircled by her husband's strong arms and by his words, Ellie had a sudden epiphany.

It should have occurred to her before. But there were too many other things on her mind.

She didn't say anything out loud. But she was sure of it:

Brett wasn't telling her the truth.

She didn't know where he'd been tonight—but it wasn't the bank. And the other nights?

No. Not the bank. And there weren't any board meetings, either.

She'd been so focused on Tyler that she had ignored the glaring, unassailable, too-obvious truth: Brett was lying. He'd been lying to her for weeks. Ever since he'd started staying out so late, not returning home until midnight or long after.

This was yet another way Tyler was ruining their lives. He'd turned his father into a liar.

And his mother into a killer.

She trembled. Brett kissed the top of her head.

He thinks I'm still upset over the close call with the gun. He thinks I'm still frightened. He doesn't know what I'm really thinking. He doesn't know I'm going to kill our son.

Just as her husband had no idea what was going on in *her* mind— she didn't know what was going on in his, either.

She had never felt lonelier.

Chapter Seven

There it was.

The Raythune County Public Library was just as Bell remembered it. The old bricks were still painted malarial yellow, and the paint was still peeling, still flaking, in all the same places.

Well, maybe a few more places, too. She could see that now, courtesy of the morning sunlight.

The green metal box on the sidewalk out front, with BOOK RETURN stenciled on the side in look-at-me white lettering, still had the same dents and gouges in all the same spots.

Everything was the same.

Everything was completely different.

This wasn't the first time Bell had walked through the heart of downtown Acker's Gap since her release. But it was the first time she'd been here so early in the day, with no one else around. Usually she went right home when her shift at the clinic ended, avoiding these streets and their closely packed cargo of reminiscences.

Morning, she realized, changed the place. It was as if the memories coiled deep inside each object—parking meter, streetlight, mailbox—moved closer to the surface for just a few minutes, knowing she was the sole witness.

She read the sign on the door: Yes, the library still opened at nine. She'd be back after she got some breakfast.

It was very cold this morning. Surprisingly cold, given the fact that it was only October. The young sunrise had yet to dent the intense chill. The surrounding ring of mountains looked as stern and black as a barrel stave.

A blast of wind flung a red plastic cup end over end along the brick street. The clatter made her turn and look. Bell zipped up her jacket, hunching her shoulders. Her hands found their way deeper into her pockets.

She kept walking.

She passed an empty storefront. This had been Waltrip's Furniture. Jesse Waltrip had finally given up a few years ago, after a good half-century in business. A sheet of plywood covered the space that once had been a broad picture window, behind which the beautiful accouterments of a perfect living room—couch, coffee table, end tables, wing chairs, fireplace—offered up a cozy little fiction.

As a girl, Bell remembered, she used to stand in front of this window and dream. She had known perfectly well that the fireplace was fake, but warmed herself by the happiness it promised.

She came to another empty storefront. This one still had glass in the window but that glass was filthy, smeared with dried mud and gray scabs of bird shit. The hand-painted sign on the crumbling door had faded almost to invisibility, yet if you looked close, you could barely make out the once-peppy lettering: CAPPY'S SHOE REPAIR AND CUSTOM-FIT ORTHODICS. Cappy—Billy Capperton—used to own the place.

He'd died a good ten years ago. Or was it fifteen?

Now she was coming up to JPs, the diner where she'd had so many conferences with Nick Fogelsong, late at night or early in the morning, for so many years. He used to be the sheriff.

And I used to be the prosecutor.

Bell shook her head. She had a bad case of the used-to-bes. There was no cure—at least none she'd ever heard of, other than just putting up with the sadness, the melancholy, caused by wandering through a dense thicket of her yesterdays.

This town was where she'd grown up. Yes, she'd gone away to college, then law school. She'd lived in the D.C. area for a while after that.

Then, in a move that surprised herself as much as it did everyone else, she had returned.

Newly divorced, with her sixteen-year-old daughter in tow, she had come back. She'd had a vague, poetic notion about rescuing Acker's Gap. Ripping it free from the fist of darkness that seemed to hold the town in its smothering grip. Drugs, alcohol, poverty, crime, despair: The roll call of afflictions was dreary. And endless.

Had she been she naïve? *Of course,* Bell thought. *And idealistic and probably arrogant, too. So sue me.*

Her first act had been to run for prosecutor. Nick Fogelsong's favorite joke still rang in her head: *And the bad news is—you won.* But they'd made a great team, she and Nick. For years. Sheriff and prosecutor. Colleagues. Good friends. Fighting the good fight—at least until Nick resigned five years ago and took a job in private security. A year ago he and his wife, Mary Sue, retired to Florida.

Christmas cards, emails: not the same. Not the same at all.

He'd visited her often at Alderson. The visits were always awkward. He didn't agree with what she'd done—her guilty plea, her demand for prison time—and his disappointment, while wordless, still dominated their time together. He was her oldest, dearest friend, and she didn't really know him anymore.

He'd said the same thing about her, back when she first told him her intentions: *I don't know who you are, Belfa, when you talk this way. For God's sake, don't do it.*

She was still bitter about his defection. Instead of supporting her decision to request prison time, he had lectured her. *Lectured* her. She was throwing away her life, he said. She was making a meaningless sacrifice. Playing the martyr card.

On and on.

I'll never forgive him, she thought. *To hell with him, anyway.*

She had reached JPs. God, the memories! How many times had she and Nick sat across from each other in one of the high-backed, dusky-red Naugahyde booths, drinking coffee by the gallon, arguing by the hour, laughing, kidding each other, talking over cases?

Hundreds. At a bare minimum.

She tried to push open the door.

It wouldn't budge.

"Check the sign," said the woman who'd just come up behind her. "Doesn't open 'til eight."

Bell turned around. "As of when?" She'd seen the woman's reflection in the glass window, which is why she didn't jump from the shock.

"As of—well, I don't rightly remember, but recently," Rhonda Lovejoy said. "How are you, Bell?"

"I'd be better with a cup of coffee and one of Jackie's cinnamon rolls—but I guess it can't be helped." Jackie LeFevre owned and operated JPs. "Anyway, it's good to see you, Rhonda."

A brief hug ensued. It was awkward for both of them. But it also was the thing to do, and so they did it. And then they broke apart.

Rhonda Lovejoy was a broad-faced, big-shouldered woman with a curly luxuriance of orange-blond hair that was, right now, mostly tucked beneath a black beret. She wore a belted beige trench coat over what Bell could see was a navy pants suit. Black heels. Businesswoman's attire.

And why not? Bell told herself. This was a workday. For everyone.

Almost everyone.

"What brings you downtown so early?" Rhonda said.

"Finished my shift at Evening Street. Realized I wasn't the least bit tired. So I thought I'd have breakfast at JPs and then do some work at the library." Bell crossed her arms and shivered. "Damn this cold." She tilted her head. "How about you? Pretty early to be heading to the courthouse."

Rhonda smiled. "Not really. Compared to the hours you used to keep—I'm already late."

It was the wrong thing to say. Or maybe it was the right thing. Who knew?

In any case, Rhonda had gotten it out of the way before it had a chance to become a burden, the Great Unsaid Truth that would brood over their conversation like a patient, I've-got-all-day vulture:

She was the prosecutor now. Bell's job.

Rhonda had kept in touch with her over the past three years, first driving over to Greenbrier County to the prison as often as Bell would allow it, and later stopping by Evening Street Clinic. The visits were brief—they had to be, because Bell's time was strictly supervised—but they were regular.

And so this wasn't the first time they'd seen each other since the momentous change in Bell's life.

But it was the first time that such an encounter had occurred in the shadow of the Raythune County Courthouse—*the granddaddy,* Bell realized, *of the used-to-bes.*

That courthouse stood in all of its foursquare, limestone glory on the very next corner, an ancient, gray symbol of enforced rectitude. In a heavy fog, it might be mistaken for a whaling ship, its tarnished gold dome poking up through the murk like a crow's nest. The wide lawn rose at a slow incline to meet a sweeping expanse of steps. The steps led to a massive double door flanked by four white pillars, two on either side. Such a massive, ornate structure seemed wildly out of place in a downtown so humbled and shrunken, so scraped raw and pounded down by decades of adversity and lack.

But out of place or not, Bell still loved every inch of it. She'd been immensely proud of what she and Nick had done at the courthouse—the cases they had solved, the lives they had saved, the children and elderly people they had rescued. And the justice they had tried, in their own imperfect but steady and determined way, to serve.

And now she was exiled from it. Forever. She'd never work there again.

"You look great, Rhonda," Bell said hurriedly. She needed to get her mind back to the here and now.

"Got a big trial starting today. Aggravated assault." Rhonda lifted her right foot, frowning as she turned the uncomfortable-looking heel this way and that. "It's Judge Tompkins. You know how it goes. If you show up in his courtroom and you're not dressed fit to kill and cripple, he'll tell the bailiff to throw you out—if you're female, that is."

Bell nodded. Certain courtrooms were the last bastions of misogyny; judges were the absolute rulers of their domains. Yes, you could complain—but God help you when you made your next motion before that judge. You'd be cut off so fast and so completely that your sentence would need a tourniquet to keep it from bleeding out.

"Oh, yeah," Bell said. "I remember."

"So I guess I'd better go," Rhonda said, after another brief but awkward stretch of silence. "Lots of prep work to do."

A pickup truck rattled by, shedding sparks from a dangling muffler that bumped along the bricks. The driver honked; Rhonda waved.

"Sure," Bell said. "I understand." Once, she'd been the one who had to cut short the conversations; she'd been the one with the impossible schedule and the ludicrously overstuffed to-do list.

"We're having that dinner we talked about, right?" Rhonda said. "Soon as you're settled and all. We can catch up then." A grin. "I've got some news."

"Really. Do I get a hint?"

"Nope. I want your curiosity honed to a fine edge. I want you to be jumping out of your skin until I spill the beans." Rhonda's grin got bigger.

And then it disappeared altogether, as if she only allowed herself a few seconds of levity in any given morning. It was clear that Rhonda had something else she needed to say, something serious, something somber.

The words came out in a ragged rush.

"Truth is, Bell, things're bad. Really bad. As bad as they've ever been. I don't know how much you've heard, but the overdose deaths are still piling up. The drug gangs are worse than ever. Bolder. More vicious. Even kids from good families—kids who've had every advantage, every break in the damned world—they're getting involved, too. Starting early. Pills, then heroin. Fentanyl. It breaks your heart. You know?"

Before Bell could reply, Rhonda said, "Of course you know. You saw it, too. We saw it together. No stopping it. Not then, not now." She looked down at the sidewalk, and then back up again, meeting Bell's eyes.

This isn't the Rhonda I knew, Bell thought. Sunny, fun-loving, optimistic Rhonda—where had she gone? *The job's gotten to her.*

How could it not?

"Let me tell you about a crazy dream I had," Rhonda said. Her voice had shifted again. It was softer now, less agitated, even though her words were still grim. "More like a nightmare, really. Sometimes—right before I fall asleep—I see us heading for some final crisis. Some kind of

Appalachian apocalypse. Where the whole damned place just . . . *explodes.* It all goes up in a big old ball of smoke and flame and it's all wiped out—and then we have to start over." A bemused half-smile. "Well, not 'we'—I guess we'd be dead. But somebody. Somebody starts over. From scratch. And this time around, nobody invents any drugs." She touched Bell's arm. "Gotta go."

"I know."

But it was a bad note to end on. Bell could sense Rhonda's hesitation to leave, with the terrible vision hanging in the air.

"The good news is," Rhonda said, "Jackie's been able to keep JPs open. Hell of a struggle, tell you that. Things've been real slow."

"Is that why she changed the hours?"

Rhonda nodded. "Wasn't getting the early morning business off the interstate anymore. All those truckers, the ones who didn't mind a little detour to get a plate of eggs over easy with hash browns and rye toast? They started minding, I guess." She shrugged. "Jackie's hanging on, but barely."

Like all of us, Bell thought.

As soon as Rhonda had gone she peered in through the big picture window, cupping her hands across her forehead to create a makeshift visor. Even without the lights on she could still make out the booths with their bench seats and battered wooden tables, slotted against the walls. Tables and chairs in the middle of the room. Cash register and coffee urn on a shelf at the side. Across the back was a long bar. Four leather-topped bar stools in front of it.

Carla, she remembered, used to love perching on a bar stool and twirling and twirling. She'd laugh and—

Stop it, Bell scolded herself. *Enough with the used-to-bes.*

She dropped her arms and turned. She rammed her hands in her pockets. The cold was cutting through the fabric of her jacket, as if it wasn't even there.

She'd drive up to the interstate, find a place to get a cup of coffee, and then come back when the library opened. She had work to do.

She wasn't a prosecutor anymore. Law enforcement was out of the picture for her now. That much was true.

But maybe there were other ways of saving a town.

Chapter Eight

Tyler Topping sat on a curb at the edge of the student parking lot at Acker's Gap High School. The lot was on a hill next to the low-slung clump of dull pink brick, accessed by a short run of concrete steps.

He passed the time by repeatedly poking his heel in and out of a mound of trash that had wedged itself against the curb. The intrusion created a satisfying little rattle, thanks to the preponderance of empty brown McDonald's bags, straw wrappers, and assorted other paper-based trash.

Last night's high was gone, but he wasn't yet ravaged by the need to get high again, either. That would come, and soon, and it would be brutal; it would claw at his guts and smack his brain around like a tennis ball. Right now, though, he teetered on the thin margin between the savor of one high and the desire for the next one, an interval that never lasted long but that provided his only meaningful opportunity for enterprise and forward motion.

He'd spent most of yesterday in various parking lots—Dollar Tree, the Skin U Alive tattoo parlor, Lymon's Market—trying to sell pills, because he owed a lot of money to Deke Foley. This was his first stop this morning. He was waiting for the kids to start arriving, at which point the lot would be flooded with students.

Or as he now thought of them: customers.

He felt around in the pouch of his hoodie. Yep, there they were: three baggies filled with white Oxycontin pills. Not as good as heroin, because you had to charge more to make any profit, but at least it was something. He'd bought them with the money he'd gotten from his mom's billfold. Started out with five and this was what he had left. Selling the two had taken him almost all day yesterday. *Way* too long. He'd lost the magic touch. His old haunts didn't work anymore. Not when you only had pills. Everybody wanted heroin now. Heroin, though, was harder to get, especially when he already owed so much money.

"Hey. You."

Before he looked up to see who had addressed him, Tyler slid his hand—slowly, *slowly*—out of the pouch. If you moved too fast, you looked like you were way too self-conscious about what was in there.

Be casual. Be cool. That was the best way to play it. Always.

"Yeah," Tyler said. He squinted up at the large figure looming over him, blocking the sun. He hadn't noticed the kid's approach; he'd been too intent on his troubles. He was certain he'd never seen this person before: overfed body, the big pimply face topped off by a tan Peterbilt cap, and the standard county-boy uniform consisting of a brown Carhartt jacket, camo cargo pants, knockoff Red Wing boots. Tyler pegged his age at fourteen, fifteen, although the size could be a fooler; he might be younger. Big ones generally looked older than they actually were. It was only when you started talking to them that the kid part showed through.

"You can't be doing that shit around here, man," the kid said. He spoke in a mild, nonthreatening way, with a slight wheedle at the end of the sentence.

Tyler decided to be coy. "What shit?"

"Come on. I seen you yesterday over at Lymon's. I know why you're here. All I'm sayin' is—they won't stand for it. They'll chase you right outta here, soon as they see you. Mr. Bricker—he's the assistant principal—he checks the parking lot every hour. He's a real SOB."

Ed Bricker. Big, ugly Ed Bricker with his stupid crew cut and his sneery lip and his lazy eye and his blubbery gut and his fat ass. So he was still here. He'd been here two years ago, the last time Tyler was enrolled as a student. As far as Tyler or anybody else knew, Ed Bricker had been here forever; he was one of those school administrators synonymous with the building, meaning he dated back to the 1950s and had never had a single upgrade.

Tyler kicked again at the slurry of trash. "Don't know what you're talking about, bro."

The kid looked confused now. Tyler could read his mind: The kid was wondering if Tyler was telling the truth. Maybe he'd been mistaken about the drugs.

Could anybody be that dumb?

Yep. This kid could.

Then again, Tyler asked himself, who was the dumb one? Selling this shit in the school parking lot was asking for trouble, just like the kid said. He knew that. But he was desperate. Rock-bottom, end-of-the-line desperate. The other places weren't working. The few people who came along told him to go away, or to repent and give his life to Jesus. Or they just threatened to call the sheriff.

If he didn't sell the rest and get the money to Deke Foley by tomorrow, if he didn't make at least some kind of payment on the shitload of cash he owed him, well . . .

Tyler shivered. Foley was serious business. He didn't care about anything but his money. Tyler knew a guy who'd tried to cross him once. Nobody ever heard from that guy again.

"I'm talking," the kid said, "about what you got in your pocket there." He'd been temporarily emboldened by Tyler's preoccupation. "You got pills in there, ain'tcha?"

"What?"

"I ain't stupid."

"Didn't say you were." Tyler hauled himself to his feet. He was tired of sitting on the curb. His butt hurt. "Why're you up here, anyway? First bell's not for a while. Used to go here myself."

The kid's eyes changed. "Really? How long ago?"

"Not long."

"Really." The kid looked intrigued. "You look older'n that. Like you been out a while."

Now that he was standing up next to the kid, Tyler could smell his breath. It was a sweetly foul combination of Dubble Bubble and smokeless tobacco. There was another scent, too, sweeping off this Big Goober of a kid; to his amusement, Tyler realized it was AXE body spray. The country boy's go-to aphrodisiac. This kid might as well have taped a hand-lettered VIRGIN sign to his forehead and been done with it.

Before Tyler could brag to the kid about how bad a student he'd been, and how many times Bricker had kicked his nasty ass, his cell rang. With the money he'd swiped from his mom he had picked up a burner phone last night and texted the number to Foley. If he hadn't, Foley would've tracked him down and done some damage. Foley didn't fool around. He needed to know where you were and what you were doing. He kept tabs on you. Always. You couldn't call him but he could call you whenever he wanted to.

"Yeah," Tyler said.

Silence.

"Anybody there?" Nervousness made his voice shake.

"You got the money yet?"

"Working on it."

The click on the other end of the call was abrupt, unnerving. Like an unspoken threat. That was impossible, Tyler knew; a click was a click. But when the person at the other end of the call was Deke Foley, that's how it was.

He was afraid of Foley.

Only a friggin' idiot *wouldn't* be afraid of Foley.

And Tyler Topping was no idiot. In fact, he was smart. And so he had a plan. He had a little something up his sleeve. Foley was going to find that out. If everything came together the way Tyler wanted it to—and it would, because the plan was good—then Foley was in for a big surprise. He'd understand real quick that Tyler Topping wasn't just another one of his dumb-shit employees. You could only push Tyler Topping so far, right?

Sooner or later, a guy like Tyler Topping was going to turn the tables on you. Because he had a brain. Not like those other guys.

"I'm tellin' you—Bricker's gonna be coming up here real soon," the kid said. "You better go. Before he throws your ass out."

Tyler turned his head. He had forgotten all about the Big Goober.

"Mind your own damned business," he muttered to the kid. Students had started to arrive, swarming the lot. It was showtime. Tyler only had a few minutes to mingle, make it clear what he had, and strike quick deals. The kid was in his way.

Potential customers swept past him, the guys in Levis and T-shirts despite the fierce cold, the girls in blouses and skirts and leggings and peacoats, a jostling, jumpy, noisy crowd. The sea of teenagers that engulfed him also brought an unwanted slap of nostalgia: He'd been one of them himself, just a couple of years ago. He, too, had talked shit about homecoming and about what an asshole Bricker was and about how hot Sharon Cullen was—she was the popular girl back then, and he could still remember the dirty jokes about her, God, her tits were *spectacular,* and when Charlie bought that additive stuff to put in his Dodge Charger, the red plastic bottle with STP on the label, it was Tyler who said, *You know what STP stands for, right? It stands for Sharon's Tough Pussy,* and everybody cracked up and he felt like a king, like the friggin' king of the world, because nothing felt better than making your friends laugh.

Well, there was one thing that felt better: getting high.

Only sometimes at first, and then more often. And then, before he knew it, all the time. He forgot about his sacred ambition of getting into Sharon Cullen's pants before graduation.

He forgot about Sharon Cullen.

And graduation? Shit—who cared about *that* anymore?

He blinked and shivered, shaking off the stupid memories. No time for that crap.

"Hey," he said, sliding up next to kid after kid, pulling his hand slowly out of the hoodie pouch, thumbing the edge of the baggie. That's all he ever had to say: "Hey." Nothing more. He'd known it would be easy, lucrative, like shooting fish in a freakin' barrel, but he'd tried the other places first because the school parking lot was high-reward, high-risk.

Bricker would be out here any second.

The Big Goober wasn't right next to him anymore. He'd been pushed back by the crowd as word spread that the guy in the hoodie over by the curb was selling. Tyler finished a transaction and looked up and he somehow saw the Goober's face again, staring at him mournfully, and he wanted to shout *Quit looking at me* or *Get lost* or something—anything—that would make the kid go away.

A soft voice interrupted his irritation.

"Tyler? Is that you?"

His heart gave a little lurch. Jesus Christ—it was Sara Banville. Alex's little sister. She was a junior this year—how had he forgotten that? When they were kids, he and Alex and Sara had hung out all the time. Played together, rode their bikes, built forts, caught crawdads in the creek in the woods out behind the Banvilles' house.

"Hey," he said.

She'd turned out pretty. Not just pretty: friggin' *gorgeous*. He'd forgotten that, too. The gawky kid with the sawed-off hair and the braces and the horsey face was, like, a babe now. Lean and tall. Legs for days. He hadn't seen her in—how long? He couldn't remember. Before his last rehab, anyway.

"Tyler Topping," she said, as if she needed to state both halves of his name to make the reality of it being *him* stick.

And then, just before she was bumped aside by a jagged wave of her classmates, as more car doors popped open and people wheeled past, she gave him a look that infuriated him because it seemed to be made up mostly of pity, with some bafflement thrown in there, too, and a dash of abstract curiosity, and she said, "You used to be the coolest guy."

You used to be the coolest guy.

He felt a roaring in his ears. His face was hot, even in the cold air. Sara had always had a major crush on him. She'd begged him and Alex to let her hang out with them, back when they were kids. He was a king. But not anymore.

Tyler couldn't stand to be here another minute, not another friggin' *second,* and so he yanked the dirty gray hood up over his head and he drove his balled fists into the pouch and he hunched away.

He wasn't leaving because of Bricker. To hell with Bricker. *Bricker can kiss my ass,* he thought. To hell with Sara, too. To hell with everything. He wanted—no, he needed, and he needed it *now*—to be high. To wipe this shit out of his head.

Correction: to fill his head with another kind of shit.

He'd get out on the highway and hitch a ride. Find somewhere to chill.

He started walking faster. He took a quick look back over his shoulder, scouring the lot. He wondered if Bricker was really going to show up, or if the Big Goober was misinformed—if the kid, that is, was just as full of shit as everybody else in the whole friggin' world.

No sign of Bricker.

He relaxed. Forward, march. The highway was just ahead.

But he had missed it.

He didn't notice the man who had hidden himself behind a rocky outcropping on the ridge above the parking lot, watching him.

It wasn't Bricker.

Chapter Nine

Ellie Topping stood in front of her kitchen counter, staring pensively at the two chicken breasts she had thawed out to make a late supper for her and Brett. The chicken breasts were still in the package, still positioned on a thin yellow cardboard slab and covered tightly in plastic.

She planned to bake them, not fry them. Brett preferred fried chicken, of course—who didn't?—but Dr. Salvatore had been clear. Brett needed to get his weight and his blood pressure back under control. The excess pounds were putting pressure on his joints, Dr. Salvatore had explained multiple times, in a voice more neighborly than censorious, and definitely forgiving, being as how the physician himself carried at least thirty extra pounds packed around his middle like ballast in a cargo hold. *Fat doctors,* Brett had remarked with a wicked grin on their way back from the last appointment, *are a real blessing, you know?*

She wasn't sure what time Brett would be home. He'd told her that he was addressing a regional civic improvement association meeting over in Swanville.

Did she believe him? No, she didn't. But her skepticism didn't matter to her, and she pushed it aside. She didn't care about where he was. Maybe he was having an affair. She doubted that, but maybe it was true. She didn't care enough to speculate.

Only the fact of her resolve to kill her son mattered to her anymore.

She unwrapped the chicken breasts and arranged them in a shallow baking dish. Her plan was to let them marinate in Italian dressing for an hour or so in the refrigerator, and then bake them in a 350-degree oven for forty-five minutes. It was her go-to recipe, the first dinner she'd ever cooked for Brett, just after they met.

She had been working at the Walgreen's photo counter. He came over and introduced himself. Before she knew it, Ellie had invited the big, handsome, older man with the nice smile to come to her house for dinner. And—wonder of wonders—he showed up, driving his fancy car to the log home at the end of Briney Hollow, shaking hands with her sisters and brothers and her father, charming them all.

A year later, she had married him.

She turned the temperature dial on the front of the oven to pre-heat it.

Still no word from Tyler. He could be anywhere, doing anything. Which was nothing new. Which was why she'd decided to do what she had to do.

Her thoughts took a wild swing.

Here I am, sprinkling a bottle of Kraft Italian over chicken breasts—and the next time I see my son, I'm going to kill him.

Here I am, pressing Saran wrap around the edges of the baking dish—and the next time I see my son, I'm going to kill him.

Here I am, putting the baking dish in the fridge—and the next time I see my son, I'm going to kill him.

The juxtapositions had been popping up in her mind ever since she had made her decision. Ordinary life rubbed up against the profound thing that loomed over her, the thing that dominated the horizon the way a mountain range does, throwing a shadow over everything.

The two-part chime of the doorbell crashed into her thoughts. Startled, she lurched away from the oven and almost blundered into the butcher-block island, catching herself before her hip smashed against it.

Her mind clicked through the possibilities. Brett wouldn't ring the front doorbell, would he? No, of course not. He always came in through the garage door.

Tyler. Could it be Tyler?

Her gun was up in the doll room. Two stories away.

This is all wrong.

She felt like a fool. Like the universe was playing a joke on her. Because when she *had* the gun—it wasn't Tyler.

And when it really might *be* Tyler, she didn't have the gun.

Ellie waited another few seconds, letting her breathing go back to a semblance of a normal rhythm. And then she walked to the front door. She felt light, almost hollow, as if she were watching her own actions from a high and distant perch, and she was curious to see what she might do next.

But it wasn't Tyler.

It wasn't Brett, either.

Standing on the wide front porch, each palm cupping its opposite elbow, dressed in a pretty lavender sweater and pressed khaki slacks, was Sandy Banville. Her short blond curls looked coppery in the brightness of the porch light. At the moment Ellie opened the door Sandy's head was turned; she appeared to be scanning the darkening neighborhood, her head whipping around in quick, birdlike jerks.

"Sandy?" Ellie said.

The head zipped back around to face forward. Sandy smiled at her and laughed. It wasn't a real laugh, though; Ellie knew what it was, because she did that herself. It was a nervous, embarrassed reaction to stress. Almost every woman of Ellie's acquaintance was a nervous laugher. None of the men were.

"Oh—hi," Sandy said. Another short laugh, as she winced in the porch light. "Sorry to just come by like this."

"It's fine. Is everything—"

"Everything's great. Really great."

Ellie waited. In years past she would have automatically said, "Get in here, you," and she and Sandy would've sat around the kitchen and talked, maybe having a glass of wine, maybe not, but the talk was always animated and fun. *Sandy's a riot,* Ellie would tell Brett, because it was true. *An absolute riot.* They went back and forth all the time in those days, she and Sandy; they were in and out of each other's houses, chatting about children, husbands, current events.

But they hadn't been that close for . . . what was it now? A year and a half? At least. At least that. Ellie had lost track. What had divided them was Tyler. And his problems.

"I just wondered," Sandy was saying, "if you saw anybody around here tonight."

"What? Who?"

"Oh, I just mean—has there been anything—like, unusual?"

She was fishing, but for what? Ellie knew she ought to invite Sandy inside. It was getting chilly out there. But she held back. The invisible wall between them was higher and harder than ever; the hurt Sandy had inflicted upon her—telling their other friends about the problems with Tyler, leading the unofficial neighborhood campaign to isolate the Toppings—was still there, still hot and bristling. *They treat us like lepers,* Ellie thought, *and Sandy here, my good friend Sandy—ha!—is the ringleader.*

So—nope. Freeze your ass off, for all I care. I'm not inviting you into my house. Not anymore.

"No," Ellie said.

"Okay, well. I just thought—it's just that I was out walking and I thought I saw something." Her smile looked astonishingly fake to Ellie. "But you're sure."

"Yes."

Sandy nodded. She had abandoned the palm-cupping-opposite-elbow stance by now and crossed her arms, tightly hugging her own torso.

"Well, okay, then," Sandy said. The phony grin subsided, replaced by an expression of concern that looked equally phony. Ellie knew this expression well; she was fairly sure Sandy refined it by watching *Dr. Phil.* "Like I said the other day, if you ever need anybody to talk to, we can sit down with a cup of—"

"I've got dinner in the oven. Better go check on it."

Ellie shut the big front door before Sandy could utter even one more pointless, insultingly inane and insincere platitude. The lines were clear: The Banvilles were superior—blessed, even—because their children were thriving. The Toppings were lesser because their son was a mess.

Simple as that.

Ellie stood in the living room, breathing hard, watching the closed door as if she expected it to do something. Fly open, give her sass—something. She didn't give a damn what Sandy had seen or hadn't seen in the neighborhood tonight. She wasn't the least bit curious.

She had a theory: Sandy was probably just snooping. Hoping to catch the Toppings in some dramatic moment, with Tyler raving, Brett threatening, her cowering, a scene that Sandy could then describe to the Blankenships and the Coverdells and the Martins and every other damned family, up and down the block. Everybody knew Tyler was living at home again. Hard to keep it secret, when he showed up on the street all the time, grinning that stupid grin, falling down.

Ellie turned and walked back into the kitchen, wondering along the way if Brett would prefer green beans or salad with his dinner. Truth was, he didn't like either; what Dr. Salvatore called "healthy choices" made Brett roll his eyes. He wanted burgers and curly fries and milkshakes. All the things that are bad for you. But really—who didn't?

Finally, *finally*, Brett was home. It was long past ten o'clock.

Hearing the front door open and close, Ellie took a deep, grateful breath and unlinked her hands. She had been sitting at the kitchen table, eyes closed, head bowed, thinking about . . . about what she always thought about these days, which was: the time before.

Before all of this. Back when she was happy.

The chicken breasts had been ready a while ago; the baking dish waited on top of the stove. It wasn't hot to the touch anymore. She could reheat it in the microwave. Although chances were, Brett had stopped at a drive-through burger place on his way home. That was okay. He hadn't called in advance of his arrival, either, and that was also okay; she didn't care.

She waited for Brett's booming, "Honey? Ellie? You still up?" She was cold, but she knew that she wouldn't be cold anymore once Brett's arms were around her. For that reason, she stayed seated. She loved it when he leaned down and embraced her from behind, nuzzling the back of her neck. She still got goose bumps when he touched her.

"Mom?"

It was Tyler.

Ellie stood up abruptly.

It was her son, and he had been using. "Using" was the preferred term; she and Brett had learned that, and now it came to them naturally. At first, it hadn't. You used shovels and fabric softener and fountain pens, didn't you?

No. In their family, the word "using" was now reserved exclusively for drugs.

She could tell right away. The "Mom" sounded slurred.

She felt a surge of panic in her stomach, the twist and the gouge.

Tyler ambled into the kitchen and fell into a chair. He lifted his face, sniffing the air. Even though the chicken had cooled, a trickle of its scent was still in the air, the sweetly acidic tang of the marinade. Tyler scowled, as if it was a bad smell, which it wasn't; the scowl came from his attempt to identify it, which he couldn't. His brain, Ellie knew, was functioning like a pudgy runner in mud. She knew that because she'd read articles about it.

About what happened to a brain when you marinated it in drugs, the same way she'd marinated the chicken breasts in Italian dressing.

He looked at her and grinned. "Hey," he said.

His eyes were glassy. There was a large red scrape on his right cheek, as if he'd face-planted into a sidewalk somewhere. Now she saw that the backs of his hands, too, were scraped raw. Ellie wondered where and how it had happened. Tyler, she knew, probably wouldn't be able to tell her, even if he wanted to; he didn't remember.

He didn't look as if he remembered much of anything right now—except for the way home. That, he'd mastered. That, he'd kept intact and accessible somewhere in that mealy-soft, slow-dissolving brain of his. He always found his way right back here.

So that he can torment us. So that we'll never be free of him. Never.

Tyler smacked his lips. He ran the tip of his ugly, salmon-colored tongue around the rim of his mouth; those lips, Ellie saw, were dry and cracked.

"Hey," he said. The way he said it—the slow, lazy drawl—infuriated her.

She stood by the table, looking down at him, and she was filled with a disgust that, in turn, repulsed her as much as Tyler did right now. *I'm disgusted by my own child. Truly, truly disgusted. If he needed me right now, I wouldn't want to touch him. I don't even like looking at him. Being this close to him.*

So who was the real monster here?

That was what she asked herself. Was it Tyler—or was it the mother who couldn't stand the thought of touching her own son?

Now he slumped over, like a puppet with cut strings. His forehead clunked on the tabletop.

She wasn't worried. She knew he'd just fallen asleep. Boom—just like that. She'd found him this way before. Many mornings she had come downstairs and there he was, her son, curled up on the kitchen floor, snoring and twitching, his skin gray, his clothes torn, his hair filthy, drug paraphernalia scattered carelessly around him like fallen leaves.

Paraphernalia. That was another word they'd learned was the appropriate term. A funny-sounding word, really, if you said it out loud a few times; it sounded like a carnival ride or a fancy hat. She didn't think she'd be able to spell it.

She watched him for another minute, keenly regretting the fact that Brett was going to come home and find this in the kitchen, along with the nice, healthy dinner: His son, his child, passed out at the table, snoring. A filthy lump.

Welcome home, Daddy.

Unless.

Unless she followed through with her plan. Right now. She had time, didn't she? Brett hadn't called. So he wasn't close.

She could do it. Tonight. Right now. And then she could somehow move Tyler's body and . . . *Wait.*

How? How would she do it? How could she move him? Her son was skinny, but he would still be too much for her to handle, too heavy, too awkward, too cumbersome, too everything. And the cleanup. How would she—

Never mind. Never mind.

She didn't remember climbing the two flights of stairs—first floor to second floor, second floor to attic—but she must have done that, and then back down again, because she stood where she'd been standing before, right behind him . . .

And now she was holding the gun.

Everything would be okay.

Tyler stirred. He farted. It was a prolonged, squeaky wheeze that would've been funny, Ellie thought, if it had happened around a dinner table with other kids. Everyone would've laughed and teased him. Back in the hollow, with her brothers and sisters, a loud fart was a happy excuse for mayhem; there were groans and boos and sisters pinching their noses shut and brothers jumping out of their chairs so they could crumple to the floor, pretending to faint dead away from the noxious odor. Henry always started it; he was always the one who coughed and gagged the loudest, rubbing his eyes and staggering around. He was hilarious.

God, she missed Henry.

Her brother never knew about Tyler and the drugs. That was a blessing. She'd managed to keep all this from him. Henry had died without knowing. He died still thinking Tyler was a sweet boy.

She raised the gun. Aimed at his head.

He had settled down again. He wasn't moving. He would be an easy target.

As far as what would happen after—who cared? She didn't. All she cared about was getting rid of this pain. The terrifying conviction that she couldn't live even a second longer with this sorrow. It was crushing her.

The crown of his head was a scraggly mess of black frizz. When he was a little boy she had kissed him in that exact spot each night, right on the top of the head, after she'd read him a chapter or two of *My Side of the Mountain*. She didn't leave his room until he had fallen asleep.

Another long, languid snore.

She moved the gun into position. It always felt heavier than it really was, as if the gun itself was aware of the profoundly grave use to which it was about to be consecrated, as if it channeled a density of weight simply from the implications of its existence.

She took a breath. Calmness suddenly overwhelmed her, a kind of spreading, beatific contentment, replacing the internal chaos, the anxiety.

This was the right thing to do. She knew it. She *knew* it.

She was ready.

She took another breath.

Now, she told herself. *Do it now.*

And then she lowered the gun.

She could not do it. She would never be able to do it. She had been fooling herself, thinking she was hard enough and cold enough and brave enough to perform this act.

It had been a fantasy, and for a few precious days, it had sustained her—the idea that she could rescue herself and Brett from all that their lives had become, from the drama and the strangeness and the ravening sadness.

But she couldn't. Because Tyler was flesh of her flesh, bone of her bone.

It was over. She would put the gun back in the box and put the box on the high shelf in the garage, and that would be that.

Now she was truly helpless, and she knew it. There was no escape.

Chapter Ten

"I thought we had an understanding."

Molly Drucker's voice was neutral. Not mean, not unfeeling—just not especially warm. She stood in front of Jake, holding the snout of an empty Rolling Rock bottle between the thumb and forefinger of each hand.

"Jake? You listening?"

"Yeah." He rolled his chair back and forth on the living room carpet, just a tenth of a turn each way. Forward, back. Forward, back. He needed to have something to do. Somewhere to funnel his chagrin.

"Then tell me what's going on," Molly said. "We had an agreement, right? Two beers a day. Tops. I get here tonight and I start fixing dinner and I find these in the trash. Plus the one you're working on right now. That makes three."

He started to make a smart-aleck crack about her counting skills and how impressive they were but he held off. It wasn't funny. And besides, she had a point.

Molly's habit was to stop by his house when she had a night off. He hadn't asked her to. She just did it, falling into a rhythm before he could come up with a plausible reason why she shouldn't. Sometimes she brought Malik; sometimes not. If she brought him, she had to leave a little earlier, to get her brother home to bed.

In the first few months after he'd gotten out of the hospital, Jake hired a home health care aide to come by each day. It was all paid for by his disability check. But it didn't work out. Jake hated him. Well, maybe not "hated." The guy bored him. Judged him. Condescended to him.

Or maybe none of the three, Molly had said, when he complained bitterly about the guy. *You just don't want some stranger hanging around. Even though he means well. And even though you need him.* Jake's reply was needle-sharp and cobra-quick: *I don't need anybody.* Molly didn't bother to soften the blow when she replied: *Yeah, you do.*

After the first guy there was an aide named Melissa, and then one named Bobbi Rae, and then there was nobody. One by one, he told them all to get lost. He'd go it alone.

A month and a half into Jake's ill-fated experiment with independence, Molly began stopping by in the afternoons. Good thing: He'd come down with a urinary tract infection because he didn't clean his catheter correctly. The infection almost killed him. He also had an infected bedsore on his butt that very nearly took him down the same way. And his house was nirvana for cockroaches, because he couldn't clean the kitchen properly after meal preparation. The sink was too high. Instead of dealing with that problem he'd just stopped eating regularly. He lost fifteen pounds in six weeks. The sweatpants and T-shirt dripped from his pared-down frame.

Molly had made things right again.

She came by two or three times a week to check on him. She didn't fuss over him. She would replace a lightbulb in the hall or drop off a prescription she'd picked up for him or collect the empty Rolling Rock bottles on the coffee table and take them to the recycling bin in the church lot at the end of the road.

He was sometimes overwhelmed with the depth of the feelings he still had for her, even after all that had happened, all the changes. He loved watching her hands. In his former life he had worked with her for years, arriving at accident scenes and parking the Blazer next to the square white truck with RAYTHUNE COUNTY FIRE RES-CUE painted on its sides in blocky red letters, and in all that time, he'd never lost his fascination with Molly Drucker's hands. They were black, like the rest of her—she and her brother were among the few

African-Americans in this part of West Virginia—and there was a beauty to her hands, a strength and a power that made them almost like art objects for Jake. He would never, of course, have said such a silly thing out loud.

"I'm waiting for an explanation," Molly said. "About the beers."

Malik laughed. Jake couldn't get mad at him. Molly's little brother had been born with profound cognitive and physical challenges. And besides, it *was* pretty funny: Molly lecturing Jake about drinking too much beer, hovering over him like a spitfire wife in a sitcom. And Jake, sitting in his chair, nicely buzzed, grinning, letting her do it.

"Had a lot to think about," he said.

"Yeah—and beer's always such a great help when you're trying to think clearly." Molly marched back into the kitchen. There was a brief tinkle of glass as she tossed the bottles into the recycling box under the sink.

"Hey," Jake called. He wanted her to come back. "Hey. I'll explain, okay?"

"Just a sec," she answered. She didn't need to raise her voice for him to hear her; the kitchen wasn't that far away in the tiny house. "I've got to finish slicing carrots for the stew. I need to get everything in the crock-pot before three. So it'll be ready for your supper."

He waited. Malik sat on the couch, playing with a deck of cards. It wasn't a card game—Malik was not capable of that—but it was a game with cards. He pulled six cards out of the deck and placed them faceup on the couch cushion beside him, and then he drew out another six and did the same thing with those, just below the original row. And then he scrambled the cards all together and started again. Sometimes, Jake saw, he added a third row before scrambling the cards.

Molly came back into the living room. She untied the strings of a red-checked apron as she walked. When she got close enough to the couch, she lifted the apron and dropped it playfully over Malik's head.

"Hey!" he yelled, and then he giggled. He pulled off the apron and flung it back at her. She caught it in one of her sturdy hands.

Jake liked watching them goof around. He knew how easily a relationship that was permanently out of balance—a relationship in which one person took care of another—could become toxic, with resentment from both ends, from both the beleaguered, overworked caretaker and the helpless, needy recipient of that care. Molly, he'd noted from the day he met Malik three years ago, avoided that trap. She kept their interaction as light and fun as she could. She was in charge, and Malik was a burden—but he wasn't *only* a burden. He was her little brother, too.

He wondered how their relationship—his and Molly's—would evolve, now that everything had changed for him. He wouldn't be anybody's damned burden. He'd run his chair straight off a high cliff before he'd let that happen.

"So just put whatever stew's left in the fridge tonight," Molly said. "Tomorrow night you can heat it up again. It'll taste even better."

"Why's that?"

"Flavors mingle." She sat down on the couch, careful not to jostle Malik's row of cards. Jake understood: For the rest of the conversation, she didn't want to loom over him.

"So," she went on. "This thing you've been thinking about. This thing that requires the assistance of three beers."

"Sheriff came by," he said. Molly nodded, waiting for him to go on, to justify his broken promise. "Job offer," he added.

A light leapt into her dark eyes. "Oh, Jake—is she going to—"

"No, no, no," he said hastily. "Nothing like that." He hadn't meant to mislead her, even for an instant. But part of him was pleased: Molly knew how much he wanted to be a deputy again, and she really believed it might be possible. If she didn't believe it, she wouldn't have reacted that way.

"Then what?" she said. Her voice had gone flat again.

"Dispatcher. They need somebody on the night shift for a few months."

"Well, it's something."

He shook his head. "Come on. We both know what it is. It's a shit job. Offered out of pity."

She nodded. "You're probably right." There was a rigorous honesty about her. It was one of the things—one of the many, many things—that had made him fall in love with her, all those years ago. He had waited too long to tell her, though.

And by the time he did, just a few hours before he was shot in the spine, she had turned him down. After that, he had a few more important things to deal with than his unrequited love for Molly Drucker.

Like: How to survive the rest of his life as half a person. Because that's precisely how he regarded himself. He'd been severed. Sliced in half, body and soul.

"Maybe you could do it for just a little while," she said.

"Maybe."

For a few seconds the only sound was the soft scrape of the cards against the couch fabric as Malik dished them out and plucked them back up again, one after another.

Then Molly said, "So that's it? That's why you broke your promise and had the extra beers? Come on, Jake."

"It wasn't a promise."

She nodded. He was right. It hadn't been a promise, just an agreement.

"Still," she said. "Pretty lame."

Before Jake could react, Malik uttered a long screeching yodel, sweeping both rows of cards onto the floor and then dumping the rest of the deck on top of them. The yodel wasn't distress, Jake knew; it was excitement. Malik dropped to his knees, wedging himself between the couch and the coffee table while he scooped up the cards.

"Got to go check on the crockpot," Molly said, standing up. Jake got it: She was using Malik's outburst as a way of closing off the moment. As much as she helped her brother, her brother often helped her, too—in ways Malik himself would never be able to appreciate. "And then I have to get this guy home," she added, "so I can go to work." She leaned over and rubbed Malik's head. He grinned up at her.

"Hey," Jake said.

"Yeah?"

"Thanks," he said. "For the stew, I mean." He thought about adding *And for everything else, too,* but he knew how much she'd hate that.

"No problem."

"And I've decided."

"Decided what?"

"I'm going to take the dispatcher's job. I'll tell Harrison I can start right away."

He knew how much Molly wanted to hear that, but he also knew how hard she'd try to hide it. She wasn't effusive.

"Okay," she said. She couldn't fool him. He'd heard it—the little hitch in her voice, the slight catch. She *was* pleased. And that, in turn, pleased him.

Chapter Eleven

When Brett came home an hour and a half later, Ellie was still in the garage, sitting on the concrete floor, her back to the wall, her knees up, her arms looped around those knees. She had put the gun back in its original spot on the high shelf.

And then she'd sunk to the floor, and stayed there.

Tyler was still asleep back at the kitchen table. He'd probably be there all night. When he passed out, he could stay that way for hours.

She heard the chipper little hum as the garage door opener was hailed by the remote in Brett's vehicle, the edges of the door rolling up smoothly in the sleek aluminum grooves. But she didn't lift her head. She heard the Escalade slide into its spot, right next to her Audi.

She heard the garage door going down again. She heard the door of the Escalade open and close. She reacted to none of it.

Brett was leaning over her. He couldn't squat; his knees were too bad.

"Sweetie?" he said. "Are you okay?"

She looked up at him but she didn't answer. He reached down and took her elbow, helping her up. He put his arms around her. She was crying but she did it gently. There were times in the past when she had sobbed into his chest but this was not one of those times.

Finally he stepped back from her, still holding her upper arms. He needed to look at her.

"Are you okay?" he repeated. It was a silly question, of course; they had not been okay, either of them, since Tyler had started his descent. But it was still the question one asked at such a time.

"He's back," she said.

At the moment, that was all she needed to say. It explained everything.

Brett nodded. "I'm sorry I'm so late. Things got—well, the meeting was pretty intense."

"The meeting."

"Yeah."

She put a hand on his lapel. She looked into his eyes. When you'd been married as long as they had been married, there was no expectation of total honesty all the time; that was an impossible standard, she knew. People lied. They lied out of kindness, sometimes, or out of expediency, when the truth was too complex. Or maybe too hurtful. Lies weren't always cruel, horrible, deceitful things. Some lies were just softeners. Shortcuts. Avoidances of controversy.

Hence forgivable.

"I made chicken," she said, "if you're still hungry. If you've already eaten, I can just save it for tomor—"

The sudden noise was shattering. It blasted through the garage like a linked chain of mini-earthquakes. Several seconds went by—and another flurry of punches—before Ellie realized it was coming from the closed garage door. Someone was attacking it from the outside with a series of massive, heavy blows.

"Get in the house," Brett said. His voice was firm but not agitated, not panicky. He tried to turn her around, pushing her toward the open doorway that led back into the kitchen.

"What's happening?"

"In the house *now.*"

She didn't go and he didn't have the time to make her. Sweat, she saw, instantly swamped his brow. He fumbled for the cell in his pants pocket as the pounding accelerated. Dents were popping through the aluminum in rhythm with the blows.

Pop, pop, pop. Three dents in the middle of the door.

Pop, pop. Two more, off to the right.

Pop. Another one, on the left.

Pop, pop. Back in the middle again, a little higher this time.

The white door instantly looked like a page of braille. Her best guess? A baseball bat.

Brett's shaky thumb kept slipping off the screen but finally he steadied it enough to press. "He's here," he muttered into his cell. The phone dropped with a clatter onto the concrete. Brett was in the corner now, grabbing for the shovel, pawing his way past the other garden implements to get at it: rake, hoe, broom.

"How soon until the police get here?" Ellie said, raising her voice so that he could hear her over the tremendous noise, the *BoomBoom-BoomBoomBoom* echoing through the garage.

"That's not who I called."

"Who did you—"

"I said to get in the goddamned house!"

Still no shock in his voice. Just irritation at not being obeyed. Again she ignored him, knowing it wouldn't matter past the next three seconds because his attention was elsewhere.

She watched as her husband advanced toward the right side of the garage door, the fabric of his blue suit bunched across his back, holding the shovel like a minuteman with a musket. He looked silly, but that wasn't the kind of thing you were supposed to think at such a time— was it?—and so Ellie let the thought drop out of her head. She was frightened—of course she was frightened—but she was also curious. Their long ordeal with Tyler had left her immune to the more primitive forms of panic.

With the heel of his hand Brett slapped the lighted square of the inside opener. The wounded door stuttered upward with a groan and rattle and a tinny shriek, inch by difficult inch, as if reluctant to rise and reveal its own tormentor.

And there he was.

Hunched in their driveway in a sort of semi-crouch was a man with a shaved head and a matched set of lethal-looking hands. He clutched a baseball bat in the right one.

In the splash of artificial illumination from the floodlight, Ellie could see his face. It was contorted in a snarl. He was dressed completely in black: black jacket, black jeans, black boots. For all of his menacing brio, though, his face looked soft to her, malleable, as if his youth kept peeking through the hard veneer.

His vehicle—or what she assumed was the vehicle belonging to him, a low-slung, black sporty thing with a white racing stripe down the side—was parked at a crazy angle, half on their driveway, half on their lawn, its engine still spitting and growling.

From across the street, an outside light went on at the Tudor-style house. The oversized front door with the gold sunburst inlay separated itself reluctantly from the ostentatious frame. *Ed Coverdell*, Ellie thought. *Nosy bastard.*

"Everything okay over there, Brett?"

"Just fine, Ed!" Brett yelled back. He waved. "Got it under control!"

The door across the street closed again. With relief. The light snapped off.

Truth was, Ellie knew, the neighbors were no longer surprised by anything that happened at the Topping house. Loud, crazy noises didn't faze them. The Toppings were in a special category now, on account of Tyler. The category was: People Whose Lives Have Spun Totally Out of Control. They were, she knew, a joke. The neighborhood punch line.

Tonight's little disturbing-the-peace drama was far from the worst thing that had ever happened at the Toppings' house. Far, far from it. She knew what Ed Coverdell was telling his wife, Sherry, right now: *It's that junkie kid of theirs again. Gotta be. Whacked out on something. Tearing their house apart. Oughta lock him up. Lost cause.*

"Lookin' for Tyler," muttered the young man in the driveway.

"Get out of here." Brett panted hard, and then he closed his mouth to suck in air through his nose.

"Who the hell are *you*?"

"Tyler's father."

"Okay, Tyler's Father." The man cackled at his own witticism. "He owes me four thousand dollars, okay? He gives me the money—I go away."

Of course, Ellie thought. Tyler was involved in some kind of drug business with this man. It had happened before—people showing up at all hours, drug people asking for Tyler, demanding that he show himself until finally he did, and they all left in the same rusty van—but tonight felt . . . different.

The others hadn't included any door-bashing. This man bristled with rage. He was holding the rage in check right now, but the hand with the bat was never still. It quivered like a tuning fork that never lost its connection with his deep, endless anger.

"I said you need to leave," Brett said.

"Listen, old man. You step aside. Right now. Tell that lying sack of shit to come outside and pay me. Else I'll rip down your whole fuckin' house with my bare hands, you get me?"

"Leave."

The man's response was to cackle once more and peer at the baseball bat in his own hand. Up and down, handle to tip. Up and down. Then he looked back at Brett.

"Your choice, old man."

"Hey." Brett's voice had changed. Ellie heard something different in it. A confidence. A certainty. It was hard and sure. "We don't want you around here," Brett went on. "We want you to leave. Now."

Another cackle. "Shut up. Go get Tyler."

"I did some research. I know who you are. Your name's Deke Foley." The man, Ellie saw, definitely reacted to *Deke Foley*. Her husband was still talking: "You think you're a real tough guy, don't you, Deke? You think you're some kind of big-time gangster. Well, you're not. You're a loser. A bully. A small-town punk. So listen up. You stop this, okay? You leave my family alone."

Foley stared at him.

"I've been watching you," Brett continued, his voice getting stronger and more sure of itself the longer he talked. "You and Tyler both. I've been following Tyler when he goes out to meet you. I take notes, okay? Been doing it for months, ever since he started living here again. I write it all down—dates, times, places, license plate numbers. I know Tyler's selling for you. I've even got pictures, okay? I've got an entire *file* on you, Foley. You and your associates. And there are some surprises in there. Some names that I don't think you'd like other people to know about. So you leave us alone—or I turn that file over to the police."

Foley's jaw flexed and shifted. Ellie could almost feel it in her own jaw: upper and lower rows of teeth grinding against each other. The pressure.

"Did you hear me?" Brett said. He was panting even more heavily now. The sweat on his face was so copious that he looked as if he'd just stepped out of the shower. Fresh notches of sweat blossomed under the arms of his suitcoat. "Did you?"

"Yeah," Foley said. "I heard you."

While Brett was uttering his last two words, Foley had changed his grip on the baseball bat. Added his other hand. He looked like a batter stepping up to the plate. Ellie felt a wave of fear rippling through her guts.

Foley was talking again. "You get that file and you give it to me. You got ten seconds." He took a few practice swings.

"Leave," Brett said.

"Nine."

"I told you to—"

"Eight."

"You better—"

"Seven. Six."

Another sound. It caught the attention of the man and Brett alike; they turned simultaneously and stared as a light-colored sedan barreled straight toward the house, swerving at the last minute so that it ended up sideways in the driveway. It had nearly clipped the end of Foley's car. The man who emerged from it looked like a slimmer version of Brett: suit and tie, shiny shoes. He had a thin, middle-aged face and a goatee.

"What's going on here?" Goatee said, in the kind of too-loud voice that reminded Ellie of the tone a first-time teacher uses to bring a class to order. He stood on the balls of his feet, arms curved out from his body, ready for action. "You need some help here, Brett?"

"Depends," Brett said. "If Foley is ready to leave, then we're okay. If he's not, then we've got a problem."

Okay, right, Ellie thought. Now she understood. Brett must have formed a partnership with some other dad who had the same problem, the same lost son or daughter.

She remembered Brett's complaints, the bleak and bitter asides, the soundtrack to every long drive they'd made in the past few months: *The sheriff can't handle it. Too much for her. Too much for anybody, maybe.*

And later: *Only way to get anything done is to do it your own damned self.*

Just as she'd concocted her own secret plan to liberate them—Brett had his plan, too.

She'd lost her nerve. But Brett hadn't.

Foley spat a rubbery wad of phlegm on the driveway. It sparkled on the concrete. His gaze shifted between the two men. Ellie felt as if she could almost see his thoughts as they slouched across his brain, gray lumps of caveman cognition: *New guy changes the odds. Longer I stand here, better the chance some nosy friggin' neighbor calls the cops. Time to go. Settle this later.*

Foley switched the bat back to one hand. "Ain't over," he muttered. "Both of you's gonna be *real* sorry for this." He took several backward steps down the driveway, shaking his head. Reaching his car, he spat one more time. Then he tossed the bat through the open door and flung himself in after it.

He made sure to leave by way of the wide and beautifully groomed lawn, flattening a chunk of the shrubbery that lined the long curving walk.

At the end of the street Foley's taillights swooped flamboyantly as he executed a crazy-fast left turn. And then he was gone.

Ellie's eyes returned to the driveway. Neither her husband nor his friend had moved.

And for a moment, the scene—two human figures caught in the spectral glare of the floodlight, the flesh on their faces bone-white—looked, she thought, like something out of a movie. Like a scene she had paused with her remote, while she went to the kitchen to refill the chip bowl.

There was Brett and there was Goatee.

Two men poised on a gray expanse, frozen in a tableau of frustration and false bravado. Something stirred in Ellie. It wasn't pity—or it wasn't *only* pity. It had elements of admiration in it, too. *They're trying,* she thought. *They're doing what they can.*

They were good, decent, honorable men, going up against the

unthinkable—thugs and money and all the ugliness in the world—with the only weapons they had, namely their courage and their absurd, touching gallantry. They were too old and too tired to be doing this.

"Go on home, Pete," Brett said wearily to Goatee, and now Ellie knew his name. "It's late."

"You sure?" the man said. "What if he comes back?"

"He won't. Not tonight. I'd bet on it. And thanks for getting over here so quickly."

The man shrugged off the gratitude. "That's the pact we made. And besides—you'd do the same for me."

"Yes," Brett said. "I would."

Brett clamped a hand on Tyler's shoulder. He shook it roughly.

Tyler didn't raise his head. He had slept through the whole thing—the assault on the garage door, the confrontation in the driveway, the threats, the yelling. Drug sleep was not like regular sleep. Ellie had learned that. Their boy could sleep through anything.

His face was thrust into the filthy nest formed by his crossed arms on the kitchen table. He groaned and smacked his lips and shifted his shoulders, trying to get out from under his father's hand.

"What the hell," Tyler mumbled. "Leave me 'lone—lemme—"

"Up," Brett said. The word sounded like a dead weight that dropped with no echo. "Get up."

Ellie watched. She didn't intervene. Brett glanced at her at one point, to see if she might be tempted to try and stop him; she had done just that in the past, when Brett had found Tyler passed out on the front porch, stinking of vomit, and tried to rouse him. *Don't hurt him, Brett. Don't. Don't. Please—don't.*

Not tonight. Tonight, Tyler was on his own.

"Get up—or else," Brett said.

Tyler's response was a cross between a mumbled *FugYou* and a wheezy moan.

In a move that came so quick it thoroughly surprised Ellie—she didn't know that her husband could summon such strength and speed—Brett jerked the chair out from under him. Tyler tumbled onto the floor, yelping like a kicked puppy.

"*Dammit,* Dad, what the hell are you—"

"I told you to get up." An iciness in Brett's voice now.

A few minutes ago, as his friend was getting ready to leave, Brett had introduced Ellie to Pete Pauley out on the driveway. "Pete lives over in Swanville," Brett said. "Runs a carpet place. Sales and installation." The way Brett said that—*sales and installation,* as if he were reading it on a business card—tipped her off that Pete Pauley was probably a bank customer. Pauley had likely come in one day to go over the terms of his business loan and started chatting with Brett Topping, one of the VPs, and before long, they realized what they shared: both of them had a kid in rehab. Again. Because nobody went just once. Both of their families had been eaten alive by drugs. And both of them were ready to fight back. They weren't willing to cede the region to the dealers, to just hand over everything precious to them.

And then Pete Pauley had walked down the driveway and gotten back into his car, as if his visit had been an ordinary one, as if he hadn't raced over here late at night to serve as backup in a standoff with a drug dealer.

The world, Ellie reflected, was only barely recognizable to her any-more.

When she and Brett had walked from the garage into the kitchen, Brett headed straight for Tyler. A few seconds later, Tyler was sprawled on the floor.

"Whaddaya want?" their son muttered in a whiny, slurred, poor-me voice. He tried to stand but couldn't manage. So he flopped right back down on his butt again.

"Your buddy came by," Brett said. "Deke Foley."

The name seemed to hit Tyler like a slap. He flinched, his head snapping back so that he could look up at his father.

"How do you know Deke?"

"I know a lot of things."

Tyler shook his head, trying to clear it. He blinked and he coughed, and then he looked up at Ellie, who stood several feet away from Brett.

"Mom?" Tyler said plaintively. "Help me up, okay?" He stuck out his arm. There was a hint of impatience in the way he waved the hand at the end of that arm. *Of course* she was going to help him up. She was his mom. Mothers did that. She'd always helped before, right? No matter what he'd done? She always capitulated. Always crumbled. She couldn't resist. Couldn't stop herself.

Every instinct in Ellie's body told her to reach down and take Tyler's hand and help him up.

But, no. Not this time. She would back up her husband.

"Your father's talking to you," she said. "You'd better listen."

Tyler dropped his arm. Whatever. He shifted his eyes back to Brett. "So how do you know Deke?"

"I've been following you. Keeping a record. I've seen you meeting with him. You and other people, too. Plenty of times. Got an ID from his plate number."

Now Tyler was focused. "You *what*?"

"Surveillance. For months now," Brett declared. Ellie heard the note of pride in her husband's voice. "That's where I was tonight. I saw you making your rounds, trying to sell that shit. I've been watching you. Saw you at the high school. I know what you do. I know where you pick it up. I know how Deke Foley runs things."

"You didn't tell him that." Tyler made it a statement, not a question.

"Yeah. I did. That's why he hightailed it out of here."

Tyler stood up on his own. He fought against his wobbliness, grabbing the table edge. Ellie saw fear in her son's eyes. Fear and panic.

"Dad—listen, okay? Deke Foley's a really bad guy. I mean it. He's dangerous. You shouldn't have told him—"

"Don't worry. The file's in a safe place. If Foley shows up here again, those notes go straight to the sheriff. It's what we call leverage, son."

"You don't understand," Tyler said. He swayed toward his father, clawing at his arm. Ellie realized that Tyler was crying. Crying! "Dad," he said, "please, *please* listen to me. You can't threaten Deke Foley. It doesn't work that way."

"Sure it does." Now Brett, too, noticed Tyler's tears. Ellie could feel her husband's surprise. Maybe he'd forgotten that drugs could do that: make somebody emotional. Strip off the top layer of a person's self-control.

"Good Lord, Tyler," Brett said. Brisk, businesslike. There'd been a problem to be solved—and he had solved it. Executive-style. "Get hold of yourself. I just told you—Foley can't do a thing to us now. We've got him. He'll stay away. He knows my file could shut him down. So this is your chance, okay? You've got to straighten up. Quit working for him. Get clean. We're talking last chances here, son. I mean it. No more empty promises. No more excuses. You stop *now*. Tonight. And your mother's backing me up on this. We're in this together." He turned to Ellie. "Right, sweetie?"

"Yes," she said.

Tyler stared at the floor, shaking his head, breathing hard, using upward strokes of his palm to wipe at the ropy dazzle of snot on the bottom half of his face. Then he staggered toward the back door, churning his arms as if the air itself was putting up a fight, as if it was too thick with doom to let him slide through with no resistance.

"You don't know what you've done, Dad," Tyler muttered as he lurched forward. There was a darkness in his voice that startled Ellie, a quality of frank foreboding that chilled her right down to the bone. "You don't know. *You don't friggin' know.* They're gonna kill me. They're gonna kill all of us." He blundered out the door.

Chapter Twelve

"Excuse me, ma'am."

Startled, a little confused, and definitely unsettled, Bell flinched and shuddered. Her head jerked up as she searched for the source of the sound. A stranger—harmless-looking, but you never knew—stood on other side of the broad table, regarding her with curiosity.

Okay, Bell thought. *Okay. Right.*

She took a quick second to ground herself. It was all coming back: *You're in the public library. You're sitting at a table in the reference section. You're fine. Absolutely fine.*

Nothing like a couple of years in a state-run facility to put you on edge. Permanently.

"Yes?" Bell said.

"It's getting late."

"What?"

Bell looked around. The rest of the room was deserted. The tall windows were black. The green carpet bore the marks of a vacuum cleaner's evenly plowed rows.

You mean somebody vacuumed *in here and I didn't even notice it?*

Her gaze swung back to the ragged stack of documents on the table in front of her: printouts, file folders, newspapers, magazines, books folded open to pages marked with fluttery yellow tassels of Post-it Notes. There was a pencil in her hand, an open notebook at her elbow, and a chunk of numbered bullet points on the page in handwriting she recognized as her own.

"What time is it?" Bell asked.

"Almost ten."

"Almost *ten?*" Bell was incredulous. Also slightly panicked. Her shift at Evening Street started at 11 P.M.

She looked sheepishly at the woman. She was young—no more than twenty-five, Bell surmised—with a sturdy square body, soft brown eyes and a thick rope of chestnut-colored hair draped across her left shoulder.

"I guess I was preoccupied," Bell said. "Sorry. You're probably getting ready to close."

"Um—we actually closed a couple of hours ago. But you were so focused, I didn't want to disturb you. It's just that—well, I have to get home. I've got a dog, and she needs to—"

"Jesus. Of *course.* Sorry." Bell stood up. She put a hand on her lower back. She'd been sitting way too long.

She was annoyed with herself. How had she gotten so deeply preoccupied with her reading that the real world slipped away? She knew better. She couldn't lose track like that. It had become a scary habit in Alderson. The danger didn't come from the character of the facility itself—Alderson was more depressing than perilous, and the gravest threat came from too many empty hours and too much self-reflection, not from other inmates.

What worried her was the mental drift itself. The lack of self-control.

After which, all hell could break loose inside her.

"So the rest of the staff went home—and you stayed on my behalf?" Bell said. She'd grabbed her jacket from the back of the chair and was poking her fists through the arm holes.

"Um—there's actually no 'rest of the staff.' I'm it." The woman smiled.

Of course, Bell reminded herself. *This is Acker's Gap. Two librarians? An impossible luxury.*

"Well, I really appreciate it. Let me help you put these things away. So you can get home to . . . ?"

"Virginia Woof." The woman spelled out the surname so that Bell would get the joke. "She's a black Lab. And I was an English major."

Bell smiled approvingly. "Home to Virginia Woof, then." Bell had fostered a dog a few years ago, a wonderful shepherd-retriever mix named Goldie. Goldie's sweet brown eyes swam up from the special place in Bell's memories that she reserved for her. "And please pass along my apologies."

The librarian touched the top of the stack. "If you're coming back tomorrow, you can just leave these things here."

"That would be great. I know you spent a lot of time digging up all this information for me. Are you sure it's okay?"

"We don't get a lot of patrons these days. Nobody'll touch it."

Bell nodded. She had recognized a kindred spirit in this young woman when she'd met her early that morning, shortly after Libby Royster had unlocked the rickety front door and flipped on the overhead lights, about a quarter of which didn't work. Bell was right behind her.

She had outlined what she needed. Libby had nodded thoughtfully, a finger on her chin in what Bell assumed was a gesture taught in library school, and then snapped her fingers. "Coming right up," she'd said.

That proved to be overly optimistic. The topic about which Bell had requested information—anything relating to a multinational company known as Utley Pharmaceuticals—produced a massive trove of material after even a cursory data search. "Give me a few hours," Libby said, "and I'll have even more."

And so Bell had returned later that afternoon. She went directly to the square wooden table in the far corner. The butternut surface was broad and burnished, with occasional blotches marking the places where forbidden beverages had spilled, leaving indelible stains. In the center was an enormous pile of materials.

"I set a Google news alert for 'Utley' and 'McMurdo' and it went a little crazy about two P.M.," Libby had explained. "A couple of congressmen announced a hearing for next month on opioids—yeah, I know, *another* hearing, same old same old—and the minute you hear *opioids*"—she made air quotes around the word—"Utley's back in the news, big time."

Bell had nodded. She'd picked up a printout of a *Wall Street Journal* article on the top of the heap. Skimmed the first few paragraphs.

"This one," Bell said, "has all the usual comments from the CEO." She found the sentence she was after. "Here you go. Right in the first paragraph. 'We provide a valuable product to millions of people suffering from debilitating pain' and 'If our products are not used properly then we join with Congress in rising up to demand an accounting of'—blah, blah, blah. You get the gist."

"Yeah."

Bell already knew the players well. The name "McMurdo" was a reference to Roderick Utley McMurdo, CEO and chairman of the board, grandson of company founder Sebastian Utley.

She had moved eagerly through the top items on the stack. "You've really helped me a lot. You've found things in places I didn't even know *existed.*"

"Well, good. Glad it helps."

"By the way, my name is—"

"I know who you are."

Bell had felt a quick spasm of disappointment. It figured: Her story was three years old, but gossip had a long shelf life. Scandal, an even longer one.

She had wanted to be just another patron. She had wanted to be somebody that nobody knew anything about—not a former prosecuting attorney who'd admitted to a long-ago murder. She could hear Carla's voice: *Then you ought to get out of Raythune County, Mom, just as quick as you can. And go as far away as you can. That's the only way you're ever going to outrun who you are. Who you were.*

Libby had continued to talk. "I knew from the moment I saw you. I wasn't living in Acker's Gap when you were prosecutor, but I recognized you from your picture in the paper. I didn't say anything because—well, I didn't want to embarrass you. And when you told me what you were interested in—Utley Pharmaceuticals—it was perfect, because I have a good bit of interest in that company, too."

"Really? Why?"

"You're not the only one looking for answers to this epidemic. The law enforcement part—the dealers, the addicts—that's one side of it. You and your colleagues fought that war for a lot of years. But that's not the only battlefield. More and more, people are turning to another one."

"The drug manufacturers."

"Right." Libby's nod had been quick and resolute. "The illegal drug trade is bad—sure. Absolutely. But the appetite for pain pills in these parts wasn't created by the dealers. It was created by Utley. And by the doctors who were more than willing to prescribe highly addictive pills—as long as it kept the assembly line moving along. The line of desperate people."

"You sound like you know a lot about this."

"More than I'd like to."

"What do you mean?"

Libby had paused, but only briefly. "My maiden name was Washburn. Howie Washburn was my brother."

She thinks I'll know the name, Bell had thought. *And she's right.* Because everyone knew the name. Howie Washburn, a nineteen-year-old deputy in the Collier County Sheriff's Department, had been killed on the job five years ago. A car had passed his county-issued SUV on Highway 14 just after 2 A.M., traveling at a high rate of speed. Deputy Washburn flipped on his lights and siren and gave chase. The car pulled over. Washburn approached. The driver's door popped open. In seconds the deputy was on the ground, drilled in the center of the forehead by a slug from the driver's handgun.

But that wasn't the end of the story. The reason everyone remembered it was because, when they pried open Deputy Washburn's locker at the Collier County courthouse to clear out his belongings, his colleagues made a surprising discovery: a stash of Oxycontin massive enough to supply a dozen pharmacies for the better part of a year.

Deputy Washburn was dealing.

Because Deputy Washburn was using.

"I'm sorry," Bell had said to Libby. Here was proof once more that the tentacles of the drug crisis spread out in every direction, metastasizing with ghastly speed. Bell had always understood that on an intellectual level.

But sometimes she could still be brought up short by the visceral *feel* of that pervasiveness, by the sense of its relentless reach into unexpected places—like, for instance, the life of an able and good-natured reference librarian in a small county library.

Nobody gets away clean, Bell had reminded herself. *Nobody.*

That afternoon, before Bell got down to work, Libby told her the rest of the story. "I knew he had a problem," she'd said, speaking in the slightly trancelike way that Bell had heard in the voices of other people when they recounted this kind of narrative, as if it was some perverse fairy tale, heading toward the polar opposite of a happy ending.

"Started with a football injury. High school. Unbearable pain. Right knee." Libby reached down and tapped her own. "Hyperextended after a nasty tackle on a kickoff return. Doctor told him he'd fix him right up." Her tone grew even darker. "And he did. Boy, did he ever." She tucked in her lower lip. Shook her head. "Howie liked the way the pills made him feel. Simple as that. So he couldn't stop. It got hold of him and—that was it. He hid it pretty well at first. I mean—he got hired as a deputy. Proudest day of his life. Mine, too. But after a while, I figured out what was really going on. So I did all kinds of research on addiction and treatment—what works, what doesn't. I was sure I was going to save my brother. I just knew it. What I *didn't* know"—she swallowed hard—"was that he'd already started dealing. His job helped him out. He was around dealers all the time. It was the only way he could pay for what he needed. By the time he died, he'd moved on to heroin. He had to. It was cheaper than the pills." The pain in her voice was hard for Bell to hear. "Heroin. My brother snorting heroin. Impossible. But—no, not impossible."

"You've read a lot of this material, too, haven't you?" Bell had inclined her head to indicate the stack of printouts.

"Yeah."

"So you know the numbers. Four out of five heroin users started out taking prescription pain pills."

"And Utley made forty billion dollars last year," Libby declared. "*Billion.* They like to say they didn't understand how addictive their pills are. And once they knew, they started warning physicians. But you know what? I think they *did* know. They knew—but they didn't care. They were making too much money." Her voice shook slightly with a livid anger she was trying hard to suppress.

"You may be right. Hard to prove, though."

"Is that what you're doing?" Libby had asked eagerly. "Getting enough information so you can go after them?"

"No. Nothing so grand as all that. I'm not a prosecutor anymore. I'm not even a practicing lawyer."

"Well, somebody better do *something*." Libby's face had changed. It was hard now, and pinched. The soft lines seemed to tighten up. The anger was winning out. "Those bastards. Those *bastards*. They've got to pay for what they did—what they *do*—to Howie and a lot of other people like him. Decent people. Honest people. People who get hurt and go to the doctor in good faith and do what they're told to do and who never *dream*—not in a million years—that they'll ever end up—"

Libby broke off her sentence, breathing with an effort. She had a look in her eye that Bell had seen before. It was the look that came when someone's belief in justice was destroyed.

It was more than just normal disappointment. There was a sense of betrayal—not just by the bad guys, but by the good guys who didn't seem to give a damn about what was being lost, what was dying right before their eyes.

"I'm sorry," Libby said. "I didn't mean to go off like that."

"It's okay."

"That's what happens to me now. I think I'm over it and then something reminds me and . . ." She couldn't finish.

Bell didn't have the heart to tell her that there was no "over it." So she nodded and put a hand on the closest stack of printouts. Her meaning was clear:

Back to work.

Out on the dark, cold street, Bell pulled up the collar of her jacket. God, it was freezing.

She looked around. No one else in sight. No cars in the street, either. Just the shadow-black outlines of the closed businesses—some closed until tomorrow morning, some closed forever—brooding over the broken sidewalk. Towns like Acker's Gap became ghost towns at night.

She hated this town. But she also loved it. That didn't make sense, but it was true.

Maybe, she thought, you couldn't truly love a place until you'd gone through a spell of hating it, too. If you didn't care about it at all—and she knew plenty of people who didn't give a damn about their hometown, who left it behind as quickly as they could, never giving it another thought—then you couldn't summon up the passion to love it, either. The hatred enabled the love. You hated it *because* you loved it— and because it had broken your heart, over and over again.

Bell raised her eyes to the mountains. The great dark shapes eliminated a big chunk of the sky, blocking entire constellations. Each season, there were stars that the people of Acker's Gap never saw.

Sometimes she sensed that those mountains weren't just innocent bystanders, after all. Sometimes she sensed that they secretly dreamed of swallowing this place whole.

Might be a blessing, she thought.

Chapter Thirteen

The next night, in the narrow living room of a small house in one of the scruffier neighborhoods of Acker's Gap, a lithe young woman stood in front of a man in a wheelchair. She leaned over and picked a small thread from the sleeve of his shirt.

"Quit fussing," Jake snapped.

"I'm not fussing. Just want you to look nice."

"Are *too* fussing."

"Maybe I am. But it's for a good cause." Molly checked out the rest of his shirt, concentrating, looking for imperfections, like a jeweler pricing a gem.

He was wearing dark green corduroy trousers, brown socks, and brown loafers, plus that chambray shirt. The shirt was so new that it still featured the creases caused by its long-term internment in a flat plastic package.

The shirt was a gift from Molly. She'd brought it along with her tonight when she showed up with Malik to make dinner.

"Nobody'll know what I look like," Jake said. "I'll be sitting in a damned room. Alone. Taking calls."

"You'll know what you look like."

"Yeah? So?"

"It matters. If you look sharp, you'll *be* sharp." She continued to study him with an appraising eye. When she leaned forward again and tugged at his collar, straightening it, he caught a whiff of the soap she used. He didn't react—not outwardly—but inside, he was thrown into a tumult of longing. He had declared himself to her once, three years ago, and she had explained all the reasons why it wouldn't work. He didn't fight her on it. Maybe, he'd thought at the time, he would try later. Make his case again.

And now, of course, everything was different.

He had no idea why she kept coming around. When he tried to talk about it or—God forbid—to thank her, the glare he received in return was intense, prolonged, and definitely unpleasant, and he backed off. Molly Drucker was a hard person to thank.

She turned to the couch, where Malik sat with his card deck.

"What do you think, Malik?" she asked. "Does Jake look like he's ready to go to work?"

Malik grinned. "Yeah," he said. He added a squeal, and then he tossed the entire deck up in the air. He scrambled on his hands and knees amid the delirium of scattered cards.

She turned back. "Okay, then. There you go. By the way, I can drop you off at the courthouse. I'm not on the duty roster tonight, so I can pick you up after your shift, too."

"That's just *dandy*." The word, the way he said it, was heavy with sarcasm. "No thanks. I'm not a kid on his first day at school. I don't need your help."

"Yeah. You do. Your van still needs a new transmission—unless there was maybe a spontaneous healing that you forgot to mention."

They glared at each other for a few seconds, him looking up at her, her looking down at him. That was the thing about Molly: She always spoke her mind. She didn't sugarcoat things. He was dependent on other people for some basic necessities—things such as cleaning himself and his environment, and lately, until he came up with the money to get his van fixed, getting places—and while it irritated the hell out of him, it was a fact, stark and simple. No hiding the reality. Other people hemmed and hawed, coming up with coy conversational work-arounds so that his needs weren't always front and center—but not Molly.

If she didn't drop him off and pick him up, he'd have to call the county van, the one used to haul Medicaid patients and special-needs kids to their doctor appointments. Chances were, he'd be late for work; the county van was notoriously unreliable, especially at night. Jake had been depending on it ever since the transmission on his van conked out.

"Let me get a comb," Molly said. "I think that hair of yours could use another pass-through. Anybody ever tell you that you've got a cowlick there in the back?"

"Noticed it myself a time or two." He didn't mind her ribbing. In fact, he sort of relished it.

She stood behind him, pushing the comb through his springy brown hair. His hair was longer now than at any previous time in his adult life, falling almost to his shoulders. As a deputy, he'd kept it razored short for many reasons: No time to fuss with hair when you were answering emergency calls. Plus the deputy's hat—brown, flat-brimmed, with a circle of gold braid around the crown that he was supposed to think was silly but that secretly pleased his vanity—fit better over a smooth head than one unruly with too much hair. The new deputy, Dave Previtt, had thick blond hair, so thick and so blond that some county employees had taken to calling him Surfer Dave behind his back, and Jake always wondered why he kept it that way. Surfer Dave's hat always looked ready to pop right off, the hair forcing it out like the charged-up waters of Old Faithful.

Jake closed his eyes. Molly took a few minutes combing his hair. To steady herself while she did it, she put one hand on his left shoulder. The feel of that hand was something he would remember through his entire shift, he thought, and maybe his entire life. He let himself be melodramatic in his thoughts in a way he'd never let himself be out loud. The feel of her hand—strong and true—centered him. Back when he first realized he was falling in love with her, he'd watch her do her job at accident scenes and it was her hands that drew his appreciative gaze. He had a job to do, too, at such times, from unwinding the yellow tape to taking notes to collecting evidence to shooing away rubberneckers, but when he could, he'd sneak another look at Molly's hands.

"There," she said. "All done."

She lifted her hand from his shoulder. The loss of that pressure instantly grieved him; he felt as if he might fly right off the face of the world, without her hand there to hold him down. But that was silly, and he knew it.

She thrust a mirror in front of his face, a small round one with a pink plastic handle.

"What do you think?" she said. She held on to the handle.

He pushed the mirror away. "Jesus Christ, it's not a beauty pageant, okay?"

"Just didn't want you looking like you don't give a damn."

"Maybe I don't." He was feeling restless now, moody. He didn't know what to do with his feelings for her, the ones that still lingered, even after all that had happened. They annoyed him, those feelings. They were too intense. He wished they'd go away.

Sometimes.

"If I thought that was true," she said, "I wouldn't be here." She put the mirror down on the coffee table.

"Where'd you get that thing, anyway?" he said. "That's not mine."

"It's mine."

"What's with the pink?"

"I like pink."

"You like pink."

"Yeah. You got a problem with that?" She said it in a mock-tough style, like a wannabe gangster.

Malik's voice flapped in the background: "You got a problem with that? You got a problem with that?" If he heard a line that he liked, or that was familiar to him, he had a tendency to repeat it. This one scored on both counts.

"No," Jake said, once Malik had settled down again. "No problem."

Truth was, pink seemed a little—well, a little *girly* for Molly Drucker. Pastels didn't suit her. To him she was all about primary colors: the dark blue of her EMT uniform, the trousers and the shirt; the black of her skin. When he was growing up in Beckley, West Virginia, he had seen exactly one African-American. One. That was it. Not three, not five—one. West Virginia, he'd read, was one of the least diverse states in the country, and he believed it.

Sometimes when he felt sorry for himself—usually first thing in the morning, when the reality of his handicap came slamming back into his newly roused consciousness—he thought about Molly, and what it must have been like to be an African-American growing up in Raythune County, West Virginia, the loneliness, the unabashed stares from the old-timers. The muttered comments. She'd never said so, but he knew there had to have been muttered comments. There always were.

"Time to go, Miss Congeniality," Molly said. "I'll go start up the truck. Can you help Malik with his coat?"

He grunted and obliged. He was still thinking about her hand on his shoulder and how good it felt. Too good.

"Ever tell Sheriff Harrison how you really feel about the job?" Molly asked. They had almost reached the courthouse.

"Don't have to. She knows." Jake leaned his head out the open window as Acker's Gap went rolling by. Brick streets, parked cars, mailboxes, houses, empty lots.

He liked to feel the cold wind on his face. Found it bracing. He tilted his head, looking up. The sky had started out starless but at some point had cleared up. Dashes of light now rippled across the black fabric.

"So she's a mind-reader now," Molly said.

Malik sat between them, jittery as always. Humming.

"I mean I made it clear by my attitude," Jake countered. "When she first offered it."

"And you think she picked up on the subtle little signals you were sending out."

"Sounds silly when you say it that way. Not what I meant."

"How would she know if you didn't tell her?"

He considered the question. "She knows me, doesn't she?"

"Maybe."

Molly swung the truck into a parking spot just up the street from the courthouse. At this hour, there was only one other vehicle parked along the block, a small yellow hatchback. Jake assumed it belonged to Beverly Epps. The courthouse was a brooding presence off to the right, three stories of tired stone heaped into a dull, massive square, fronted by a series of wide concrete steps with a wrought-iron railing on either side. Only one window was lighted, on the bottom left-hand side; that was the dispatcher's office. Beverly Epps was waiting for him in there, to show him the ropes.

Like he couldn't figure out how to punch a button all by himself.

"Okay," he said, as soon as Molly had shut down the engine. "I'll tell Harrison that being a dispatcher is beneath me. Great way to start out a new job."

"Might be another way to phrase it. Just so she knows you're on the lookout for something else. If it comes up. That's all I meant." She patted Malik's arm. "Sit tight, buddy. I'm getting Jake's chair out of the back. Then you and me will head home."

She helped Jake into the chair and they moved toward the courthouse. A handicap entrance had been added on the north side. The ramp predated Jake's injury—the county commissioners had wanted to head off a federal order—but he knew that a lot of people resented the cost of it and somehow considered him responsible. The timeline didn't work out, but they didn't care about timelines. So far he was the only one who really needed the ramp. A couple of elderly people used it, but they'd managed the steps before the ramp was available—a fact about which certain citizens still muttered, their eyes dark with judgment, while they scratched the back of their necks.

Molly pushed his chair up the ramp. Jake had tried to argue her out of it; he could get himself up a damned ramp, couldn't he? But then it dawned on him, as she ended the argument by grabbing the rubber-capped handles that jutted out at his shoulders and guiding the chair up the incline, that this wasn't about his disability. She was aware of the fact that he could do this for himself.

She wanted to be with him a few more seconds, before they said their brusque good-byes.

He didn't know how he knew, but he did. He just did.

"So," she said, "if I get a call to go in to work and can't get back here by the end of your—"

"I'll call Steve," he said. "He's on duty tonight. When he gets a break he'll swing by and take me home."

"You'll have to wait."

"Used to that."

She nodded. "Don't take this wrong, but I hope you have a boring night."

"Yeah. Know what you mean." A boring night meant no emergencies. No sudden blooms of violence, with attendant human misery, to deal with. Just a long, unbroken stretch of black Appalachian night.

"Thought you would."

Still she didn't leave. The awkwardness increased by a tick.

"Okay," Molly finally said. "See you around."

He nodded. "Thanks again for the lift. Tell Malik I said he needs to brush his teeth before he goes to bed—even if he doesn't want to."

That brought a smile. "He never wants to. But I'll tell him."

Then she hit the buzzer—again, he could do it himself, and she knew that, but she did it quickly, before he could lift his hand, and she said, "They'll have to get you your own key."

"Already been discussed. Bev's got one ready. Going to give it to me tonight."

"Okay."

And then Molly did leave, turning and heading back down the ramp. Jake suddenly wondered—he let the thought rise and fall in his mind before dismissing it, because it couldn't be true, could it?—if she had secretly wanted to kiss him good-bye.

Maybe that was the reason for her hesitation.

They had kissed only once. Three years ago, on the night his life changed forever. They had kissed and then she'd rejected him, rejected everything he was offering her—his heart, his devotion, his entire life— and then he had driven away in his Blazer. He was grateful for its heft and its speed, because he had needed to be enclosed right then, wrapped up in something larger than himself, something that could contain the rapid spread of his sorrow. Something that could form an impervious barrier, stopping his immense sadness from seeping out into the world.

Also, he'd needed to get the hell out of there for the simple sake of his pride, which is why the speed mattered, too.

Later that night, he had walked into a gas station and a cowardly punk had shot him. And that was that.

He and Molly were friends now. The relationship was easily explained: He was a cripple, helpless and needy, and she was a kind woman. In any case, he was in no position to offer anything to anyone. End of story.

But still. Something in the way she'd stayed with him at the court-house door tonight, before she rang the buzzer—that pause, that fraught moment—did a terrible thing: It gave him hope. Hope for something more with Molly.

He hated hope, hated and feared it. Hope had betrayed him, over and over again. Hope was cruel. Hope, he knew, was for suckers and for idiot assholes—but damned if that wasn't what he was feeling right now, just the faintest, frailest edge of hope, and it was like an unraveling hem, like something you shouldn't touch because you might make it come apart even faster, dissolving before your very eyes.

The desk was not the right height. The wheels of his chair didn't fit under it, and so Jake had to stretch forward to reach the equipment he would need to answer the phones and send deputies or EMTs to locations in need of them. It was awkward, but it was okay.

"No problem," he said. "I can make do."

"You sure?" Beverly said. "I mean—we could tell them that from now on we need something else . . ."

"Really. It's fine." What he wanted to say was: *This is not a perma-nent gig for me, lady. No point in changing the furniture.*

Bev put both hands under her belly and staggered clumsily across the room toward the utility table. She was short, blond, and stout; she had been stout even without her pregnancy and with it—"Just call me Shamu," Bev had told him cheerfully when he first arrived. "Won't bother me a bit. Truth's truth, I always say."

She wanted to show him how to work the shiny red Keurig coffee-maker, even though he had assured her repeatedly that he could figure it out on his own.

Watching her lurch from her right foot to her left foot, right to left, right to left, with only a modicum of forward progress, Jake realized that he moved more smoothly—and definitely faster—in his wheelchair than Bev did on two good legs. But that was not the sort of thing you could say out loud.

"—and then you just mash this little button and you're all set," she said. "The only thing that's tricky is remembering to put your cup down there. If you forget, the coffee goes all over the place. Heck of a mess, I'm here to tell you."

"Got it."

Next she showed him the computer, the log sheet, the quirks of the phone system. Jake did a lot of nodding. He had liked Bev from the moment he arrived here. She didn't fuss over him, which was a great relief. She asked about a few friends they might have in common—her ex, Bobby, used to do the oil changes on all the county-issued Blazers, had he ever met Bobby, who was a real sonofabitch when he'd been drinking but was basically good people?—and none of the names sparked a memory in Jake. It was probably better that way, he thought. They could start fresh, the two of them.

When he'd first come to Acker's Gap he assumed that everybody automatically knew everybody else. Surely that was how it worked in small towns. But no: There were just as many isolated pockets and tucked-away places for various cliques and gangs and posses here as there were in more populated areas. Acker's Gap was a shrunk-down version of the larger world, with the basics remaining intact; it was not a different world altogether.

He found himself wondering if Bobby was the father of the baby whose arrival seemed worryingly imminent—but again, that wasn't the kind of thing you could ask about. You had to wait for the information to be offered. And it hadn't been offered.

Bev had agreed to stay through most of his first shift, but after an hour, he could see how tired she was. They hadn't had any calls yet.

She plopped down in a metal folding chair across the room from the dispatch desk. She spread her legs—she was wearing black stretch pants and a dark blue sweatshirt with WVU in swirly gold letters across the front—and giggled. "Hope you don't mind if I'm a little informal here, Jake." He smiled, shaking his head. She giggled again and then she pulled a Little Debbie Swiss Roll out of her purse and ripped off the cellophane with her front teeth. She offered to break off a piece for him.

"No, I'm good," he said. "Hey—why don't you go ahead and take off? You look beat."

"I *am* beat." Bev sighed. She took another bite of the cake roll. "Did you bring a snack?"

"Not this time."

"You're gonna want to do that. Trust me. Along about ten, eleven P.M., your stomach'll commence to growling."

"I'll do that."

"You can get these at the day-old bakery store up on Route 7." She looked stricken. "Well, I guess you might not have a way to get there. I'm sorry I brought it up."

"Sure I do. I can drive myself."

"Really." She was truly shocked. He could tell.

"Yeah. I've got a van. Needs a new transmission, but soon as that happens, I'll be all set."

"I could talk to Bobby. We're still in touch."

"Taken care of. But thanks." He read the next question off her face. "Hand controls—that's how it's done."

"Gotcha." She rubbed her belly. She looked at the big clock on the wall above the dispatch desk. "Quiet tonight. Don't get used to it. I've had nights when I couldn't take a bathroom break for hours. Too busy."

"How long have you worked here?"

"Close to ten years."

"Bet you've heard just about every calamity known to man."

"That I have. That I have." She chuckled. "I used to see you, you know."

"See me." He repeated back the words, with no inflection.

"Yeah," she said. "Around the courthouse. Late at night. I'd be getting off my shift, heading home, and it'd be midnight, one A.M., and you'd be bringing somebody into the jail. You always had a way about you."

"A way." He was still in a repeating mode.

"Oh, yeah. You were kinda—kinda arrogant, I guess I'd say. But not in a bad way. You had a swagger. Like you owned the world and you damned well knew it, too." She looked down at the wooden floor between her feet. "Bet I passed you in the courthouse at least a dozen times. Probably two dozen. Not surprised that you don't remember me, though. You were a real hotshot."

He couldn't think of anything to say back to her. Everything she was saying was exactly right—he'd thought he was all that. And more.

She was talking again. Still looking at the floor. "I was real sorry when you got hurt, Jake. Real sorry."

"Appreciate it."

"Damned shame, that's what it was."

The phone sang out before she had finished her sentence.

"Can I get that?" he said.

"Knock yourself out."

But it was nothing. Kids, playing around, one of them pushing 911 on his cell because the cable had gone out. "Is *too* an emergency!" the caller yelled back at Jake, when Jake pointed out that they needed to keep the line clear for true emergencies. Jake could hear lots of background noise, the raucous, untethered kind that told him it was a party, the heavy-duty rap music and over-the-top laughter. He further informed the caller that making a false claim to a 911 operator was against the law, and that he had their address from the caller ID and in ten seconds he'd be sending a deputy over there to explain to them why they shouldn't—

"They hung up," Jake said, turning to Bev. He lifted the headset over his ears and set it down on the desk.

She laughed. "You'll do fine at this job, mister."

They were both quiet for a few minutes. The only sound was the hum from the computer. The windowless room was small but somehow that made it feel cozy, not cramped. Desk, chairs, computer, printer, phone console, two-drawer file cabinet, utility table, coffee fixings, bulletin board, a small fire extinguisher hanging on the wall: If you made a list of the room's contents, Jake thought, it would be a very short list.

Bev stood up. It was a difficult maneuver, given her condition, and she had to grab the back of the chair, but she made it. "Well, I might take you up on your offer to fly solo tonight. Even though it's my last shift for a while." She put a hand on her belly and spread out her fingers. "Pretty soon this little one'll be here and I can get back to work."

"You scared?"

Jake hadn't known he was going to ask her that until he did.

"Scared?" she said. "Of what?"

"Of having a baby."

A smug smile. "I already have four of 'em. My youngest came too quick and I had to have him at home. That's why I named him what I named him—Early. Early Epps. But—scared? No way."

"Not what I meant. I didn't mean childbirth itself."

"Well—what, then?" A trifle impatiently. He could see that she didn't like riddles.

He thought about it. What *did* he mean?

"I mean—just being responsible for another living creature."

"Like I said—not my first rodeo. Brought four others into the world."

"Not this world."

Now she understood. He watched the understanding spread across her brain the same way he'd watched her fingers spread across her belly. The progression was clear in her features.

This was not the town they knew. Not the town she'd grown up in, and not the town Jake had come to, five years ago. The character of the place had changed. It was dangerous now, in a way it had not been dangerous before. Drugs had eaten a hole in the center of it, like an acid spill. And the damage just kept on growing, going deep and digging in. Everyone knew it, but they didn't talk about it much because there was no point. It was a knowledge that was shared wordlessly, for the most part, and the only way you could tell that someone was feeling the same thing you were feeling was by finding their eyes and seeing the sadness there, the helpless regret, the sense that they had all lost something precious and irrecoverable before they'd had a fair chance of appreciating it. It was gone forever before they'd found the time or acquired the wisdom to rightfully acknowledge that it had been there in the first place.

"Didn't have much choice, tell you the truth," Bev said. "Let's put it this way. I'm seriously thinking of naming this little fella 'Surprise.'"

He laughed, which lightened the moment considerably.

"As long as you don't name him Jake," he said.

"Why's that?"

"Too many Jakes already. If you throw a stick in this town you'll hit a dozen Jakes without even trying."

She waddled over to the utility table. She'd left her purse there.

"You've got my number," Bev said. "Anything comes up tonight that you've got a question about—you give me a call."

"It's getting pretty late. I'd hate to wake you up."

Big grin. "Jake, Jake. Weren't you listening? I got four little ones at home. How much sleep you figure I get on a normal night?"

"Not much, I guess."

"You guess right. Somebody's always puking or having a nightmare or trying to sneak back to the TV set to watch something they ought not be watching. Oh—one more thing."

He waited. He was half-afraid to hear about some burgeoning crisis he needed to be aware of, some imminent threat or likely peril.

"I'm gonna tell you something," Bev continued, "that I didn't tell the last guy who held down the fort here when I went on vacation. I didn't tell the guy before him, either. In fact—I've never told anybody." She cleared her throat. "I'm telling you because I like you, Jake."

He leaned a little forward in his chair. Dropping her voice to an ominous hush, Bev said, "I keep my Little Debbies in the back of the cabinet over there. Private stash. You help yourself. Take all you want."

Chapter Fourteen

The massive black Escalade made the same smooth turn it had made so many times since the day Brett Topping purchased it at Doggett Motors. He could've gotten a better deal, no doubt, at a larger dealership in Charleston, but Doggett Motors was local, and he was a community banker. He did business with Alton Doggett because Alton Doggett did business with him.

Brett loved the Escalade. It was as big as a tank but it moved like a ballerina—that's what he told Ellie on the afternoon he brought it home three years ago, having test-driven it and then written a check on the spot to Alton Doggett.

On this Friday night, as he guided the Escalade into his driveway, something reminded him of that special day. He touched the button to turn off the engine, instantly missing its comforting purr. The floodlight attached to the front of the garage was on; it made the car's black leather interior look almost liquid.

He didn't engage the garage-door opener just yet. The door had been replaced the very next morning after Deke Foley's assault upon it, and was once again a seamless sheet of creamy white. Instead Brett simply sat, indulging himself, recalling with pleasure the first time he'd parked the Escalade here. He deserved such a moment, didn't he?

He wasn't a show-off. He wasn't the kind of man who bragged about his wealth. There were lots of ways to brag, he knew, and only some of them involved talking. Buying things was another way. He didn't like his colleagues who heaped up expensive toys as if trying to achieve a sort of critical mass, tangible proof of their superiority.

The Escalade was his one true indulgence.

He had always had nice cars, large and shiny ones, but this was the pinnacle, the best he'd ever owned. It reminded him of how big his dreams had been. For his family. His son.

He didn't have those dreams anymore. He didn't know what was going to happen. Not to him and Ellie—and not, God knows, to Tyler. He could never say so to Ellie, but sometimes he wished the boy was dead.

There: He'd said it. Only in his mind, but still.

He wished his own son was gone. Just gone. All of him: skin, bone, drug habit. He wished the boy was out of their lives for good.

A little peace: That's what he wanted for Ellie. For himself.

The first time he'd played catch in the yard with Tyler, he noticed the boy's powerful arm—even at six, the kid had a cannon—and Brett thought: *Well, maybe professional sports.* Unlikely, but—hey. He was a dad. Dads had dreams.

And then later, when he helped Tyler with his math homework in middle school, he'd thought, *Maybe an engineer. Or a physicist. The boy's got a really good grasp on mathematics. A fine mind.* More dreams.

Brett was cold now, sitting there in the Escalade with the engine off. Time to go inside.

He decided to leave the Escalade in the driveway tonight. Not pull it into the garage. He didn't see any lights on in the house, which might mean Ellie had fallen asleep. If she had, the sound of the opener would awaken her. He didn't want to do that.

He climbed down out of the vehicle. Had Ellie gotten the mail? Maybe not. She almost never remembered to do that anymore. She lived in a sort of daze. Brett didn't like to think about it, but it was true.

He walked down the long driveway toward the big black mailbox. TOPPING, the letters spelled out on the side. The front of the mailbox, where he had to stand in order to open the metal flap and reach in to pull out the contents, was just outside the circumference of the flood-light. He stood in darkness.

That was why, when the figure approached him, Brett was so startled. The figure, too, was in darkness. Brett didn't know where the figure had come from. Nor, at first, could he make out any facial features.

And then the figure reached calmly into the pocket of a hooded coat. Drew out a handgun.

The front edge of the hood shifted. Now Brett did see the face. He recognized it. He began to sputter, going into bargaining mode: "Wait— hold on—you don't have to—you know I'd never tell anybody about—"

Three shots—*pop pop pop*—pinged almost musically against the cold night air. The first two came quickly, followed by a pause, and then a final one.

Brett Topping was still upright when the second shot struck him in the chest. The mail he'd recovered from the box—a *National Geographic*, a gas bill, two credit-card statements, a flyer from Lymon's Market that listed the weekly specials—flew out of his hand as if he were tossing confetti in a parade.

He staggered backward into the driveway. By the time the third shot came, also hitting him in the chest, he fell. His head slammed against the concrete. The impact fractured his skull.

At that point the bleeding in his brain was massive and irreversible, and in all likelihood he would have died from that alone, had the bullets not already done the job.

At fourteen minutes before midnight, Jake was getting ready to flip the big silver toggle switch, the one that would send all subsequent calls over to the regional call center in Blythesburg. It was only his second night on the job but already he had the system down cold.

He'd had only two calls tonight, neither one serious. The first was from a trailer park; a woman who sounded drunk, stoned, or possibly both had complained of "funny business" in a double-wide at the end of her row. She would not be more specific. Jake told her he'd send a deputy when one became available. The second was from a motorist on the interstate who had passed a broken-down pickup with people inside. Jake notified the state police. The interstate was their bailiwick.

He had a few minutes before the end of his shift, and so he decided

to follow Molly's advice. He logged on to his Gmail account and com-
posed a quick email to Sheriff Harrison:

> Hey. Just wanted to make sure we're clear on something. I
> don't mind working dispatch but if anything else comes up,
> any other way I can help out—I'm your guy. Just feels good
> to be back in the saddle. You know?
>
> Jake

He read it over. Fine. He hit SEND.

It was now two minutes before midnight, the time at which he was
required to switch the calls over to Blythesburg. His job would be over
for tonight. He could go home.

Six hours from now Tina Lawton, who worked the early shift at the
Raythune County Sheriff's Department and who generally arrived at
the courthouse between 5:30 and 5:45 A.M. but in any case never later
than 5:55 A.M., would flip the switch again, rerouting the calls right back
here. And then she would download the list of calls logged by the overnight dispatcher in Blythesburg—usually that dispatcher was Harriet
Brandenburg, but if Harriet was ill or on vacation, it was Bradley Simmons, Deputy Simmons's stepbrother—and print out the file. Sheriff
Harrison would find the single sheet of paper—it was never more than
one sheet—on her desk by 6:15 each morning, along with a yellow Post-
it Note affixed to the top that featured Tina's bouncy handwriting:
Have a great day, Sheriff!!

That was Tina. She was sunny even when the data she was passing
along was grim and grindingly ordinary: squad runs for terrible car ac-
cidents, drunk and disorderlies, thefts, domestic entanglements that
had gone from merely unpleasant to downright deadly. If anything truly
horrific had occurred, the sheriff, of course, would already know about
it; Pam Harrison was accustomed to being called out at all hours. But
usually, the list was made up of predictable calamities, the kind that the
night-shift deputies could handle on their own.

Jake had to compile the same kind of list for the sheriff, tracking the calls that had come in during his shift. But he didn't affix any Post-it Note to the top. No happy, casual greeting. If he had anything to say to Harrison, he'd damned well say it in person.

Or by email, he corrected himself, recalling the note he'd just sent.

At approximately one minute before midnight—to be precise, it was fifty-seven seconds until twelve—he was using a pencil to check off the items on his report. He'd already printed the report for the night. It was a little premature, printing it before his shift was officially over, but what could happen in the final fifty-seven seconds?

His eyes and his pencil-tip traveled down the list of calls. He made a small mark beside the ones that had required a squad dispatch. He paused, using the eraser end of the pencil to scratch the left side of his head.

And then he dropped the pencil.

Jake leaned over in his chair to try to retrieve it, but couldn't; it had rolled too far away. He scooted forward, but overshot the mark. Now he needed to scoot backward.

"Damn," he muttered. Cursing out loud when there was nobody else around was a special kind of pleasure, he'd discovered. You didn't have to apologize to anybody. You could really let loose.

And all I can come up with is "Damn"? Well, it's late. And I'm tired.

There. Finally he was able to reach the pencil. He grunted, sitting up straight in his chair again.

It was now twenty-eight seconds past midnight.

Had he not dropped the pencil—this would occur to Jake a few hours later, as he lay in his bed and pondered the night's big event, one obviously destined to have consequences stretching into the weeks and months ahead—he would have flipped the switch precisely at midnight, the designated time, and the call would have gone to Blythesburg.

He would not have known what had just happened in the driveway of the home belonging to Brett and Ellie Topping.

He would have found out later, of course. This was Acker's Gap, and eventually everyone knew everything. But there would have been a delay of several hours before the news came back around again to its birthplace. In the meantime, the Blythesburg dispatcher would have summoned whatever unit was closest—Raythune County or Collier

County, it didn't matter, just as long as somebody got there—and Jake could have slept through the night, perhaps not peacefully, because after all he never slept peacefully, but at least without the heavy psychic residue of the knowledge that attached itself to him when the call came in at approximately thirty seconds after midnight, and he answered, and a ragged, desperate voice invaded his headset:

"Help me—please—help me—Oh my God, Oh my God—" she screamed, high and wild.

Second night on the job, Jake thought. *Figures I'd get more than a cat up a tree.*

"Ma'am, what's the nature of your—"

"Help me—my husband—please, please—" Again the words were hijacked by screams.

"Are you located at . . ." Jake snapped off the address that had popped up on his screen. *Good neighborhood,* was the thought that occurred to him. Unusual: Typically 911 calls came from the same few trouble-prone sectors. He knew that from his days as a deputy.

"Yes," the out-of-control voice confirmed. "Oh my God—please—"

"What's going on? Do you need an ambu—"

"He's in the driveway! Oh my God—"

"Are you in danger? Do you need—?"

"No—I just came home and found my husband—I don't know—" She screamed again, as if the screams were somehow grounding her more effectively than his words did.

"Ma'am, I'm sending a squad right now." Jake kept his voice professional and calm but that was not an accurate reflection of what was going on inside him. As a deputy, he'd had plenty of perilous moments and he was known for keeping his cool, but that was three years ago. And now, unlike then, he was stuck in this chair. He felt as helpless as this woman must feel, his heartbeat clattering in his chest.

He called the number for any available squad. Would it be Molly and Ernie Edmonds, her partner? She wasn't scheduled to work tonight—it was her second night off in a row, an unbelievable luxury—but that meant nothing. She was often called in when the shifts got too busy.

Jake rattled off the address. It was read back to him through a thorny forest of static.

"Squad's on the way," he said, switching back to woman. "Be there in minutes. What's your name, ma'am?"

"Ellie Topping."

"And you're sure you're safe."

"He's *dead*. I know he's dead." She let out a new kind of scream, an animal scream that reverberated through Jake's entire body, at least the parts of him that could still feel. At the same time, he could hear the sound of a distant siren through the phone line; sounds traveled far and fast on cold autumn air.

"Ellie," he said, using her name, the way Bev had advised him to do. Establish a rapport. "Listen to me. The squad's coming. Just wait right there. They'll know what to do."

"Brett—*Brett*—oh my God. Oh my—"

He kept talking to her, trying to wedge in his words through the shrieks. He didn't know how much time passed. Only minutes, he'd find out later, but it felt like hours. He could only imagine how long it had felt to her: days, maybe.

Then, through the phone, Jake heard shouts, the heavy scrape and pant of a very large engine, the stomp of heavy boots on concrete. More screams from the caller. He heard people talking rapidly, giving instructions. And then the line cut off.

The professionals were there. He'd done his job. He could stand down.

He started to make his report, add the last call to the log. But he found that he couldn't type. Not just yet. His hands were shaking too much. He swallowed several times; suddenly there didn't seem to be enough saliva in his mouth.

Even though the call had ended, Jake somehow kept hearing the woman's screams. He knew that didn't make any sense. He knew he wasn't really hearing her screams—but still. They were there.

Yes: They were there. He imagined that he could see the screams now as well as hear them; they were vivid red streaks against the iron blackness of the night. Her screams were anguished and lost, rising and rising until they had clawed their way to the tops of the mountains, the visible limit of this sunken world.

Three years previously

Bell came back out onto the front porch. Shirley sat on the swing, It was dark—neither of them had any desire to turn on the porch light, and Bell had turned off the living room light when she left the house—and so Bell could not see her sister's face.

She didn't need to. Not really. She knew every line in that face, every hollow. She knew the sad eyes and the way the flesh on her neck separated into vertical folds.

Bell would carry a picture of that face forever. She would carry it not the way you do an actual photograph—in a phone or a computer file or a wallet or an album—but in a much safer place.

She would carry it in her bones.

"So you did it," Shirley said. Her words seemed to come from a long way off, as mournful as the hoarse call of a faraway train. "You wrote a letter of resignation."

"Yeah. I'll deliver it to the courthouse in the morning," Bell said.

"You don't have to do that."

"I know."

"I didn't tell you those things so that you'd blow up your life."

"I know that, too."

"So why are you doing it?"

Bell rose and moved restlessly around the porch. Her pacing did not have any particular pattern. It was motion without direction. Action without the expectation of progress. *Kind of like my life from now on,* she thought, and then she banished the thought from her brain because it reeked of self-pity. Stank of it.

The death of their father, Donnie Dolan, when Bell was ten and Shirley sixteen, was the defining moment of their lives. Tonight, Shirley had told Bell the truth: It was Bell, not Shirley, who had killed him. It was Bell, not Shirley, who had slit the throat of the abusive man they always called "the monster."

Yet Shirley had taken the blame. In the last few desperate minutes they had together before the authorities arrived, she had made Bell believe that she—Shirley—had murdered Donnie Dolan.

Not Bell. Not the real culprit.

And so it was that Bell went on to college, law school, and then the prosecutor's job. Shirley went to prison.

A terminal cancer diagnosis had brought Shirley here to Bell's front porch tonight. Her mission was simple: She needed Bell to know the truth at last. To wipe the slate clean between them, so that she could die in peace. But things had quickly moved beyond Shirley's control. Bell—her stubborn, headstrong, infuriating, beloved little sister—was going to tell the whole world.

"I wanted to keep it between us," Shirley said, speaking again because Bell hadn't. "This is nobody else's business. You can go on being prosecutor. Nothing has to change."

"Everything has to change," Bell said.

"I don't know why you have to—" Shirley's cough came upon her quickly. It was violent and prolonged, and it made her whole body shake. That shaking, in turn, made the swing twist and shimmy.

"Can I get you a glass of water? What can I—"

"No." Shirley, recovered now, took several deep breaths. "Happens." She patted the spot on the swing next to her. "Sit. That's what you can do for me."

Bell sat. "What did the doctors tell you?"

"Not much. I'm supposed to get my treatment plan in a couple of days. In Charleston."

"No. Not Charleston. I'm taking you to another hospital. A better one. Somewhere else. We're going to fight and fight *hard*." Delivered like a manifesto. Bell Elkins, on the case.

"Won't matter, Belfa." Shirley's voice was calm, a soft repudiation of Bell's drive and determination. "Lung cancer—it's the kind of thing you don't recover from. We both know that. I don't want you going to all that trouble for something that's not gonna make a difference. Okay?"

Bell felt Shirley's hand on her knee. That protective hand, the one she'd felt even when Shirley wasn't present, when Shirley was far away, locked up. Shirley had always taken care of her.

Now it was Bell's turn to take care of Shirley.

"We have to fight," Bell declared.

"Do we?"

Bell shook her head. It was after midnight. The level of fatigue in her sister's voice was alarming. "We can discuss all of this in the morning, okay? I'll let it go for now."

"Deal." Shirley coughed again, but this time it didn't go on quite so long. It didn't make her entire body shudder, the way the earlier cough had. "Too damned tired to argue." The next time she spoke, a tease had made its way into her tone. "Besides—who in the world ever won an argument with Belfa Elkins? Nobody, that's who."

Bell teased her right back. "Oh, but sometimes I let you win, right? Just to keep things interesting."

A week and a half later they walked through the glass double doors of the James Cancer Center in Columbus, Ohio. Shirley had agreed to an appointment with a top oncologist there.

That was the exact term Bell had Googled: "top oncologist." Too many names emerged in her initial search and so she refined it, adding "lung cancer" and "Eastern and Midwestern US." The name "Frank Karsko, M.D." popped up enough times to catch Bell's eye. His office was at the James, on the Ohio State University campus.

Bell had driven them here, rented a room at the Holiday Inn Express near the hospital. The day of the journey was lovely. The colors of the leaves along the way had seemed especially emphatic and intense, the reds and yellows and russet browns, as if they were all clamoring for attention, like dressed-up characters in a parade. Shirley slept for most of the three-hour drive. Bell was sorry that she had missed the leaves, but it didn't seem worth it to wake her up to see them.

She knew that she'd worn Shirley down to get her to agree to the appointment. *How's it feel, little sister?* Shirley had said, a saucy grin on her emaciated face. She'd awakened just as they pulled into the motel parking lot. *You pressured a helpless cancer patient. Browbeat a sick person.* Bell grinned right back and said, *Too easy. It was a snap.*

Then, seriously: *But thanks, Shirley. For doing this.*

By now, Bell's resignation from the prosecutor's post was old news. A special election was scheduled to replace her. Rhonda Lovejoy was acting prosecutor. Bell's trial date had been postponed while she dealt with the opening stages of Shirley's treatment.

They had a long wait until Dr. Karsko could see them. Two hours and fourteen minutes after their appointment time, they were escorted into a small room with brown walls and minimal furniture. Karsko swept in, the bottom of his white lab coat flapping around his knees as if he always moved so fast that the hem never had a chance to settle. He was a lean, fierce-looking man with a sharp nose, black crew cut, ice-blue eyes, swarthy complexion, and absolutely zero interpersonal skills, which was just fine with Bell: She wasn't looking for a pal.

While they sat and watched him, Karsko read the report from the Charleston hospital. He held floppy scans up to a lighted box. He checked something on his laptop. He did not react to anything he saw. At no point—Bell was struck by this fact—did he touch Shirley, or even seem particularly interested in her. His attention was solely focused on data. Test results. Shirley's prognosis was a matter of figures now, of percentages and ratios and graphs. Lung cancer came with long, daunting odds. *But I don't care about your damned numbers*, Bell wanted to shout at the man. *This is my sister—and she'll be the exception.*

And then they had to wait. Again. Waiting was their new reality.

Waiting, Bell realized, would henceforth define her sister's life: waiting for a bed to become available so that she could start her chemo; waiting in a line of other people on gurneys for her radiation treatments;

waiting for the nurses to deliver pain medication; waiting for the fleeting, infrequent visits by Dr. Karsko.

His coldness was consoling. He didn't care about them as people. Bell could tell that he didn't remember their names from one visit to the next, and had to check the chart each time. Shirley was a packet of information to him. Nothing more. He wasn't distracted by anything warm or personal. *Good,* Bell thought. *That's how it should be.*

So many times, in her own career, she had let emotions cloud her professional judgment. If you saw people as individuals, you were doomed. To be effective, you had to deal in aggregates.

The night before Shirley's first round of chemo, a Tuesday dominated by an endless chilly rain, Bell and Shirley went out to dinner near their hotel. She made Shirley pick. Shirley had no appetite and didn't care where they ate—"It all tastes like sawdust anyway"—but Bell still insisted that she make the selection. "Fine—Applebee's, if they've got one," Shirley said. She shrugged when she came up with the name.

"Everybody's got one," Bell said.

They settled into the booth. Told the too-cheerful waitress that, no, they didn't want any appetizers and yes, they'd need another minute. Myriad streaks of rain had made a smeary mess of the dark window. The parking lot upon which they looked out was a wavy lake of drowned-looking cars.

"So I'm doing what you wanted," Shirley said. "I'm fighting."

Bell looked at her sister over the top of the tri-fold menu. Where was this going?

"And so," Shirley went on, "you owe me."

Bell closed the menu and set it to one side. "Meaning what?"

"Meaning I don't want you to stand trial. I know what people are saying. You don't have to do it, Belfa. Nobody wants to punish you. You were a *kid.* And I lied to you. Tell me how it makes any sense—any damned sense at all—for you to go to prison. You've already resigned as prosecutor. That's enough. Right?"

Bell didn't answer. A gust of wind drove a fresh spatter of raindrops hard against the window, as if even the weather was trying to get her to relent.

"Belfa?"

"Better figure out what you want to eat. The waitress will be back any minute."

"Belfa—listen to me." Shirley was agitated now, leaning forward, her bony elbows on the wooden table. "All the years I was in prison—I can't get them back. They're gone. Is that what this is all about? I lost my life—and so you have to lose yours, too? It doesn't work that way. It means that *two* lives get ruined. Not just one. What's the point?"

"The salads looked pretty good. The burgers, too. Want to split an order of fries?"

"Is this some kind of martyr thing? Is that what it is? Because that won't help anybody. Not me, not you—nobody."

No reply.

"*Belfa.*" A hectic gleam had come into Shirley's eyes. "Why are you doing this? Tell me why. At least do that, okay? Just tell me. Nobody wants to punish you—so why are you so bound and determined to punish yourself?"

Bell picked up the menu again. She opened the sections and began to study it earnestly.

"Okay," Shirley said. Defeat in her voice. She fell back against her seat, too tired to keep on trying. "Okay. You just be that way, little sister. You just keep your damned secret. Lord knows, you and I have had a lot of practice at that. We're the best there is."

Two days later, leaving the hospital by herself in the middle of the afternoon, Bell paused. She had just cleared the glass double doors on her way to the parking garage.

Up in the room on the eleventh floor, Shirley was in the midst of a grueling series of chemo treatments. Bell was going back to the Holiday Inn Express for a short break. She needed to be strong for Shirley, and right now, she was exhausted.

Yet something caught her eye. Two people had passed her, going in the opposite direction—a pretty, middle-aged woman and a much older man. The man was leaning heavily on the woman.

"Excuse me," Bell said. This was totally out of character—accosting a stranger—but she couldn't help herself. "I know you, don't I? Don't you live in West Virginia? Acker's Gap?"

"That's right." The woman blushed slightly. "I thought I recognized you, too. Aren't you Bell Elkins?"

"Yes." Bell snapped her fingers. "Now I remember. You're Brett Topping's wife, right? We met at the county commission meeting last year. For the new stoplight." A group of citizens had petitioned the commission to change a four-way stop near Yeager Elementary School to a stoplight. Too many drivers were blowing through the stop sign. "I'm sorry—I don't remember your name," Bell said. "I know Brett through the bank."

"I'm Ellie. And this is Henry Combs. My brother."

"Hello, Henry." Bell shook his hand. Now that she was closer, she saw that the man with the pale blue eyes wasn't as old as she had thought he was; illness, not age, had carved the lines on his face and rubbed the flesh off his bones. "I guess you don't live in Acker's Gap, like your sister here."

He shook his head back and forth, very slowly. It cost him a great deal, Bell saw. It was as if every expenditure of energy had to be measured out by the teaspoonful.

"No, I live I Charleston," he said. "But I grew up in Briney Hollow. Same as Ellie."

Ellie started to say something to Bell. She hesitated, and then pushed ahead. "Are you being treated here? Are you—?"

"It's my sister," Bell said. "Lung cancer." There. She could say it out loud now without feeling a sharp wedge of pain push through her chest.

Ellie touched Henry's arm. "They're taking great care of my brother." When she said "brother," Henry smiled. Hearing his sister say the word seemed to bring him an instant, simple pleasure.

And then there was nothing more to talk about, because they did not know each other, and the only bond was the accident of being from the same small town. Running into someone from home wasn't such a remarkable coincidence, Bell realized; many people from West Virginia with serious illnesses went to university medical centers in relatively close big cities like Columbus and Pittsburgh.

Ellie said she would give Bell's regards to Brett. Bell wished Henry good luck with his treatment.

Only later did it strike Bell: *She doesn't know.* Ellie Topping didn't show any signs of having heard the news. She probably had no idea what was happening to Bell—the resignation and the pending trial, the gossip and the drama. Bell had seen, in Ellie's eyes, no curiosity, no appraisal.

Nothing but anxiety for her brother.

Maybe it was still too new to have worked through the layers of townspeople, the way a bad burn moves through layers of skin. Or maybe—more likely—it just didn't matter to her. Ellie was wrapped up in Henry's mortal illness and so the fate of her local county prosecutor— one who had murdered her father when she was ten years old, and then blocked it out and let her sister suffer the punishment—was irrelevant.

Each of them was locked inside her own private universe of pain. That was how it seemed to Bell. They could look out and the see the world, but people in the world could not look in, could never really know what was going on behind the smile and the brave, patient words.

PART TWO

Chapter Fifteen

Rhonda Lovejoy looked around the room.

Present in the prosecutor's office at 2:14 A.M., roughly two hours after Brett Topping had expired in his driveway, was the prosecutor (*check*), the sheriff (*check*), the assistant prosecutor (*check*), the on-call deputy (*check*), and an additional deputy summoned out of a sound sleep to help out (*check*).

Everything looked slightly blurry and fuzzed to her at this hour, the walls and the furniture as well as the faces. There was a middle-of-the-night mistiness that clung to it all, softening the edges: the chestnut paneling, the pressed-tin ceiling, the chunky wooden desk, the small sofa, the mismatched chairs.

In the corner, the ancient drip coffeemaker fussed and harrumphed, preparatory to disgorging its bitter bounty into a shifting series of grimy mugs.

It was just like the old days, just like the meetings Bell Elkins used to convene in the first fraught hours after a major incident.

Except, Rhonda reminded herself, it really wasn't like the old days at all. The first major difference: the prosecutor wasn't Bell Elkins.

It's me.

The thought did not give her confidence. Or fill her with any sort of satisfaction.

The second major difference was the fact that the sheriff wasn't Nick

Fogelsong. It was Pam Harrison. Pam was smart and tough and courageous and efficient—but she wasn't Nick. There were things Nick knew that Pam didn't know.

And one of the things Pam didn't know, Rhonda reminded herself ruefully, was the fact that she didn't know everything.

Nick was well aware of his limitations. He'd often say, "Well, we've swiftly come to the end of my expertise. Here on out, we're dealing in rank speculation, and that's worth about as much as it costs you on the open market."

Harrison wasn't like that. A sheriff, she'd lectured Rhonda on many occasions—and "lectured" was the only word that fit—had to be confident. Self-assured. Hard as nails. Had to maintain an air of infallibility. No second-guessing any decision. Admitting a mistake was the biggest mistake you could make. Harrison had definite rules about how to do the job.

But then again, she had never really been tested yet. Neither had Rhonda.

In three years, they had not faced a homicide with significant implications. There had been violent deaths, of course, but nothing like this. Nothing that interacted with the town at so many different points of contact.

Brett Topping was a bank vice president (*check*), a quasi-kingmaker in local politics (*check*), a husband (*check*), a father (*check*), a friend to other prominent local citizens (*check*). He was—in the parlance of Rhonda's childhood—Somebody, a word that was pronounced around here with the stress on the second syllable: Some*body*.

Translation: He mattered. Theoretically, of course, every human being mattered, but you didn't grow to adulthood without learning the cynical but inarguable truth that Some People Matter More Than Others.

Thus the murder of Brett Topping constituted Rhonda's first real challenge as prosecutor, and Harrison's first as sheriff.

Domestic disputes, drug deals that backfired amid profane accusations of double-crossing and shortchanging—those homicides had all fallen well below the level of long-term consequence. Rhonda could've prosecuted them in her sleep.

She and assistant prosecutor Hickey Leonard, a rangy, rumpled old man who had worked with Bell, too, and who had encouraged Rhonda to run for the top spot after Bell's resignation, had mastered their jobs. They saw the same general sorts of offenses, committed by the same general sorts of people, with the same general sorts of outcomes, repeatedly.

This was different.

"Who secured the scene?" Rhonda asked. She coughed. Her voice didn't sound quite right to her. Maybe it was the lateness of the hour.

Or maybe it was something else.

"I did, ma'am." Sawyer Simmons took a single step forward, chin up, arms tight at her sides.

She and her colleague, Deputy Steve Brinksneader, had positioned themselves against the wall by the door. Sheriff Harrison and Hickey Leonard had, by virtue of rank in the former case and age in the latter, naturally gravitated to the two chairs across from Rhonda's desk.

Simmons was a thirty-five-year-old former bodybuilder from Moundsville. She'd been told one too many times that she ought to put those biceps of hers to better use than just winning trophies to spread across her mantel to gather dust. And so when an opening came up—former deputy Jake Oakes's injury in the line of duty—here came Simmons. She'd proven to be a quick study. Excellent markswoman.

Best of all, she had the temperament for the job, possessing two out of three essential qualities thereof: She was slow to anger. She didn't mind hard work at all hours.

And now, Rhonda thought, they would find out if she possessed the third: keeping her poise—even when forced to deal with a shocking trauma, such as finding the body of a prominent local citizen at the foot of his driveway, his life having ended abruptly on account of three bullet holes and a traumatic brain injury.

"I arrived just after the EMTs," Simmons went on. She was breathing a little too fast. She took off her hat. The color of her straight blond hair—Rhonda recognized the shade—came courtesy of L'Oréal. Simmons wore it trimmed short, parted in the middle. "The wife of the victim—Ellie Topping—was standing in the driveway. She was hysterical, but I got her settled down enough to ask her a few questions. Said she'd come home, found her husband in the driveway, called 911."

"Where'd she been?" Rhonda asked.

"At a cemetery. Took a basket of flowers to her brother's grave."

"Pretty late for a cemetery visit."

"He's buried in Charleston. She ran into traffic on the way back."

"Describe the scene." Rhonda was making notes on a legal pad. "I'll read your full report, but just give me your general impressions now. What sticks in your mind." She'd heard the excitement in Simmons's voice and wanted to slow her down, keep her focused on the facts at hand.

Simmons fetched a deep breath.

"Mrs. Topping's car was in the middle of the lawn," she said. "It was—"

"What kind of car?"

Simmons looked peeved at the interruption. *Does that matter?* her expression said.

Rhonda could've explained, but didn't want to take the time: *Details. The key to the case will be in the details, not in generalities.* She'd learned that from Bell Elkins.

"Audi," the deputy said. "Silver. Nice."

"Okay. Go on."

Simmons nodded. She was still slightly miffed. "Car was running when I got there. Driver's door hanging open. Mrs. Topping was standing in the driveway, about ten feet from the body. She said that she'd turned the corner, come up the street, saw it was her husband. There's a big floodlight that lights up the driveway. Her first thought was that he'd had a heart attack. At that point, being so upset and all, she lost control of her vehicle. It jumped the curb. Plowed right up into the yard. She got out, called 911."

"Did you see a weapon?"

"No, ma'am."

"Back to Mrs. Topping. Had she touched the body?"

"No. Too scared. That's what she said, anyway."

Plausible, Rhonda thought. Most people, when spotting a body on the ground—even when it was a loved one who might need assistance—didn't want to go anywhere near it. Something primitive took over.

Something that made a live human body recoil from the blunt reality of a dead one.

"But she knew something was wrong," Simmons added. "Didn't look right."

"Forensics will settle it. If she touched the body, we'll know when we get their report."

Communities as small as Acker's Gap didn't have their own scene-of-crime units; they had to request a team from the state crime lab. That sometimes meant a long wait.

"Speaking of forensics," Rhonda went on, "when did the state folks get there?"

"Pretty quick this time. They'd been just up the interstate on another case. Roped off the scene and got to work. We're supposed to have some results—type of bullets used, distance between the shooter and the victim, any footprints or other evidence—real soon."

"Good." Rhonda flipped to a new page of the legal pad. "So where did Brett Topping go tonight?"

"Business meeting. His wife didn't know where."

"She say anything else?"

"She was hard to understand, being so upset and all, but basically she kept saying a name over and over again. Took me a minute to figure out what she was saying—it was Deke Foley. Said we need to find him. Claimed he'd threatened her husband earlier this week. Has to be him. She's sure of it."

"Deke Foley," Rhonda said, letting the name bob around in her brain. "Drug dealer, right?"

"Yeah," Sheriff Harrison answered, taking over for her deputy. "We've already sent out an alert to nearby counties. They're looking for him. Frankly, I wasn't too surprised to hear Foley's name in connection with this. I'm familiar with the Topping family and their . . . situation. A situation that would put them on a collision course with a Deke Foley." She paused again. "I've arrested Tyler Topping on multiple occasions over the past two years or so. At first it was for things like public intoxication and selling pot. Lately it's been possession of narcotics without a valid prescription. Twice for domestic issues, when

Tyler assaulted his father. Mr. Topping had attempted to keep Tyler from stealing household items."

"Jesus." Rhonda shook her head. "I knew Brett just to say hello to—and I'd heard some rumors about his son's problems. But I didn't know it had gotten out of hand like that."

"Happens quick," the sheriff said.

Hickey lifted a gnarled index finger. "I dealt with those cases," he said, his voice gravelly with fatigue. "The fights between father and son—well, Mrs. Topping always talked her husband out of pressing charges."

"Where's Tyler now?" Rhonda asked.

"He got lucky," the sheriff replied. It was an odd thing to say, given the fact that the boy's father was dead. The room fell heavily silent. Harrison, too, realized, that it was a peculiar comment to make and so spoke quickly to augment it. "He was picked up yesterday afternoon over in Bretherton County. Trying to sell pills in a 7-Eleven parking lot. He was sitting in a jail cell at the time his father was shot. Best alibi on the planet."

Rhonda nodded. She took a swig of her coffee. Awful stuff. She hadn't paid attention to measurements. If she'd been by herself, she would've spit it right back into the cup. But with witnesses, it didn't seem ladylike.

"What's the condition of the house?" she asked, after a painful swallow.

"I did a run-through," the sheriff answered. "Front door lock was busted. The place had been ransacked. Furniture overturned, cupboards emptied out onto the floor. A real mess, top to bottom."

Rhonda frowned. "No security system?"

Simmons took the question. "Ellie Topping didn't set it when she left for the cemetery. Said she just forgot. Got a lot on her mind these days. That's why she went to her brother's grave. It's where she goes when she gets upset. Settles her down."

"Okay," Rhonda said. She tapped her pen against the legal pad. "Let's go with the obvious thing first. A burglary? That got interrupted? Maybe Brett Topping pulls in the driveway, the burglar hears him, comes out, shoots him to cover the theft."

"Maybe." The sheriff scratched her cheek. "It's a theory, anyway." The cheek-scratch was her tell, Rhonda recalled. She didn't think that was it. But she didn't have a good enough reason to dismiss it yet.

Rhonda looked down at her notes. "So—to summarize. Mrs. Topping arrives home a few minutes after midnight. Finds her husband lying at the end of the driveway. He's dead—from what will later be established were three gunshot wounds to the chest." She looked up. "Nobody else in the neighborhood called the cops? Three gunshots in the middle of the night and—what? They turn up the volume on *Jimmy Kimmel*?"

Deputy Brinksneader arched his back against the wall, trying to stretch out the kinks. He was three decades younger than Hickey, and so the lateness of the hour shouldn't have affected him quite as drastically, but he, too, seemed slightly dazed with weariness, same as the old man was.

"I did a preliminary canvas of the surrounding houses," he said. "Most said they either didn't hear—or they thought it was a car backfiring. Or something else. I got the idea, ma'am, that the whole neighborhood's pretty well used to trouble at the Topping house. They've learned to ignore it. They just don't get involved anymore."

"They're used to gunshots?" Rhonda's voice was incredulous.

"Well, maybe not that, but everything else." The deputy pulled a small spiral notebook out of the breast pocket of his shirt. "The guy across the street—name of Ed Coverdell—did say that there'd been an incident a few nights ago. Somebody pounding on the Toppings' garage door. A lot of shouting, he said. Garage door got beat all to shit."

"And Coverdell didn't call the sheriff's office?" Rhonda asked.

Brinksneader shrugged. "Same story up and down the block. The Toppings didn't want any interference. They wouldn't even acknowledge there *was* a problem, even though it was obvious. Wouldn't answer questions. If anybody tried to help—Brett and Ellie Topping would just smile and shut 'em right down. They were handling it themselves."

Rhonda leaned forward in her seat. She sifted through the crime-scene photos that Sheriff Harrison had deposited on her desk just before they'd gotten started. The pictures were stark and gruesome.

Brett Topping's large body had been flung backward onto the smooth concrete of the wide driveway. His stumpy legs had ended up angled in different directions; one was tucked up under him, the other was hyperextended sideways from the knee in a way that was excruciating to look at. His shirtfront had popped out of his trousers and was twisted up around his neck and shoulders, revealing the massive ring of white fat around his middle. His bare belly looked gelatinous in the blinding glare of the floodlight.

His chest had three bloody tears in the vicinity of his heart. Blood had run out of his mouth and dried on his chin and neck. On the pavement behind his head was another circle of blood.

Rhonda did not react to the photos. Her eyes flicked over to Sheriff Harrison. "Where's Ellie Topping now?"

"The hospital. EMTs transported her, right after they dealt with the body. It was their call. They said she was hysterical, might need sedation. A neighbor rode along."

"Who?"

The sheriff consulted her own tiny notebook. It was identical to Brinksneader's. Rhonda wondered if the sheriff's department ordered them by the gross. "Sandy Banville," Harrison said. "Apparently she and her husband, Rex, are old friends of the Toppings."

"Okay," Rhonda said. "I'll go over there and talk to Mrs. Topping while her recollection's still fresh. Looks like Deke Foley is our man, but let's cover all the bases before we go headlong down that road. Which means, Sheriff, that you and your deputies need to poke around in Brett Topping's life. Get a list going of anybody who might've wanted him dead. Assuming it was deliberate."

Simmons nodded toward the photos. She snickered. "Looks pretty damned deliberate to me."

"Yeah? Well, here's the thing, Sawyer," Rhonda said. She was annoyed by the surly sarcasm in the deputy's tone. "Your opinion—it doesn't count."

Simmons wasn't backing down. "What *does* count, then?"

"Only one thing." Rhonda stood up. "The facts. And we don't have them yet. So let's go."

Maybe this was going to be an easy one.

Maybe Deke Foley had killed Brett Topping. Just like it seemed.

Rhonda felt a surge of relief. Her first big case—and it was going to be a snap. Easy-peasy. Foley's conviction would put a major drug dealer out of circulation, too.

Could she be that lucky?

Well, why not?

She had dismissed the others ten minutes ago. Perversely, the office felt much smaller now than it had when it was filled with people. Not larger, like you'd expect. Almost as if the room automatically adapted to whatever its current circumstance happened to be. Stretched or shrank as needs required. Shape-shifted to accommodate an ever-changing reality.

Or maybe she was just so tired that she was hallucinating.

Rhonda sat behind her desk, her hands on the arms of her chair, thinking. She wore black slacks ribbed with dog hair—Rhonda had three dogs, all rescues and all excessive shedders—and a white sweater with an unraveling sleeve and scuffed brown loafers. She usually dressed up for the office but not when she had to fumble frantically around her bedroom after a call at 1 A.M.

By this point she had turned off the overhead light and switched on the desk lamp, preferring its soft, creamy, horizontal light to the fusillade of fluorescence from above. Her eyes itched and her head felt as if it were stuffed with foam peanuts.

Price of the job, as Bell Elkins would say.

Sunrise was less than an hour away, and so going home was beside the point. Not that Rhonda had been tempted to. If she *had* felt such a temptation, it would have vanished just seconds after she asked herself The Question—the one that seemed to hover at her elbow every minute of every day in this office:

What would Bell do?

And one thing she knew for sure: Bell would not have gone home. She'd be sitting here just as Rhonda was, creating a to-do list on her legal pad.

During her first week on the job three years ago, Rhonda had contemplated a shortcut. She'd considered asking her Aunt Millie to make her a needlepoint with the message:

WWBD?

But she didn't. She needed to handle the job her own way, on her own terms—which was, Rhonda knew, exactly what Bell would have advised. So perversely, the answer to *What Would Bell Do?* was:

Bell Would Do Whatever She Wanted to Do, and Would Advise You to Do the Same.

Or: BWDWSWTDAWAYTDTS.

Which might, Rhonda realized, be a little too much for a needlepoint, even for Aunt Millie.

She knew what she had to do. She needed to create a timeline for Brett Topping's final hours; compile a list of Deke Foley's known associates; procure warrants to search his home and his car; confirm Ellie Topping's alibi; get Tyler Topping transferred to the Raythune County Jail so they could find out what he knew about Deke Foley; follow up with Sheriff Harrison for a list of what had been taken from the Topping home.

And in a few minutes, she needed to head to the Raythune County Medical Center to interview Ellie Topping.

But before she did any of that, Rhonda had another crucial task that she was most definitely not looking forward to.

She had to call Mack and give him the bad news. She knew him well enough by now to know that he'd prefer to get the news right away, even if it meant waking him up.

They'd have to postpone the wedding—which, on the scale of human tragedies, was not even in the same universe of pain and anguish as that suffered by someone whose loved one had been brutally murdered.

But it was still damned irritating.

Chapter Sixteen

Bell still wondered how news spread so fast in a small town. When she was prosecutor, she'd look on with amazement as people who never watched TV or listened to the radio, never read a newspaper, didn't have a telephone—neither landline nor cell—and who barely left the La-Z-Boy in their own living room for anything except bathroom breaks always seemed to know, instantly and accurately, the minute particulars of any given crime anywhere in Raythune County, seconds after said crime was perpetrated.

She'd once theorized to Nick Fogelsong that there must be a secret sound emitted at the moment of a homicide or an armed robbery or a drug deal, a sound that, like a dog whistle, could only be heard by certain ears—in this case, the ears of lifelong residents. Or maybe it was a mysterious change in the air pressure that only registered on particular kinds of skin.

Could be, he'd replied, sipping his coffee and giving her a pitying look over the rim, as if she'd lost her mind. *Sure, Bell. We'll go with that.*

But it was true. And she'd just seen it in action, yet again.

When she arrived home this morning to the big stone house on Shelton Avenue, after her final night of work at Evening Street Clinic, Bell looked across the street. She waved at her neighbor, Sally Ann Turner, who'd just come out on her porch.

Frost glittered on the driveways and sidewalk. The mountains in the near distance wore a dusting of snow on their spiky shoulders. This was Bell's favorite time of day, when the sun had just begun to tip over the tops of those mountains. After this moment, everything would go downhill.

Her shift had been busy. She was tired. And she had a lot to do today, including the nap that she was already anticipating with great relish. Carla was coming over for dinner tonight, Saturday being her daughter's only full day off from her job in Charleston. There was a house to clean, food to shop for.

Still, Bell knew that a conversation with a neighbor was a non-negotiable in Acker's Gap. It was an absolute requirement. Unless you wanted to be slapped with the nickname "Boo Radley," superficial sociability was a must.

"Sally Ann," Bell called out. "Good morning."

"Hey, Bell." Sally Ann was a tall, skinny, woman with yellowish-white hair that she wore in a long rope down her back. She was in her late eighties but was still spry and nimble, with a spine as straight as the handle of the broom with which she was vigorously sweeping her front steps. She'd buried three husbands and, as the neighborhood well knew from the strange cars that often left Sally Ann's driveway at the comparatively late hour of 9 P.M., was working assiduously on acquiring a fourth.

"Cold out here," Bell said. She waved, indicating the fact that Sally Ann was in shirtsleeves, corduroy skirt, and sneakers. No coat. No hat.

"My people always run hot," Sally Ann answered. "Feels good to me. Hey—how you doing?"

That would serve as Sally Ann's sole reference to the fact that Bell had now fulfilled the terms of her obligation to the state of West Virginia's Department of Corrections. Other neighbors, Bell knew, would follow suit. They might gossip about her behind her back—okay, so she knew for certain that they *did* gossip about her behind her back, and who could blame them?—but to her face, they were polite. They didn't pry.

"I'm good," Bell said. Social obligation now officially concluded, she turned and began to unlock the front door, a thick slab of battered oak that attested to the house's antiquity.

"Hang on," Sally Ann called. "You hear the news?"

Bell turned around. "What do you mean?"

"Brett Topping." Sally Ann and her broom had finished with the bottom step and now started back up at the top again. Might have missed a spot. "Murdered in his driveway last night."

"What?"

"MUR-DER," Sally Ann yelled, breaking the word in two and doubling the volume of her voice. "Brett Topping."

Bell didn't answer right away. Sally Ann's news had startled her, causing a sense-memory to ripple through her body in a sharp, almost painful wave: It was the visceral feel of a violent event, momentous and disruptive even though it had happened to somebody else, even though she hadn't witnessed it.

Back when she was the prosecutor, Bell had experienced this kind of dark, startled wonderment several times a day. She'd been at the bull's-eye of all the bad things that happened in the county, from the first 911 call down through the arduous aftermath: investigation, arrest, interrogation, trial, and, if the cosmic coin-flip of the criminal justice system decided on a whim to get it right, sentencing and incarceration.

"Bell? Did you hear me?" Sally Ann hollered. She swept as she talked, going up and down, back and forth, worrying the front steps over and over, just as she did every morning and most evenings, too. Bell was surprised that there was any wood left by now. "You knew him, right?"

"Yeah. They arrest anybody?"

"Nope. But it's gotta be the drugs. Not Brett—it's his boy, Tyler. Fell in with the wrong crowd. Same old story."

Bell had indeed known Brett Topping. Not well, but enough to be able to picture him: Big face. Solid handshake. Friendly. Prosecutors and bank vice presidents traveled in some of the same circles. Civic groups, county commission subcommittee meetings.

She remembered his wife even better. Ellie, was it? Yes, Ellie. Blond hair, pretty. From three years ago came a flash of memory: Ellie, going into the James Cancer Center the same moment Bell was leaving it. Ellie's brother, leaning on her arm. Both of them—Bell and Ellie— there to take care of someone they loved. Their meeting that day was an accidental rhyming of undeserved fates and soon-to-be tragedies.

Three years ago.

Back when Shirley was still alive. Fading, dying, but alive.

Bell needed to change the subject in her own head. Right away.

"That's a shame," she called back across the street.

"Yeah. Way I hear it, the boy maybe owed some money to the wrong people. Real bad people. Tyler wouldn't pay up—and so they went after Brett."

Bell's thoughts suddenly fell into a familiar groove, clicking along, hitting all the marks she knew so well. She was thinking like a prosecutor: *Make the kid give up his sources, track down the dealer, use the aggravated murder charge against the dealer and the possibility of lifetime imprisonment as leverage in a plea bargain to get—*

She stopped herself.

You're not the prosecutor. That's Rhonda's job now.

But she could march inside and call Rhonda, right? Give her advice? Suggest some avenues to pursue, some techniques to try? It would be a public service. Definitely. And Rhonda wouldn't resent it. She couldn't. Bell had all those years of experience, and she'd be a valuable source of—

No.

But—

No. Just stop it. Now.

Sally Ann was staring at her. Bell wondered if she'd been talking to herself. Mumbling, maybe, as the fierce debate had raged inside her head.

Jesus, she thought. *If I do this too many more times, they'll be calling me a lot worse names than Boo Radley.*

Being a bystander was going to be hard. Very, very hard. Much harder than she'd anticipated.

When she was in Alderson, she'd deliberately avoided the news from Acker's Gap. She knew how it would eat at her—each crime, each case, the trials. If she followed every detail, every turn, she'd make herself crazy. And so she didn't. Instead, she generally confined her reading to investigative reports about Utley Pharmaceuticals and how the company had grown rich off the miseries of West Virginians.

And then, during her time at Evening Street, when it was impossible *not* to pick up on the local news, there hadn't been any major incidents. Just run-of-the-mill mayhem and low-level lawlessness.

So this was the first. The first time that the new reality hit her: *You're not the prosecutor anymore. If you offer any tips to Rhonda Lovejoy, you're not helping her—you'll be getting in her way. That's all. You'll be just another nuisance.*

She had to stand down. Let Rhonda do her job. And embrace a new life—one that didn't include being at the center of law enforcement efforts in Raythune County.

Bell took a deep breath. Right now, she needed to shift her thinking away from the emptiness that had suddenly engulfed her, a feeling that edged close to despair.

She'd go in another direction entirely. Now was a good time, she decided, to dig out the truth, once and for all, about how people like Sally Ann Turner got the news ahead of Facebook, Twitter, Instagram, and a dozen or so satellite uplinks.

"Hey, Sally Ann—how'd you find out about the murder so fast?"

The old woman stopped sweeping. She contemplated the question.

"Oh, you hear things," she said. "Bits and pieces. Here and there. Always keep my ear to the ground."

Chapter Seventeen

"How long?"

Rhonda was baffled by Ellie Topping's question.

"Ellie, I'm not sure I understand what you're—"

"How long? How long?" Angry, desperate, Ellie reached out and grabbed the sleeve of Rhonda's coat. "How long?"

"If you could give me a general idea of what you—"

"How long?"

Rhonda turned to the other woman in the room, hoping she could help. Sandy Banville shook her head. Widened her eyes. *I'm as clueless as you are,* the head-shake and the eye-widening implied.

"Ellie," Rhonda said. "I want you to take a deep breath. I'm Rhonda Lovejoy. The prosecutor here in Raythune County. And I have some questions for you." She spoke slowly and carefully, the way she'd watched Bell speak to newly bereaved people. "I know you're still in shock. I'm really sorry for your loss. But right now, time makes a big, big difference. We need to find out who did this to your husband. So I have to ask you some—"

"How long?" Ellie repeated again, but this time she said it softly, wonderingly, not angrily.

That felt like progress to Rhonda. She waited. Her instinct was correct: Ellie was settling down. She was ready to explain herself.

"How long will I feel this way?" Ellie asked. "I can't—I don't know what I'm—" She swallowed hard. She looked down at her hand, and realized she was clutching Rhonda's coat sleeve. She released it and uttered a small moan. "I'm so sorry. I didn't hurt you, did I? I didn't mean to—"

"I'm fine." Rhonda lifted her arm and shook it. "All good. See?"

They were sitting in a small room next to the ER. The nursing supervisor had offered the space when Rhonda said she needed a private place in which to talk to Ellie Topping. The sign on the door said simply: FAMILY ROOM. But Rhonda knew what the room really was, behind the polite euphemism. She had been here before.

This was where the hospital chaplain met with the next-of-kin of someone who'd been brought into the ER—after that someone had unfortunately died. In here, the conversations generally started with the solemn words: *The doctors and nurses did all they could, but I'm very sorry to have to inform you that . . .*

Lime-green walls. Nubby orange chairs. Blue-and-white striped carpet. *Comfort colors?* Rhonda always wondered. *Or just lousy decorating instincts?*

Lamp. End table. A small red artificial flower, rising perkily from a plastic bud vase.

Sandy Banville and Ellie sat next to each other. Rhonda had moved the third chair around in front of them, so she could face both women. Ellie, as the nurse had reported to Rhonda in a discreet whisper, was sedated, but only mildly; she should be able to handle a few questions, as long as they were delivered with sensitivity.

"You're in shock, hon," Sandy said. She reached for Ellie's hand.

To Rhonda's surprise, Ellie quickly pulled her hand away. Weren't they supposed to be neighbors? Friends?

"Don't you touch me," Ellie snapped. "Why are you here?"

Sandy nodded, as if she'd expected this. "Because you asked me to come along," she said patiently. "In the ambulance. You were scared, hon. You needed somebody."

Ellie seemed confused. She looked at Rhonda.

"I can't remember. My mind—it's just—I'm—"

"It's okay," Rhonda said. "Let's take it slow. Like your friend says, you're in shock. And if it wasn't really important, I wouldn't be bothering you now. I'd let you rest. But we have to find out who did this. You understand that, right? We're doing this for your husband. For Brett."

The mention of her husband's name had done the trick. Ellie seemed to channel strength from it. She sat up straighter in her chair. She nodded and looked directly into Rhonda's eyes.

"Yes," she said. "I'm ready."

"Okay." Rhonda pulled a legal pad from the briefcase she'd propped next to her chair. "I know you already spoke to Deputy Simmons. And normally she'd be talking to you now, too. But we're short-handed. So you get to deal with me. Lucky you, right?" She smiled. Sometimes that brought an answering smile from an otherwise nervous, distracted person: the lighthearted sarcasm, the self-deprecation was a sort of universal solvent.

But Ellie didn't react to it. She spoke in a deadpan voice.

"I didn't go to him. I left him there. I didn't help Brett."

"There was nothing you could've done," Rhonda said. "He had already passed away by the time you got there."

"You're sure? The paramedics said that?"

"Yes." Rhonda wasn't sure, and the paramedics had said no such thing. But she had to keep Ellie Topping calm. Regret and recrimination wouldn't help their cause right now. "According to what you told Deputy Simmons at the scene, your husband recently had an altercation with a drug dealer named Deke Foley."

Ellie gasped slightly, remembering. "It was terrible. Foley came to our home the other night because Tyler owed him money. He had a bat and he—he smashed the garage door. Again and again."

"So Tyler was working for Deke Foley."

Ellie flinched. Her eyes widened in horror. A thought had just occurred to her, one that Rhonda easily guessed: Could her son have had something to do with this—more, that is, than having brought such ugliness, such brutality, into their lives in the first place? Was Tyler specifically involved in the murder of his father? Could he have—

"Did you find him?" Ellie asked. Her voice was ragged with agitation. "Tyler didn't come home tonight. He might be—"

"We know where Tyler is, Mrs. Topping," Rhonda said evenly. "And he didn't do this. He was in police custody in another county at the time of the shooting."

The enormity of her relief made Ellie's entire body slump forward. She put a hand to her forehead.

"Thank God," she murmured. "Thank God for that, at least."

Sandy patted her arm. "Yes. Thank God."

Rhonda let a moment go by. She folded back the top page of the legal pad, exposing a fresh sheet. "Tyler's drug problems. They began—when?"

"High school. Junior year," Ellie answered. "Until then, he was—he was a wonderful boy. Never got into any trouble at all. He was good. He was—" She faltered.

"He really was a fine young man," Sandy said, finishing the sentence for her. She gave Ellie's hand a squeeze. This time, Ellie didn't pull away. She let herself be comforted. "He and my son, Alex, are the same age. They were best friends. And then poor Tyler just got swept up in the drugs. It wasn't his fault. This whole town—everywhere you look—" She broke off her sentence, shook her head. "You can't blame Ellie and Brett. They're good parents. Did the very best they could."

Rhonda was making notes.

"You sent him to rehab," she said to Ellie.

Ellie nodded. "Over and over again. In Florida."

"And—?"

"And it's a joke." Ellie's voice was bitter now. "That place made it *worse*. He made contacts down there. People who led him to Deke Foley. So he had even more sources. Every time he came back to us, it took him less and less time to relapse. We sent him three times."

"Four," Sandy said. "It was four, hon."

Ellie shrugged. Whatever. "I lost count, I guess."

"Okay," Rhonda said. "So Deke Foley was angry at your husband, too. Not just at Tyler. Why?"

"Brett told Foley . . ." Ellie paused.

"What, Mrs. Topping? What did Brett tell him?"

She looked down at her hands. "I didn't know what Brett was doing. I didn't know until that night. The night Foley came by. Brett never told me. If he had, I would've begged him to stop."

Rhonda leaned forward. "What did he tell Foley?"

"That he'd been following him."

"Following him."

"Yes. Spying on him, I guess you'd call it. Keeping a file on Foley's business. He was writing down the times when Foley bought his drugs, and where, and who he sold them to. Brett said he'd been doing it for months. Ever since Tyler got back from rehab."

"Why did your husband take that kind of risk?"

"He thought it might keep Foley away. Away from our son. If Brett had that file, he could convince Foley to back off. To pick on somebody else's kid. Foley wouldn't want all that information given to the sheriff— and so maybe he'd go away. Leave us in peace."

Rhonda didn't say what she was thinking:

Tyler would've just found another dealer to work for. Tyler's problem isn't Deke Foley. Tyler's problem is Tyler.

Out loud, she said, "So on Foley's previous visit to your home, he confronted your husband and made specific threats. Is that right?"

Ellie nodded. "He said awful things." She told Rhonda about the arrival of Pete Pauley, about the agreement between him and her husband. They had been working together. Taking turns watching Deke Foley. Compiling a file that was better than a weapon.

Rhonda excused herself for a moment. She knew Tyler was safe— he would be transferred soon from the Bretherton County Jail to Raythune's facilities, and never out of sight of law enforcement—but she was concerned about Brett Topping's associate. She sent a quick text to Sheriff Harrison:

> *Need protective detail ASAP*
> *@ home of Pete Pauley*

Harrison would find Pauley. If it turned out that he wasn't a resident of Raythune County, then the sheriff would request protection from the department of whatever county in which he did reside.

Because Deke Foley did not seem like the forgiving sort. Chances were, he'd just murdered Brett Topping. He would want to take out Pauley, too, in his search for the file and its incriminating data.

Rhonda put away her cell. Ellie was sobbing quietly now. Rhonda dearly wished she could leave this woman alone now, and let her begin to come to terms with the enormity of her loss.

But she couldn't. There were questions she had to ask.

"Mrs. Topping," Rhonda said. "Do you know what your husband meant by 'file'? Did he mean a computer file? Or something that could be carried externally—say, a thumb drive? A USB flash drive, I mean. Or maybe he meant a physical file—an actual piece of paper. Any idea?"

Ellie shook her head.

"Okay," Rhonda continued. "Someone broke into your house. It might be that Deke Foley ransacked it after killing your husband. He was looking for that file. And maybe he found it. But if he didn't find it, then he might come back and—"

A tiny click notified Rhonda that she had a new text. She excused herself one more time in order to check it.

She expected the text to be from Sheriff Harrison, acknowledging her request for protection for Pauley and letting her know she was on it. And that was indeed the gist of the first line.

The remainder of the text, however, made Rhonda grip her cell a little harder:

> *Brett Topping's office at bank*
> *ransacked an hour ago*
> *Masked assailant*
> *held janitor*
> *at gunpoint*
> *and demanded entry*

Rhonda knew what that meant. It meant Foley hadn't found the file in the Topping home. If he *had* found it there, he wouldn't have needed to break into Brett Topping's office at the Mountaineer Community Bank.

It meant Foley was still in a desperate panic. He needed to get that file. And a desperate Deke Foley was a dangerous Deke Foley.

Maybe, though, he'd found the file in Topping's office at the bank.

Another click signaled a quick follow-up text from the sheriff:

JULIA KELLER

Janitor unhurt
but says assailant
was angry. Search of
office unsuccessful

So there it was. The file was still missing. Foley hadn't found it at the bank.

"A forensic computer specialist will go through all of yours and Brett's computers," Rhonda said. "If it's on the hard drive, we'll find it. But if your husband meant another kind of file, it's going to be harder. Do you have any idea where he would've hidden it?"

Ellie shook her head. The dazed look had returned to her eyes. She didn't seem to be focusing on anything.

Rhonda could see that the window had closed. She'd gotten what she could out of Ellie Topping. And it might be a while before she had another chance; the doctors, she knew, would send the grieving woman home with generous doses of medication to allow her to sleep.

Funny thing about painkillers, Rhonda thought ruefully. *On the one hand, they're destroying us. On the other—they're saving us.* She hated to think about Ellie Topping trying to make it through the next few weeks on her own. Good thing she wouldn't have to. She had her son.

"We'll be bringing Tyler back to the courthouse later today," Rhonda said gently. "Would you like to see him?"

Ellie appeared to be considering the offer.

"Not right away," she finally answered. "He's safe. I'm glad to know that. But to see him right now—after what he brought into our lives— all of *this*—" She shook her head. "When I think of Brett lying there in the driveway, I just—" She closed her eyes. She shuddered. "Soon. Just not yet."

Chapter Eighteen

Jake Oakes finally answered his phone after six rings. Bell had almost given up, but decided to stick with it. Maybe, she reasoned, it took him a while to get to the phone.

"Yeah."

"It's Bell Elkins. Haven't caught you at a busy time, I hope."

He laughed.

"Yeah," he said. "Right. A busy time."

Self-pity: That was something she'd never expected to hear from Jake Oakes, no matter what had happened to him. It momentarily threw her off. Self-pity didn't become him.

But then again—maybe he was kidding. Mocking himself. That would be more his style. She'd know for sure after they talked for a few minutes.

"So what can I do for you?" he went on. "What's Bell Elkins need from a guy who pisses in a plastic bag?"

Jaunty Jake. That was more like it.

His jauntiness used to irk her, back in the day. Back when he was a deputy and she was the prosecutor. She'd wanted her staff to be focused, their tone reflecting the gravity of their task. That task was keeping the peace or, if the peace had been broken, bringing the law to bear upon those who'd done the breaking.

But Jake Oakes was never like that.

He'd grinned his way through the world. He made jokes when jokes were inappropriate. He had annoyed her endlessly. Worse yet, he seemed to sense that he did and thus doubled down on the very behavior that got under her skin. He took visible pleasure in infuriating her on a regular basis.

Funny thing, though: When it came right down to it, there was nobody she'd liked working with better than Jake Oakes. Nobody she trusted more.

"Did you hear about the murder last night?" she said. *Some icebreaker,* Bell thought. But it was a natural topic; time was, she and Jake would already be on the case, reviewing evidence in her courthouse office. Debating theories. Running down alibis. Dousing their insides with the harsh black coffee that Bell favored.

Caring about criminal justice in Acker's Gap was a hard habit to break.

"Yeah," he said. "I took the 911 call. I'm helping out at the courthouse. Nights. Working dispatch."

Bell didn't know what to say. That didn't sound like the kind of thing that would satisfy Jake Oakes.

At least not the Jake Oakes she remembered.

"Good for you," she said.

"Not my first choice, I'll grant you. But I don't have a lot of choices these days."

There it was again: self-pity.

"You free right now?" Bell said. "I'd like to come over. If it's convenient."

He laughed again.

"Yeah, I'll cancel all the important stuff I've got on my schedule today," he said. "It'll be hard, but for you—anything."

She needed to tell him to work on the self-pity. She knew from experience how seductive it could be. And that kind of conversation always went better in person.

His directions were good, but they didn't need to be. Bell knew the neighborhood. She'd lived two streets over from Jake's street when she was in high school; one of the foster families with whom she had spent a portion of her youth had rented a house there. She remembered the neighborhood better than she did the foster family.

The one-story homes were modest but decent. Small front yards were caged by chain-link fences. The porches were concrete slabs the size of postage stamps. She didn't need to check for the house number; Jake's was the one with the wooden ramp.

He opened the door and then backed away so that she could come in.

"Something to drink?" he said.

"I'm good." She looked around before she sat down. "You've made a real home for yourself here. I'm glad."

He grunted. "Let's not get carried away. It's a piece of crap. But yeah—I'm surviving." He watched her sit down on the couch. "How about you? Community service all done?"

"Yes."

"'Bout time. Never understood why they threw the book at you in the first place. Didn't expect you to serve any time at all, matter of fact. Nobody did. I mean, come on—it was thirty, thirty-five years ago, right?"

"Thirty-eight."

"*Jesus.* And you were just a kid."

She'd stay on this topic for another ten seconds, she decided, and then they'd move on for good. "I let my sister go to prison for me. Deliberately."

"Not the way I heard it. I heard that you didn't remember it at all. That your sister convinced you that she'd done it. And that you pretty much forced the judge to give you time. Insisted on it. What the hell?"

Ding! Bell thought. *Time's up.*

"Okay, Jake. Doesn't matter anymore. Right? Point is, I'm out. Can we move on?"

"Sure." He flipped the hair off the back of his neck. "How's your daughter?"

"Doing well. Works for a nonprofit in Charleston. They've got a crazy idea about making the chemical companies clean up the Kanawha River."

"Bunch of crazy hippie dreamers, you ask me," Jake said. He was teasing her. His grin was so familiar to Bell that she felt a secret ache when she saw it. This was the old Jake—playful, sarcastic, but for a good cause. "Next thing you know, they'll be asking for clean air, too. And food's that not tainted with chemical crap. It just never ends with those do-gooders."

She laughed. "Exactly."

"So how about you? Your daughter got that hippie DNA from *somebody*. I'm betting you've already figured out some nasty old corporation to go after."

"Wow. Sounds like you've been giving the psychic hotline a workout. That's right."

"Once a prosecutor, always a prosecutor." He tilted his head, looking at her with a more serious expression on his face. "So who are the unlucky bastards this time?"

He knew her well. "The people who are killing our children," Bell declared. "Who ruined this county. This state. Hell—if you ask me, they destroyed the whole damned country. And they're not finished yet."

"Oh. You're talking about the drug dealers." Jake couldn't keep the disappointment out of his voice. Been there, done that. He'd spent a good part of his career arresting dealers and hauling unconscious addicts off to the hospital, so that they could recover from their overdoses and then go back to the activity that had brought them to his attention in the first place.

But that's not what she meant at all.

"Screw the dealers," Bell snapped back at him. "I'm talking about the bastards who made the stuff in the first place—and then told everybody it wasn't addictive. And got stinking rich off other people's agony."

She'd had a lot of time on her hands at Alderson, she explained to him. And she'd spent it researching Utley Pharmaceuticals, a company that seemed to have tagged West Virginia as a lucrative dumping ground for its signature painkiller. She'd added to what she knew by visiting the Raythune County Public Library earlier in the week.

"Kind of premature, isn't it?" he asked.

"What do you mean?"

"Well, if you ask me, it might be jumping the gun a little bit to dive right into the middle of a big old hairy mess. When you were prosecutor, you averaged about a dozen big old hairy messes per week. Maybe you ought to take a short break?"

"I did take a break. And it wasn't short. It lasted about three years."

He groaned. "Guess I should know better than to argue with Bell Elkins."

"Yeah," she said. "You should."

He put his hands on the tops of his wheels. "Strikes me that I'm being a pretty piss-poor host. I can rustle up some snacks if you're hungry."

"No, thanks. Didn't come over here to raid your refrigerator."

"Then why did you come over?"

"To see you. To say hello."

"To check on me," he corrected her. A hardness had suddenly barged into his voice. "To make sure I haven't turned into a bitter old man, crying into his beer because he's stuck in a damned chair for the rest of his damned life. Because everything's changed now."

"For both of us."

He glared at her. "Yeah. For both of us. We're a couple of has-beens, Bell. A couple of broke-ass, useless nobodies. Dammit—we used to *matter*. We were doing something important with our lives. Something good. Something *big*. We made a difference."

"We still can. I just told you about Utley."

"I heard you. But I don't believe it. Not for a single goddamned second."

"Then maybe that's why I'm here."

"And why's that?"

"To change your mind."

Chapter Nineteen

"Deke Foley."

Tyler had repeated the name so many times by now that it rang in his ears like the chanting of a monk—a monk with, as it happened, filthy hair and dirty sneakers and a puke-stained T-shirt and a bloated face and a black eye, but still: *DekeFoleyDekeFoleyDekeFoley.*

It was having no effect. Nobody was doing anything. Nobody was jumping up and scurrying around to grab weapons and racing out to hunt down the bastard.

Instead, they were pretty much ignoring him.

"Hey!" Tyler called out. "Hey!"

He smacked the tabletop. Even that mild effort was a bit too much; he felt an acute wave of nausea pulse through his gut. The drugs had dissipated by now. He was facing the world as it was: cold, hard, ugly.

"Hey—somebody! I'm telling you—it's Deke Foley! That's who you need to go after. He killed my dad, okay? Deke Foley! *Deke Fucking Foley!*"

They had brought him here, to one of two interrogation rooms in the sheriff's office in the Raythune County Courthouse, and left him. Left him. *Left him!* Jesus Christ. Could they do that? Wasn't there a law or something? Couldn't he sue them?

First they'd grabbed him out of the Bretherton jail, hustled him into a big SUV with a metal grille separating him from the driver, let him bounce around in the back until his brains were scrambled, and then they'd dumped him here.

This place, he knew. This was Raythune County lockup. He'd been here dozens of times.

On the drive, they told him. His father was dead.

When they first said it, he thought he was dreaming. He was still a little bit high; traces of what he'd snorted were still moving around in his body, tiny flickers of light. He'd gotten beaten up behind that 7-Eleven, after the guys he sold to said they weren't going to pay him and he tried to argue with them. Bad mistake: They knocked him down—that punch in the eye was aching again—and kicked him in the ribs and belly, and he'd puked on himself. He went into the 7-Eleven and he swiped a few things and he sold them right down the street— you had to know what to take, what would sell in minutes—and he bought some drugs with the money and that would've been fine, except that he got greedy.

He went back into the 7-Eleven again and now they weren't so busy. They must've been watching him this time. When he tried to walk out with another bunch of shit tucked up under his shirt the manager was in his face, and the guy was all *Calling the cops* and *Stay right here* and *I'm so tired of you fucking junkies.*

Fine, Tyler had thought. *Call the cops. Do it. Like I care.*

And then he was not in jail anymore. He was in the back of the SUV. The words about his dad, when he heard them, weren't real. They couldn't be real.

The deputy behind the wheel—Tyler thought he recognized him, but you never knew around here, everybody looked like everybody else, just a big dumb blur—said, "We got some bad news, Tyler." How did they know his name? Anyway, they did.

The other deputy—it was a woman—said, "Your father was shot to death. Do you know anything about that? Anybody you know who mighta wanted him dead?"

Finally the words sunk in. By the time they put him in the dingy room with just the metal table and two chairs, he was feeling it. Feeling the words.

Your father was shot to death.

His dad's face swam up in his mind, the big head with the little round chin sunk in a roll of fat. Always in a suit and tie, even when he wasn't at work. These days, at least. It wasn't like that when Tyler was a little boy: His dad wore sweatshirts a lot back then. And jeans, sneakers. They'd play catch in the yard. Alex Banville might come by and join in; his dad would smack a pop fly and he and Alex would both try for it, elbowing each other out of the way. Laughing. His dad would laugh, too, because usually they'd end up knocking each other down and neither one would get it.

Take your time, boys, his dad would say. *Teamwork. That's the key.*

Alex. He hadn't seen Alex in a while. But he'd seen Sara Banville, Alex's sister. She was why he'd gone off like he had, matter of fact.

The look on her face. The appraisal. The judgment. Miss High and Mighty. Like she was *better* than him. Like he was scum. Like they hadn't grown up in the same damned neighborhood, with her begging him to let her play with him and Alex.

It stung him, that look in her eye. Snooty bitch. So he'd hitched over to Bretherton County. Might as well get fucked up. Might as well.

His memory jerked forward. It lurched until it hit the moment when they'd yanked him out of the Bretherton jail and then he was bouncing around inside the SUV. The fog lifted and the words started to make sense—"Your father was shot dead"—and Tyler panicked. That's when he started his chant: *DekeFoleyDekeFoleyDekeFoley.* He'd kept it up, all through the march down the corridor and then the moment when they put him in here.

He'd warned his dad, right? He'd tried to tell him. You *do not* mess with the Deke Foleys of this world. You *do not* do that.

The deputy came in once and said, "We know all about Deke Foley." But Tyler didn't believe him. And so he kept saying it:

DekeFoleyDekeFoleyDekeFoley

He didn't know what time it was but it had to be morning by now. Had to be.

Somebody was coming in. The door opened with a buzz and a scrape and it was another cop in a big hat and a uniform. Another woman. Wow, he was surrounded. Where were all the guys? What was this, anyway—Planet Bitch?

That triggered something in his mind: *Mom*. He hadn't even asked about his mom.

"How's my mom? She's not—?"

"She's okay. She's alive."

"So Deke didn't—"

"No. She wasn't home when it happened. As you can imagine, though, she's very upset. Doctors had to give her a sedative." By this point the woman was seated across the table from him. Yellow pad in front of her. A pen on it. "I'm Sheriff Harrison. We've met before, Tyler."

He nodded. Whatever. "My dad—what the hell happened? And you know Deke Foley did it, right? He threatened him. Said he was going to kill my dad. You've got to find Deke Foley."

"Why, Tyler? Why did Foley want to kill your father?"

"The file. My dad had a file."

"What kind of file?"

"About Foley. His operation."

"I don't understand," the sheriff said. She was infuriatingly calm. Why wasn't she off chasing Deke Foley? Why was she just sitting there?

"What? What don't you understand?" Tyler was starting to feel the pinpricks running up and down his arms. His scalp was on fire. His gut churned. He felt like somebody was ripping out his toenails, one by one. He felt like they'd sewn ants under his skin. He needed something. Fast. They didn't get it. He was going to be sick. Unless. Unless they helped him.

Hell, I need a sedative as much as my mom does. Why aren't they giving ME *a friggin' sedative?*

"I want to know," the sheriff replied, the calmness oozing out of her, "why your dad would've had a file on Deke Foley's operation."

Tyler sputtered the words like toothpaste he was spitting into the sink. "Because I *work* for him, okay? I work for Foley sometimes and my dad knew that. He'd followed me. Taken notes. Wrote some shit down. He said he needed leverage. So Foley would leave us alone. Okay? Okay? Now—would you please just let me out of here and go after Foley? Before he gets away? He killed my dad. Dammit—goddamn all of you, every friggin' one—*go get Deke Foley!*"

"Any idea where Foley might be? Other than his trailer, which we've already checked?"

"Starliner Motel, maybe. That's where they drop off the shit he sells. Or maybe Skin U Alive. The tattoo place."

"We've checked those places. Anywhere else?"

"Highway Haven, maybe. Around the back. He does a lot of business there." Tyler tried to think of the names of the other places, places that everybody didn't know about already, new places, but his mind wasn't sharp. He needed that file to jog his memory. The file his dad made. The one that got him killed.

"It'll be in that file," Tyler muttered. His eye sockets burned. He started to shake. He was close to being dope sick. Damned close.

"Speaking of the file. Any idea where your dad was hiding it?"

"His computer, maybe? He's got a big one on the desk in his den. And one at work."

"Any other possibilities?"

"Hell—*I don't know*, lady, okay? Why're you wasting time? Go find Foley. For Christ's sake—"

"Okay." The sheriff pushed the legal pad across the table. She did it slowly, which had a fingernails-on-a-chalkboard effect on him. He really, *really* needed something to take the edge off. His whole body felt like it was cramping up, like somebody was trying to fold him up and make him smaller so that he'd fit in a box. The soles of his feet were starting to ache. His nose was running; he could feel the snot on his upper lip.

Like they couldn't give him a friggin' *Kleenex?*

The sheriff was still talking: "Write down everything you just told me, Tyler."

"What the *hell*—it's *Deke Foley* you ought be worried about and not—"

"Write."

Tyler grabbed at the pen. Anything to get this bitch out of here, anything to make sure she started tracking down the bastard who'd killed his father.

Killed his father. Something about that idea bumped up against a concept that was already in Tyler's head.

He remembered. His mother had said that to him, many times, her voice heartbroken rather than angry: *You're killing your father. You know that, right? You're killing your father. The things you do—the drugs, the police, the terrible things you bring into this house—you're killing him. Killing him.*

But that was different, right?

She meant it another way. Not this way. Not for real, like what Deke Foley had done. She meant it—what was the word?—symbolically.

He knew his mother hated him sometimes. He'd seen it in her eyes. She loved him, but she also hated him, too. He could sense it.

And speaking of killing—there were times when he knew she wanted to kill him. She probably thought he didn't know that, but he did.

"Write," the sheriff repeated.

Tyler realized he'd been just sitting there, holding the pen, staring at his thoughts. Staring at his mother's face, the face she wore when she was hating him. Which happened more and more often.

Well, he hated himself, too. That was the thing. After a while you didn't need anybody to tell you what a worthless SOB you were, what a useless, pathetic sack of shit—because you already knew it.

In fact you knew it better than *they* knew it.

So why didn't they just shut up?

The sheriff was talking again. "By the way, you caught a break."

Tyler waited. He wasn't aware of any breaks. He wanted to peel off his own skin, starting at the top and working his way down to his toes, the strips curling up like potato peels. Might bring some relief.

"That clerk at the 7-Eleven," the sheriff went on. "He's not pressing charges on the shoplifting. Minute he heard that you'd lost your dad, he got real sweet and sentimental. Might even give you a free cherry Slurpee and a Slim Jim, next time you drop by."

Chapter Twenty

"So I invite you to dinner—and lo and behold, you bring dinner with you," Bell said. She stepped to one side so that her daughter could come in. Carla needed both hands to wrangle the very large, very flat cardboard box from which spicy smells twined and drifted.

"I suppose," Bell added, "that's a pithy commentary on my culinary skills."

"Just figured you might not have time to stop by Lymon's Market."

"You figured right."

Carla continued on past her into the kitchen. She set the box down on the table. "Might need to be nuked in the microwave. Had to get it before I left Charleston." The one and only pizza place that had ever existed in Acker's Gap had been called A Separate Piece—the owner was an English major—and it opened and closed in the same month a decade ago.

A few minutes later they were settled in the living room, plates on their knees, Bell scrunched up in her favorite armchair, Carla stretched out on the couch. Those were the same positions they had always taken in here—for TV watching, for casual chats, for arguments, for revelations, for family councils.

"Bet you have a lot better things to do with your Saturday night," Bell said, "than hang out with your mother."

"Actually—no. Brad Pitt called and canceled our date."

"Probably just as well. He's still hung up on Angelina. You can tell."

"And all those kids," Carla said. She made a face. Then she picked a curled-up piece of pepperoni from her slice and popped it in her mouth. "Too, too complicated."

Bell smiled. God, she loved this girl. Carla was twenty-five now, all grown up, with a responsible job and a full life, but Bell would always think of her as a little girl: a passionate climber of trees, an all-day bike rider, a feisty kid who cherished reading and running and justice—all the things that had defined Bell, too, when she was that age.

She'd put Carla through so much. The divorce. Moving back to Acker's Gap. Taking the ferociously demanding job of prosecutor, which meant her daughter was on her own for long stretches of her young life.

But the worst thing she'd done to her, the absolute worst, had happened some three years ago, when Bell confessed to killing her father and asked to be sent to prison for the crime.

Bell would never forget the night she told Carla what she was going to do. It had happened right here, in this very room. Her daughter had instantly shut down, like a circuit that was suddenly overloaded. She didn't cry. She didn't get mad. She'd simply stared at her mother, her dark eyes reflecting a shocked incomprehension that went beyond mere surprise.

Carla had visited her at Alderson at least once a week, bringing books and magazines, bringing combs, new toothbrushes—bringing anything Bell requested and a lot of things she didn't. Their conversations about how Bell had ended up there—the act of violence so many years ago, the act of contrition much more recently—were mostly awkward and halting, filled with silences that seemed to grow longer with each visit.

But somewhere along the way they had reached a fragile sort of equilibrium about things, about Bell's decision to request prison time and the havoc that decision had wrought upon their lives. When Bell was discharged from Alderson, Carla had helped her get this house back in shape so she could return to it. She came on the weekends, driving down from Charleston. She listened to her mom's stories about Evening Street.

"Heard about the murder last night," Carla said. "It was on the morning news. God. How awful."

Bell nodded. "The sheriff has her hands full. Rhonda, too."

"Did you know the guy who got shot?"

"A little. He was a VP at the bank. Good guy, from what I remember." Bell took a bite of her pizza slice.

"They're thinking the wife did it, right?"

"Why would you say that?"

A droll glance. "Mom. Come on. I'm the daughter of a prosecutor—*and* I used to watch so many *Law & Order* reruns back in high school that I named my hamsters Munch and Finn, remember? It's *always* the spouse."

Bell laughed. She'd had another porch-to-porch chat with Sally Ann Turner that afternoon. Garnered more details.

"You're right," Bell said. "Usually is. But apparently she has an alibi. So does their son, Tyler. He's about six years younger than you. Did you know him? A lot of drug problems, I guess."

"I'd need more than *that* to go on, Mom. Hardly a distinguishing characteristic around here." Carla shook her head sadly. She'd finished her slice while Bell talked. "So many of the kids I graduated with—they're lost. Just lost. The drugs. So many." She shook off the memory. "Anyway, no. Doesn't ring a bell. This Tyler guy was too many years behind me. Six years—that's a lifetime."

Her mother nodded. "Ready for another piece?"

"In a minute. Any other suspects they're looking at?"

"Sally Ann Turner says no. And her sources are a lot better than mine."

Carla laughed. "God. Sally Ann Turner. What a snoop. I remember how she'd watch me from that front window of hers. I'd be coming home late from a date—and I'd look across the street and see that curtain moving. There I was—sixteen years old—and I had the neighborhood FBI on my tail."

"I have to say, though," Bell murmured, "that those surveillance tapes she gave me were pretty interesting."

Carla started to react, then relaxed. "Very funny."

"I thought so."

"Anyway," Carla said, "I bet Rhonda wishes Nick Fogelsong was still in town."

"Pam Harrison knows what she's doing."

"Sure. But she's not Nick." Carla studied the crust on her plate. "Do you miss it, Mom?"

Her daughter had tried to make the question seem spontaneous, but Bell knew better. Carla had probably wanted to ask her that from the moment she heard about the murder.

"Do you mean working on a capital case?" Bell asked.

"I mean—being part of the team," Carla clarified.

No point in pretending. "Yeah. I do."

Carla seemed to be waiting for her to say something else. Bell changed her position in the armchair, tucking the other leg beneath her rump. She did have more to say.

But not about the murder.

"You know, sweetie—I've been wanting to tell you—we've never really discussed—" Deep breath. Full speed ahead. "I never wanted to embarrass you. With my time at Alderson, I mean. With any of this. You or your father."

"What?"

"That's one of my big concerns. That I embarrassed you. Both of you."

"*Embarrassed* me?" Carla said. "Is *that* what you think?"

"A mother in prison." Bell's voice was matter-of-fact. "For murder. And in Sam's case—his ex-wife. That can't have exactly made him proud over there in D.C., with his fancy friends."

"Oh, Mom." Carla's voice was firm. "You've got it all wrong. I'm not embarrassed. I've *never* been embarrassed by anything you've done. I'm proud to be your daughter. I've *always* been proud to be your daughter. You know that."

"I used to."

Carla put her plate on the coffee table. When she spoke next, it was softly and carefully:

"You know what, Mom? This is going to sound corny but I don't care. Okay? Listen—you're my hero. You're Dad's hero, too—did you know that? No, you couldn't possibly know that. Because he'd never tell you. But you are. I'm sure of it. I hear how he talks about you to other people. The things you did—coming back to Acker's Gap, running for prosecutor. Doing incredible things. Important things. Things nobody else would've done." Carla shook her head. "And then when you found out what really happened with you and Aunt Shirley. And your dad. Mom—I can't imagine the pain you went through. The pain of the truth. And then after all that—to lose Shirley—"

"Okay, okay," Bell said. "I hear you, sweetie."

"You still can't talk about her, can you? Or have anybody else talk about her when you're around." Carla didn't wait for a reply before pressing on. "So you're wrong. I'm not embarrassed because you went to prison. I mean—I don't understand why you had to do it and I never will—but I love you and I trust you. I know you could've kept it between you and Shirley. I know everything could've gone on pretty much the way it was. You could've swept it all under the rug. But you didn't do that. You *couldn't* do that."

Bell stood up. She went over to the couch, leaned down, and put her hand on the top of Carla's head.

She was aware, as she was each time she had the slightest, most casual physical contact with her daughter, of the still-astonishing reality of this person she had created, of the hair and the eyes, the bones and the skin. As always, awe blossomed in Bell's mind at the beautiful, ever-perplexing mystery of it all:

This is my child. I made her.

And then, this: *But she's not mine at all, of course. She belongs to no one but herself.*

"I never wanted to hurt you by what I did," Bell said. She'd returned to the armchair now. "Or Sam, either." Despite her differences with him, her ex-husband had always been an excellent father to Carla. Even after he remarried, he was still kind and attentive, still lovingly involved in his daughter's life.

"But you *didn't,* Mom. The only person you hurt was—*you*. You lost so, so much. Your home and your profession—everything. You lost the life you had. And now you have to start all over."

"I'll be okay. I'll figure something out."

Carla let a moment go by. "You're never going to tell me, are you?"

Bell didn't answer.

"At first," Carla went on, "you said you might. Someday. But lately, I've had my doubts."

"It doesn't really matter now, does it? Shirley died. It's over."

"Mom." Carla's voice was grave. "You know better than that. It's *never* going to be over. Not really. I respect your decision, but—it's a life sentence. In a way, that's what it is. You'll be dealing with this forever. And I don't even know *why.*" An edge of frustration now crept into Carla's tone. "You didn't have to confess. Aunt Shirley told me that. She didn't tell me much—but she told me that. She wanted me to know that she didn't pressure you into anything. She was fine with just the two of you knowing. She didn't want you to ruin your life."

"No. She didn't."

"So—why? Why did you do it? Why did you tell the judge you wouldn't accept any sort of probation or deferred sentence? It's like you *wanted* to suffer, Mom. Like you *wanted* to have everything taken away and—"

"Sweetie. Please—don't."

"Okay. Fine. Fine." Carla's voice backed down a notch. "But for the record—I'm worried about you. About how your life's going to be from now on. I *know* you—and I know how much you need meaningful work. Something you can believe in. Something that does for you what being a prosecutor did."

"I'll be fine." Bell thought about her research into Utley Pharmaceuticals. She didn't want to talk about it tonight with Carla. The conversation was heavy enough already.

"You know what, Mom? Sometimes I wish . . ."

"What?"

"I wish you'd think about getting out of here. Moving away. Even just to Charleston. You could live with me. I'd be happy to—"

"Carla." Bell's voice was sharp. "No. We've been all through this. I can take care of myself. Good God. I'm almost fifty years old."

"Everybody you run into, every single day, is going to know who you are and what happened. They're going to know that you used to be the prosecutor. They're going to know you pleaded guilty to murder. They're going to know *everything.* Wouldn't it be nice to be somewhere else? Where nobody knows you and you don't know them, either? A fresh start—that's all I mean."

"This is my home."

Carla took a deep breath. She knew it was a lost cause, but she had to try.

"Got it, Mom. But sometimes I can understand why Nick and Mary Sue Fogelsong retired to Florida. Can't you? I mean—really? They see different things now. Not the same old crap they saw every day. Not the same people they've been looking at their whole damned lives."

Bell didn't answer.

"How about just a mini-vacation?" Carla went on. "A day trip somewhere?"

An idea stirred in Bell's mind. It was a way to connect her work on Utley Pharmaceuticals with Carla's suggestion.

"You know what, sweetie? I think you're right. And I just thought of the perfect destination—D.C. I'll go Monday morning. It's a four-hour drive. And I already know the way."

That night, long after Carla had left to drive back to her apartment in Charleston, Bell's cell rang.

"Didn't wake you up, did I?"

"I've been working nights, Nick. It'll be a long time before I go to sleep at a regular hour."

"Point taken. So how are you, Belfa?"

"Fine. I'm fine." She had been expecting his call. She just hadn't realized how much until she'd heard the sound of his voice.

She had known this man since she was ten years old. Nick Fogelsong had been the deputy on duty the night that everything changed for Bell and Shirley—the night their father died and their trailer burned to the ground. After that, their lives had dissolved into chaos. But for Bell, the young deputy was a guiding light, a helping hand, a steadying influence—and later, when she came back to Acker's Gap, her colleague as Raythune County sheriff.

Nick was as much of a father as she'd ever known. Even when he gave up the job he loved and excelled at—a decision that troubled and disappointed her as much as her decision, a few years later, had troubled and disappointed him—she still cherished him, and trusted him, and counted on him.

As long as Nick was a part of her world, she could endure whatever bad luck and bleak fortune came her way.

Thus it was entirely fitting that he was calling her tonight, her first real night of freedom in almost three years.

She just wished he didn't have to be doing it from Florida.

"Guess you've heard about Brett Topping's murder," she said. She knew that Nick kept up with the news from Acker's Gap.

"Yeah. Knew him pretty well. Tragic." His voice shifted, signaling a desire to move on. "But I don't want to talk shop right now, okay?"

She started to point out that, technically, it wasn't talking shop, because he wasn't the sheriff and she wasn't the prosecutor, but held back. Because she wanted to tell him about Utley Pharmaceuticals and her plan to make them pay.

And briefly, that's just what she did.

"So what do you think, Nick?"

"I think," he said, after a long pause, "that you oughta let yourself relax a little while, Belfa, before you go riding that big white horse of yours toward another damned windmill. Settle in. Plant some flowers."

"It's fall, Nick," she retorted brusquely. She was miffed and didn't mind him knowing. "Long past flower-planting season. But—okay. If that's what you think—then, okay."

Only later, an hour they'd hung up, did she realize that he hadn't mentioned his wife, Mary Sue, at all. Mary Sue struggled with severe mental illness. It was kept in check with medication. Bell wondered if she was doing poorly, and if maybe that was why Nick hadn't talked about her.

Although there might have been another reason, too.

Maybe Mary Sue was doing better.

Bell had always wondered what would happen to Nick's marriage if his wife no longer needed him every minute of every day, if his role as rescuer and protector wasn't required anymore.

Well, he'd never bring it up, and Bell would never ask. She had other things to think about, anyway. What had he said to her? Oh, right:

Windmills. White horses. And—of all things—flowers.

She was irritated all over again.

Chapter Twenty-one

"Missed you at church yesterday, Rhonda," Lee Ann Frickie said.

"Busy time. We're dealing with Brett Topping's murder, plus all of the other cases that we still have to—"

"Don't tell *me*." Lee Ann cut her off, adding a small sniff of pure unadulterated self-righteousness. "Tell the Lord."

"Will do." Rhonda took off her coat and folded it onto the bench seat beside her, cheerfully ignoring the old woman's sanctimony. JPs did not have a coat rack anymore; the previous one had cracked beneath the stacked-up burden of too many heavy-duty parkas and ankle-length down coats on a memorable day last winter. Jackie hadn't gotten around to replacing it yet. "Good to see you."

Lee Ann, she knew, meant well; she simply believed that nothing was more important than church attendance.

And she may be right, Rhonda thought. But she hadn't had a choice. She and Sheriff Harrison had spent their Sunday morning in Rhonda's office, reviewing a list of people who might have had a reason to want Brett Topping dead. The roll call included a slew of disgruntled bank customers whose homes or businesses had been foreclosed upon, and a former colleague who had lost his job twelve years ago when Brett sided with a female bank employee who had accused the man of sexual harassment.

Long shots, every one of them. In Rhonda's mind, all roads still led to Deke Foley.

"I do appreciate you meeting me," Lee Ann said primly. "Of course I've heard about Brett Topping, and it's just so shocking and sad. Such a tragedy."

"Yeah, well—tell you the truth, Lee Ann, I don't have a lot of time right now, because I'm got a conference call scheduled with—"

Lee Ann held up a bony hand to stop her. "I know about a prosecutor's schedule, Rhonda."

Yes, she did. Gray-haired, long-faced, and stick-thin, Lee Ann was seventy-nine years old and had worked for eight different prosecutors during her long career at the Raythune County Courthouse. She had retired shortly after Bell's resignation.

An hour ago, as Rhonda sat at her kitchen table in her pink plaid pajamas, finishing off a carton of strawberry banana Light & Fit yogurt, her cell rang. To her surprise, the screen told her it was Lee Ann Frickie.

Lee Ann asked Rhonda if she could spare a minute or two on her way into the courthouse this morning. Maybe meet her at JPs?

Whereupon Rhonda, to what would turn out to be her everlasting regret, had said, "Sure."

They were the only customers.

Lee Ann had worn her dress coat, Rhonda noted, a powder-blue wool one with a muff around the collar, from which her long, wizened neck emerged. She didn't take off her coat. She looked older every time Rhonda saw her, which was usually just at church, because the old lady rarely came downtown anymore. The lines on her face cut deeper, and her pale, sad eyes were extra watery, pushed deep into nests of crinkled skin.

Rhonda signaled across the diner to Jackie, a tall, muscular woman with straight black hair that cascaded down her back until it nearly reached her waist. She wore a red flannel shirt tucked into a pair of black jeans. The jeans, in turn, were tucked into hiking boots.

Jackie brought over the coffeepot. She set a white china mug in front of Rhonda, filling it with a thick black ribbon of coffee. She didn't bother setting a mug in front of Lee Ann. Lee Ann didn't drink coffee. Everyone knew better than to ask her why not—and if you forgot and *did* ask, you'd be on the receiving end of a long and rhetorically ornate lecture on the dire health risks of caffeine in particular and the sinfulness of stimulants in general.

As usual, Jackie said nothing beyond a murmured *Mornin'*. She was not a purveyor of small talk. She had run this diner for almost a decade now, naming it in honor of her late mother, Joyce—the "JP" was for "Joyce's Place"—who had also run a diner in this spot for many years with her partner, Georgette.

Coffee poured, Jackie looked at Rhonda. Rhonda shook her head. The meaning was clear: *No food right now. Thanks.*

Rhonda was always amused by the fact that she'd had entire conversations sometimes with Jackie and not a word was ever spoken.

Now she looked across the table at Lee Ann. "Okay," Rhonda said. "I really do have a ton of things to do this morning. So if we could wind this up in just a few—"

"Understood."

Lee Ann took a deep breath.

Since her retirement she had, Rhonda knew, devoted more and more of her time in service to Rising Souls Baptist Church. Three years ago the church had weathered a scandal when its former minister, Paul Wolford, had admitted to fathering a child out of wedlock, and ever since then the parishioners had accelerated the pace of their good deeds, as if they hoped to prime the pump of penance—penance for a sin that none of them had personally committed, Rhonda reminded herself.

Such an activity, sadly, was typical of a lot of women in these parts. They atoned not only for their own shortcomings, but also for those of the men in their midst.

"The time has come, Rhonda," Lee Ann declared. "We've decided to take a stand."

"'We'?"

"The Ladies League of the Rising Souls Baptist Church."

"Okay." Rhonda sipped her coffee. It was satisfyingly scalding. She had inherited Bell's taste in coffee temperature as well as her public office. "A stand against what?"

"Against what's happening to this country."

Rhonda felt the beginnings of a stomachache, and it wasn't from the introduction of harsh black coffee into a belly already partially filled with strawberry banana yogurt. It was from the passionate gleam she'd just noticed in Lee Ann's translucent blue eyes.

"Look, Lee Ann, you know I can't discuss politics. It's just not—"

"This isn't about *politics.*" Lee Ann said the word with a shudder of disdain. "It's about right and wrong. Good and evil. Jesus and the devil."

Oh, Lord. Rhonda had heard from a few different sources that Lee Ann—and Rhonda hated the words they used, even though she knew how well those words communicated a certain state of unhinged fanaticism—had gone off the deep end, religion-wise, since her retirement. Jesus-crazy, some called it.

Lee Ann, most likely, had too much free time. And she used those empty hours to brood over the world's wicked ways, and the responsibility of God's army to rid that selfsame world of the scourge of sin and faithlessness.

"Lee Ann," Rhonda said. She hoped that the simple saying of her name might get the old woman back on track.

No dice. "We want to put up a pillar." Lee Ann's words swept forward in a confident tsunami, coming faster and getting bigger the longer she talked. "A big stone pillar on the courthouse lawn. We've been saving our money and we think we've just about got enough. We've been selling quilts and having bake sales, rummage sales—anything and everything we can do. Because Acker's Gap has become a place of darkness and iniquity, and unless we fight—and I mean *fight*, Rhonda, fight the fight of our lives—we're looking at the end times. The prophecy is *very* clear. The signs are all around us."

She wasn't finished.

"The pillar has to be tall enough so that we can get all the words on it, starting at the top and going right on down the line. The words of the Ten Commandments. We're going to hire somebody to chisel them on there in capital letters. Evelyn says her cousin over in Romney could do it. But if we don't use him, we'll find somebody else. The Lord will send us somebody. That's for sure."

Rhonda looked down at what remained of the contents of her coffee cup, at the little circle of black liquid. Her queasiness had increased in direct proportion to the length of Lee Ann's speech.

"We've got it all planned," the old woman went on. She leaned forward. Rhonda smelled talcum powder. That was the only scent you ever detected on Lee Ann Frickie; she dusted the back of her neck with Johnson's Baby Powder every morning. "We're going to put the Ten Commandments on that pillar and it's going to have these big Roman numerals in front of each commandment. We have to remind people, Rhonda. Remind them of what we've all forgotten about. And this way—putting it on the courthouse lawn—everybody'll see it." She paused, needing to reacquire some oxygen, and then plunged right back in. "We need your support. If we can tell people that the prosecutor is on our side—it would go a long way toward—"

"Lee Ann." Rhonda interrupted her, but she did it gently. She looked into her friend's eyes. She reached across the table, putting a hand atop Lee Ann's spindly, arthritic one. "You know I can't do that."

"I *don't* know it." Lee Ann's voice had an odd pitch to it. "I don't know that *at all.*" Abruptly she pulled her hand out from under Rhonda's. Then she turned her head, looking out the large window along the front wall of the diner that offered a cloudy view of Main Street.

Rhonda suddenly realized, to her astonishment, that the old woman was crying. She did so quietly, but there was no mistaking it: a tear slipped slowly down the side of her face that was visible to Rhonda.

In all of the years she had known Lee Ann Frickie—and that was her entire life, because Lee Ann was already the secretary in the prosecutor's office the year Rhonda was born—Rhonda had never seen her cry. Never. Not even once.

Not when she was almost hit by a bullet that came crashing through the courthouse window.

Not when Charlie Mathers, a retired deputy and a good friend, was killed three years ago during a drug raid.

By now the lone tear had been bolstered by others. Rhonda didn't know what to say or do—Lee Ann was the proudest woman she had ever known, and the notion of an emotional display in public would, at least in times past, have been as painful to her as an attack of sciatica.

And so Rhonda took another drink of her coffee.

Lee Ann wasn't looking out the window anymore. She unsnapped the black patent leather purse on the bench seat beside her. She drew out a small package of tissues. A few sniffles and dainty nose-wipings later, she had recovered.

"They told me you would say that," Lee Ann murmured. "The other ladies told me, but I said—no, no, she won't, because Rhonda's a good girl. And she loves the Lord. She goes to our church. She'll help us. She'll find a way."

"You know it as well as I do, Lee Ann—the courthouse is a public facility. There can't be any religious displays there. Because the First Amendment to the Constitution says—"

"*Fiddlesticks*," Lee Ann cried out, interrupting her with the strongest epithet she ever used. "The courthouse is exactly where we *need* religion. Don't you see that?"

All I see, Rhonda wished she'd had the gumption to say, *is a conscientious old woman whose entire working life was spent at the crossroads of all the sorrows—violence, alcoholism, drug addiction, a dying economy—that can befall a community: the courthouse.*

I see a good soul who is heartbroken over what's become of the home she loves, and who believes in the power of the church—and only in the power of the church—to fix it all.

Lee Ann knew the church-and-state mantra as well as any lawyer. Right now, it didn't matter to her.

Something had tipped her over the edge. It might have been Brett Topping's murder, but it also might have been something else, too. Because the tragic, inexplicable events were piling up. The winds were rising, the mountains were crumbling, and to Lee Ann Frickie, God seemed mighty displeased with His servants here on earth.

"Nothing more to talk about," Rhonda said. She spoke quietly, but firmly. "There can't be any pillar with the Ten Commandments on the courthouse lawn. You need to go back to your friends in the Ladies League and make that very clear to them, okay?"

Lee Ann's jaw tightened. "I won't. I won't tell them that."

"Well, that's your choice. I just thought it might be easier if it came from you—because you can explain to them the reasons why. You worked in the prosecutor's office, Lee Ann. You understand these things."

"No, I don't understand them. Not anymore." All at once the old woman leaned across the table, startling Rhonda with the vehemence in her voice. She picked up Rhonda's coffee cup and set it to one side, clearing the way for her to snatch up Rhonda's hands and squeeze them. "I'm going to try one more time here. I've *got* to. Rhonda—please. *Please*. Help us. The Lord is watching."

Squeezing even tighter, Lee Ann added, "Think of it. Every day, people going in and out of the courthouse would see that pillar. They'd read the commandments. And if even *one* heart was changed, if even *one* wayward soul heard the call of Jesus and decided to—"

"I've got to get to work." Rhonda extricated her hands. Her patience had officially expired. She scooted out of the booth and stood up.

"The Lord is watching," Lee Ann said, glaring up at her. This time it sounded like a threat, a warning.

"Have a good day, Lee Ann."

"I mean it. *The Lord is watching*." Her eyes narrowed. "We're going to fight you on this, Rhonda. I hate to say it, because I know your parents so well and your whole family and I've watched you grow up and I've been so *proud* of you, so proud—but you're dead wrong this time. You're on the side of the devil. From now on, you're the enemy."

"I'm sorry you feel that way."

There was nothing more to say.

As Rhonda walked out, she caught a quick glimpse of Jackie over by the cash register, thumbing through a stack of old receipts. JPs was a small establishment, and so it was impossible not to hear customer conversations, especially when those conversations were intense.

Jackie raised her dark eyes. She offered Rhonda a single curt nod of solidarity.

But Lee Ann wasn't finished. Before Rhonda had cleared the front door, she heard the old woman's voice again, rising behind her like a fiery whirlwind of righteous conviction:

"The Lord is watching you, Rhonda! The Lord is watching!"

A heretical thought occurred to the weary prosecutor as she made a right turn toward the courthouse: *Oh, yeah? Well, I wish He'd do more than just watch. Wish He'd pitch in and help. We've got a helluva lot to do and not enough people to do it.*

Chapter Twenty-two

"I bet the scenery's spectacular this time of year," Sam Elkins said. "The leaves and all of that."

Bell nodded. "Yeah. Sure is."

Leaves. Okay, so they'd talk about leaves first.

Sam leaned back in his chair, a high-backed one crafted of sumptuous black leather and featuring a complicated undercarriage of sleek steel.

She waited for the creak. The desk chair she'd used for eight years back in the Raythune County Courthouse had always creaked at the slightest application of pressure. When she leaned back, the way Sam was doing right now, the creak would unleash an assortment of unbearable shrieks and moans. Anyone loitering in the corridor probably assumed that the prosecutor had undertaken a series of executions with the ruthless, *next-next-next* efficiency of a stylist at Great Clips.

There was no creak from Sam's chair, of course. Because this wasn't the courthouse, with its older-than-dirt furnishings and a budget you'd need an electron microscope to locate.

This was a partner's office at Strong, Weatherly, and Wycombe, an international lobbying firm toward which other wealthy firms and individuals insisted upon slinging millions—no, billions—of dollars each year.

"I do find myself missing those hills," Sam said.

"I bet you do."

He gave her a sharp look. Was she being sarcastic?

She wasn't, but she enjoyed his uncertainty.

"It's good to see you, Sam," she said, and this time she hoped her sincerity was obvious. "I'm glad you had a moment to chat. And on such short notice."

If she was going to take on Utley Pharmaceuticals, she needed advice on the best way to approach the company's CEO, Roderick Mc-Murdo. Bell knew only one person who worked daily with CEOs, who could think like a CEO, who had a CEO's money and power and influence—and ego:

Her ex-husband, Sam Elkins.

She had been forced to wait for over an hour in the lobby of the slim, magnificent, glass-cladded structure that rose into the sky like an exclamation point. Dropping in the way she did—with no appointment, and not trailing a retinue of obsequious hangers-on—had thrown the security staff into a dither.

Just who *was* she, exactly? And what was her business with Mr. Elkins?

Her ID was checked and double-checked. The clasp on her purse was examined with the meticulous precision of a bomb-disposal expert checking a detonator. She was photographed—"It's for a temporary ID, ma'am, and it expires at midnight tonight," the guard explained—and his female colleague was summoned to pat her down.

Finally Bell had been allowed access to the tenth floor, where the top managers of Strong, Weatherly, and Wycombe had their offices—but not *only* their offices. The floor also included a private dining room, private theater, private gym and sauna, and—naturally, she thought—private lavatories. *God forbid those precious executive butts should have to share the same porcelain as the humble folk*, she told herself, as the same female guard who had run her gloved hands down Bell's backside and across her breasts escorted her to the fabled tenth floor.

Her observations were snotty and childish, and she knew it. The truth was, the scrupulous security was justified; Sam's company did business with a number of nations whose reputations prompted the fanged envy and murderous ire of adjoining countries. Vigilance was imperative. And she had, after all, shown up here on a whim. Even small-town prosecutors—like she had been—were hard to see on a moment's notice, much less big-time lobbyists like Sam.

And as for the luxurious accommodations—*I could have had all of this, too,* Bell reminded herself.

There was a time when she'd wanted it. Definitely. She had left Acker's Gap to go to college and law school, and by the time she and Sam had married and settled in the D.C. area, her ambitions were fixed: big firm, big salary, big responsibility, big life.

Then she had changed her mind. She gave up all of it—the firm, the salary, the life. The only thing that still remained big, after she divorced Sam and moved back to Acker's Gap to run for prosecutor, was the responsibility part. Life and death: those were the stakes she'd dealt with, every day.

Not even the complex, billion-dollar transactions of Strong, Weatherley, and Wycombe could match *that* for significance.

"Carla tells me that you intend to stay in Acker's Gap," Sam said.

"For the time being, yes."

"Is that a good idea? With all that's happened?"

"I don't know. But it's what I've decided."

He nodded. He lifted his chin and changed the direction of his gaze, moving it away from her and toward the expansive window that took up an entire wall of his office. Sunlight glinted crisply against the tidy flanks of the surrounding buildings.

Sam was a handsome man. He had the kind of dark-haired, green-eyed, chiseled-chin good looks that usually fade and blur in middle age—but in his case, hadn't. Bell had fallen in love with him when they were both sixteen-year-old sophomores at Acker's Gap High School, not because of those looks, but because of what he represented: stability. The thing her life had theretofore notably lacked.

The marriage had not survived her return to West Virginia. But the two of them had always been cordial, and they stayed in each other's lives because of Carla. Sam, Bell had learned over the years, was an absolutely first-rate father.

Like everyone else, he had not understood her decision to plead guilty to a crime for which she was manifestly not responsible. He had argued with her. The argument had become quite heated.

Yet in the end, Sam gamely observed that, once again, Belfa Elkins had done exactly as she pleased. And would live with the consequences—without complaint.

"Can I do anything to help?" he asked.

"Yes."

He was intrigued. She'd always rebuffed his offers of assistance.

"Do tell."

"Utley Pharmaceuticals."

Sam waited for more.

"I'm not a prosecutor anymore," she continued, "so I won't be chasing down dealers and putting them in prison. But I still want to do something about the opioid crisis. So how would I approach Roderick McMurdo?"

"What do you mean?"

"I mean—there's a lot his company could do to help West Virginia recover from this. He has a moral obligation to—"

"Come on, Belfa," Sam said, interrupting her. He sounded impatient. She understood: He'd probably expected her to hit him up to cosign a car loan. Not weigh in on moral culpability. "Rod runs a billion-dollar company. If somebody occasionally abuses the drugs he produces—that's not his fault."

"'Rod'? Sounds like you know him personally."

"I do. We sit on some of the same boards. I've played a few rounds of golf with him." Sam offered her a puckish grin. "I whipped his ass."

"So how does he justify the fact that one hundred and forty-five people a day die of opioid overdoses? Or that more people died of overdoses in 2016 than were killed in the Vietnam War? His company makes a fortune selling the drugs that have created this crisis."

"The same drugs that have helped millions of people deal with their pain."

"Look, Sam—we could debate this all day. And you don't have all day. I just thought you might be able to suggest a way of getting McMurdo's attention."

"Some way other than a lawsuit, you mean."

"My lawsuit days are over. I was thinking of soft power."

"What?"

"You know—gentle persuasion."

Sam laughed, but not in an unkind way. "Look around you, Belfa. All of this"—he swept a hand in a wide half-circle to indicate the sump-tuous breadth of his office and the pristine view beyond the window— "is completely dependent upon the fact that there's no such thing as 'soft power.' There's only the hard kind. Hard and blunt. The kind that people pay for, and that other people are intimidated by. If you can't sue Rod McMurdo, and you're not in a position to lobby some federal agency to impose penalties on his company and thereby affect his bottom line— then he's not going to deal with you. Why should he? What's in it for him?"

"I don't know. Maybe a good night's sleep?"

"So you think Rod has trouble sleeping?"

"A guilty conscience can do that."

Exasperated, Sam stood up. He took a few steps back and forth behind his desk, hands in his pockets, frowning down at the carpet. Then he stopped. He looked at her.

"I can assure you that Rod sleeps just fine," he said. "Utley's prod-ucts didn't create this crisis."

"Then what did?"

"Too many greedy, irresponsible doctors writing too many prescrip-tions. And too many people looking for a quick fix for complex prob-lems—or sometimes, just an easy high. There's a lot of blame to toss around, Belfa. But in the end—what good does it do?"

"Better than doing nothing, I guess." She was searching for another way to explain herself. "If McMurdo and his pals didn't know, and just kept pushing these pills because they honestly thought they weren't so ferociously addictive—then, fine. But there's mounting evidence that they *did* know, Sam. And if you know the truth—but you don't admit to knowing it—isn't that the worst sin of all?"

"Sin. Now, there's a word." He smiled. "Sounds like you've been hanging out with Lee Ann Frickie and that crowd from Rising Souls Baptist Church." He knew the same people she did. His roots went just as deep into the soil of Raythune County as hers did—although he'd spent the majority of his adult life thus far trying to hide that fact.

He had yet to sit back down. It was, she realized, a signal that it was time for her to go.

She rose. They regarded each other across a gulf much wider than a strictly numerical measurement of the space could have accounted for.

When he spoke, his voice was bemused. "Sounds to me like you're looking for a new crusade. Now that you're not a prosecutor anymore. But why *this* one? It's hopeless. Utley will never admit that it did anything wrong."

She didn't reply. She knew the answer—but she couldn't share it with Sam. She couldn't share it with anyone. It would come too close to revealing the secret—the one buried so deep in her, the one that was so impossible to bring to the surface that it might as well be part of her bone structure.

The one that only Shirley had known, and only then at the end of Shirley's life.

Sam was talking again. "How much of this—this battle against Utley, I mean—is to take your mind off things?"

He didn't need to identify the "things." He knew what Shirley's death had meant to her. After Carla, Shirley had been the most important person in her life.

Bell shrugged. She didn't mind him bringing it up. They had known each other a long time. Because of Carla, she and Sam were family. They always would be.

"I don't know," she said. "I really don't."

He accepted that. "I wish I had more time today." A quick look at his wristwatch. "But I've got a conference call in a few minutes."

"No problem. I need to start for home, anyway. Long drive."

"But a pretty one, right? Those leaves."

So it was back to leaves again.

"Thanks for your time today, Sam. Hope we can revisit the topic sometime."

He didn't answer, and his face was noncommittal.

She was almost to the door before he asked the question.

"Are you ever going to tell me?"

She stopped. Again, she didn't need any clarification.

"I don't think so, Sam."

Some tension in his voice now. He'd held it under wraps but this was his last chance. "It wasn't your fault. That's what I don't get. You were a traumatized little kid. You didn't even remember what you'd done. How did it make any sense for you to go to *prison*, for God's sake? You threw away your whole life, Belfa."

"No. I didn't throw it away. I still have it. It's just different now."

"You're telling me." An alarm sounded on his cell. "Damn. My call's starting in one minute."

She waved, leaving him to his work. And his pretty things. And his questions.

Chapter Twenty-three

The waitress led her to a table back by the fireplace, weaving a path around a forest of round tables covered with identical white tablecloths and flowery centerpieces.

Empty tables, Bell noted.

"Sorry I'm late," she said. She draped her coat across the back of the chair. "Just got back from D.C. Met with Sam. Had some things to go over with him."

"How is he?" Rhonda asked.

"You know Sam. Always polite. No matter how annoyed he might be."

"Well, count your blessings. He didn't go all hillbilly on you. Didn't take out a shotgun and spit a wad of smokeless on your shoes."

They both laughed at the incongruity of the image: dapper, debonair Sam Elkins, toting a firearm and ruining his perfect white teeth with a pinch of snuff.

Bell looked around the room. It was past the regular dinner hour, but there still should have been more customers. This was the Chimney Corner, a restaurant in Blythesburg that had been here roughly forever, with no discernible updates to the menu—but was still the best dining option in the area.

Rhonda had texted her that afternoon, proposing dinner. Bell was a little surprised—surely Rhonda was up to her eyebrows with the Topping murder case?—but she was pleased. She dearly missed conversations with the woman who'd been her best friend in Acker's Gap, as well as her trusted colleague. And there was the small matter of Rhonda's secret and the promised revelation.

Sure, she'd texted back.

Rhonda's reply: *Chimney Corner @ 7*

Bell had swept in at 7:12, trailing cold air and apologies.

"Used to come here as a teenager," Rhonda said. She looked around. "It was that kind of place, you know? The kind where you have lunch with your mom when you're sixteen years old, after you've gone shopping for school clothes. And your mom's pissed at you because nothing fit you. Not even the skirts from the section of the store they called 'Chubbette.'" Rhonda laughed, and so Bell did, too. "And then," Rhonda continued, "you sit down at one of these tables and your mom makes you order the 'Dieter's Plate'—it's the restaurant version of the 'Chubbette' section—and the waitress brings you a little mound of cottage cheese topped by a single pineapple ring. And it's garnished with this sad, limp lettuce leaf."

"Maybe we should've gone somewhere else," Bell murmured.

"Oh, no—it's fine," Rhonda said. She laughed again. "If we avoided all the places in this county where we'd had some unpleasant experiences, we'd never leave the house, right? Anyway—I've got some nerve. Your childhood was not exactly a bed of roses."

Bell shrugged. She was just about to ask Rhonda about the Topping case when her friend cut her off, leaning across the table and grabbing Bell's hand.

"Besides, none of that really matters. That news I wanted to tell you about—well, hold on to your hat. I'm getting married." Rhonda blushed fiercely. The blush ran up the side of her face and bloomed across her cheeks.

"Rhonda! Really! That's *terrific.*"

At which point Rhonda Lovejoy, prosecuting attorney of Raythune County, a position filled with significant duties that she performed each day with tremendous dignity and skill, promptly began sobbing.

"Hey—hey, come on, Rhonda, what's the matter? This is wonderful. Just wonderful."

"I thought—I guess I thought you'd say—" Rhonda was trying to talk through sniffles. "I thought—" She turned in her seat, reaching for the purse whose thick turquoise strap she'd looped across the back of her chair. She dug out a tissue from its crowded depths.

After an extended goose-honk of a nose-blow, Rhonda was ready to try again.

"I thought that maybe—maybe you'd tell me it was a bad idea."

"A bad idea? Why would I say *that*?"

"Because—well, because over the years, whenever we talked in general about marriage, you seemed a little—well, kind of down on it. I mean, you're divorced. And we saw the consequences of so many bad marriages, there in the prosecutor's office. Love always seemed to end up in fights over money or property or custody of the kids or whatever. And sometimes violence. And you and Clay never—well, you know."

Clay Meckling had been Bell's longtime boyfriend. After several years of an on-again, off-again relationship that was fairly tormenting to both of them, Bell had finally ended things for good, just before her life blew up in her face. Six months into Bell's time at Alderson, Clay had written her a brief letter. He told her that he and a woman named Monica Dean—he'd met her in Charleston, where he'd taken a job with the state division of highways—had been married that weekend. They were moving to Dayton, Ohio. Clay had gotten a managerial job there with a construction firm.

"I just figured," Rhonda added, "that by this time, maybe you were—well, philosophically opposed to the whole institution."

Bell shook her head and smiled. "I've got nothing against marriage, Rhonda. I just draw the line at *me* getting married." She looked up at the waitress, a woman in her late eighties who had just arrived tableside. Bell recognized her. "Hello, Pauline."

Pauline's watery, olive green eyes reacted. "My goodness. Belfa Elkins. How long have you been—" Apparently she couldn't think of a polite way to say "out of prison," and so the woman with the tight white bun and the corrugated yellow skin simply stopped, blinked, and handed each of them a menu, falling back into her spiel. "The special tonight is chicken-fried steak. The sides are mashed potatoes with gravy and green beans. Oh—and we ran out of the meatloaf, in case you were thinking in that direction." She gave them a tired smile and left them to their decision-making.

Bell set her menu aside without looking at it. She needed to make sure Rhonda understood her.

"I'm very happy for you. I want you to know that. Okay? Now—back to business. Do I know the guy?"

Rhonda grinned. She finished dabbing at her eyes with the fourth tissue she'd pulled from her bag, a repetition that had begun to remind Bell of a magic act with a top hat and an endless stash of silk scarves.

"I think so," Rhonda said. "It's Mack Gettinger."

Bell thought about it. *Did* she know him? Yes. She did. She had a hazy recollection of an older man, at least twenty years Rhonda's senior, with a hawk nose. Eighty-five percent bald. Thin gray mustache, dark eyebrows. Tall. Lean everywhere except in the belly. Quiet.

"He works for Claussen's," Rhonda said. "He's their top sales associate."

Norbert Claussen's company had started out specializing in janitorial supplies but expanded over the years into uniforms, floor mats, vending machines, restaurant equipment—the works, Bell recalled. The collection of warehouses in rural Raythune County covered an acre and a half.

"Mack's got the accounts for the whole southern half of West Virginia," Rhonda said. Bell was touched by the pride she heard in her friend's voice. "And they're going to be expanding, too."

"He's from around here, isn't he?"

"Born and raised. We started dating a while ago. I was fine with things as they were. And then last month—out of the blue—Mack just said, 'Dammit, let's do it.'" Rhonda laughed. "Romantic, right? That's what he said. No more, no less. Next thing, I know . . ." She held out her left hand. The stone was small and the setting was a simple one, which is why Bell hadn't noticed it, but she could sense Rhonda's pleasure in the fact of it, and so she uttered the expected murmur of admiration.

Rhonda slid her hand back into her lap as Pauline returned. The woman took their orders and departed again.

"I suppose I can understand," Bell said, "why you'd think I didn't believe in marriage."

"Yeah. And I guess I was sort of afraid that—that if I was happy, it would be sort of a reproach to you. And everything that's happened."

"So those times you came by Alderson—you didn't tell me that you and Mack were dating because you thought I'd *resent* you? For God's sake." Bell was exasperated. She sat back, crossing her arms. "I thought you knew me better than that."

Rhonda's answer came quickly: "Nobody knows you, Bell."

Bell waited. "Point taken," she finally said.

"Anyway, I know this is a shock, but it's next week. At Rising Souls. We had to be quick about it. Church gets booked up early." Her voice was bubbly again. "I would've been fine just taking some vacation time and heading to Vegas—but with my family, that's impossible. My great-aunt Lulu said she'd tan my hide if I didn't get married in a church. Mack doesn't care one way or another."

"Sounds like a good man."

"He is. Even Lulu's impressed. And she's the kind of woman who finds fault with everybody. Thinks Jesus should've trimmed the beard and ditched the muumuu."

Bell laughed. Something occurred to her, and she changed the subject. "You know what? I think this is a new record."

"For what?"

"Longest we've ever gone without talking about the drug problem."

"You're probably right."

During her visits to Alderson, the topic had always returned to the opioid addiction crisis, which took up a huge chunk of Rhonda's time as a prosecutor—just as it had taken up a huge portion of Bell's tenure, too. If it wasn't the illegal drug activity itself, it was everything that followed in its wake: robberies, home invasions, car thefts, prostitution.

Bell lifted her water glass in a salute. "Here's to you, Mack Gettinger, for helping us to change the damned subject."

Rhonda smiled and lifted her glass. She took a sip and set it back down. "So you and Carla'll come, right? I've got your invitations in my purse. Wanted to make sure you got them in time."

"You can count me in. I can't speak for Carla—her work schedule's always erratic. But I know she'll try. She thinks the world of you, Rhonda."

"Mutual."

Their dinners arrived. They had both ordered the chicken-fried steak. Not because they had a craving for it—but because it had been suggested and was easier than picking something else. Pauline set the steaming platters in front of them and then stood back, draping the towel she'd used as a pot holder across a skinny forearm. She clasped her knobby hands and awaited the verdict on how it all looked.

"Everything okay?" she said.

The waitress was referring to their dinners, Bell knew, but she decided to interpret it in her own mind as a general question about Acker's Gap.

And the answer was: no.

Everything was *not* okay. Not by a long shot. Dark forces were destroying it from within and from without. There'd been a horrific murder of a prominent local citizen in his own driveway just a few nights ago.

Yet for the first time in eight years—the realization came to Bell once again, as she tapped a finger on the rim of her water glass, a signal to Pauline that she'd like a refill—she wasn't a prosecutor. She had no public position at all. No staff and no budget and no power and no portfolio. It wasn't her responsibility to fix things.

So why did it feel as if—somehow—it still was?

Rhonda and Bell had each made a valiant attempt to conquer the chicken-fried steak, but without measurable success. Their plates looked remarkably the same as when Pauline had dropped them off. The food was overcooked and tasteless, but it wasn't just that; they had too many topics to address, such as Mack's three adult children from a previous marriage and how Rhonda might go about handling that delicate situation.

Rhonda also filled her in on Lee Ann Frickie's faith-based stubbornness. Bell had had her own battles with the woman. "She was a great secretary," Bell said, "but she could be a real pain in the ass when it came to that church of hers."

And then it was time to talk about the Topping case.

"How's it going?" Bell said. "I know you can't discuss specifics, but—"

"I don't mind discussing specifics. For heaven's sake—you were the prosecutor for a lot of years."

"I'm a civilian now."

Rhonda grinned. She used her fork to point at her entree. "You're about as much of a 'civilian,' Bell, as this thing was ever an actual cow." She set the fork down. "Frankly, progress is pretty slow. We still haven't recovered the gun. All we know is that it was a handgun. Nine-millimeter slugs."

"I hear his wife was cleared as a suspect."

"Well, we always start out close to home. But Ellie Topping's alibi is solid. She says she was at a cemetery in Charleston, putting flowers on her brother's grave. Stayed all afternoon and late into the evening. Several independent witnesses put her there when she says she was— the caretaker, three families who were also visiting. And it's a trip she makes frequently—in case you were thinking what I was thinking."

"That she went there specifically the day of the murder, in order to create an alibi," Bell said.

"Right. But that seems unlikely. We also checked her odometer and the receipts for gas purchases. As far as the specific moment she claims that she arrived home—minutes after the murder—that, we can't prove *or* disprove."

"Did she have a motive? Or access to a weapon?"

"Motive, no. Weapon, yes. The Toppings had a registered firearm. It's missing. And Ellie knows how to shoot."

"So does nine-tenths of Raythune County," Bell muttered.

"Exactly."

While Rhonda took a long drink from her water glass, Bell said, "Their son's drug problems are common knowledge, yes? I assume that's the next best possibility."

Rhonda nodded, filling her in on Deke Foley's threats and the file that Brett Topping had been keeping.

"Topping and a friend of his—a man named Pete Pauley—took turns following Foley," Rhonda said. "Pauley reported back to Brett Topping and then destroyed his own notes. Names and locations of drug deals. License plate numbers of buyers and sellers. The kind of thing that could put Foley out of business. Topping added his own observations. Kept the master file."

"Pretty reckless," Bell declared. "I assume Pauley's been ruled out as a suspect? I mean, maybe he and Topping had a disagreement. Did he have an alibi?"

"Airtight," Rhonda answered glumly. "He was speaking at a sales training seminar in Swanville in front of about four hundred people." She lifted her hands off the table, preparatory to forming air quotes with her index fingers. "The topic was—and I quote—How to turn a 'Hell, no' into a 'Heavens, yes.'"

"Quite a challenge." Bell shrugged. "Well, he's a brave man. Brave or stupid, I guess. To join up with Brett Topping and go after Deke Foley." Bell shivered slightly. "I remember Foley. One of the meaner SOBs I ever ran across. First arrested when he was thirteen years old. Stealing cigarettes from a 7-Eleven. There was a look in his eye—even way back then—that told you he was trouble." She shook her head. "By the way, his name's not really Deke. Just calls himself that. He thought Randy sounded lame. Not nearly cool enough or tough enough."

Rhonda's voice was darkly certain. "We'll get him."

"Know you will." Bell had spotted her opening. "And once you do— and once this wedding business is out of the way"—she toyed with the salt shaker, moving it an inch across the tablecloth—"you'll have a little free time. Right?"

"Emphasis on 'little.'"

"Okay, well—I might need your help with something."

"Do tell."

Bell briefly recounted her research into Utley Pharmaceuticals. "So maybe," she said, "we can persuade them to take some responsibility. For what their product has done to the people around here. The misery it's brought—the lives it's ruined, all the premature deaths."

Rhonda didn't answer right away. She lifted her fork and gave her mashed potatoes a poke. They offered no resistance, so it was not a satisfying activity. "Responsibility," she said, repeating Bell's word but making it sound far more dubious.

"Right." Bell snapped her fingers. "Wait—I get it. You're thinking like a lawyer. I don't mean *financial* responsibility. I'm not talking about lawsuits. Yes, lawsuits have been a part of all of this, and will continue to be—if you've got lawyers, you've got lawsuits. But those would have to come from the state attorney general. That's not where I'm going with this. I mean *moral* responsibility. I mean getting their CEO to understand just how the opioid crisis has hollowed out these mountains—even worse than strip-mining has."

Pauline popped up again, asking about dessert. They both said no so emphatically that the old woman took a step back. They weren't being rude; they were simply absorbed in their conversation—to which they returned before the waitress had even cleared their airspace.

"That's fine, Bell, but I think you're being a bit—well, let's say *optimistic.*"

"The word you really want to use is 'naïve,' right?"

Rhonda frowned. "Okay, fine. Yes. Naïve. That's it. I'm sorry, but it's the truth. No CEO on the planet is going admit any kind of culpability for something like that. The minute they do—boom, that's when the lawsuits come flying in from every direction. You're talking about tens of millions—no, *hundreds* of millions, even billions—of dollars at stake for a multinational pharmaceutical. I'm sorry, but it's a total lost cause."

"We have to try, don't we?"

"No. We don't. Not unless we enjoy getting our hearts broken over and over again."

They looked at each other, knowing exactly what the other was thinking: Their roles had reversed. Bell was now the starry-eyed idealist; Rhonda, the grim voice of reason.

Neither could have predicted such a turn of events, all those years ago, when they sat in Bell's office—now Rhonda's office—in the Raythune County Courthouse, with Rhonda arguing for the positive side of an issue and Bell pushing the negative. With Rhonda enthusiastic, Bell somber and grounded.

"I guess," Bell said, "we've both changed over the last three years."

"Yeah. That seems to be the case." Rhonda's voice was neutral. "The truth is, you're right. Pharmaceutical companies like Utley *should* be held accountable. But that's the global view. That's way up here." She raised a hand over her head, waggled it, and then let it drop. "I've got to worry about things a little closer to ground level."

"Like illegal drugs. Not legal ones."

"Right. And like the dealers. The local scumbags who get the drugs into the hands of addicts. I don't have any power over the Utley executives. But I *do* have power over the dealers that Sheriff Harrison tracks down for me to prosecute. I can put their sorry asses in prison."

"But those dealers would have a lot fewer customers if it weren't for those executives."

"Maybe."

"*Maybe?*"

"Okay, then. Yes. Definitely." Rhonda's irritation was growing. She was being forced to say things that Bell already knew, things they both already knew from their years of working side by side in the prosecutor's office. "Yes, it's true that if Utley and other drug companies hadn't dumped their crap here by the boatload—and if doctors hadn't prescribed the pain pills because that's a hell of a lot easier than really listening to what's bothering people or ordering some physical therapy—yes, for sure, the dealers wouldn't have a market to sell to. People get hooked on the pills and then the next thing you know, they're not buying from Walgreen's anymore. They're buying from some guy in a Dodge Charger in a Walmart parking lot.

"But you know what, Bell? I can't do a damned thing about Utley. On the other hand, we're actually making some headway against some of the most active dealers. The Deke Foleys."

Bell nodded. She'd gone after the same kind of dealers when she was prosecutor. It was about as effective as killing cockroaches. Step on one—and there were still a million more to go.

But she understood why Rhonda kept on fighting on the local level. Amid all the uncertainties, there was one irrefutable certainty: A drug dealer in jail meant one less drug dealer on the street. And that could never be a bad thing.

"So why not do both?" Bell asked. "Why not go after the dealers *and* the CEOs?"

"I guess because—last time I checked—there were only twenty-four hours in a day." Rhonda's voice was steeped in weariness.

Hard to argue with that. Bell didn't answer for several seconds. She buttered a roll that she had no intention of eating. Rhonda watched her.

"Okay," Bell said. She set down her knife and set down the roll and dusted off her hands. "So what's the verdict?"

"What do you mean?"

"I'm asking if I can count on you to help me, despite your doubts. I'm going to get in touch with Roderick McMurdo—he's the CEO of Utley—and see if I can make any progress. Point out what his company has done and ask him to help make things right."

"How? How can he do that?"

"I've got lots of ideas. College scholarships, maybe, for kids graduating from Acker's Gap High School? Rehab centers? Funding for neuroscience research on addiction? Or even—this is blue-sky thinking, so bear with me—how about building their next manufacturing plant right here in Raythune County? Or another county in West Virginia? That would provide a substantial number of good-paying jobs. Why shouldn't they make their medicine in one of their prime markets? All kinds of ways a big corporation like that can do good. Getting the CEO's attention is just the first step." Bell leaned forward. "So are you with me? Will you help?"

Rhonda let her gaze wander around the restaurant. They were the last two customers.

Her eyes returned to Bell's expectant face. "No. I can't. Brett Topping's murder is the biggest case we've had in years. You remember what that's like. My first responsibility is to the office that I—"

"Never mind," Bell said. "Forget it."

Silence.

Rhonda finally broke it. "I'd like to be able to count on your help with the Topping case. Off the record."

Bell waited.

"Sure," she said, after a pause that spoke for itself.

Solve your own damned case. That's what she wanted to say.

But no one—especially not Rhonda—would ever have believed that she meant it. And they would have been right.

Chapter Twenty-four

The next morning, Rhonda shut off the engine of her cherry-red CRV. She rubbed her hands together. The day was sunny but very cold, and the drive from her apartment to the courthouse had not lasted long enough for the car to heat up properly.

She had just pulled into the parking space directly in front of the courthouse. This spot was, as the sign stated, reserved for the exclusive use of the county prosecutor. The sign continued to note that violators would be towed. No exceptions.

Rhonda found that declaration to be deeply satisfying. Rarely was a crime and its punishment so clearly and unambiguously delineated.

Something caught her eye. She peered out the window at the courthouse lawn. On the east side of it—visible to her only now that she had swung her gaze away from the wide gray steps and the arched double-sided doorway—was an unusual sight.

No. It couldn't be.

No.

Please, Lord—tell me this isn't happening.

Three elderly women with white hair and stooped postures had placed themselves in the vicinity of a large galvanized steel washtub. They looked, Rhonda thought, like arthritic witches around a would-be cauldron. All three wore mustard-colored work boots, baggy Levi's and oversized sweaters. Two of them had tucked the sweaters into their jeans, which made the area around their hips balloon out unbecomingly. But clearly they didn't care.

They talked earnestly amongst themselves, pointing at the tub and then at the ground, and then back at the tub again. Next to the tub was a stack that included a mattock, two shovels, and a garden hose. Alongside the tools was a mound of yellow-and-black sacks of Quikrete.

One of the women picked up the mattock. The other two nodded and backed away.

The mattock-bearer, Rhonda noted with dismay, was Lee Ann Frickie.

She jumped out of the CRV, crossing the sidewalk and marching up to the trio. The dew had frozen on the grass overnight. Rhonda's heels crunched with every step.

Lee Ann watched her approach. Lifting her chin, clutching the heavy mattock with two knobby hands, shaking her head back and forth, she was the very portrait of extreme stubbornness.

"You keep away, Rhonda Lovejoy," Lee Ann declared. "I gave you ample notice of what we are called to do here and we are surely going to do it. I offered you a chance to be on the right side of this. You declined."

The heads of the other two women bobbed enthusiastically. Rhonda knew them, too: Eloise Drummond and Amy Purcell. Amy, in fact, had once been her Sunday school teacher.

Lee Ann started to swing the mattock up over her head. Rhonda caught the handle before the old woman had managed to get it much above waist level and pulled it out of Lee Ann's hands. Rhonda was gentle about it, but firm.

"Lee Ann," she said. "Please."

"Give that back to me. Give it back."

"What are you doing?" Rhonda held the tool just out of Lee Ann's reach.

"Just what it looks like. We're breaking ground for the pillar this morning. Eloise knows how to mix Quikrete." She motioned toward her friend, who waved, and then toward the tub. "We'll be sinking in the poles that'll keep the pillar straight. The carving of the Ten Commandments won't come 'til later. Got to get the pillar in first." She held out both of her hands, palms up. "I'd like my mattock back, please. That's my property. You are holding on to it unlawfully."

Rhonda blew out a long, slow sigh. "Really, Lee Ann? *That's* where you want to go? You want to start talking about the law? The three of you are getting ready to deface the courthouse lawn. Public property. The law is not on your side."

"Well, maybe the *law* isn't—but *Jesus* is." Lee Ann's voice was strong. Her friends clapped. The claps rang sharply in the cold morning air.

Rhonda sighed again. "Okay, then. If you all keep this up, if you won't stop right now and go away, I'll have no choice but to have you arrested."

Amy moved closer. "Look around you, honey. World's falling apart. So it's time. *Past* time, really. Folks need to be reminded of—"

Rhonda cut her off. "I'm not going to debate this with you, Amy. This isn't the place for that."

Amy gave her a long, sad look. "Guess you weren't paying attention in Sunday school, Rhonda. Not like I thought you were."

"I paid attention to every word," Rhonda replied, somewhat testily. Why was she letting the old woman get under her skin?

By now a small crowd had gathered at the edge of the courthouse lawn. Eloise smiled at the people, giving friends a thumbs-up.

"Anybody who loves the Lord is welcome to join us!" Eloise called out. "Anybody who's on the side of the devil can fight us—like Rhonda Lovejoy here is doing. She may mean well, but we all know that God's law is way more important than man's law."

While Rhonda was busy looking out at the crowd, to make sure no one was charging at her in the name of the Lord, Lee Ann snatched her mattock back. "Instead of wasting your time trying to stop us, Rhonda," Lee Ann snapped, "you can find me a spigot for the hose. Once I break ground, we'll need to get the water going to mix up the Quikrete."

An old man in the crowd laughed. Two younger girls hooted, and a dog barked. *Even the dog's making fun of me,* Rhonda thought.

This had gone far enough.

She pulled her cell out of her skirt pocket, holding it up for the trio to see so they'd know she meant business. Its sleek edges winked in the morning sunlight. "You were warned. All three of you. I'm calling Sheriff Harrison. If you don't move this stuff right now—just pack it up and get it on out of here—I'll tell her to read you your rights." She pointed at Lee Ann. "And if you dig up even a spoonful of the courthouse lawn, you're going to be in a lot of trouble."

The crowd booed. Several people, sensing that the drama was winding down, ambled away. The workday was commencing; they had places to be.

Lee Ann looked Rhonda squarely in the eye. Rhonda wanted to look away—there was no menace or meanness in the old woman's expression, but there was deep disappointment, which was somehow harder to take than those other two things—but she found that she couldn't.

Finally, still glaring at Rhonda, Lee Ann motioned to her friends.

"Ladies," she said, "let's do what she says—for now. I don't want any trouble with the authorities." As she said the "A" word, she winced ever so slightly; there was a healthy dose of *How could you?* in her rheumy eyes.

Amy and Eloise each took a handle of the washtub. Lee Ann slung the mattock over her narrow shoulder.

"We'll come back for the Quikrete," Lee Ann said. "The wheelbarrow's in the truck Eloise borrowed from her grandson. We parked it on the other side of the courthouse." Her friends began a slow trudge across the lawn, balancing the shiny washtub between them.

Lee Ann followed. She stopped, though, before she'd gone more than a few feet. Her voice was still resolute, but quieter now. She wasn't playing to the crowd. She had a message to deliver, and it was for Rhonda alone.

"Just to be clear," she said. "This isn't over."

Rhonda didn't answer out loud, but in her mind, she was giving Lee Ann an earful: *Of course it's not over. Because nothing is EVER truly over around here.*

It was all on one continuous loop, all the same dilemmas and peccadillos, the same challenges. Same despair. Same problems, different day.

She knew that wasn't what Lee Ann meant; Lee Ann meant that

she and their friends would just sneak back here when they thought Rhonda and Sheriff Harrison were occupied somewhere else.

Hell—the three of them might even be planning a lawsuit.

They would lose, of course. There was no doubt about that. No doubt at all. Rhonda didn't even have to look up the case law. It was well-known, and it was clear. But the three old ladies could make a lot of trouble before they lost, further inflaming a town that was already jittery over the murder of Brett Topping.

Rhonda was a prosecutor, an officer of the court. She knew with absolute certainty which side she was on.

And yet there was a small part of her—so small that it barely registered in her conscious mind, only sending out a weak pulse every now and again like a distress beacon from a skier buried in an avalanche—that recalled her Sunday school days, and the simple lessons taught by Amy Purcell, and how good the words had made her feel, how cherished. How they'd lifted her up. And how they secretly soothed her still.

Chapter Twenty-five

"Do you want the bad news first—or the bad news?"

Rhonda raised her eyes from the paperwork on her desk. Sheriff Harrison was framed by the doorway.

It was just after noon. There'd been no additional visits that morning by Lee Ann Frickie and her posse.

"I think I'll take the bad news," Rhonda said.

"Good choice."

Harrison took two steps forward and dropped her narrow butt into the chair facing Rhonda's desk. That was unusual. Typically the sheriff stood while she delivered her bulletins. But then again, this wasn't a typical time; they had both been working exceptionally hard since Brett Topping's body was discovered.

"Still no sign of Deke Foley," the sheriff said.

Rhonda groaned.

"Hold on, hold on," Harrison added. "We're getting a lot of cooperation from law enforcement in all the adjacent counties. He'll turn up sooner or later. Trust me—some other piece of scum will want to make a deal. They'll sell him out quicker'n a minute. But in the meantime—"

"In the meantime, we've got to assume he's still looking for that file."

"Right."

"Did the bank custodian have any useful information?"

"Name's Evelyn Smith. She was too scared to notice many details," the sheriff replied. "She starts her shift at five A.M. Shuts off the alarm and uses the back door. The guy was waiting for her. Jumped out, put a gun to the back of her head and ordered her to let him in. Didn't talk much. Just enough to say what he wanted. Once inside, he went to Brett Topping's office and tossed the place."

"Was there anything to verify that it was Foley?"

"His face was totally covered by a black ski mask, she said. Black gloves. Black turtleneck. Dressed in black, head to toe."

"Could've been Foley."

"Yep."

"Chances are, it *was* Foley."

"Yep."

"But we can't prove it."

"Nope."

Rhonda pushed back her chair and stood up. She reached out her arms to either side, made a few small circles in the air. Let them drop. "God, that feels good. I've been sitting here way too long. Got about six other cases I'm trying to finish up so I can concentrate on the Topping murder."

"Can't Hickey Leonard give you a hand?"

"He does what he can, Pam. He's an old man."

The sheriff rubbed the back of her neck. "I hear you. When I dropped him off at his house after our conference here Friday night, I had to help him all the way up the steps and into the living room. Thank God his wife took him the rest of the way. I didn't exactly relish putting old Hick to bed. What's your bet—boxers or briefs?"

Rhonda laughed. Levity was just what they needed. That, and coffee.

"Okay," she said, handing Harrison the mug she'd proceeded to fill. She topped off her own mug and then sat back down. "I assume the second helping of bad news is when you tell me you're fresh out of ideas about where to find that file."

The sheriff nodded. "My deputies turned the Topping house upside down. Three times. Just in case Brett Topping kept it in a notebook or stuck in an empty jar of peanut butter or an old shoe or whatever. But we didn't find it."

"And nothing in any of the family computers, either?"

"I had Dirk Chenoweth take a look. You know Dirk. Teaches all the computer classes at the community college. That kid's a whiz. He double-checked the laptop that Brett Topping used at home and the desktop at work. Nothing. We returned the computers to Ellie Topping. No reason to hang on to them."

"The bank was cooperative?"

"Oh, yeah. Bent over backward. Dot Burdette's still shook up over the janitor being held at gunpoint—not to mention having her colleague murdered. Wants to do whatever she can," Harrison said. Dot Burdette was president of Mountaineer Community Bank. "Every computer Brett had access to, they opened right up for us. Nada."

"Ellie Topping—did she have any suggestions about likely hiding places?"

"She's barely coherent. Home from the hospital now, but still out of it. Not sure when—or if—she'll recover. They were married a long time. Seemed like a real love match, from what folks say."

Rhonda twirled a pencil on her desktop. She couldn't remember ever having heard Pam Harrison use the word "love" before.

Hell. I didn't use it much, either—until recently.

"You've got somebody watching the house, in case Foley comes back to hunt for it again?"

"Twenty-four seven."

"And Tyler?"

"Trying to be helpful and answer our questions, but he's managed to screw up his brain pretty damned well with all the drugs. Not sure he remembers much of anything these days. Mainly just sits in his cell and grabs his belly and howls. Detoxing is no picnic. We've got him under medical supervision, but being dope sick is still a rough road."

Rhonda's sigh was deep and discouraged-sounding.

"Back to the computers," she said. "Some people know how to hide files." Grasping at straws now. "We know that from when we busted that online pedophile ring last year."

"Rhonda." The sheriff leaned forward, setting her empty coffee mug on the desk. "Dirk's a pro, okay? He knows about files hidden behind other files. It's not there. It's just not there."

"So what do we—" Rhonda's private phone line rang, sparking a frown. "Hold on. Let me get rid of this call." She answered it gruffly. "Yeah." In a softer voice, once the caller made himself known: "Hey, sweetie. I'll call you back, okay? Great. Okay. Soon. Promise." She hung up and gave Harrison a sad little smile. "That man's a saint."

"It was Mack, I take it."

"Yeah. I've had to put off the wedding so many times now that he's gotten skittish. Needed to know if next week looks safe. Some out-of-town relatives are still pretty pissed about change fees for their flights." She reached for Harrison's mug. "You want more?"

"My stomach lining still hasn't recovered from the first cup."

"That's a no, I take it. Or is it a yes?" Rhonda grinned and settled back in her chair. The grin disappeared. "Okay. So we don't know where Deke Foley is. But wherever he is, he might assume that Ellie and Tyler have the file—or that Brett told them what's on it."

"Meaning they could be in danger for a long, long time."

"Exactly."

"Well, Deputy Previtt's parked in their driveway," the sheriff said. "And Tyler's here at the courthouse. Both of them are safe for the time being."

"And after that?"

Harrison crossed a black-booted foot over a knee. "Let me be honest here, Rhonda. County doesn't have the money for any sort of long-term witness-protection detail. Even if we housed them in the same location to cut costs—it's still a burden. The expenses for a full-time deputy, plus a motel bill and meals for Ellie and Tyler? There's just no way."

Rhonda nodded. "I concur."

"You 'concur'? I swear, Rhonda, this job's getting to you. What happened to plain old 'Yeah'?"

This was a secret side of Pam Harrison. Few people had ever seen her smile, much less make a joke.

"I'm rising above my raising, to be sure," Rhonda said, grateful for the brief chance to smile. "From now on, you'll get nothin' fancier from me than 'Yep' and 'Nope.' Learned my lesson."

Harrison and Rhonda had utterly different personalities—Pam was quiet and self-contained, Rhonda gregarious and irrepressible—but they had one crucial element in common, Rhonda reminded herself: Both had been born and raised in Acker's Gap. They knew this place and its people, and were in turn known by it. Their bond was a thing of the soil.

They were two women doing jobs—prosecutor and sheriff—traditionally done by men. That was part of their bond, too.

"So tell me this," Rhonda said, serious again. "How do we protect Tyler and Ellie Topping?"

The sheriff took a minute to think about it. She recalled an email she had received on the night Brett Topping died, a message that came in before the murder. She had checked her phone a few minutes prior to midnight and there it was—a brief note from a man who was, she knew, sorely in need of proof that he still had something to give, proof that the broken part of him didn't go all the way through to the bone.

"I don't think Ellie Topping is the one in danger," Harrison said. "Think of it from Foley's point of view. We haven't disrupted any of his operations yet—which we surely would have, if we knew the locations. So he knows *we* haven't found the file, either. It's not in the Topping house—that's the only certainty. I'll still have a deputy keep an eye on her, but I think Ellie Topping's safe at home. She can start to pick up the pieces of her life, as best she can.

"But Tyler's a different story," the sheriff continued. "He worked for Foley. Which puts him in a hell of a lot of danger." She leaned over and rubbed at a spot on the side of her black boot. Just a dash of dried mud, but it bothered her. "If it's okay with you, I'm going to name Jake Oakes a special assistant to the sheriff's department."

"Special assistant. Is there such a thing?"

"There is now." Harrison rose. "Tyler can stay over at Jake's house while we're sorting this thing out. We'll keep it quiet. A need-to-know basis. He'll be safe. Jake is the best marksman my department ever had. If there's any trouble, he can protect him." She tucked her thumbs into her belt, proud of herself for coming up with the idea. "Think of it as our own version of a federal witness protection program."

"I hate to bring this up, but what about Tyler's addiction?"

The sheriff smiled. "Jake was a deputy sheriff. He's got no patience for that shit. He'll have that kid getting up at sunrise and making his own bed. My guess? Tyler won't know what hit him."

Rhonda shrugged. "All right, then. In the meantime—"

"—we'll get back to work tracking down Foley." She put on her hat, adjusting it until it felt right. "Which leaves only one thing for you to do."

"What's that?"

"Call that guy of yours back. He's a good man. I've known Mack for years. Never seen him so happy." A shy grin. "And you seem kind of pleased, too, about how it all worked out between you two. Hang on to that, Rhonda. You didn't ask for any personal advice from me, but I'm going to give it to you, anyway. Happiness is a rare thing. Got to tend to it daily. Protect it. Baby it. Think of a flowerbed when a bad frost is on the way. Can't be too careful. Because around here"—she was at the door now, ready to go—"a bad frost is *always* on the way."

Before she returned Mack's call, Rhonda needed to use the ladies' room.

And that was when her day got a lot more complicated.

"Lee Ann. What the hell are you *doing*?"

A poor choice of words under the circumstances, perhaps, but Rhonda was bristling with shock. When she opened the door to the ladies' room off the main corridor of the courthouse, she saw Lee Ann Frickie, Eloise Drummond, and Amy Purcell in a line, facing the white-washed plaster wall in the lounge area that came just before the row of stalls.

Each woman held a can of red spray paint. One of them—Rhonda suspected it was Amy, because she was renowned for her careful artis-tic hand and had painted the nativity scene on a big piece of scrap lum-ber that the church propped up in its parking lot every Christmas—had made a penciled list of the Ten Commandments on the white wall.

Clearly, the trio was about to trace over the large letters with spray paint. Amy's template would ensure the uniformity of the Thou Shalt Nots.

"I'll thank you not to curse," Lee Ann said primly.

"What are you *doing*?"

Rhonda advanced into the room as she spoke. The wooden door swung shut behind her.

"It was supposed to be a surprise," Eloise said. "When people come in to use the facilities, they'll be in the presence of these sacred words. A few might even give themselves to the Lord, thinking this is some kind of miracle." She gave a cheerful shake to the paint can.

"It's your fault, Rhonda," Lee Ann stated. "You won't let us put up a monument on the courthouse lawn. So this is the next best thing."

Amy nodded. She was less defiant than Lee Ann and even sounded slightly maternal. "Rhonda, dear, we'll be out of here soon. You look tired, honey."

Rhonda crossed her arms.

"If anybody so much as touches the button on a spray paint can for *one single second*," she declared ominously, "I will put that person in jail for defacing public property. I mean it."

"Well, I think *that's* a little excessive." Lee Ann's voice was filled with umbrage.

"No, it is *not* excessive," Rhonda shot back. "I've been over and over this. The courthouse is a public facility. You can't put up any sort of religious signage here because it clearly violates the Constitu—" Rhonda stopped.

She didn't say anything for a full minute. She just stood there, looking at the three women.

They looked back at her.

"Dear?" Amy said. Her forehead was wrinkled with concern. "Are you having a stroke?"

Rhonda shook her head. "No, I'm not having a stroke. Although that does sound rather appealing at this point. I could use the bed rest." She smiled a tight little smile. "No, I'm fine. I'm just thinking about how those commandments are going to look with passages from the Koran painted in between every line."

"What's that, dear?" Amy said.

"The Koran. I'm going to call up the mosque over in Blythesburg. Tell them I'd love to have excerpts from the Koran decorating our ladies' room wall. I'm sure they'll be happy to send someone over to do that. Of course, it'll cut down on the space you have for the Ten Commandments."

Lee Ann touched Amy's arm. "Pay no attention. She's bluffing."

"*Am* I, Lee Ann? *Am* I bluffing? I don't think so," Rhonda said. "I mean—even with the threat of arrest, I can't seem to make you stop trying to display your religious message. What should I do? Keep a deputy on duty all night long, to head off any sneak attacks by your friends, armed with spray paint and self-righteousness? I don't have the manpower. As you might have heard, we're trying to track down a murderer right now. So—I'll go in another direction." Rhonda tapped a finger against her chin. "And I'll also contact that witches' cult that just started up over in Simmons County. They've got some wonderful Satanic art to share. It'll be lovely right next to your commandments."

Lee Ann stared. Amy looked confused. Eloise set down her paint can on the front of one of the sinks.

"Rhonda Lovejoy," Lee Ann said. There was deep reproach in the way she said the words.

"If one group gets to post their message," Rhonda intoned, "then all groups do. Or—and this is the path I hope you'll choose—we can just agree, here and now, to keep the walls and the lawn clear. We can all worship as we wish. Start any church we like. But we keep the church as the church—and the courthouse as the courthouse. What do you think?"

Amy and Eloise kept their eyes on Lee Ann. They would follow her lead.

Lee Ann bowed her head.

Was she praying? Rhonda couldn't tell.

If lightning strikes me in the next three seconds, Rhonda thought, *or a mighty wind comes along and lifts up the courthouse and carries it away—I'll know for sure I'm on the wrong side of things here.*

A few more seconds went by.

Lee Ann raised her head.

She turned to her friends. In a crisp, businesslike voice, she said, "Ladies, let's go home." To Rhonda, she declared, "You've won. You've beaten us. I hope you're proud of yourself."

"It's not a matter of pride. It's Constitution 101, Lee Ann, and if you'd just—"

"Don't." The old woman cut her off, a soft quaver in her voice. "Just don't. I'm following your orders, doing what you tell me to, because I believe you. I think you might've actually *put* those nasty words up there, just to spite me. And I can't have that. I won't abide having that sort of blasphemy on the walls of this building I love. But you know what, Rhonda? I don't have to listen to your lecture on top of it. If anybody gets to give a lecture, it's me."

She waited. Rhonda didn't interrupt her, so she went on.

"My heart breaks every single day when I see what's become of this town. It breaks and then it breaks again. It's finding new ways to break, all the time. I was born here and I was raised here and I'm going to be buried here, and I can tell you for absolute certain—it's never been this bad before. *Never.* We've crossed over. Crossed over some terrible line. We're on the other side now. In the darkness."

She took a breath and then went on. She didn't speak melodramatically, but in a driven monotone that was somehow more sorrowful-sounding than histrionics would have been:

"Our children are dying and we can't stop it. They're dying right in front of us, every day. They're filling their bodies with poison. Babies are born at Evening Street and they're already sick with the same poison. We've been trying to fix it your way for a long time, Rhonda, and you tell me—where has that gotten us? How is that working out? The law's way, the way of arresting people and putting them in jail and then arresting other people and putting *them* in jail, too—where will it end? I worked here at the courthouse for a lot of years, Rhonda. You know that. And I can tell you this—the law's way has failed us. We need to try the Lord's way."

"Good afternoon, Lee Ann," Rhonda said. She said it quietly, wearily. The argument was over, as far as she was concerned. "I'll just wait here while you all clean up this mess and then I'll walk you out."

Amy reached over and patted Rhonda's arm. She was smiling. "Hope we see you at church this Sunday, sweetie."

"Oh, my, yes," Eloise said. Her pale blue eyes were shining.

For the two of them, Rhonda saw, this had been a bit of a lark. A grand and spirited adventure, the likes of which ladies in their late seventies and eighties did not often get to indulge.

But for Lee Ann, it was different. This had been no lark.

Lee Ann did not join her friends in scrubbing the pencil marks off the wall with a couple of blue sponges or gathering up the spray paint cans and putting them back in the tan Home Depot bag. She watched them work. Occasionally her eyes moved from Amy and Eloise over to Rhonda.

There was something in Lee Ann's expression—a hardness, a bleakness, the stark residue of a long and bitter knowing—that Rhonda found a little disturbing.

Each time Lee Ann looked at her, she looked away.

Chapter Twenty-six

"So here's your room." Jake stopped his wheels at the threshold of the tiny bedroom. Tyler, following too close behind, bumped hard against the back of the chair.

"Sorry," Tyler mumbled. He didn't sound sorry at all.

The young man backed up and flattened himself against the wall of the corridor, so that Jake could maneuver his chair out of the way and they could switch places, with Tyler in the lead. He stepped into the small room. There was a single bed, a particleboard chest of drawers, a small closet, a tiny window.

"Sheets are in the linen closet out here in the hall," Jake said. "There's a quilt in there, too. Ought to work for a month or so, until the cold really gets going. Then I'll dig out the comforter."

"A *month* or so?" Tyler was incredulous. "No way. I'm only here until they find Foley. That's it."

"Whatever." Jake backed up his chair. "Check out the room. Figure out what else you're gonna need—the sheriff told me to send her a list. No guarantees, but they'll do their best. Shampoo, toothbrush, razor, whatever. Up to you. Then meet me back in the living room."

He wanted to let Tyler have some time alone so that it could sink in: This is home now, bro. So get your mind right.

Truth was, Jake wasn't any happier to suddenly *have* a housemate than Tyler was to suddenly *be* a housemate. When Sheriff Harrison had called this afternoon, Jake's first reaction was to laugh, and when Harrison didn't respond to that, his second reaction was to say, "You're kidding, right?"

She wasn't kidding.

They needed somewhere to stash a kid whose father had just been gunned down by a drug dealer—the emergency for which Jake, in his capacity as dispatcher, had ended up summoning the EMTs and the sheriff's department—until the aforementioned drug dealer was caught. "You don't have to accept the assignment, Jake," she said. "But it comes with a title—special consultant to the sheriff's department." They had thought of calling him an assistant, she said, but Rhonda Lovejoy had researched a few relevant statutes and decided that "consultant" would look better as a budget line than "assistant."

"And by the way," Harrison had added, "it comes with a salary, too. Because it's an official job. I'll get somebody else to run the dispatch."

Jake had agreed. He didn't relish the idea of being a babysitter—and when he heard about Tyler's drug problems, he was even less charmed—but this was, he thought, a way back into the department. A proverbial foot in the door. Today, a special consultant; tomorrow, maybe . . . something else. Maybe a deputy.

It could happen, couldn't it? Sure it could.

Steve Brinksneader had brought the kid over from the jail just before suppertime. As awkward moments go, the introduction wasn't the *most* awkward one that Jake had ever endured—that distinction probably belonged to the first date he'd ever had, a trip to the movies with Lola Saylor back in Beckley, when his overeager fourteen-year-old self had tried to unhook her bra and ended up spilling a jumbo Mountain Dew all over her white silk blouse—but it was close.

Tyler had come in first. He hovered on the threshold, looking around the dinky living room with an expression that was half-wonderment, half-revulsion. Steve, right behind him, muttered, "Get on in there, willya? Ain't got all day."

The kid took another step and then he noticed Jake, in his chair over by the couch, and that's when the awkwardness really kicked in.

"Shit, man," Tyler mumbled. "You're in a fucking *wheelchair*? And you're supposed to *protect* me? Jesus. I guess I better hope Foley's got a couple of broken legs, right? To even up the odds?"

Steve tapped the kid's shoulder to get him to advance farther into the house. He wanted to shut the front door as soon as possible. Once that was done, Steve had turned on the kid with the full force of his fury at seeing Jake humiliated that way.

"Listen, you," Steve huffed. "This guy here was the best deputy Raythune County ever had. You read me? You're damned lucky he's agreed to keep an eye on you."

Jake, annoyed, shook his head at Steve. He could fight his own battles. Besides, Tyler had just lost his father. Cutting him slack was no problem. Temporarily.

"Thanks, Steve," Jake said, "but I can take care of this." He shifted the wheels slightly, so that he was facing Tyler head-on. "Foley won't know where you are. That's how we intend to keep you safe. Not with gun battles." He smacked the top of the wheels with his palms. "And not with foot chases. But if this doesn't meet your high standards, let's break clean. I'll call the sheriff, tell her you want to stay in a jail cell instead. That's your only other option."

Tyler's eyes swept the room. His disgusted gaze took in the ratty couch, the battered coffee table, the patched carpet. From here you could see into the matchbox-sized kitchen with its toylike dinette set and the short hallway, along which were visible the hollow core doors to the two bedrooms and the bathroom.

Jake could read his thoughts: The house was cheap and depressing and small. Jail probably seemed downright palatial in comparison.

But then again, jail was . . . *jail*. And the kid didn't look to be a fool.

"Hate that stinkin' place. Been there enough times," Tyler muttered. "I'll stay."

"Okay, then," Steve said. Brusque now, in a hurry. "I need to go check out the perimeter. And then the rest of the neighborhood." He realized he'd neglected to make formal introductions. "Jake—this is Tyler Topping. Tyler, your host here is Jake Oakes." To Jake, he said. "We're bringing you a scanner tomorrow so you'll know what's what. For tonight, if you hear anything—I don't care if it's a hoot owl that's making you jumpy—you call me. You got that, buddy?"

"I got it." Jake grinned at his former colleague, a big, slow-talking man of refreshingly uncomplicated motives. Steve did the best job he could, every day. Jake had always liked him.

For a while there, right after the night Jake had been shot, envy and resentment had edged out the affection. Steve, after all, still walked upright, still wore the uniform.

But now Jake was back to simple liking.

"And you." Steve addressed Tyler. "We'll be picking you up every day to take you to Narcotics Anonymous meetings. We'll vary the locations. But that's the deal. The sheriff isn't kidding. If we're doing this, you're going to stay clean. There'll be some medical supervision, too. But mostly it's on you. Okay?"

Tyler waited a long time before he said, "Okay."

As soon as Steve left, Jake had wheeled down the hall to show Tyler where he'd be sleeping.

Now he waited for the kid in the living room. He had a little speech of his own to make.

Tyler slouched his way in from the hall. He plopped down on the couch, immediately slinging his feet up on the coffee table.

"Get your feet off the furniture," Jake snapped.

Tyler took his time, first lifting one foot, then the other. He made a snickering noise in the back of his throat.

"What's that?" Jake said.

"What's what?"

"That sound you just made. Like you've got a joke you want to tell. You got something to say to me, you say it. Don't make your funny little sounds."

"Okay." Tyler laced his fingers and propped them on his belly. "I will. I think it's pretty damned funny that you're so particular about your coffee table here. Making me keep my feet off. Hell—it's a piece of crap."

"You're right. It's definitely a piece of crap. Only thing I could afford."

"So why can't I put my feet on it?"

"Because I told you not to. My house—my rules." Jake moved his chair. He didn't like looking at the kid at an angle. He wanted to face him head-on. The symbolism was right. "That's rule number one. Number two? I drink beer. But you can't. You know why you can't. Because you're a drug addict. You're not going to be touching anything that messes with your brain chemistry. No drugs, no booze. I catch you with anything like that, your ass is out of here. But just so you know—the Rolling Rocks in the fridge are counted. Which brings me," Jake said, moving his chair again, just an inch, making sure he still had the kid's attention, "to my final point. You said something earlier about me 'protecting' you. I'm not doing that." His palms smacked the wheels. "Obviously. Thing is—you're protecting yourself. I'm just giving you a place to stay. Same thing with your recovery. You do it yourself. Other people can help—but the work's up to you, my man. Nobody else."

Tyler looked a little stunned. Finally he nodded. But there was no sarcastic subtext to the nod this time.

It was just a nod.

"I gotta go pee," Tyler said, standing up.

"Wait—that reminds me. I forgot a rule," Jake said. "Random drug tests. Just so you know. No postponing them, no ducking them. When the doc comes by, you'll be here and you'll cooperate."

"I still gotta pee." Tyler shuffled away.

While he was out of the room, Jake dialed the sheriff's cell. Watching this kid was going to be a thankless job, filled with annoyances both trivial and momentous, and more than a slight chance of danger. Nobody else would want to do it. So Jake figured he had some leverage. Time to wield it.

"Everything okay?" Harrison said.

"Fine. He's settling in. But I want a favor."

"I'm listening."

"I want you to make Bell Elkins a special consultant, too."

"Why?"

"I might need backup. And we've got a real good track record of working together."

"I don't know, Jake."

"Come on. You're paying me shit wages. Paying *two* people shit wages isn't appreciably different from paying *one* person shit wages. Right?"

"I'll check with Rhonda. And the budget. Get back to you."

"Taking that as a yes."

Jake had made his special snack for late-night TV viewing, one that required little effort or creativity but yielded large dividends—because it was his absolute favorite: He dumped a bag of Wavy Lay's in a clear plastic bowl, put the bowl on his lap, and wheeled himself back into the living room.

Tyler sat on the couch in a slouch, the kind that made his bony knees stick up in front of him like two fence posts and lowered his neck almost to the level of his hips. His eyes moved lazily around the room. Occasionally he'd reach up and pluck at his bottom lip.

He had gotten settled in the spare bedroom in what seemed like seconds, a process that consisted of sitting on the bed and then standing up again, opening the closet door and then closing it.

And now the remainder of his first night in Jake's home was unspooling slowly. *Excruciatingly* slowly. He knew he'd have trouble sleeping tonight, which was a common junkie problem. That, and nausea. And chills. And sweats. And a deep craving that felt like his body was turning itself inside-out every few minutes.

He didn't want to read a book—Jake's offer of a few paperbacks, all mysteries, all by Michael Connelly, was rebuffed with almost comic abruptness—and he didn't want to watch TV and he didn't want to call or text a friend because his friends were all out getting high and he didn't want to hear about it. Jake had suggested all of those things, the reading or the TV-watching or the friend-contacting. No-go.

So what *did* he like to do?

He liked to do drugs. Period.

Tyler didn't say that out loud, but Jake knew all about the tunnel vision of your average junkie. Drugs did a lot of lousy things, but one of the lousiest things they did was to erase the pleasure of everything else in life. All Tyler wanted right now was something that would make him feel other than the way he felt. He was, Jake saw, nervous and jumpy, and at the same time, listless and lazy. Classic combo.

Suddenly Tyler jerked, as if somebody had poked him with a stick. "You hear that?"

"Hear what?"

"That." Tyler cocked his head.

"Nope." Jake wheeled his chair back into a spot beside the couch. From here, he had an optimum angle for watching TV. "Toss me the remote, willya?"

"Hold on." Tyler's head was still tilted to one side, in an exaggerated *I'm listening* pose. "There it is again."

"You're paranoid, brother." Jake scooted forward. He retrieved the remote himself and clicked on the set.

"Turn it off!" Tyler yelled. He sat up.

"Chill."

"Don't tell me to chill—and turn off that damned TV! There's somebody out there. In the backyard."

Jake hit the button. "Fine. I'll listen. See if I hear anything." A few seconds later, he said, "Nope. Nothing."

Tyler's face was strained with the effort of vigilance. He still hadn't leaned back against the couch cushion again. The slouch was forgotten.

"Let's talk for a sec," Jake said mildly. "Take your mind off the backyard. Want some chips?"

"No."

"Tell me about your dad."

A shrug, followed by: "He was a good guy. Good father."

"You didn't resent him? Hate him, even?"

"Why would you ask me that?"

"Because you were happy to self-destruct right in front of him. Day after day. I just figured you must've hated him."

"You figured wrong."

"So—why?"

"Why what?"

"Why'd you start using drugs? And why do you keep on doing it?"

Anger moved into Tyler's face. "Don't start. Okay? Just don't. I've already been to a bunch of shrinks. They always have them at those rehab places. I don't need you and your friggin' questions. Answered too many of 'em as it is."

"Okay. Settle down. Tell me about the rehab places, then."

Tyler ran his hands down the sides of his thighs. "Worthless. You come out worse than when you went in."

"Really."

"Yeah. My parents had real good insurance, so it was easy to sign me up. The last one was down in Florida. Went a whole bunch of times." He shivered. "God, the staff there was a joke. I swear—half of the counselors were dealing themselves."

"You know that for a fact?"

"Naw. Just a nasty suspicion."

"You? Suspicious? I'm shocked." Jake leaned over and bumped Tyler's arm with a fist, as if they were teammates in a huddle. "Anyway, you survived it, right? And so you come back up here and you—"

"And I relapse." The self-loathing in Tyler's voice had the thickness of sludge.

"From what I hear, that's pretty standard. Most people do. Dozens of times, before they finally kick it for good."

"Unless they're smart enough not to start in the first place." Tyler kicked at the carpet with the heel of his shoe. "Like my buddy Alex."

"He didn't go down the same road, I take it."

"Shit, no. He's got a life. A future. Goes to WVU."

"So—why *did* you start?"

"Jesus Christ. There you go again." Tyler grimaced, shook his head. "You got a license to be a therapist, mister? Or are you just a nosy SOB?"

"Let's go with 'nosy SOB.'" Jake popped a chip in his mouth. "Just wondered if you had a theory. I mean, your buddy—what was his name?"

"Alex."

"Yeah. Alex. So maybe it's not like he's a better person. Maybe it's something inside you that's not inside him. Some kind of switch. Certain people—they use drugs one time, and the hooks are in. Part of how your body works. "

"What's your point?"

"My point? My point is—life's a bitch. Nothing fair about it. I can tell you all about how unfair it really is, dude." He rolled forward and back in his chair. "You can get lost in that."

"Lost in what?"

"In the unfairness. It'll always be there. Anytime you need an excuse to use—there it is. Just waiting for you. Eager to serve. Anyway, it's like they say—the whole secret of life comes down to one thing."

"What's that?"

Jake grinned. "Low expectations."

Chapter Twenty-seven

The lights inside the Raythune County Public Library were still on. At this hour—it was two minutes until 9 P.M.—the bright orange glow constituted the only illumination in the heart of downtown Acker's Gap.

Yes! Bell thought, offering up a mental fist-pump as she tried the front door and it swung open. She knew she was cutting it close.

Can't count on Libby staying late every night. She's got Virginia Woof to think about.

Bell had been here several more times over the past few days, always sitting at the same table, working her way through the documents that Libby dug out for her: Utley's annual reports. Speeches given by McMurdo. Complaints filed with the FDA. News reports.

During yesterday's visit, Libby had explained why her husband, Levi, couldn't take care of Virginia Woof when she had to stay late at the library.

Levi Royster had moved out three months ago. They'd be getting a divorce as soon as they could afford it.

"Lots of things caused it," Libby had told her, even though Bell didn't ask. "Main thing is—Levi says I'm stuck. Says I can't move on. Can't get past my grief." She had gone on to describe how her brother's death had taken over her life. How the bitterness burned inside her. How the desire for vengeance filled every square inch of her, absorbing her attention, distracting her. Levi had had the nerve—the *gall*—to tell her that she had to let it go. That it was destroying their marriage. That it was an unhealthy obsession. That not every wrong thing in the world could be righted.

That—sometimes—there was nothing you could do.

"Can you *believe* he said that?" Libby had said. She'd crossed her arms, gathering herself in. Shuddering as she spoke. "So guess what I told him back? I said, 'Levi, you're right. I *can't* get past it. I don't *want* to get past it. I want somebody to pay—big time—for what happened to Howie.'" Then she had looked intently at Bell, her eyes filled with hope. "That's why I'm so glad you're working on this. We can finally—*fi-nally*—make those bastards at Utley admit what they did. Hanging's too good for them. You know?"

Bell did know. She knew a lot of things. But there were also a lot of things she *didn't* know. And for those things, she relied upon Nick Fogelsong.

She could have endured the disapproval of Sam Elkins. She could even have fought back against Rhonda. But there was one person she couldn't ignore: Nick Fogelsong. He had meant too much to her, for too many years, for her to be able to shrug off his judgment.

And he'd said, in effect: *Wait.*

So Bell had decided to come by and talk to Libby. She needed to let her know that, for now, the campaign against Utley Pharmaceuticals would have to be put on hold.

"I'm not giving up," Bell said. "I just need to take some time and think about what's going to be the most effective strategy to get Utley to acknowledge their responsibilities. I don't want this to just be some lame Twitter campaign. Something that comes and goes in twenty-four hours."

Bell had finally acknowledged to herself why Utley's behavior so galvanized her. She'd need more time to think about that, too. In private.

Libby listened. There was one other customer in the library, a young woman with heavy spectacles and a shapeless gray wool coat and flya-way brown hair. She had already checked out her books—they were, Bell saw from the stack of spines, all self-help books—and was ready to go. Libby waited until the woman had cleared the door before she replied.

"I can't believe this," she said. "All the work we've done, totally wasted—"

"It's not wasted. I just have to figure out another way to approach the problem."

"Justice delayed is justice denied," Libby muttered.

That'll teach me to debate a library science major, Bell thought. *They've got all the right historical quotations.*

"Sometimes, yes," Bell said out loud, "but not always. Sometimes, you need to take a step back."

"A step back."

"Yes."

"Okay." Libby pointed to the wall clock. "I have to lock up. You need to leave."

"Look, I'd still like us to be frien—"

"It's after nine. That's closing time." Libby turned her back on Bell and walked away. Her brisk steps carried their own reproach.

She's me, Bell thought ruefully. *That's how I used to behave. It was my way or the highway.*

Was she more mature now? Or was she simply losing her edge, losing her passion for justice, losing the thing that had brought her back to Acker's Gap in the first place and kept her going through all the crap and disaster?

Bell zipped up her jacket. It was cold outside and getting colder; frigid air had dropped in between the mountains and lodged there like an ax blade in the meat of the tree, refusing to budge.

Chapter Twenty-eight

The next morning, Tyler asked Jake if he could go back to his house and pick up some of his stuff.

"Not part of the plan," Jake said. "Steve'll swing by and get you what you need."

"Okay, so it's not about my stuff."

"What, then?"

"My mom. We haven't really talked since Dad died. Everything happened so fast. I mean—she was in the hospital, and you guys brought me over here. We had a phone call, but that lasted, like, a minute. She couldn't really talk. Too upset. Cried the whole time. I wasn't much better." He rubbed an eye. "I'm sure she blames me for my dad getting shot. Why wouldn't she?"

"Did she say that?"

Tyler shook his head.

"Well," Jake said, "I guess I'd wait until she says it outright before I'd start feeling sorry for myself. Although you do seem to enjoy wallowing in self-pity. I can understand why you'd like to get a head start."

"You're a real shit, you know that?" Tyler said, but he didn't say it meanly. "So can I go?"

"I'll call Steve. See if he's free to take you over there. Hang out 'til you're done."

"How about you taking me? There's a van in your driveway, in case you hadn't noticed."

Jake grinned. "I noticed. I also noticed that it needs a new transmission. You buyin'?"

"Okay, fine. Call him."

Steve wasn't available until the afternoon. He picked up Tyler a few minutes after three. A short while later, the county-issued black Chevy Blazer pulled into the long driveway of the big house with the mailbox that had TOPPING painted on it.

Tyler didn't get out right away.

"This *is* the place, right?" Brinksneader said. His voice was as playful as it ever got. "I mean, mailboxes don't lie, do they?" When Tyler still didn't move, the deputy added, "You do remember where you live?"

"It's the place." Somberly, Tyler added, "And no—sometimes I didn't remember where I lived. When I was high. Sometimes it was like a fog rolling over me. Things would happen—and then I couldn't tell you, two minutes later, what they were. I'd just forget. Everything."

Another thirty seconds passed.

"Well," the deputy said, "I need to make sure everything's cool. If you don't mind, you'd better go on inside and get started, while I check around."

Tyler still didn't budge.

"You okay?"

"My dad died right at the end of this driveway," Tyler said, the words coming in a husky rush. He rubbed his sleeve roughly over his nose. He was trying hard to keep the tears from surging. "You know what? After all I did to him, after all the trouble I caused and all the crap I brought to his life—my dad still loved me. My mom, too. And guess how I repaid them? I got him killed. That's what I did." Tyler thrust his face in his hands.

"Go on inside, kid," Brinksneader said gently. "Go be with your mom. You guys need to stick together now."

Ellie met him at the door. She couldn't speak right away. At first she just stared at him. Then she led Tyler into the living room.

Now it was his turn to look at her. His expression said that he was ready to take whatever came next: a slap or a kiss.

She folded him up in her arms. They held on to each other, mother and son, both crying soundlessly, both trembling from the massive sadness that shook them.

Finally she moved back a step. She searched his eyes.

"You're—"

"Yeah. I'm clean, Mom. I'm fine. I'm not high."

He read the reply right off her face: *But for how long?*

Because she knew him. The promises, the pledges, the whole cross-my-heart hit parade of empty affirmations. He had managed days of keeping himself straight, weeks sometimes, once an entire month.

And they both knew that he always went back.

Always.

The promises were the easy part. It was easy to fill himself up with purpose and ambition. *This is it,* he'd tell himself. Day one.

And then . . . things happened. They always did.

There was a knock at the door. They looked at each other.

"The deputy's out there," Tyler said. "It's okay."

Steve Brinksneader stood on the porch. Beside him was Sara Banville.

"This young lady says you guys are friends," Brinksneader said.

"We are." Tyler didn't know what to say next. Sara looked beautiful. Her hair was pulled back into a ponytail and her face was shining, but there was concern in her eyes. "Do you want to come in?" he said.

She nodded. A smile broke over her face. The deputy stepped aside.

The moment she was inside, she gave Ellie a hug. His mother, Tyler saw, didn't participate; her arms stayed straight down at her sides.

"My mom saw the deputy's car," Sara said, "and we wanted to make sure everything was okay."

"Everything's fine." Ellie's voice was empty.

"Okay," Sara said. She was a little embarrassed now. A spot of color dotted each cheek. "I wanted to—we were worried about—"

"It's just a hard time right now," Tyler said. "But it was cool of you to come by. Really. Maybe we can talk later. When this is all over."

Once upon a time they had all been friends: him and Alex, with Sara trailing along behind, begging to be included. Usually they'd say,

Sure, yeah, come on, and off they'd go, the three of them. Riding bikes or building forts or reading comic books. Later, other things, too.

That was a long, long time ago.

But maybe . . .

"Great," Sara said. Her eyes went to the coffee table. A laptop and an iPad were stacked up next to a monitor and CPU. "So the cops finally brought back your computers? I heard they were going through them. Looking for something, right?"

"Yeah. Looking for something."

"Guess they didn't find it."

"Guess not." Tyler shrugged. Jake had told him not to talk about the case with anybody other than law enforcement. And his mom. "So. Like I was saying. Maybe we could hang out."

"Sure," Sara said. "That would be great. Let me know. I'm around." She turned. Then she turned back. She smiled. She had a wonderful smile. "You take care of yourself, Tyler. Okay?"

Now it was just the two of them again. Him and his mother.

And their unfinished conversation.

"Really," Tyler said. "No more drugs, Mom. I'm clean and I'm going to stay that way."

His mother, he saw, had aged years in a matter of days. Her prettiness had always been fragile, a ghostly overlay of nice features and daily beauty rituals that enhanced a few natural advantages. But the beauty had gone away now. The long tragedy of their lives—his addiction, the mess he'd made of everything—had finally exploded in one last horror: his father's death.

All of it had gathered in Ellie's face.

"How are you doing, Mom?"

"It's hard. It's so, so—hard," she said. "And not knowing what really happened—it makes it harder. Losing Brett but also—not knowing if he said anything. At the end."

"They're going to get Foley, Mom," Tyler declared. "They're looking for him and they'll find him. He'll pay for what he did."

She nodded. She seemed dazed, as remote as a star. He wasn't sure she had even heard him.

"They're keeping me safe, Mom. Just like they're keeping you safe. Okay? Listen—I need to get some of my stuff," he said. "In my room. Some shirts. Underwear. To take with me. I'll be right back."

She nodded again. He started to move away, toward the big polished staircase, but abruptly he came back to her.

"It's going to be okay, Mom. Swear. I'm going to stay clean. For you. For Dad. I'll do it. I really, really will."

She looked at him. Her expression pierced him. Because her eyes spoke plainly: *We both know that isn't true, don't we?*

Chapter Twenty-nine

The recipe came from Sam's mother, which meant that Bell had been carrying it around in her head for almost three decades, give or take. It also meant that each ingredient, as she added it to the big pot on the gas stove, came with a memory, a flashback, an invisible tether to previous times and other places she had made the sauce.

Thus it was more than ground beef, parsley, oregano, onions, diced tomatoes, and all the rest: It was Buckhannon, West Virginia, where she and Sam had shared a small apartment while they finished up at West Virginia Wesleyan. It was Morgantown and another small apartment, when Sam was in law school. And an even smaller apartment in Alexandria, Virginia—the rents had made their heads snap back in astonishment—when Sam had started his first job and Carla was a trouble-seeking toddler and Bell had just decided to apply to law school herself. And then it was an enormous house in Bethesda, first of the ever-more-enormous houses they lived in, as Sam's career achievements went up, up, up, and his income level rose right along with it. The Elkins family sauce made frequent appearance in each place—first out of economic necessity, later from nostalgia.

After the divorce, it was this rambling stone home on Shelton Avenue in Acker's Gap. The years as prosecuting attorney.

Another Saturday night, another dinner invitation to Carla. The water for the pasta had just come to an enthusiastic boil when her daughter arrived.

"Hey—I'd know that smell anywhere. Grandma's famous sauce," Carla said, zipping into the kitchen. She didn't even take off her coat before picking up the wooden spoon to sample it. "Yep. The taste of judgment and prejudice and recrimination. With a pinch of bitterness and bile. *Mmmmm*."

Bell laughed. "Okay, so Bessie could be a little—"

"A little racist, sexist, homophobic, and misogynist? Um, yeah." Carla took another sip from the spoon. "But her sauce rocks. I'll grant you that."

"Seemed like a good idea for my first real meal here in a long time. Other than the Big Macs and fries I've been inhaling, I mean."

"Don't forget last week's pizza. You know what, Mom? You've been living like you're in a frat house."

"Until now. Here—hand me that pot holder. The steamed broccoli's ready."

They sat down at the big wooden table.

"I read another story today in the *Gazette* about that murder," Carla said. "Only time Acker's Gap ever makes it into the news—drug overdoses and murders." She tore off a hunk of crusty bread. "I guess they haven't arrested anybody yet."

"No." Bell took a bite of pasta. "Do you remember Jake Oakes?"

"Oh, yeah. The deputy. *Really* cute guy."

"He's too old for you. Anyway, you remember how he was shot."

Carla's lightheartedness vanished. "Of course. How is he?"

"Better, I think. He's had a lot to deal with. But he's adjusting." Bell filled their water glasses from the glass pitcher. "We keep in touch. He's been working for the sheriff's department. Something called a special consultant."

"Well, he knows a lot about law enforcement. Sounds like a good idea. Maybe he could help you out with the Utley Pharmaceuticals thing. Pressure the CEO—Lord Voldemort, right?—to make amends."

"Lord Voldemort would probably resent the comparison. And— sure, maybe. Maybe he can help. But in the meantime, Jake got the same deal for me."

"Same deal?"

"Yeah. Special consultant. It's a temporary thing. Rhonda called me the other day. Said they could use some extra hands with the Topping case."

"Doing what?"

"Checking out a rehab place in Florida, for starters. Just making phone calls. Tyler Topping was in court-ordered rehab a bunch of times. Rhonda thinks he might have made some friends—and I'll let you add your own quotation marks around the word—down there. Addicts who might've kept up with Deke Foley. He's the main suspect."

"Phone calls," Carla murmured.

"What?"

"I just mean—*Jesus*, Mom. Phone calls? You have a law degree from Georgetown."

Bell took a long drink of water.

"Let me tell you a little story," she said. "When your Aunt Shirley first came back, I gave her a lot of pep talks about fresh starts and new horizons. Encouraged her to get her GED, find a good job—all of it. Blah, blah, blah. She probably wanted to strangle me. Or stuff a sock in my mouth." Bell smiled. "But she didn't. She listened. And she tried. In the end, though, she wound up where a lot of people who've been to prison wind up—in a crummy, low-paying job with no prospects. It's damned hard to break through. Like it or not, we all carry our past around with us."

"Mom, come on. You were in a *minimum*-security prison. That's not the same thing. I mean—you can't be comparing your situations. You're not like Aunt Shirley."

Bell couldn't speak for several seconds.

"You're right about that," she finally said.

Carla, who had missed her mother's meaning entirely, stood up. "Unless I'm way off base here, we're having ice cream for dessert, right? I mean, you haven't totally abandoned the frat house lifestyle?"

"Bowls are in the same place in the cupboard they always were. Oh—and there's Hershey's syrup in the fridge."

"Score!"

*   *   *

They were loading the dishwasher when Bell's cell rang. She levered it out of her pants pocket.

After a quick check of the caller ID, she swiped a finger across the bottom of the screen.

"Hey, Nick. What'd you find out?"

"Plenty. Got a pen?"

"Hold on." Bell lowered her cell. "Sweetie, is it okay if I'm on the phone for a minute? I asked Nick to make some inquiries down there. He knows Florida a lot better than I do. Being as how I don't know it at all."

"Sure."

Bell withdrew into the living room.

"Okay," she said. She wedged her cell between her chin and her shoulder while she hunted for a pen and notepad in her purse. "Go."

"It's common knowledge nowadays that Florida's crawling with drug rehab facilities. Because there's huge money to be made in rehab now. Tons of desperate parents with addicted kids. And insurance companies, legally required to pony up the big bucks for inpatient treatment. It's like a grim new kind of Disney World down here."

"Right."

"So I drove up to the last rehab place where Tyler Topping was admitted. It's about an hour and a half north of here. Naturally they wouldn't give me any information. HIPAA laws, confidentiality rules, et cetera."

"None of which slowed you down in the least."

"Of course not."

She smiled. Same old Nick.

"I hung out at the convenience store across the street," he continued. "Sure enough—ten o'clock rolled around and some staff members took their smoke breaks. I struck up a conversation with a guy we'll call Camel Filters. Now, they've hiked the price of cigarettes so high that you have to take out a second mortgage to buy a carton. So in exchange for some folding cash, my new friend agreed that—once he was back at his desk—he'd give me a list of the residents who were there during the past six months. But here's where it gets interesting."

"Do tell."

"Twenty minutes later Camel Filters called me. Kept his voice low. 'You said you're checking on a resident from West Virginia, right?' I said, 'Right.' And he said, "Acker's Gap, right?' I said, 'Right.' And he said, 'Got him right here. Name's Alex Banville, right?' And I said, 'Whoa.'"

"Something's not right. Alex Banville is Tyler's neighbor. Goes to WVU. A good kid. Clean."

"I thought so, too."

"You know him?"

"A bit. His father, Rex Banville, is an acquaintance. And now it turns out—and I had Camel Filters double-check it, just to be sure—that Alex was admitted to that rehab center a few weeks after the last time Tyler left. Not for the first time, either. You could've knocked me over but it's true—Alex Banville is an addict. And."

"There's more?"

"He was just readmitted two days ago. He's there right now. Had a major relapse."

Chapter Thirty

As writing surfaces go, the dinette in Jake's kitchen was not the most ideal foundation upon which Bell had ever worked. It wobbled. It shimmied. It shifted. The uneven top was marred by nicks, trenches, gouges, scratches, burns, and sticky spots. He explained to her that he'd bought it used—the one from his other house was too big to fit in the tiny kitchen—but then he corrected himself: *It's not just used. It's used up.*

"Doesn't matter," Bell said. "We've got work to do."

She had arrived at his house a little after noon. The night before, Bell had sent Carla back to Charleston with a kiss, a Tupperware container of leftover spaghetti, and a promise to call her if there were any breaks in the case.

The natural thing would have been for Jake to come to Bell's more spacious quarters, but there was a problem with that: The house on Shelton Avenue wasn't wheelchair-accessible. Getting Jake and his chair up the seven steps onto the porch was a daunting prospect.

So they'd given up the big, beautiful, polished table over there for the teensy, ugly, unstable one right here.

"It'll keep you humble," Jake said. He guided his wheelchair up under the table so he could share it with her. "Want a beer?"

"Really, Jake? A *beer*?" Bell gave him a withering look. "This isn't a social occasion."

"Okay, okay." He rolled his eyes. "Clean forgot that Mother Superior had decided to fly down from heaven and grace us with her perfection."

He was teasing her, an activity in which she fully expected him to engage on a regular basis. And she ignored him, which was precisely what he'd expected her response to be.

Thus they had fallen smoothly, effortlessly, back into their old partnership.

The first thing Bell did was to arrange her work materials across the dingy, scarred top: two legal pads, a box of Bic pens, a scattering of photos. These were copies of photos Rhonda had requested from Ellie Topping: happy, smiling people, the Toppings and their friends.

"Where's Tyler?" Bell asked, looking around.

"One of his NA meetings. Sometimes you have to drive a while to find one when you need it, but Steve Brinksneader is always around to give him a lift. So far, they've done wonders for the kid."

"Good to hear. Did you get a chance to ask him about Alex?"

"Yeah. Gave him the news this morning. He was shocked. Said he was, anyway. He admitted that Alex had gotten high a few times. All three of them had—Tyler, Alex, and Alex's sister. But Tyler didn't know that Alex was dealing with his own addiction."

"What do you think? Is Tyler telling the truth?"

Jake did as she'd requested. He thought about it. "You know, if you'd asked me a few days ago, I wouldn't have known how to answer. Addicts lie. They lie even when they don't have to lie. They lie just because it's the one thing they know how to do. And they do it so well. But now? Yeah, I believe him. I don't think Tyler had any idea that Alex was in that kind of trouble."

Bell nodded.

She sifted through the photos, setting aside the ones of Brett, Ellie, and Tyler, from various vacations. She found what she was looking for: a photo of Tyler and Alex and Sara Banville. Their names had been written at the bottom.

Tyler and Alex were sitting on their bicycles, facing the camera, long, tanned arms hanging over the handlebars, squinting into the sun. Sara squatted on the ground on the right, holding a jar filled with some kind of insects. She looked like a young Jodie Foster. She had lean limbs and freckles and sun-bleached, straw-like hair. Bell called that style "I-don't-care-about-my-hair" hair, which Bell knew about because she'd had that kind of hair, too, when she was that age. The girl in the photo simmered with a quiet, understated beauty-to-be, a loveliness that rested just under the surface, ready to rise when she hit puberty.

Sara was gazing longingly up at the boys, as if she was hungry to be part of their adventure but had been told to play with her grasshoppers instead.

All three were in shorts and T-shirts. The photo said "Summer" so clearly that Bell almost thought she could hear the word being whispered.

"What are you looking for?" Jake asked.

"Nothing in particular. Just getting a sense of these kids. Take a look at Tyler and Alex. Clear eyes, great smiles. They've got their whole lives ahead of them. Why in God's name would kids like that start messing around with drugs?"

"I don't know, Bell. I guess I'm more surprised these days at the kids who don't—more than the kids who do. 'Cause most do." Jake was not so jaunty right now.

Bell's next move was to reach for the legal pad she'd brought along. As they talked, she made notes on it. Each time the table wobbled, she slid the pad to another quadrant to stabilize it.

"Okay. So Alex Banville is an addict," Bell said. "Contrary to what everybody apparently thought. Relevant?"

"You're damned right it's relevant. Maybe he was working for Deke Foley, too. Just like Tyler."

"How would that change things?"

"Maybe Foley sent Alex to kill Brett Topping. As part of his job."

Bell checked her notes from her call with Nick. "No deal. Alex went back into rehab in Florida the day before the murder."

"Damn."

"Right. So we're still back to Foley."

"And he's still on the lam." Jake let out a frustrated sigh. "Okay, well—then how about another employee, since Alex Banville's out of the picture? Guy like Foley must have a slew of low-level losers who do his dirty work. Tyler Topping can't be his only flunky. Even if Foley didn't specifically send the shooter, anybody who worked for him would've been in Brett Topping's file. Ergo—they'd have a reason to want Topping gone. And to get that file."

"'Ergo'?" Bell looked amused.

"Had a lot of free time lately. Been reading."

"Good. It'll keep you out of trouble. So—you're right. If it wasn't Foley, then it could've been anybody on his payroll."

"But it's got to be Foley," Jake said.

"Hard to argue against it. Who else had reason to be angry at Brett Topping?"

Jake pondered the question. "Anybody who made less money than he did. Topping drove an Escalade, right? Nice ride."

"If he'd been another kind of person, I might agree," Bell answered. "But by all accounts—and from what I remember—he was a decent, likable guy. Low-key. Personable. Not some arrogant asshole. The Escalade was his only real indulgence."

"How about that house?"

Bell shook her head. "I still don't see it. I don't buy some jealous person happening to come by on a Friday night, gun in hand, to shoot Topping. And then to go tear up his house—and not take any valuables."

Jake groaned. "So—Foley." He smacked a hand on the tabletop, making the whole thing shimmy precariously. "I *hate* it when we end up right where we started," he declared. "Just *hate* it."

"Better than spinning our wheels all night long." The words were out before Bell could catch herself. "God, Jake, I didn't mean to—"

"Forget it," he said, interrupting her. "But with your permission, now I *will* have that beer. You sure you won't join me?"

Bell's cell rang.

"It's Rhonda," she said, eyeing the caller ID.

She listened. Jake waited politely to get his Rolling Rock out of the fridge until she was off the phone.

When Bell clicked off the call three minutes later, she was tempted to indulge as well.

Because the case they'd assumed would be wrapped up the moment they tracked down Deke Foley had just blown wide open.

Yes, Deke Foley had been found.

But he could not have murdered Brett Topping.

"What the *hell*?"

Jake's voice sounded more angry than interrogative. So angry that he forgot all about his Rolling Rock.

He hadn't been privy to Rhonda's explanation over the phone, and so when Bell set down her cell and relayed the news to him—Deke Foley had an absolutely airtight alibi—he glared at her and sputtered his response.

"It's true," Bell said.

"Come on! That rat bastard's pulling something. Alibi? Come *on*. Either he paid somebody to lie for him or he—"

"No. No, Jake. He didn't do it."

Bell abruptly rose from her chair. The chair was so spindly that the force of her motion knocked it sideways. It bounced twice on the cheap yellow linoleum.

Jake didn't notice. He was still seething.

"So you tell me," he demanded, pointing a finger at her, "and you tell me *right now*." He had to keep moving that finger because Bell was pacing now, back and forth, back and forth. It only took two and a half steps to get from one end of the kitchen to the other, but she still found the activity satisfying. "Tell me how a drug dealer who knew Brett Topping had been keeping a file on him—a file that could mess up his whole danged operation—and who had *threatened* Topping—somehow takes himself out of the running as a suspect when Topping turns up shot to death in his own driveway?"

"Okay," Bell said. "I'll tell you."

And she proceeded to repeat to Jake the information Rhonda had just imparted to her:

On the afternoon of Topping's death—six hours before the murder— Deke Foley lost control of his car on a stretch of interstate in Bulger County, three counties away from Raythune. His vehicle struck a tree at a high rate of speed. He had no ID. The car had stolen plates. So nobody knew who he was. Suffering from a traumatic brain injury as well as multiple fractures and significant blood loss, he had been unconscious since the accident.

He had awakened a few hours ago and was finally able to mumble his name to hospital authorities. They notified local law enforcement.

At which point an alert Bulger County deputy had recalled the bulletin from the Raythune County Sheriff's Department. The one that asked for cooperation in apprehending a murder suspect named Deke Foley.

"Damn," Jake said. Throughout Bell's story he had gradually settled down.

"Yeah."

"So if Foley didn't kill Topping and ransack the house, then who did?"

"You're half-right."

"Huh?"

"Foley didn't kill Topping. But he did ransack the house. Only he did it *before* the murder was committed," Bell said.

"What?"

"Foley showed up at the house that afternoon. Ellie Topping had already left for Charleston. And Tyler was in Bretherton County. So nobody was home. Foley tossed the place, but he didn't find the file. His plan was to come back later that night—after his trip to Bulger County. He had a big drug deal going on over there. When he came back, he'd confront Topping. Force him to give up the file."

"But he never made it back."

"Right. He didn't."

"So how do you know it was him who broke in that afternoon?" Jake asked.

"Once he regained consciousness this morning, Foley admitted it." Bell picked up her chair. She sat it back down again at the dinette. "As I recall from my conversation with Rhonda just now, Foley's exact quote to the Bulger County deputy was, 'Yeah, I tore up that damned fancy house, but I sure as hell didn't off the guy. I'm a drug dealer. I ain't no murderer.'"

Jake shook his head. "Sorry we offended his tender sensibilities by accusing him," he said. "Selling narcotics that ruin lives and destroy

families and cause a shitload of misery—yep. Killing somebody—nope."
He made a snorting sound. "Time to break out the halos for that boy."

Bell went back to her legal pad. She tore off the top sheet and wadded it up into a ball. She flipped it at Jake.

"Think fast," she said.

He caught it in one hand and then side-armed it into the trash can, banking it off the side of the refrigerator.

"What's next?" he said.

"What's next is starting over."

He groaned. "I'm listening."

"Okay. So Foley didn't kill Brett Topping. And he didn't break into the bank a few hours later, either, to keep searching for the file. Because at the time, he was flat on his back and hooked up to a ventilator. But that doesn't mean he wasn't involved somehow. Foley obviously knows more than he's saying."

"How do we find out? Even if we got ourselves over to the Bulger County Hospital, Foley's not going to tell us a damned thing." Jake's smile was grim. "In fact, more than likely he'll tell us to go screw ourselves."

"You're right. But he might be a little more forthcoming with one of his colleagues."

"I still don't see how we could—"

"Where'd I leave my purse? I need to get a business card out of my billfold."

"Hi, Glenna. It's Bell Elkins." Having punched the number into her cell, Bell slipped the business card back into the slot where she'd kept it since her last conversation with the night nursing supervisor at Evening Street Clinic.

"Bell! Oh, my goodness—so great to hear your voice. How are you?"

"I'm doing well. Thanks. And listen, Glenna—I'd love to catch up, but I'm pressed for time right now. I need your help."

"Sure."

"Do you know anybody who works in the ICU of Bulger County Hospital? A nursing school colleague, maybe? Anybody?"

"Oh, yeah. This is a small region. The nurses and doctors all pretty much know each other. The head of ICU over there is an old friend of mine. Sheila Baugh. You want her number?"

"I'd be much obliged. Oh—and how'd your granddaughter do? At the pageant in Charleston?"

Pride gleamed in Glenna's voice. "She was wonderful! Came in second place. First in the talent competition. You ought to see that child twirl a baton. Poetry in motion. Okay—got the number right here. Sheila will do whatever she can for you. Good gal. Be sure and tell her you're a friend of mine."

"I will."

"And stop in and say hello sometime, okay? You know where to find me."

An hour and a half later, Bell had what she needed.

Jake had watched her work, listening to her side of calls, both outgoing and incoming. He'd craved a beer but stuck to a bottle of water—and got one for her, too, from the fridge—because he wanted to stay as sharp as she was.

"Let me finish making my notes so I can call Rhonda," Bell said, "and then we'll talk."

He waited. A few minutes later, Bell put down her pen. She rubbed her eyes. Finished off her water bottle.

"Okay," she said. "First—Shelia Baugh really came through. You heard me ask her to hang out in Foley's room if he started to make any phone calls. And he did. When she called me back just now, she gave me a full report. Now, if I was a prosecutor—I couldn't use it. It's hearsay. And Foley hasn't had a Miranda warning. But I'm not a prosecutor anymore. So I can run with it."

"Is this where I talk about silver linings? Or making lemonade out of lemons?" Jake said, a puckish grin on his face. "You lose your job—but it frees you up to solve this case?"

"No, this is not where you talk about that," Bell said, "unless you want another paper-wad missile aimed at your head. Anyway—Foley called one of his thugs. Shelia made that assumption based on how Foley talked. Like a boss. He praised the person he was talking to. Best she could tell from Foley's side of the conversation, Foley was going over details with the person. Mentioned the fact that he'd contacted him before his car accident, complaining that the file wasn't in the Topping house. His search that afternoon had turned up bupkis. So apparently Foley's employee showed some initiative. Took matters into his own hands. Went to the bank the next morning, put a gun to the janitor's head, forced her to open the door. Searched the office for the file. All without having to deal with the bank's security system."

"So who was it? Who did Foley call?"

"Don't know. There was no way for the nurse to tell. Foley never used the guy's name."

"But at least we know your theory was right—somebody was working with Foley. And that somebody went to the bank and kept searching for the file," Jake said.

"Yeah."

"How about the murder? Did Foley talk about that in his call?"

Bell shook her head. "He was about to, Sheila thinks, when he got interrupted. Tech came in the room to take him for his MRI. That was it."

"Damn those pesky life-saving procedures," Jake muttered.

"Yeah."

"And then you called Sandy Banville. Anything useful there?"

"She sounded terribly upset. Really agitated. Semi-hysterical. When I told her how sorry I was about Alex, she started sobbing."

"I was kind of surprised," Jake said, "that you didn't push her harder about covering up his drug addiction."

"Why would I? Rhonda had already done plenty of pushing. I called Rhonda last night, relaying Nick's information about Alex. She made an appointment with the Banvilles for first thing this morning. She texted me on my way over here. She talked to Sandy and Rex for several hours. And Alex's sister, Sara."

"Anything useful?"

"Rhonda's not sure yet. Still going through her interview notes. They claim Alex never would've worked for a man like Foley, but—who knows? They also hid his drug addiction. Or at least Sandy did. Rhonda doesn't think Rex even knew. He travels a lot for his business. Seemed out of the family loop, Rhonda said. He was just devastated by the news of Alex's addiction. Sandy, it turns out, has been the point person on hiding their son's troubles. Took it all on herself." Bell moved her neck back and forth, and then around in a circle, working out the kinks. "I didn't want to echo the same line of questioning that Rhonda had used. Sandy would be expecting that. Anyway, by the time I called her, *not* mentioning Alex's problem was the better strategy."

"Because . . . ?" Jake asked dubiously.

"Because she kept waiting for me to. Incredible stress. By the end of the call, she was barely coherent."

He nodded.

"How about your third call?" he asked. "That guy you were talking to—from what you were asking him, he's like an ATF agent, right?"

"He is. Frank Martz. I knew him back in D.C. Long time ago. We were pretty close."

Jake waggled his eyebrows suggestively.

"Oh, stop," Bell said. She rolled her eyes. "But—okay, yeah. There was something between us. But I wasn't divorced yet, and then once I was—well, I was leaving. No point to it." She shook her head, changing the subject. "Now that we know Foley wasn't the shooter, we can start trying to figure out who *was*. I asked Frank to check his records from shooting ranges in the area. See who signed up for handgun lessons over the past several months. If any familiar names pop up, he'll call."

"The government tracks that?"

"The government tracks *everything*, Jake."

He nodded sheepishly. "Okay. I'm a naïve dope."

"That's okay. You'll wise up one of these days."

Chapter Thirty-one

Later that afternoon, Ellie sat in the doll room and waited for the sun to work its magic. She needed some magic.

That noise.

She knew it well. It meant someone was coming up the stairs.

Why wouldn't they leave her alone? All she wanted was to be by herself—here in the only place where she could feel any peace. Here in the place that knew the worst about her but that embraced her still. The place that would always forgive her.

But someone was interrupting her. She was never safe anymore.

A knock on the door.

"Ma'am?"

The door opened. She saw a big brown hat. Flat-brimmed, with a thin gold braid around the crown. A brown uniform.

"Ma'am, I'm Sheriff Harrison. We spoke on the night your husband was killed. I'm sorry to just barge in like this, but we rang the front doorbell and waited for a long time. Then we reached your son over at Jake Oakes's house. Tyler told us that you come up here a lot. And that sometimes you can't hear the doorbell."

She stared at the intruder.

"Ma'am?" the sheriff repeated.

Now, at last, Ellie reacted. Since Brett's death she had had a delayed reaction to everything, as if her brain was operating in a different time zone from the one her body occupied.

"Yes. Yes, all right. Fine."

"I have some information," the sheriff said. She looked around the small room, at the books arranged so carefully on the shelves, the round table, the window with its neat white trim. Sunlight touched each of those items like a friendly little pat on the head. "I'd like to speak with you. We could stay up here or maybe go down to the living room where you might be more comfort—"

"Here's fine."

Harrison shifted her feet. "Okay." She took off her hat, wedging it up into her right armpit. "As you know, we've been working under the assumption that Deke Foley was responsible for your husband's murder. He needed to find the file your husband kept. We speculated that he confronted your husband in the driveway and—when your husband wouldn't agree to give him the file, well—"

"He shot him." Did they think she wouldn't say it, couldn't say it? Saying it didn't matter. Brett was still gone, either way.

"Right. And then ransacked your house. Looking for the file."

"Well, isn't that what happened?"

"No. Deke Foley could not have done it."

"What?"

"He was in the hospital. Three counties away."

Ellie shook her head, blinking rapidly in confusion. "But my house—who tore it up?"

"Foley. He did that in the afternoon, after you had left for Charleston. Looking for the file your husband told him about. When he didn't find it, he planned to come back later—but he never got the chance. A big tree over in Bulger County—and Foley's habit of driving at a high rate of speed on dangerous curves, after drinking a fifth of Jack—made sure of that."

Ellie was stunned. She was so still, for so long, that the sheriff was slightly afraid to rouse her. But she had to.

"Mrs. Topping, are you all right?"

"So who killed Brett?" she said, her voice rising. "Who did it?"

"We've actually had a confession. Late this afternoon."

"A confession? Oh, my God—who—"

"Your neighbor. Sandy Banville."

Ellie uttered a short gasp. "What? How—but *why*?"

"She holds you and Brett responsible for Alex's addiction. That's what she told us. She just keeps repeating, over and over again, that Tyler introduced Alex to drugs. Her son was a good boy. The best. And then Tyler got hold of him."

"Tyler didn't—"

"Sometimes people have to have somebody else to blame, Mrs. Topping. It's the only way they can go on." Harrison shifted her hat to her other armpit. "She told us that she'd been waiting for the opportunity to assault either you or your husband. To make you pay. She wanted you to hurt as badly as she was hurting."

"But we *were* hurting. Tyler had ruined our lives. Good God, we were devas—"

"Sandy Banville doesn't see it like that. She said you and Brett escaped any real pain. Because Tyler was . . . ordinary. Not special, like Alex. So your loss was less than hers. Far, far less." Harrison waited for Ellie to speak. When she didn't, the sheriff continued. "On the night of the murder, Brett came home first. And so he was the target. Sandy watched him pull into your driveway. Something took hold of her. An anger that was worse than any anger she'd ever felt. An uncontrollable grief. *Somebody* had to pay. *Somebody*, she said, had to answer for what had happened to Alex. You and Brett were responsible for bringing Tyler into the world. And so—she crossed the street and she did it. She murdered your husband."

Wonderingly, as if the puzzle pieces were slowly falling into place, Ellie said, "There was one evening . . . she came to my door. She was . . . not herself. She must've been searching for her son—for Alex. But I didn't know that. And I didn't know she was suffering, either. If I had—I could've been there for her and—"

"No, Mrs. Topping," the sheriff said. "You're the last person in the world she ever would have confided in."

"But our sons—we'd both lost our boys—we could've *helped* each other."

"No. She didn't want your help. She was filled with rage and sorrow over what had happened to her family. She was desperate. And finally, it was just too much for her."

Ellie touched her forehead with two fingers.

"All that hate," Ellie murmured. "How she must've hated us. Me just as much as Brett. It's so clear now. She despised both of us."

"Given that reality, maybe we ought to be grateful that she didn't kill you, too."

"Oh," Ellie quickly replied, "but she did. Can't you see that, Sheriff?"

Chapter Thirty-two

A few hours after Harrison broke the news to Ellie Topping in the doll room, Bell and Jake settled themselves into Rhonda's courthouse office.

Jake had scooted his wheelchair to the right side of the big desk. Bell chose one of the chairs facing the desk.

"You two did a hell of a lot of work in a very short period of time," Rhonda said. She set three cans of Diet Coke on the center of the desk. "I'm much obliged. Sandy Banville was booked and fingerprinted twenty minutes ago. Made a full confession." She handed a can to Bell, and another to Jake.

He stared at the can as if it were a peculiar artifact someone had unearthed from an archaeological dig, and he was in charge of figuring out to what use the now-vanished civilization had put it. "Diet Coke?" he said.

"Do you like Pepsi better?" Rhonda asked. "Or maybe Dew? I can send over to JPs."

"No, no—this is fine." Jake smiled wanly. She'd misunderstood him. He simply couldn't figure out why you'd have a gathering to express your appreciation and serve . . . soda pop. Where was the Rolling Rock?

"Okay. Good," Rhonda said. She leaned forward, elbows on the desk. "So Sandy Banville's attorney is driving over from Blythesburg. Until she gets here and the interrogation can begin, I thought we'd take a moment. We've still got some unanswered questions—but at least we've got Brett Topping's killer in custody." She opened her own soda and took a long swallow.

"I know there's not a lot to be happy about," Rhonda went on, "because this is a tragedy. A man's dead. A woman's life is ruined. Two families have been torn apart. But we did our jobs. We're going to make sure justice is done."

"Maybe we should try to Skype with Nick Fogelsong," Bell said. "Get him in on this, too. He was a big help."

"He's probably out on his fishing boat right about now," Jake said. He'd opened the can and taken one sip to be polite, and then set it on Rhonda's desk. "Blue skies. Sunshine. Beer in the cooler." He sighed.

"Maybe we'll see Nick at the wedding," Rhonda said. "I invited him and Mary Sue. They're not sure yet if they can make it."

Jake snickered. "Hell, Rhonda—*you're* not sure yet if you can make it." The many cancellations had become a bit of a joke. In the wake of Sandy Banville's confession, Rhonda had called her church and requested yet another short delay.

Rhonda winced at Jake's dig. "Okay, okay." She sat back in her chair. "I'll admit it—I was plenty worried once Foley was eliminated as a suspect. But now we know who did it. A confession is the best outcome of all. Not that we're done. Not by a long shot. We still need to get our hands on that file. It could help us shut down Foley's network for good. Believe me—even with that scumbag laid up in the hospital, his business will still be going strong."

Sheriff Harrison appeared in the doorway.

"Pam," Rhonda said. "Come on in. How did Ellie Topping take the news?"

"Not sure she's fully grasped it yet," Harrison answered. "She's in pretty bad shape. Deputy Brinksneader is taking Tyler over to be with her right now." She took off her hat and sat down on the small couch. "First she loses her husband. Then she finds out that her neighbor's the one who did it."

"So why did Sandy confess?" Jake asked.

"I guess she realized we were closing in," Rhonda replied. "Thought it might be better to get out in front of it. The noose was tightening. Bell's friend at the ATF found out that the Banvilles had purchased a firearm six months ago—and a family membership at the Hawksbridge Mountain Shooting Range. We'd asked Sandy about it."

Jake looked at Bell. "So that was your theory all along? Sandy Banville did it? Because she was distraught over her son's addiction?"

"My theory doesn't matter anymore," she answered. "We have a confession."

He looked distinctly unsatisfied. "But that's where you were heading?"

Rhonda spoke before Bell could. "Damned right it was. Both Rex and Sandy had a reason to hate the Toppings, or so they thought—their belief that Tyler had lured Alex into drugs—but Rex had an alibi for the night of the murder. Sandy didn't. And when I interviewed her friends, they said she'd been behaving erratically lately. They mentioned specific threats against the Toppings.

"It's the trifecta," Rhonda concluded. "She had motive, means, and opportunity. She knew we'd be on to her soon. Better to confess and hope that buys her some leniency."

"Speaking of means," Bell said. "What does Sandy say she did with the murder weapon?"

The sheriff lifted a hand, meaning that she'd take the question.

"She said it went missing," she said. "Her guess is that Alex stole it from the house. Probably sold it for drug money. Standard behavior for him these days, apparently. Sneaks in from wherever, robs them, and then takes off again. They find him and he's all apologetic and says he wants to get clean." Harrison shrugged. "He got out of rehab a few days after the shooting. Then it's right back in again. Vicious circle. Chances are, we'll never find the weapon."

"We'll be commissioning a psych eval, first thing," Rhonda said. "Sandy Banville's been through hell. The trauma of watching her son slide into drug addiction, plus blowing through the family's retirement savings to pay for one rehab stay after another—that kind of pressure would've broken anybody."

Bell motioned to Jake. She'd eyed the intimidating pile of paperwork on Rhonda's desk and remembered what that was like: always, always, another item on the list.

"The prosecutor and the sheriff have a lot to do," Bell said. "Let's get out of the way."

And then the two of them headed side by side down the courthouse corridor, the woman walking and the man pushing himself in his wheelchair—exiles, each for a different reason, from this place that both of them had loved and served.

"Need a ride?" Bell asked.

"I'd be much obliged."

She followed him down the ramp at the side entrance to the courthouse. "So I guess Tyler Topping will be going home again. As long as Foley's laid up, he's not much of a threat."

"Funny thing," Jake said. "Kid claims he wants to hang out at my place for a while. Says he's making real progress for the first time in a long time. Getting his head on straight. Must be my sparkling personality. Truth is, we have some good talks. In between chores, that is. I don't let him get by with any bullshit. The schedule we keep, he'd get more rest if he was in Marine boot camp." He shrugged. "Anyway, it's fine by me. He can stay as long as he likes."

Chapter Thirty-three

"This isn't what I had in mind. Not even close."

"But it's still good, right?" Bell said. "It's your special day, Rhonda. Come on."

Rhonda sighed and nodded. She looked beautiful but not altogether comfortable in a complicated wedding dress that included mother-of-pearl buttons cascading down the front, a low neckline, and a great deal of frilly white material sprouting from her backside.

"So relax," Bell added.

It was a week later and the Chimney Corner had never looked more festive. The staff had done its level best, pushing back the tables and chairs, draping swags of sparkly bunting across the crown molding, lowering the lights to create a romantic glow. *Don't know about any dadburned RO-mantic glow*, crabbed one of Rhonda's older relatives, who had sidled up next to Bell and demanded to know why the damned lights were so damned low. *Just reminds me of macular degeneration.*

On one side of the room, a long buffet table featured a row of silver chafing dishes. At the end of the table was a carving station, behind which a knife-wielding Chimney Corner employee in a white chef's hat and white tunic and black-and-white-checked trousers waited expectantly, his eyes fixed upon the steamship round of beef as he planned his next attack upon its freshly exposed, deep-pink flesh.

On the other side of the room, a four-member band—lead guitar, bass guitar, drums, and vocalist—in matching powder-blue suits and ruffled shirts offered a selection of soft rock tunes from the 1970s, that being roughly the period of time whose music stuck in the groom's brain.

It was Rhonda's surprise gift to him. "I know that's the music he loves best," she had murmured to Bell, as the reception began and a certain sameness gradually became apparent in the band's repertoire. It was, Bell realized, a good working definition of love: When you love someone, you know what they love best in all the world.

So the band played the music of The Grass Roots, Paul Revere & the Raiders, The Monkees, Tommy James & the Shondells.

Over and over again.

Rhonda took a quick swig from her champagne glass and then handed it to Mack Gettinger. His face revealed that he'd be willing to accept her empty glasses with joy for the rest of his life.

"Yeah," Rhonda said, turning back to Bell. "Not my dream venue. But the best I could expect, after canceling with the church three times. Or was it four? I lost track. Anyway, this last time was the charm."

The ceremony had been a short one. Rhonda's grandfather, a retired Baptist preacher named Enoch Lovejoy who sported a white beard nearly as wide as he was, had presided, and unlike most of his ilk, he moved things along at a brisk pace. He asked Rhonda and Mack to come to the center of the room, and then he sprinkled a few things biblical upon the assemblage and told Mack to give his bride a kiss. And it was done.

Rhonda and Bell now stood at the rim of the crowd, watching as people shifted and shimmied to a halfhearted cover of "Last Train to Clarksville." Mack had departed for a moment to procure more champagne.

"Every time I called the church to postpone it," Rhonda went on, "I had to go to the back of the line. I think at this point, my turn for the sanctuary and the fellowship hall was set to come up sometime in the spring of 2027."

"Not your fault," Bell said. "Those cancellations weren't just some crazy whim. You had a major case under way. Cut yourself some slack."

"Well, Mack was tired of all the delays. He just wanted to go ahead—

and so did I. By this point, we would've been happy to have the ceremony up at the Highway Haven, if it had come to that."

Two young women bounced up to congratulate the bride, alternating squeals with hugs. While the three of them chatted, Bell looked around the room. Through a twinkly haze of low lights and shiny decorations, couples swayed and dipped to vaguely familiar music. She caught a glimpse of Jake Oakes, who seemed to be enjoying himself.

Rhonda had finished with her friends. She turned back to Bell.

"Mack's on his way with our refills. So I'll need to make this quick."

"My, my. Keeping secrets from your husband already."

"Yeah—but not the fun kind." Rhonda lowered her voice. "Sandy Banville's attorney plans to plead diminished capacity."

"Why are you whispering?" Bell asked. It was hard to hear her over "Crimson and Clover."

"I promised Mack I wouldn't talk shop at our wedding," Rhonda replied. "Couldn't resist, though. I know you've dealt with this kind of situation. Sandy was under a ton of stress. But I still think the minimum sentence should be—"

"Hey." It was Mack. Rhonda hadn't seen him coming up behind her. "I distinctly heard somebody say 'minimum sentence.' Not a phrase you expect to hear at a wedding. Unless you're marrying one of the Manson girls, maybe." He handed his wife a new glass of champagne and kissed her cheek. "So I've got to ask. Did you break your promise? Were you and Bell talking shop?"

A moment swept by, punctuated by the opening guitar riff to "(I'm Not Your) Steppin' Stone."

"Guilty," Rhonda said. "Look, sweetie, I just needed to get her advice about—"

"Not a problem." He winked at her. "I knew you couldn't do it. In fact, I think I would've been a little disappointed if you *had* been able to pull it off. That's not the gal I married. Oh—almost forgot," Mack said, turning to Bell. "Ran into a friend of yours who was just coming in the door. He's hanging up his coat. Said he'd be right back here to find you."

"Really? Who's that?"

"Lemme see now." Mack tilted his head back, scratched his chin.

"Not sure I caught it. Might've been one thing, might've been another. It sounded like—" Mack grinned and shook his head. He couldn't stretch out the joke a second longer. He'd recognized the new arrival right away—just as had everybody else who had spotted him. "It's Nick Fogelsong."

He was older, of course, but the passing of time hadn't changed him in any substantial way. Bell spotted him across the room. He was parting the sea of people in party clothes. It hadn't been a terribly long interval since she had last seen him, but even a brief gap offered a new perspective.

Nick's face had a few more lines in it, and he'd put on some weight, but it gave him a sort of courtly gravitas. He was wearing a dark suit and a pressed white shirt, with no tie. He looked good. Like always, though, Bell was slightly jarred when she saw him out of a sheriff's uniform, even though he'd not worn one in almost half a dozen years.

Everyone wanted to shake his hand. Everyone wanted to say hello. Everyone wanted to tell him how good he looked and how much they'd missed him and how often they'd . . .

"Appreciate it, folks, I really do," Nick said, glad-handing his way across the edge of the dance floor, moving deftly between the swaying couples who were trying to sync themselves to a too-slow version of "I'm a Believer." "Hi, there. Hello. Good to see you folks. Well, thanks— you're looking pretty good yourself."

All at once he was standing in front of Rhonda. He gave her a big hug.

"Congratulations," Nick said. "You look so pretty tonight, honey." As soon as he'd finished with the bride he gave the groom a handshake and a big grin. "Mack, you're the luckiest sonofabitch in the state of West Virginia—and maybe the whole USA."

"You got that right," Mack said.

And then came one of those amazingly tender moments that Bell could appreciate, even while fully understanding that she herself would most likely never be a participant in such a moment ever again. Her role from now on would be to rejoice on behalf of her friends who *were* participants in such moments—and that was fine. That was more than enough:

Rhonda put the back of her hand on Mack's cheek and stroked it. He lifted his hand and took hers in his own. He turned over her hand and kissed her palm.

"Save it for the honeymoon!" someone yelled from across the room, and there was a spurt of laughter.

Mack laughed, too, and waved at the crowd, drawing more cheers and a few whistles.

"I never dreamed you'd be able to come," Rhonda said, giving Nick a playful shove. "'Course you missed the boring part. The vows and such. Got here just in time for the champagne and the buffet supper, you rascal." She looked around. "Did Mary Sue come with you? Where is she?"

"No," Nick said. "She couldn't make it."

Now Bell saw it: Something was wrong.

She knew Nick Fogelsong well. And she realized that this wasn't a social call.

"Nick?" Bell said.

He looked at her, and then back to Rhonda. "I'm very happy for you," he said. "You make a beautiful bride. I'm so pleased I could see you tonight, here with your family and all your friends. I want you to know that. But I have to be honest. That's not why I came."

Rhonda looked confused. "What?"

Mack had moved even closer to his wife, as if he sensed that whatever Nick had to say, it was going to involve some degree of distress for Rhonda. It was his job henceforth to help mitigate that; such was the message sent when he put an arm around her waist.

"Say what you need to say," Rhonda declared.

Nick put his hands in his pockets, sweeping back both sides of his unbuttoned suit coat to do so. He looked around the room. The band had started up again, which was fortunate; everyone but the four of them had returned to the festivities.

He moved his gaze back to Rhonda.

"Sandy Banville didn't kill Brett Topping. Her confession is false. Whoever killed him is still out there."

Two and a half years previously

Henry was home now, in his apartment in Charleston.

Ellie had set it all up. "Knew you'd handle things," Henry had said, grinning, when she told him about the move. She had hired a medical ambulance to take him from Columbus back to Charleston. At first he'd hated the idea of that. He knew what a medical ambulance must cost, he told her, and he didn't want to be a bother.

"Stop it," Ellie had said, tears in her eyes. "It's no bother and you know it. Besides, Brett and I can afford it. Believe me."

The ambulance driver and his assistant had just arrived. They were moving him from his hospital bed onto the gurney. They were very gentle with him and it was that—their gentleness, the concern of strangers—that had made Ellie cry. Not so much the fact that Henry was going home to die. She had come to terms with that reality a few weeks ago; what moved her now were the little mercies. The driver was a big, burly man and yet he handled her brother with great delicacy, as if Henry was someone beloved by him, too, and not just a client.

Once the gurney cleared the hospital room Ellie had stayed behind for a few minutes, gathering up his belongings: slacks, sweatshirt, wristwatch, dentures, a Civil War magazine that Brett had brought him on one of his brief, infrequent visits. Henry's precipitous downturn had come during the bank's busy season, and Brett had not been able to make the drive to Columbus as often as he would've liked. "Don't worry about it," Henry had said to him. "Ellie's taking real good care of me. Appreciate you letting her stay." Henry was an old-fashioned man. To his mind, a wife didn't go anywhere—and certainly didn't stay there for weeks on end—without her husband's approval.

Ellie followed the ambulance to Charleston in her own car.

Henry's apartment was on the second floor of an older building, three stories of drab, sand-colored brick with an unaccountably fancy entranceway, an arched threshold with THE LANCER ARMS chiseled in the concrete. The driver had stopped his long vehicle right there, blocking the lane. He flipped on his flashers. It was a busy street, with no legal way to park in front of the building, but this seemed like the best way to get Henry inside. A few drivers honked and gunned their engines, annoyed at getting stuck and having to wait their turn to swerve around the ambulance. *To hell with you*, Ellie thought as she heard the honks. She had stopped right behind the ambulance, daring the bastards to hit her car. *You go straight to hell. I don't care what you think.*

She already had the living room set up for Henry. Brett's secretary had researched places in Charleston that supplied home medical equipment; she had texted the list to Ellie, and Ellie made her selections. Everything had been delivered and assembled before they got there: hospital bed, bedside commode, adjustable tray table.

The next few days passed in a slow, sepia-colored blur. Henry slept. He had lost control of his bowels and his bladder just before he left the hospital, and so a great deal of Ellie's time was spent cleaning him. He no longer had the capacity to be embarrassed about having his sister see those parts of him. It did not matter to either of them.

The hospice people came and went, bringing what needed to be brought, making sure that he wasn't in pain. Ellie kept the blinds closed, because the sunlight had seemed to bother him.

"I don't want this to happen," she said.

She was sitting by his bed, watching him breathe. Sometimes he rallied and they were able to have brief conversations.

"Well, now, little sister—it's nothing that anybody can do anything about." Henry chuckled. He gave her a tired smile that was half apology, half encouragement, as if Ellie were a child who'd asked for a pony and he wasn't able to oblige this year, but maybe next.

"I'm scared, Henry."

She had not been this blunt with him before now, naming things, identifying the fate that rushed at him, but it was time. She sensed it.

"I know," he said.

"Are *you* scared?"

That was what she really wanted to know. Her confession about her own fear had been strategic; maybe it would make him come clean, too.

"I don't know," he said.

You don't know? The words bumped around in her head while she tried to make sense of them. *You don't know? How can you not know?*

"Well," she said.

Silence pooled around the little island comprised of all the words they'd already spoken. As the silence grew, the island seemed to become smaller and smaller, shrinking back into a small, hard nugget. Soon Ellie could barely remember anything they'd said, even just minutes ago.

And so she reached into the past. If the present was a vanishing island, the past was the sky—vast, permanent, always accessible.

"That doll," she said.

"Mmmm?" He'd been dozing. He did that now; he fell asleep all the time, sometimes in the middle of his own sentences. Weariness engulfed him.

"That doll," Ellie repeated. "Do you remember?"

He murmured something.

"You got it for me," she said. "I was five years old. I'd never had a doll before. Lillian was so jealous. She tried to grab it away from me. But you told her to stop that. You said, 'This is for Ellie.' That was it. You didn't give any reason. You just said, 'This is for Ellie.' And that satisfied her. She walked away. She didn't even argue. Can you imagine that? Lillian loved to argue. You remember. If somebody said the sky was blue, Lillian would say, 'No, it's pink,' just to get an argument going." Ellie's head was suddenly filled with images of her sister. Lillian was never pretty, the way Ellie was pretty, and she let that fact define her life. She was heavyset, with lank brown hair that tended to be oily looking even right after she'd washed it. She had died eight years ago of a stroke. Alone in a trailer.

Henry's eyes fluttered open. He didn't move his head—he seemed too tired for that—but his pupils slid over in Ellie's direction.

"The doll," he murmured. "I think I remember it now."

She didn't know if he was telling the truth or if he was just being polite. Chances were, he probably didn't remember the doll: a small plastic one, obviously secondhand, that didn't even have hair. The butterscotch-colored hair was painted on and the paint had already rubbed off in several places by the time Ellie held it to her heart that day, loving it at first sight.

No, he surely didn't remember it. One small gift to his little sister, a gift for no reason, amid a lifetime of events—it wasn't that important. She had lost the doll somewhere along the way, anyway. It was one of the reasons she loved Henry as much as she did, but it wasn't important, not the thing itself. All that mattered was the fact of the giving.

"If I still had that doll I sure know where I'd keep it," she said, talking softly. "Our house in Acker's Gap has a doll room. In the attic. Tyler couldn't wait to show it to you, remember? When you visited us? It was Thanksgiving. Ten years ago. Tyler was just a little boy. The dolls weren't there anymore but I still called it the doll room. You thought that was funny. A doll room with no dolls."

Henry had closed his eyes again, drifting off. She didn't know if he could hear her anymore, but she didn't care. Tyler's troubles had recently started—the principal had called two days ago, her son was being expelled for selling pot to his classmates—and Ellie was tempted to tell Henry about it, seek his sympathy. And then she thought: *no.* The things of this world were receding from Henry Combs now, sliding back, falling away from him. One by one the little threads tethering him here were disengaging. Thread by thread, memory by memory.

"I go up there and I sit," she said. "I can remember things better in that room. So many things. Sometimes I think if I could just stay there—stay in that room forever—I'd be fine. I'd never be sad or scared again. I'd have my memories and that would be enough. Briney Hollow and all the fun we had—do you remember, Henry? How much fun it was? All of us together?"

His eyes suddenly opened. It startled her. She reached for his hand. Something was happening.

"Ellie," he said.

His hand felt small in hers, the skin papery and dry, the bones infinitely fragile.

"Ellie," he said, and then he was gone.

Each time Shirley took a breath, her body seemed to register it as a separate and distinct event, as if each breath was being counted. Breathing was an ordeal now.

The hospital staff had moved Shirley into a larger room. A private one this time. Apparently that was what they did when the end was near. Bell only figured that out later. At first she was just grateful for more space, and for the absence of chatter from a TV set. Every roommate her sister had had so far was a dedicated, indiscriminate TV watcher. The set was always on. Bell tried to block it out, but that proved to be impossible.

They were down to days now. That was an obvious, if still unspoken, reality. Shirley lapsed into periods of silence; sometimes she didn't react anymore when Bell came into the room. Her head was arranged in the very center of the pillow. Her arms were at her sides. The thin white blanket had been pulled up to her chest by somebody else. She wouldn't have had the energy to pull it up herself, Bell knew.

"Hey, Shirley," Bell said. That was what she said each time she came back into the room.

Sometimes she thought she saw a response from Shirley. A flicker of an eyelash, a tremor of a finger. And even those minute motions might not have been volitional. Just the body going through its inevitable progressions as it slowly, methodically, shut down.

Bell had watched people die. There was, for instance, her ex-husband's grandfather, Chester Elkins, back when she and Sam had just gotten married. The old man had lasted a day and a half after a brain aneurysm, with various family members shuttling in and out of the hospital room, and Bell and Sam were the unlucky ones; it was during their brief visit that Chester had decided he'd had enough of this world and would take his leave of it.

Bell remembered the particulars: the low, guttural groan; a noise like heavy-duty farting; a gush of foul-smelling black liquid from the old man's sagging mouth. Later, as a prosecutor, she'd twice found herself at the bedside of a dying witness, taking a statement.

And a few months ago Charlie Mathers, a retired Raythune County deputy and a good friend, had died in her arms after being shot during a drug raid.

But those moments, as harrowing as they might have been, were nothing compared to this.

Because this was Shirley.

"Hey, Shirley," Bell said. She'd gone for coffee in the hospital cafeteria and was back now. The coffee had been a bad idea; it glowered and snarled in Bell's gut like a liquid grudge, seeping into the crawl spaces in the lower half of her body.

Bell sat down in the chair next to the bed. She had kept on talking to Shirley, every day, even after it was hard to tell if her sister could hear her. "Got a call from Carla. She's going to drive over again tomorrow." Carla had just started a new job in Charleston but came as often as she could.

Sam, too, had visited three days ago, when it had become clear that things were drawing to a close. He flew into Columbus from Reagan National. Rented a car, drove to the Ohio State campus, sat with Bell in Shirley's room for an hour, and then did the whole thing again in reverse. It was more than Bell would ever have expected. She had been divorced from the man for well over a decade, yet he came.

A few hours later, Shirley revived a bit. It started when she licked her lips. Then she opened her eyes. Bell was standing up now, hands on the bed rail, looking down at her sister.

"Hey," Bell said.

"Hey." Shirley's voice was a soft rasp. The doctors had explained to Bell that the tumor had grown so large now that it was impinging on her vocal cords.

"Something to drink?"

Shirley's head rustled slightly on the pillow. Bell took it as a nod. She picked up the plastic cup on the bedside table, angled the bendy straw between her sister's cracked lips. When Shirley was finished, Bell sat back down again.

She had promised herself that she would keep on talking to

Shirley. The silence seemed too momentous, too much a foretaste of what was waiting around the corner for her sister. Bell could not have put that thought into words but it was there, anyway, with or without words.

"Comer Creek," Bell said. "Remember that? I know you do. I was—what? Four years old? Five? I'd play in that mud and get it all over me. You'd be hopping mad. Because you had to clean me up."

Shirley murmured something. Bell leaned closer.

"What?"

"I never. Wanted." She had to rest between words. "To. Hurt. You."

"We don't need to talk about this. Not now."

"Yes."

"Okay, okay." Bell touched her sister's shoulder. "I know you didn't. I know that, Shirley."

"Telling. You. I didn't mean . . ." She came to a full stop. Her shoulders vibrated with deep, lung-scraping breaths. The effort exhausted her. But she wanted to try again. "I didn't want you. To resign. Your job. Job you love."

"Not your call."

Shirley's eyes opened wider. This had happened sometimes over the past few days; she would be in a deep drowse and then suddenly rise up out of it, capable of complete sentences, of arguing back.

"Makes no sense," Shirley said. "You do good things. And now—"

"Now I'll do other things. Different."

"Not for a while. You told them to send you to prison."

"Who told you that? Who?"

"It's true, isn't it?"

"Who told you?"

"Nobody. I read it in the paper. Connie Boyd brought me a copy." Connie was Shirley's friend. They had worked together at an auto parts store until Shirley grew too sick to work.

The judge had given Bell a month to put her affairs in order. She had four more days of freedom left.

"Never wanted that," Shirley said. "Wanted you to know the truth. Didn't want to wreck your life."

"You didn't wreck my life. *I* did that. All by myself."

Shirley closed her eyes. She was, Bell knew, trying to summon more strength so that she could make her next point. Her chest rose and fell.

"Belfa," Shirley said.

"I'm right here."

"You've got to tell me why."

"No. I don't."

"You do. I told *you* the truth—so you owe me the same. Why didn't you keep it to yourself? Why did you tell the world—and then make them punish you?"

"It doesn't matter anymore."

"The hell it doesn't." Shirley's cough was long and phlegmy. "Why, Bell? You didn't know what you'd done. For God's sake—you were a *child*. I made you think it was me who'd killed Daddy. So why did you . . ."

Bell leaned closer. She felt a frantic, rushing sound in her ears, like a million winged insects taking flight simultaneously. Her heartbeat had taken over her entire body.

They were the only two people in the world right now.

Maybe her sister was right.

Maybe she should tell her.

Maybe it would be a gift, not a burden.

"Shirley," Bell said.

Shirley's eyes looked bigger now, Bell thought, because she was listening so intently. Shirley's fragile body—stippled with cancer, the organs peppered with it, her lungs riddled with it, her bones thinned and frayed by it—was strained with this waiting, this listening.

"Shirley," Bell repeated.

Shirley licked her lips. She tried to swallow, but she was too weak; she made a small strangling sound in the back of her throat. Foamy saliva trickled over her lips.

"You didn't know," Shirley murmured. "You're not to blame. You didn't know."

It's time, Bell thought. *I have to. Before she goes. While I still have the chance.*

"Shirley," she said, "I *did* know. I knew from the beginning. I knew what I'd done. I knew that I was the one who'd killed Daddy. I just pretended I didn't know. Because I wanted a life."

Shirley's face looked startled, and then confused. "You—"

"I knew. I knew all along. That's why—now, all these years later—I did what I did. Confessing. Serving time. When you got sick, I realized that I—I had to be punished. I *had* to."

There was doing a wrong thing because you didn't know that what you were doing was wrong.

And then there was doing a wrong thing and *knowing full well* that it was wrong—and not admitting that you knew. Until you were forced to.

Very different sins. One was forgivable. The other—maybe not.

Later, when Bell read about Utley Pharmaceuticals, the realization would strike her: They knew. They knew—and they did nothing. They pretended they hadn't known.

Just as she'd pretended that she hadn't known.

A day and a half later, Shirley died.

It happened when Bell was sleeping, slumped over in the chair beside the bed. She had not left Shirley's side after she told her the truth, except for bathroom breaks. Occasionally, though, she did fall asleep.

This time, when Bell awoke, she lay with her head back against the seat, eyes still closed, and asked her sister if she'd like a drink of water. There was no answer.

Bell sat up. She looked at Shirley's face.

Her eyes were open. Her struggle was over.

Bell's was just beginning.

PART THREE

Chapter Thirty-four

"Coffee tastes the same," Nick said.

"No wonder. Same pot we were working our way through when you left off being sheriff."

"That was over five years ago, Bell."

"Like I said—same pot."

He smiled. He took another drink and then set down the white china mug. He took a look out the big front window of JPs. The morning was overcast, with the remnants of an earlier fog.

"I'll give you credit—you sure know how to spoil the mood at a wedding," Bell said. "After your bombshell, Rhonda got out of there so fast I thought she was going to knock over a few bridesmaids."

"It's a murder investigation. She wants to get it right." Nick embellished his next remark with a raised eyebrow. "Same way her immediate predecessor operated, yes?"

She shrugged. "Don't recall."

"The hell you don't." He was trying to make amends. He hadn't had time to answer Bell's questions the day before—there was too much to do, explaining to Rhonda why he'd crashed her wedding with his stunning announcement, having a quick private conference with her, making his case—and so he had asked Bell to join him here at JPs this morning.

He had blindsided her—he'd blindsided everybody—and she didn't like that. And then he topped it off by having his conference with Rhonda. Not her. She liked being in the loop.

But the loop wasn't where she lived anymore. She'd given that up.

Nick was talking. "So Rhonda convened a meeting in her office last night with Sandy Banville and her attorney. All charges dropped. Sandy was still claiming she'd done it. Whole thing got a little heated." He chuckled, despite the serious nature of the matters they were discussing. "Can you picture it? Rhonda didn't even go home to change first. So there she was at the courthouse, going over the details of Sandy's release—in her wedding gown. Gotta be a first."

Bell wasn't chuckling. "Rhonda put a lot of trust in your word. I mean—you show up at the reception out of the blue, you give her your personal guarantee that Sandy Banville's confession is fraudulent—and *boom*. Rhonda calls her attorney. And Sandy—whether she likes it or not—is home in time to watch the late local news."

"Hey." Nick was surprised at the tone he'd heard in her voice: skepticism mingled with disgruntlement. "What are you talking about? It had nothing to do with any guarantees from me. I have proof. Solid and irrefutable. Rhonda heard me out. She agreed that the new information I provided was enough to clear Sandy Banville. This wasn't some trick, Bell. No damned rabbits were pulled out of any damned hats. This was about truth. And facts. And evidence. You ought to know that."

"How, Nick? How exactly would I know that?"

It still rankled. She was on the outside looking in. She didn't know the rest of what he'd said to Rhonda last night—because seconds after he'd made his pronouncement to the prosecutor, Rhonda had left the room with him for a private conference. It was official business.

Which meant it wasn't Bell's business. Not anymore.

He could read the resentment on her face. She was feeling left out. And overlooked.

"You know what?" Nick said. "I don't think Rhonda would mind if I gave you some background. Exactly how, for instance, I came to know that Sandy Banville didn't kill Topping. Contrary to her assertions."

"Well, don't take any chances." Bell sounded petulant. "Don't betray any confidences."

"I won't."

Restless, she changed her position on the bench seat. "I'll grant you that I wasn't totally comfortable with the idea of her being the killer. Seemed a little too . . . neat. Convenient. But then again, she despised the Toppings. She'd always felt superior to them—and then her own son falls down the same rabbit hole as Tyler Topping did. She was unhinged by her hatred of both Ellie and Brett. Brett just happened to be her first opportunity. And she can't account for her whereabouts at the time of the murder."

"Yes, she can. She just didn't want to."

"What?"

"Sandy's alibi is not the kind of thing you brag about. She didn't want to embarrass Rex. And bring even more shame and humiliation on him than she'd done already."

"I don't know what you're talking about."

"No, you don't. And there's no way you could. I only know because one of my buddies from up here—Marv Cunningham—called me in Florida yesterday and filled in the picture. He told me what was going on—Sandy's confession, all the rest of it. The fact that she didn't have an alibi. Although she actually did—just not one she wanted to admit to." Nick held up a hand, to stave off more objections from Bell. "Let me finish. Marv said I needed to come up here and talk to Rhonda. Make it right. He knew she'd listen to me."

Before Nick proceeded further with his story, they decided to order some food. Nick made eye contact with Jackie LeFevre, and a moment later the lean, taciturn woman who was still a bit of a mystery in Acker's Gap, despite the fact that she'd been running the diner for over a decade, stood alongside their booth. Today she wore a turquoise flannel shirt, faded black jeans, and knee-high black boots that laced up on the sides.

She didn't use an order pad. And they didn't use a menu.

"Nick Fogelsong," Jackie said. She greeted Bell, then immediately shifted her attention back to Nick. "I don't see Mary Sue. Did she come along?"

"Not this trip."

"Okay," Jackie said. "What can I get you two?"

Nick selected the western omelet and rye toast. Bell ordered two eggs over easy and corned beef hash.

"Coming right up." By now four additional customers had slung themselves into a booth across the room, two to a side. Jackie abandoned Nick and Bell to see if the new arrivals wanted coffee.

Bell kept an eye on Jackie's retreating back. "She didn't seem too surprised to see you here. Almost as if you left yesterday, instead of a couple of years ago."

"Oh, we've communicated a time or two since I moved," Nick said.

"Really."

"Yeah. Email, mostly. A few phone calls, now and again. She had some business before the county commission a while back and needed some advice. Things like that." He finished off his coffee, knowing that Jackie had another pot going. The smell was unmistakable. "She always asked about you, by the way. About how you were dealing with Shirley's passing."

"She could've asked me herself. I still live here. I've been out of Alderson for a while now."

Nick moved his empty cup around on the tabletop.

"She's a brave woman, Bell, but she probably didn't dare." Trying to make a joke of it.

"What are you talking about?"

"Come on. It can't be news to you that you're sometimes a little—well, intimidating. Kind of a hard-ass."

Bell's umbrage was front and center. "I was a prosecutor. Being a hard-ass is part of the job description."

"But you're not a prosecutor anymore, right? So maybe you could lighten up."

Bell drew in a deep breath. She'd been hunched forward while they talked, fingers interlaced on the tabletop, and now she sat up straight. She pulled her hands off the table and brought her arms down to her sides. The chill that emanated from her had an arctic tinge to it.

"You're supposed to be telling me about Sandy Banville. Can we get back to that?"

"Fine." Nick settled into his story. "Marv Cunningham runs the Motel 6 up on the interstate."

"I know that."

"Well, he's aware of the fact that people have been known to use his establishment for purposes that aren't strictly savory. Not all of the couples who wind up there have availed themselves of the holy state of matrimony. Or if they have, it's with somebody other than the person with whom they checked in."

"This is fascinating, Nick. Is there a point?"

"There is indeed. Marv's no gossip. He figures he's got no right to judge anybody, being as how nobody's perfect. But he does keep his eyes open. That's how he knows that Sandy Banville was not in her own neighborhood on the night Brett Topping was murdered. She was at the Motel 6."

"With—?"

"With a good-for-nothing piece of crap named Bucky Travers. He tends bar over in Marbleton. They get a room a few nights a month."

"Did Rex Banville know about this arrangement?"

"He did."

"And he didn't go after this Bucky character with a two-by-four?"

Nick paused, lifting his elbows. Jackie was back with the coffee-pot. She topped off Bell's mug, refilled Nick's.

"Food'll be up real soon," Jackie said.

As soon as she was gone, Nick continued. "Stress and anxiety have been tearing Sandy apart. Not only have they been dealing with their son's addiction—but Sandy was determined to hide it. Wanted every-one to believe he was still the golden boy. His freshman year at WVU, he got high more often than he went to class. After pot, it was Oxy. And then—"

"Let me guess. Heroin."

"Yes. Sandy was frantic. But she felt she had to keep it under wraps. It was a terrible strain."

"Sounds a lot like what Brett and Ellie Topping were dealing with."

"It does, doesn't it? And that's what irked Sandy no end. She wanted her family to be the exception. *Her* kids wouldn't be like other kids. *Her* kids wouldn't go down the same dark road as so many others in this town. *Her* kids wouldn't use drugs." He let out a long, sad breath. "She finally got him into rehab."

"Same one as Tyler Topping."

"Initially, yes. Alex has had a hard time, though. He's been in several different facilities. Nothing works. He stays a week or two and then runs away. Goes back on the streets."

"Where does the Motel 6 come in?"

"You and I have seen it before, Bell—all the ways people cope with that kind of intense pressure. They drink or they start using drugs themselves. Or . . ."

He seemed to be slightly embarrassed. He looked away from her, letting his gaze rove across the diner's checkerboard linoleum floor.

"Or what?" she said.

"Or they have affairs."

"Oh. Right."

"Yeah. So—Sandy and Bucky."

"And Rex knows about this."

"He does."

"And he hasn't tried to stop her? Give her an ultimatum?"

"He loves her, Bell."

"Still not following."

"He loves her and he can see that she's drowning. Barely hanging on. A few seconds away from going under. She needs something—some way to get rid of all that accumulated pressure. Bucky Travers is just a life preserver she's grabbed onto—that's all. Rex doesn't give a damn about Bucky Travers. But he loves Sandy. In fact, he's got a real blind spot when it comes to her."

"So he's been putting up with her affair."

"For now, yeah. It's like being in a foxhole. You don't worry too much about the décor until the shelling stops, okay?"

She rolled her eyes. "Never did understand people. Crazy bastards, every single one of 'em."

"Can't argue with you there." Nick set his palms flat on the tabletop. He was getting to the heart of his story. "So I get that call from Marv Cunningham. On the night Brett Topping was murdered, Sandy was with Bucky Travers at the Motel 6. All night. There are multiple witnesses, security camera footage from the parking lot, a credit card receipt."

"Credit card receipt? Couldn't he have been there with another woman?"

"It was Sandy's credit card—not Bucky's."

"*She* had to spring for the room? Jesus."

"The Buckys of this world don't usually have credit cards. Their credit histories are—let's just call it 'spotty.' Anyway, Sandy refused to give that as her alibi. She didn't want an alibi."

Jackie brought their breakfasts. While they dived in, Nick told Bell the rest. How Marv had explained the facts as he knew them, after which Nick realized he had an obligation to fly up and give Rhonda the news:

Sandy Banville's confession had to be bogus. She wasn't there that night. She didn't kill Brett Topping.

Once Nick had laid out the evidence, Rhonda had not hesitated. She called Sandy's lawyer and arranged for the woman's immediate release.

"Hated to interrupt the wedding that way," Nick said, "but I needed to move quickly." He used his napkin to wipe his mouth. "I know you and Jake Oakes put a lot of work into this case. Can't feel too good."

"It's the truth we're after, Nick. Our feelings don't matter." Bell finished up her second cup of coffee with a quick swallow. "But we're back at square one. If Sandy Banville didn't kill Topping—and we already know Deke Foley couldn't have done it, either—then who *did* kill him?"

Nick didn't have an answer, and he also had no wisecrack to mitigate the fact that he didn't have an answer.

Bell stared at her plate. The remaining trickle of bright yellow egg yolk had encircled the tiny brown island of corned beef hash.

"I'm beginning to think I might have an idea," she said. "But I'm going to need some help proving it."

He took a sudden interest in the handle of his cup, fiddling with it. "Guess you've got Jake Oakes for that."

"I could use the both of you."

He met her eyes. His were bright. "'I'm all yours."

"Might take a few days. How long are you around?"

"Well." He cleared his throat. "Thing is, Bell—I may be coming up here a little more often. The timing's up in the air right now."

She was surprised. "I thought you and Mary Sue were enjoying yourselves in all that sunshine."

"One of us is enjoying it. One of us isn't."

Chapter Thirty-five

That night, Malik had fallen asleep in Tyler's room. He had wandered in there after supper, even though, earlier in the day, Molly had gently warned him not to.

"This is somebody else's private space, Malik. Even Jake doesn't come in here." That was what she'd said to him when she found him there the first time, sitting cross-legged on the bare floor. He wasn't touching a thing. Just looking around, lifting his face to the meager sunlight sifting through the thin curtain on the sole window.

She had reached down for Malik's hand. She drew him out of the room.

"It's not polite," she had added. "Tyler's not here, so you can't ask him if he minds or not."

She'd had to retrieve him from there two other times last week. Both times, again, he wasn't bothering anything. Just sitting. Something about the space seemed to call to him. To calm him, even.

Tyler kept the room basically clean, if not specifically tidy; the room combined personal elements—a few library books, a twenty-four-pack of Dr Pepper—with impersonal ones: single bed, chest of drawers, director's chair with a badly fraying cloth back. Anybody could fit in here, Molly thought, without having to do much adjusting or recalibrating, and maybe that was the point. It was a simple fit. No edges, no odd corners, no rough patches. Maybe that's what Malik liked about it, too. It was impersonal. Everybody belonged here.

She came out of the bathroom and looked in Tyler's room. Yep—there was Malik. Again. Except this time he was curled up on his side on Tyler's bed. He was asleep.

Molly sighed. She went back out into the living room, where Jake was having his first post-supper Rolling Rock.

"Malik's back in Tyler's room," she said. "Fell asleep on the bed. That kid."

"Don't worry about it. Tyler won't be back 'til late. He's at an NA meeting in Blythesburg. He's found a good group over there. Real supportive."

"How'd he take it? The release of Sandy Banville, I mean."

"Don't know. We haven't talked about it."

"How about you? How are you taking it?"

Jake was quiet for a moment. "Guess I'm pissed off, to tell you the truth. A false confession is a waste of everybody's time and effort."

He was suddenly tired of talking about it. Brett Topping's killer might never be found and that offended him. The gun, too, might never turn up. And the file—another lost cause.

"Well," Molly said. "I do think I ought to keep Malik out of Tyler's room." She had sensed Jake's mood and wanted to change the subject. "Now that Tyler's going to be sticking around for a while."

"He likes Malik. He won't care."

"Yeah, well—Malik needs to learn about boundaries. I know that 'Malik' and 'boundaries' don't even belong in the same sentence—but I want him to be respectful of others. It's hard for him. Almost impossible. That's what they told me at the clinic in Charleston. I took him there a few years ago. They said empathy will always be an issue. The problem is, Malik only thinks about himself and what *he* wants."

"I know a lot of other folks with the same problem," Jake murmured. "And they don't have Malik's excuse." He drained the Rolling Rock.

"That was fast."

"Hey." He angled the chair so it faced the couch head-on. "Don't do that, okay? Don't nag like that."

She stood up. "You're right. I *was* nagging. And you know what,

Jake? You can do exactly as you please. You can sit here and get shit-faced every night. Night after night. Often as you like. Not my look-out." She began to walk around the coffee table.

"Where're you going?"

"To wake up Malik. Time to go. Dinner's over, dishes are done, you don't need a ride anywhere—so we ought to be heading home."

"Don't."

"Don't what?"

"Just don't." He looked away, as if meeting her eyes was more than he could take just then. "Please. Sit back down. A little while."

For a long moment, she didn't move. Then she sat.

In a low voice, she said, "What's going on, Jake?"

"What do you mean?"

"You know what I mean. Everything's going well for you, the way I see it. You're helping Tyler turn his life around. You and Bell have been a big help to the sheriff. She'll be calling you again. I'd bet on that. If Pam Harrison trusts you—and clearly you earned her trust—she'll do everything in her power to keep you busy. And it's work you like. Public safety. Law enforcement. It's dignified work. Work that makes a difference. It's not the same as being a deputy—but it's pretty damned close."

He nodded. "Can't argue with any of that."

"So—what's eating you?"

He lifted his shoulders, let them drop. "I'm just—just restless to-night. Kind of jumpy. Sorry I snapped at you. I do drink too much beer." He smacked his belly. "Proof's easy to spot."

She tilted her head, peering at him. "I don't think you've put on any weight. Anyway, that's not the point. It's not how the alcohol makes you look—it's how it makes you feel."

"And how's that?"

"You tell me. You're the one who drinks it. Not me."

He grimaced. "Lousy. That's how. But it turns things a little murky, you know? So they're not so clear to me. Sometimes—" He broke off his intended sentence. "Never mind."

"Speak your piece."

"Okay. Okay, then. I will." He put his hands on the tops of the wheels, moving the chair a little bit forward, a little bit back. Forward, then back. It had become a nervous habit. "Thing is, Molly—I like it when you and Malik come over. I like it a lot."

"Good thing." She smiled at him. "We're here all the time, seems like. Even Tyler's been making cracks about it. You might decide to start charging us rent."

He didn't smile back. "Don't."

"What?"

"Don't joke about it, Molly. Okay? Feels like you're making fun of me."

Her face clouded over. "What the hell are you talking about?"

"Joking about it. About you and Malik living here. When you *know* how much I've dreamed of—"

"Jake. No." She was warning him. It was a gentle warning, but a warning just the same. She didn't want to talk about this. "I really do need to pack up Malik and go. Bad weather's on the way. Supposed to rain all day tomorrow. Maybe even snow. Got to get the house ready. Cover the porch furniture, make sure there's weather stripping on the back door and the—"

"What are we doing here, Molly?"

No answer.

"Molly?"

Still no answer.

"What do you want?" he asked. "What?"

He would always wonder why it happened the way it happened that night. He would never know just what changed her mind in that moment, what combination of love or lust or simple curiosity—what, exactly, was he capable of?—had moved her, causing her to shed her cool reserve and her distancing poise. She rose from the couch and she walked over to him, and before he could take his next breath, she was sitting on his lap, her arms around his shoulders, and she was softly kissing his forehead, his eyebrows, his eyelids, his cheeks, and then his mouth. He felt the knot inside himself begin to go slack and it frightened him, but *This is what you want* he told himself, and he did and oh he did oh yes he did.

They went into his bedroom and she helped him take off his clothes:

shirt, shoes, socks, jeans. It wasn't awkward and he didn't feel self-conscious, being helped out of his clothes that way. Then he watched as she undressed, too, each moment its own separate and particular marvel. He touched her and he kissed her in the places where he had long yearned to touch her and to kiss her, and when it was all over he found that he had discovered a new truth—namely, that it would never be over, that lovemaking like this lived outside of time and time's rules.

He would have this feeling within himself forever, no matter what happened between them henceforth.

Chapter Thirty-six

Ellie turned the chair around to face the window. The morning was bright but cold. Winter would be here soon.

As if it ever left, she thought. That was how the past few years felt to her: like an unbroken spell of winter. Winter had sunk its teeth into the world and wouldn't let go. When you thought it was gone, it was really just around the corner. Lurking.

The girl had come by this morning. When Ellie heard the knock and opened the front door and saw her, she thought, *Oh, my, you look so much like Sandy now.*

Ellie had known Sara Banville for the girl's entire life. How had she missed it? How had she not seen that happening, the ordinary little miracle of a child beginning to look like her mother?

"You look like Sandy," Ellie said. She meant it as a kindness, a compliment, but Sara's face changed. She didn't seem to be pleased by the observation. More annoyed, if anything. But she shook it off. Ellie had always sensed that Sara liked her. Or maybe the girl just felt sorry for her. Because of what had happened to Tyler. What he'd become.

"We're moving," Sara said. Blurting it out. "Right away. We're going to go live with my grandma and grandpa in Pennsylvania. We have to get away, my dad says. Too much has happened here. With Alex. With my mom's confession. With everything. So we have to leave. I don't even have time to tell all my friends." She winced. The words kept tumbling out of her. "We'll have to come back at some point. Or at least my mom will. She's still in trouble. For making up a story. Lying to the police. But my dad says it's going to be okay. And for now—we have to go."

Ellie nodded. "Yes."

Sara was a young woman now. Not a kid. There was a hardness to her, the glaze of maturity. But Ellie could still see, beneath that shiny, brittle shell, the ghost of the girl she'd been, all long legs and uneven bangs. Running. Trying to keep up with Alex and Tyler. So many summers gone by.

"Good-bye, Sara," Ellie said. "You take care of yourself. And Alex—is he . . ."

"He's back in rehab. Another one." Sara shrugged. She turned to go, but she'd made a decision. She had one more thing to say and so she turned back. "I know my mom blamed Tyler. She thought Tyler got Alex into drugs. But you know what? It wasn't like that. I know for sure. That's not how it happened. Alex started first. My brother was just a lot better at hiding it. For a while. Not anymore."

Ellie nodded again. Did it matter, really? No. It did not. Nothing mattered anymore.

And then Sara was gone, flinging herself forward, long hair streaming out behind her. She could have been any young girl anywhere, Ellie thought, flying into her future, running on a nice street lined with lovely homes, or crossing a dirt road in a place like Briney Hollow.

Chapter Thirty-seven

A house was really two different houses. It was one house in the day-time. And another one in the middle of the night.

Bell had learned that essential truth early in her life. The succession of foster homes—some warm and comfortable, others grim and squalid—taught her well. The superficial differences didn't matter. Because in each house, she'd experience the same moment of discovery; she'd be awake at 2 A.M., 3 A.M., after everyone else had gone to sleep, and she'd wander into the kitchen and look around at all the familiar objects—coffeepot, wall clock, saucepan—and wonder what they were. She'd wonder, too, if she was even still on planet Earth.

She looked around.

She was sitting in her own kitchen. In the big stone house on Shelton Avenue. Her watch told her it was 2:47 A.M. She couldn't sleep.

She was haunted by two questions:

Who killed Brett Topping?

Where was the murder weapon?

At least half of the homicides in any given area—big city, small town—were never solved. Bell knew that. Back when she was a prosecutor, she'd never been able to rest easy with that statistic.

She couldn't rest easy with it now, either, even though she wasn't a prosecutor anymore.

She made a pot of coffee. Then she dumped the contents of her briefcase onto the kitchen table, so that she could sort through the items, one at a time, all over again: the interview notes Rhonda had emailed to her. The forensics report. The crime-scene photos. And the family pictures, the ones that captured the Toppings and their friends in happier days.

What am I missing?

She spread out an array of photos: the Toppings and the Banvilles at Disney World. The Toppings and the Banvilles on a whitewater rafting trip. In the front raft, flung aloft by a curling surge of furious current, were Brett and Ellie and Sandy and Rex, clad in colorful life preservers, the four adults looking apprehensive and slightly sick to their stomachs; in the raft behind it, lifted even higher, with paddles jutting out at crazy angles, sunlight glinting off their helmets, faces split wide open in joyful smiles, were Tyler and Alex and Sara.

Tyler and Alex and Sara.

Bell sifted through the photos again. She found the one she'd examined the other night at Jake's kitchen table: the two boys on their bikes, with Sara below them, apart from them, looking up enviously, wanting desperately to join them in their adventure.

Three kids from the same neighborhood. A brother and a sister, and the brother's best friend.

Wherever the boys go, she wants to go there, too.

Whatever the boys do, she wants to do it, too.

Bell picked up her cell. Tyler might be awake. Recovering addicts were almost always plagued by insomnia. If he wasn't awake, he wouldn't get her text until morning, but if he was . . .

She texted: *U up?*

He answered instantly: *Y*

A second later, her cell rang.

"What's going on?" Tyler said. "Good to know somebody else is up."

"You'll get back to a regular sleep pattern once you're over the hump," she said. "Got a question for you. When's the last time you saw Sara Banville?"

"Just the other day. I went to check on my mom. She came by the house."

"What for? I mean—what did she say while she was there?"

"Not much. She wanted to see if we were okay."

"Anything strange in her behavior?"

"Strange? Like how?"

"Whatever you can think of. No matter how trivial it seems."

He thought about her question.

"It was just a regular . . . hold on. She *did* do one thing that was kind of weird. When she came into the living room, she leaned a little bit to one side. Like she wanted to see around me."

"What was in the room?"

"Nothing unusual. Well, one thing. A deputy had just returned our computers. From when they'd searched for the file my dad kept. They were all stacked up on the coffee table—two monitors, two laptops, an iPad, a couple of CPUs."

"And you think that's what she was looking at."

"It wouldn't have occurred to me until you asked, but—yeah. Yeah. That's what she was focused on. Why?"

Bell had an instant to decide if she trusted this young man. He was, after all, a drug addict, a kid who'd stolen from his parents, lied to everyone, relapsed again and again.

But Jake believed in him. Jake was rooting for him. And Jake was no pushover.

"You were the Three Musketeers," Bell said. "And two of the Musketeers got involved with drugs. Sara followed you everywhere. Wouldn't she have followed you into drugs, too?"

He took a moment to digest the question. "But wouldn't I have known about it?" he asked dubiously.

"You didn't know about Alex, did you?"

Silence.

"No," he finally said. "We'd lost touch by then. He was in Morgantown, I was here." He was thinking. "But how did Sara hide her addiction?"

"You hid yours, didn't you? At first?"

Another chunk of silence.

"Yeah," he said. "I did. And I thought I was so damned smart. So cool." He cleared his throat. Bell could imagine him pushing back his regrets, one by one. They were big and they were heavy. "So what do we do now?"

"Sara is involved in this in some way. We need to question her to find out how. We'll go over there tomorrow."

"Better make it first thing."

"What do you mean?"

"They're leaving. The whole family. Sara came by the house yesterday and told my mom. Mom called me last night and we talked about it. Moving van's already in the driveway."

"Okay. First thing, then."

Bell ended her call with Tyler. She punched in another number. This time, she was certain that she was waking up the recipient; she was also certain that the recipient wouldn't mind.

"What do you need, Bell?" Rhonda said. Her bleary, sleep-soaked, "Yeah?" had quickly given way to total focus and alertness.

"Cell records for Sara Banville. Last two weeks is fine. We'll need a warrant to give the nudge to her cell provider. Can we do that right away?"

"I know just the judge. I'll have it for you shortly."

Bell checked her email an hour later. The scanned document was waiting in her in-box. She didn't bother printing it out; she just used a handy tool that predated all of the electronic folderol—her index finger—and went down the list of Sara's incoming calls.

And there it was: a call from the Bulger County Hospital on the day Deke Foley had regained consciousness. Sara was too smart to use her cell in the regular course of business, Bell had surmised. But Foley's hospitalization was a special circumstance. He needed to reach her. To thank her for services rendered.

Bell decided that she had to wait until at least sunrise. But the waiting was excruciating.

At 5 A.M. she said, "Screw it," and got ready to go. She grabbed her purse and car keys. Two minutes later she was driving through a dark town, headed to Jake's house to pick up Tyler.

Jake was awake, too. She found him sitting at the kitchen table next to Tyler. Both looked a bit scruffy. Both had cups of coffee in front of them. There was a nearly empty carton of store-bought doughnuts in the middle of the table, the kind with the white powder that always ends up on laps and shirtfronts.

"What? No beer?" Bell said. That was her hello. "You call that breakfast?"

Jake gave her a nod. *Good one,* his nod intimated. "And a cheery good morning to you, too, Bell," he said. "Hey, Tyler here was just filling me in about what's going on. I really want to come with you guys and see what's up with Sara Banville. But I'm stuck here. I told Molly she could leave Malik here this morning. She's got a doctor's appointment."

"We'll be fine," Bell said. "What time is she dropping him off?"

Jake looked sheepish. He glanced at Tyler, whose own gaze drifted over to the sink. Neither man wanted to meet Bell's eyes.

"What is it?" she said.

"Um . . . Molly doesn't have to drop him off," Jake said. "They're already here."

Bell still wasn't following. Her mind was on the case.

"Why would Molly and Malik be—" The light dawned. So that explained the big truck parked across the street. "Oh," Bell said. "Oh, okay." Once, three years ago, she thought she'd sensed something between the deputy and the EMT, caught a hint of their mutual attraction. But so much had changed since then. Could it be?

Hope so, Bell thought. *And I hope it works out for Jake. Nobody deserves a little happiness more than he does.* She took a closer look at his face, which had lost its drawn bleakness and, despite the early hour and the bad case of bed head, was almost radiant. *Maybe a lot of happiness.*

"Yeah," Jake said. "Malik bunked in with Tyler last night. Well, Tyler's floor."

Bell was impatient. "Great. Hey, Tyler—how about putting that coffee in a travel mug? Let's hit the road."

We're too late.

That was Bell's first frustrated reaction as they rounded the corner onto the street that featured, as its far end, the rambling house where the Banvilles lived. A large green Mayflower moving van was just chugging out of their driveway.

She entertained fantasies of following the van out to the interstate, then pulling up alongside it and yelling at Tyler to take the wheel as she launched herself out of the window and grabbed the truck's side mirror with one hand, while with the other she reached in and lunged across the seat, pummeling the driver until he pulled over.

Maybe I've watched a few too many Fast and Furious *movies.* They were her guilty pleasure.

But then she consoled herself: The moving van held only the Banvilles' possessions. The family would be traveling separately. Visible now in the driveway, now that the van wasn't blocking her view of it, was the elegant square of a bright red Range Rover. Puffy little clouds of exhaust fumes drifted from the undercarriage. Someone had come out earlier to warm it up for the long drive ahead.

Bell wondered, fleetingly, about the wisdom of having brought Tyler with her. But she wanted him here. If anyone could reach Sara, and maybe head off a dangerous confrontation, it would be Tyler.

Because he was Sara's old friend. Her buddy. Her companion on a million adventures on a million summer days. The restless young girl who had begged Tyler to let her come along with him and Alex and sometimes—her heart surely leaped up at the words—he'd say, *Yeah, okay.*

A million bike rides and a long starry dazzle of endless summer nights—before it all came apart. Before the path narrowed and darkened. Before the three friends, one by one, stumbled and fell.

The big front door of the house swung open. Rex and Sandy Banville hurried out, coats buttoned and scarves tied, suitcases in hand. Trailing them was Sara. She wore a yellow parka and, on her head, a jaunty plaid beret with a fuzzy little ball on top.

Sara, as the last in line, turned to lock the front door. Bell's eye was drawn to her large backpack.

"What are you going to do?" Tyler said. "We don't have any legal authority to—"

"Legal authority's overrated." Bell parked her car with a reckless disregard of its distance to the curb.

Rex Banville had almost reached the Range Rover. As Bell and Tyler approached him, ignoring the sidewalk and crunching across the wide, frost-locked lawn, he looked startled. Confused. And a little alarmed.

"What's going on?" he said. "Tyler—what are you doing here?"

"Mr. Banville," Bell said, "we need to talk with you. And you too, Sandy. And Sara."

Rex Banville was a square-faced, heavyset, ginger-haired man. Bell knew from her conversations with Nick that he was director of sales for a chemical company just outside of Charleston. She had accepted Nick's assessment that Rex Banville was largely oblivious. He didn't know what had become of his children. He didn't want to know.

He made a great deal of money but his travel schedule was brutal, unyielding; he was rarely home for more than a few days at a time. Bell had found herself wondering if all that travel was strictly necessary—or if Rex had simply been unable to bear watching his family unravel.

Because that was what had happened, even if he hadn't been around to witness it. This was where it had all been heading: to a bleak October morning, minutes before his world was destroyed.

"Talk to us about what?" Rex said. He sounded weary, not cross. "As you can see, we're moving. Heading to Pennsylvania. This has been such a traumatic time. We can't stay here in this neighborhood. With all that's gone on. Please—please, just let us go."

Bell glanced at Sandy. The woman stood a few feet away from her husband. Her face wore the stunned, vacant expression of the recently bereaved. She'd put down her suitcase and now she simply stood there, arms at her sides, her eyes watering from the cold.

"Let us go," Rex repeated. "Please."

"Sandy," Bell said, shifting her focus. "I know why you confessed to killing Brett Topping. I know who you were trying to protect. And I understand about wanting to take care of the people you love. Somebody did that for me, too. A long time ago. Somebody tried to get between me and the terrible thing I'd done."

"No." Sandy spoke in a soft whisper. "No."

"You have to tell the truth, Sandy." Bell moved a step closer to her. "You know what has to happen here."

Sandy bristled and shrank back, as if Bell were an assailant, bent on serious harm.

In a sense, that's exactly what I am, Bell thought.

"Sandy," Bell went on, "we know. We know about Sara and what she did. And we know how you tried to take the blame on yourself. You were willing to go to prison for her. You were going to do that, weren't you? For your daughter. Because you love her."

"Yes," Sandy whispered.

"When did you find out?" Bell asked. "When did you first know that Sara had killed Brett Topping? How did you—"

Sara's harsh voice crashed through the drifting web of soft voices.

"This is bullshit! Total bullshit!'" she declared. "Dad, let's *go.* Come on. Mom—shut the hell up! We don't have to talk to these people. They're *nothing.* Mom, just keep going. Get in the car."

Sandy's face made an infinitely slow turn toward her daughter.

"Sara," she said.

Sara must have seen something in her mother's eyes—a hopelessness, a quiet surrender to the inevitable—because she became even more combative. "Mom, do you hear me? This is *complete* and *utter* bullshit. You *know* me. What these people are saying is just—"

"Yes, my darling," Sandy said, interrupting her but in a gentle way, her serenity in vivid contrast to her daughter's agitation. "I do know you. It breaks my heart, but I do. I know what you're capable of. Somehow I knew right away, even before I found the gun in your room. The moment I heard about Brett, I knew. God help me, but I knew. It just took me a few days to figure out what I had to do."

Rex blundered toward his wife, reaching out a hand for her.

"Sandy," he said. He was a baffled, stricken man. "What are you talking about? This is our daughter. She couldn't have—"

"Oh, Rex," Sandy said. Her voice was pitched low, with sorrow spreading to every corner of it. "You know, too. You've always known, sweetheart. In your heart, you know. It's both of them, Rex. Both of our children. Our beautiful babies. Both of them are gone now."

Sara was almost shrieking. "I swear—if you two don't shut up, I'm going to—"

"Going to do what, Sara?" Tyler said. "What are you going to do? Shoot them? Kill them like you killed my dad?"

"Come *on,* Tyler," Sara said. "You can't believe any of this bullshit, either." She waved dismissively at Bell. "Who *is* this bitch, anyway? You and me—we're friends. We've been friends *forever,* right?"

"If it's not true," Tyler said calmly, "then show us what's in your backpack."

Bell would always wonder if, in that moment, Sara had considered making a run for it. The Range Rover was right there. The keys were in the ignition. Bell and Tyler would've lunged to stop her, of course, but the lawn was slippery with frost; it would take them a second or so to gain traction. Perhaps her parents would have tried to stop her, too, but Sara was young and fast.

Chances are, she would have made it to the vehicle. Backed frantically down the driveway. In three turns she'd be on the interstate, heading . . . anywhere. Anywhere but here.

But she didn't do that. Maybe, Bell thought, Sara was just tired. Tired of her life. If she wanted to see where her life was heading, all she had to do was think about her brother, Alex. Or Tyler—Tyler as she thought she knew him. Just another addict in a grubby gray sea of addicts.

Or maybe what stopped her was the sight of her mother's face, the skin stretched tightly over the bones, the grief easy to spot in her eyes. Sara was looking at that face now. It was the face of the woman who had confessed to a murder she didn't commit, just to protect her. The face of the woman who'd been willing to go to prison for her.

Bell slipped out her cell and pressed 911.

"It's not your fault, Mom," Sara said. "None of it. It's—it's this *place.* This damned town. There's nothing to *do* here, okay? Except get high. Except get so completely fucked up that you don't care anymore. About *anything.* And before you know it, that's all you're doing. Getting fucked up, every chance you get. But you've got to pay for it somehow, right? Come up with the cash? Because they don't give it away for free." Her voice was harsher now. Her eyes went to Tyler. "You thought you were pretty smart, didn't you? Working for Deke Foley. Well, guess what? Deke Foley thinks you're a *joke.* He *laughs* at you. You're a fucking *amateur*, okay? You and Alex, both. *I'm* the one he counts on." She folded her hands into fists. "And then—and then your dad had to start his stupid file. He didn't know who he was messing with. Fucking dumbshit." The wave of anger passed. She looked back at her mother again. "Before you know it, you don't have a choice anymore. You just don't."

Sara shrugged off her backpack, letting it drop to the ground. She went down on one knee. Unzipped it.

"No, sweetheart," Sandy whispered. Her instinct was still to protect her child, even now that it was too late. "Wait. Don't. Don't show them anything. You don't have to. They can't make you." A sob. "I've lost Alex. I can't lose you, too."

"It's too late, Mom," Sara said. Her voice was matter-of-fact. "It was too late a long time ago."

She pulled out the contents, one by one:

A black ski mask, black gloves, a black turtleneck, black slacks, black boots.

And a gun.

They would perform the requisite ballistics tests, but Bell knew what they would find: It was the gun that had killed Brett Topping.

Chapter Thirty-eight

Ellie was back in the doll room. It was time. Time to write a note to her son that would lay it all out, detail by detail. It would be messy—her thoughts were like leaves blown around in the wind, with no pattern— but there were things she needed to explain, to clarify. And yes: to justify.

So that he would understand her. So that he wouldn't despise her.

She had been very surprised when Tyler called a few minutes ago and told her about Sara Banville. He was on his way back to the police station. The deputies had arrested Sara. So that's what the commotion had been, all the fuss and confusion at the end of this long street with its pretty homes and its pristine yards.

There had been no sirens, but Ellie had heard the heavy rumble of the SUVs. When she parted the curtains at her bedroom window, she saw that the vehicles were black, with the county seal on their sides.

So that was it. Tyler had explained things to her: Sara had been working for Deke Foley. They all had worked for him, from time to time; everybody ended up working for Deke Foley, because it was the only way to keep getting drugs. Alex, Tyler, Sara. And so many others.

But Sara—Sara had fallen under his spell. It wasn't just to pay for her drugs.

Sara had shot Brett. Because he had dared to threaten Deke Foley with that file of his. And Sara was also the one who, hours later, held a gun on the janitor at the bank so that she could search Brett's office. She knew she was in the file: all the dates and times she had picked up drugs from Foley to sell.

Which meant that Brett had known about Sara. And all the others, too. The entire operation, all spelled out. What a burden he had carried. All that knowledge. The pain of it, the disappointment.

They still hadn't found the file.

Oh, Brett, Ellie thought. *Where did you hide it? Why didn't you tell me where you—*

And then she realized that, no, of course he wouldn't have done that. Knowing the location of the file would have put her at risk.

Dear Tyler, she wrote.

She heard someone coming up the stairs.

"Brett?" she whispered.

No. It couldn't be him.

It couldn't be him because he was dead. And even though she wasn't the one who had killed him, she had *intended* to kill him—which was the same thing as if she *had* killed him. Wasn't it?

She had contemplated killing Brett because she had to save him from more disappointment.

If she couldn't kill her son—and she'd tried, but she couldn't—then she would kill her husband.

But someone had beaten her to it.

False alarm, Ellie realized. No one was coming up the stairs. There was only silence, a soothing quietness that felt like a blanket that some well-intentioned stranger had arranged over a nervous world, tucking in the sides.

She finished her letter to Tyler:

Once a week, I drive up to Charleston and I put a basket of fresh flowers on Henry's grave. I don't think I ever told you about that. Brett knew. And he understood. He knew how much I loved Henry. Sometimes your father offered to come with me to the cemetery but I always said no. I want to be there alone so I can remember Henry.

When I went that day, I took the gun.

I wanted to make sure—this time—that I had the gun with me. Other times, when I have needed it, I didn't have it. I had to be sure. So that if Brett and I arrived home at the same time, I would have it.

My plan was to kill him. And then I would kill myself. And we would be together, and we would be free. And happy.

But I changed my mind. As I stood in front of Henry's grave that day and I thought about what a good, gentle man my brother was, I realized how disappointed he would be. If he knew what I was thinking. What I was planning. I stood there for many, many hours, remembering Henry's face and the sound of his laugh.

I could not do it. I didn't want the gun anymore, either. All these thoughts of killing—no. They were wrong. All wrong.

So I pushed the gun into the basket of flowers. Put it real deep. Down under all that dirt. No one would find it there. Who would ever look in a flower basket for a gun?

I drove home. It was very late.

I turned into our street and saw him. My beloved Brett. Shot to death.

I was surprised when Sandy Banville confessed. And now it seems like she didn't do it, after all. Now you tell me that it was Sara Banville, not her mother, who killed Brett.

Is there no end to the pain of this world?

I had every intention of killing your father. I wanted to save him. And wanting to kill is the same thing as killing. Wanting to is the same as doing.

I have to go now.

I hope you find your way, Tyler, through this wilderness you find yourself in. Like the boy Sam in My Side of the Mountain. *He came home again. And so can you.*

Love forever,
Mom

Ellie folded over the piece of paper. To her surprise, she'd filled up both sides.

She placed it on the small writing table. She had brought up a glass of water from the kitchen and now she drank it, very slowly, and methodically she took all the pills that the doctor had given her in the wake of her husband's death. A month's supply.

She was getting sleepy now. She leaned her head back. Morning sunlight was filling up the doll room, and everything was so bright. She closed her eyes. She felt something warm touching her face. She knew it was the sun but she pretended, for the last few seconds of her life, that it was Brett.

Chapter Thirty-nine

Rhonda Lovejoy sat down at her desk. She faced her visitors.

The prosecutor's office was awash in the powerful scent of freshly brewed French roast, an uppercut of an aroma that could spin your head around and maybe even knock you off your feet.

But there was a catch: Rhonda had run out of mugs.

She always tried to keep the supply of assorted cups washed and sparkling. But it had been an exceptionally busy few days. And so the dirty mugs had accumulated next to the coffeemaker, congregating in a grubby little club alongside the crusty spoons and empty Splenda packets.

"Word of warning," Rhonda said. "We're all out of clean cups."

"Clean cups?" Bell said. "Half the flavor comes from the buildup of old coffee over the years. You're ruining everything with this misguided clean-cup fetish."

Rhonda laughed. "Okay, then. Help yourselves. Just don't say you weren't warned. And not a word to the county health department."

They had all taken their seats as if they'd been preassigned: Bell and Sheriff Harrison in the two chairs facing Rhonda's desk, Jake on the right side of the desk, Nick on the sofa.

"So as you all know, Sara Banville was taken into custody this morning," Rhonda said. "Her mother will be facing obstruction of justice charges for failing to report what she knew about her daughter's crimes."

"But you still haven't found that file," Nick said.

"No." Rhonda picked up a pencil. She tapped the eraser end lightly against the desktop. "Frankly, I'm not sure we ever will."

"Damned shame," the sheriff muttered. "That information could've put Deke Foley permanently out of business. Done a better job of it than his car accident—which, I'm sad to report, he seems to be rapidly recovering from. Doctors over at Bulger County Hospital say he might be released in another few weeks. Then he'll surely be back to his old drug-dealing ways. Can you beat that?"

"Maybe we can slip a few bucks to his physical therapists," Jake said. "Have them go extra-hard on him. They sure as hell never let up on me. I used to call the PT room the medieval torture chamber. You know what they said when they heard that? They said, 'Don't tempt us, buddy. We can make it a lot worse.'"

Bell stood up. She was too restless to sit.

"Appreciate the update, Rhonda," she said, "but if there's nothing else—"

"There is." Rhonda let the pencil drop. She leaned forward at her desk, clasping her hands. "Sit back down, Bell. Won't take long."

Bell complied.

"Sheriff Harrison had an idea that struck me as downright inspired," Rhonda went on. "I wanted to run it past the people in this room."

Eyes swiveled toward Harrison. She wasn't typically the source of inspired ideas. This was a surprise. Was there an actual personality hidden beneath all that brown polyester and the permafrost frown?

"It's become painfully obvious," Rhonda said, "that we're badly understaffed these days. Sheriff's department, EMTs, and, of course, the prosecutor's office, too. The county budget is just stretched too thin. And so when I heard that Nick here was planning on moving back to Acker's Gap, it seemed like a good time to consider Pam's proposal."

Another surprise.

Bell looked over at Nick. He sat stiffly on the sofa, both feet on the floor, hands on his thighs. The expression on his face was unreadable.

The prospect of his return to Raythune County made her happy, but it also made her anxious. What about Mary Sue?

"So let's hear about your proposal," Jake said. He moved his chair backward and forward.

"Okay. Here goes." Rhonda's tone was businesslike. "Assuming you and Bell are interested, we'd be willing to make the consultant positions with the sheriff's department permanent. And we'll add you, Nick, if it strikes your fancy. You three would be on call for us. Major cases, special investigations—whatever comes up. The county commission agreed. With all that's going on around here, we can bend the rules a little bit if it helps keep the peace. And clear some cases faster. Which, given the track records of the people involved, it surely will. We could even rustle up a little pay. Plus take care of your expenses. What do you say?"

Bell looked at Jake. He shrugged. She looked at Nick. He had tilted his head to one side and appeared to be considering it.

"One thing," Bell said.

"What's that?"

"Being on call is fine, but I'd want to be able to pursue my own investigations, too. For instance—Utley Pharmaceuticals."

Rhonda nodded. "I've got no problem with that. Sheriff?"

"Me, neither."

The prosecutor was eager to hear answers from the other two. "Nick? Jake? What do you all think of the proposal?"

Jake grinned. "I'm in."

Now it was time to check with the former sheriff. Time was, Bell reflected, when she'd have known what Nick was thinking without him having to speak out loud. That was how close they'd been. Their working relationship had been a thing of mutual trust and respect and—okay, she'd acknowledge it, but only to herself and never out loud—love.

She loved Nick Fogelsong. He was the father she'd never had. She didn't know him nearly as well as she once had, but the love remained. She was glad to find that out, even though it was a stealth epiphany.

"Sounds good," Nick said.

"Okay, then." Rhonda stood up behind her desk. "We'll iron out the particulars in a day or so. I've got to run."

Jake snickered. "Home to hubby, right?"

Rhonda gave him an admonishing look. "As a matter of fact, Mister Smart Ass—no. I'm meeting Lee Ann Frickie over at Evening Street Clinic. It's her first time volunteering there. Bell arranged it with Glenna Stavros. She's the head nurse. Bell suggested that that might be a more constructive way for Lee Ann to spend her time than arguing with me about church and state. And Lee Ann, bless her heart, agreed."

The prosecutor winked at Jake. "And *then* I'm going home to 'hubby,' as you so quaintly put it," she declared. "Damned happy about it, too."

Bell caught Nick at the courthouse door. She'd agreed to give Jake a lift home, but he needed to stop in the bathroom. So Bell used the time for a quick word with her new partner.

Or was it her old partner?

Never mind. They'd figure it out.

"You think this'll work?" she asked him.

"Time will tell."

"Kind of a shock. Finding out that you're coming back."

"It was a shock to me, too, Belfa. I hadn't had a chance to tell you. Sorry about that. Just got the call from Mary Sue last night. I had to notify the courthouse first thing. Address change for my pension checks." He swallowed hard. "She wants a divorce."

"Nick—I'm so—"

He held up a hand. He was never comfortable with sympathy. "I knew it might be on the way—just not this fast. Truth is, it's good news. She's doing so much better. Really thriving down there. But she says our relationship dynamic—that's the phrase she used, which makes me think she's been sitting on a couch in some fancy office and pouring out her heart to somebody she pays by the hour—our 'relationship dynamic' is way out of whack. Apparently I can't see her as anything but a patient. As somebody dependent on me. So, fine. I'll let her go. If she's happy, then I'm happy."

You don't look very happy, Nick, Bell thought.

"By the way," she said, "you were right."

He waited for her to elaborate.

"About me and my need to go charging into the Next Big Thing," she continued. "I've decided to hold off on Utley Pharmaceuticals for a while. Need to figure out first what I want for my life and how I can get it." She grinned. She couldn't resist. "Maybe I'll spend a little time on one of those couches in a fancy office."

"Glad to hear it," he said. "I'm not opposed to psychiatrists—you know that. Just don't go around talking damned nonsense about 'relationship dynamics.'"

"Promise."

I'm going to tell him, she suddenly thought. *Someday soon, I'm going to tell him why I confessed and went to prison.*

No wonder he didn't confide in me about his marriage, about coming back to Acker's Gap. I don't confide in him *anymore, either.*

They heard Jake's approach, the *squinchsquinch* sound of wheels on the old wooden floor of the courthouse corridor.

"You know what, Nick?" she said, hurrying her words so she could get them out before Jake joined them. This was private. "Working together again—it'll feel good."

"That it will."

He waved at Jake and took his leave.

Bell and Jake had almost reached her car when they heard it: the heavy, plaintive wail of a siren, growing steadily more distant as the emergency vehicle raced away from the downtown area toward the unknown catastrophe.

Her cell rang.

She answered. Jake watched her face.

"My God," she said, after listening for several minutes. "My God, Tyler—I'm so sorry. I'll be right there."

She ended the call. She stared at the phone as she spoke.

"He went over to his mom's house," Bell said. "No lights on, no sounds from anywhere—nothing. He was concerned. He ran up the stairs to the attic room. And he found her. Overdose. She'd used the pills they gave her at the hospital that night after the shooting. She'd been saving them up."

Jake winced, dropped his head. "Jesus Christ," he murmured. "Jesus Christ."

Chapter Forty

Bell and Tyler sat side by side on the steps leading to the attic room.

The EMTs had taken Ellie's body twenty minutes ago. When it was over, and the ambulance had cleared the driveway, Tyler asked Bell to stay with him for a little while.

The first thing Bell had done, after Tyler shared his mother's letter, was to call the caretaker at the cemetery in Charleston. She told him to check the flower basket on the grave of Henry Combs. She didn't want to risk anyone else finding the gun and being injured.

The caretaker—his name was Rafe Hensley—called Bell back in eight minutes. He'd found it, he told her in a shaky voice.

Bell advised him to put it in a safe place. Her next call was to the Kanawha County Sheriff's Department. A deputy would retrieve the gun within the hour.

That made Tyler feel a bit better. But he was still troubled, he told Bell, by the fact that they had never found the file.

"My dad gave everything he had to put together that file," he said. "He ended up dying because of it. And we don't even know where the hell it *is*."

"Sheriff Harrison and her deputies will keep looking," Bell assured him. "But some things, Tyler—some things, you can't do anything about. You just have to learn to live with them." She felt like looking around to see who'd said those words. Didn't sound like Bell Elkins. "Hey," she added. "Can I ask you a question?"

He nodded.

"When we picked up Sara, she said it was the town's fault. That so many kids around here get involved with drugs, I mean. What do you think?"

"I think one excuse is as good as another." Tyler shook his head. "She also said that it was too late. For anything to change. Well, I can't believe that. If I do, I'm totally screwed. Might as well go back to using."

Restless, the shock of his mother's passing still moving through him like waves of fever, Tyler abruptly stood up. "Can we go into the doll room? One more time? I don't think I'll ever come up here again. Without my mom, it's—it's just a room."

They stood in the middle of the small space. The EMTs had shoved the chair and the table against the wall as they did their work. In all the haste and tumult, some of the books had been knocked off the shelves.

The room was filled with a soft golden light. Bell could see why Ellie Topping had spent so much time up here.

"She loved it, didn't she?"

"Yeah," Tyler said. "And because of that, my dad never bothered her up here. He always paid attention to what she loved. And speaking of love . . ." He touched a purple paperback spine that he'd spotted on the bookshelf. "This was my absolute favorite when I was a kid."

Bell turned her head sideways to read the title: *My Side of the Mountain* by Jean Craighead George.

Tyler smiled. "I know the first line by heart: 'I am on a mountain in a tree home that people have passed without ever knowing that I am here.' My mom read that book aloud to me all the time when I was a kid."

It hit them both at the same moment.

Brett knew what Ellie loved. Ellie loved Tyler. And Tyler loved *My Side of the Mountain.*

Bell let him be the one to pull the book off the shelf. He immediately felt the slight bulge in the back.

Taped to the final page was a thumb drive.

"Where's your laptop?" Bell asked, trying to keep her excitement at a reasonable level.

"Living room."

"Let's go."

Thirty seconds later, Tyler thrust in the thumb drive. The small symbol appeared on the screen. He clicked on it.

Nothing.

"It's password-protected," Tyler said with a groan. "That was my dad—Mister Security. Comes from working in a bank, I guess."

"Our forensics people can probably crack it," Bell said.

"Bet they can." Tyler was still disconsolate. "But you know what? I kinda wanted to do it first. Because it would mean I knew my dad well enough to guess the password." It was a tiny point of pride, he explained. It was a last link to his parents, proof that he was part of them, proof that he hadn't been the total selfish bastard that everyone thought he was—proof, in fact, that their love for him was justified, even though they would never know it.

"I bet it's a name," Tyler said. "Somebody important to Dad."

"Give it a try."

He nodded and typed: ELLIE

Nothing.

He tried again: TYLER

Nothing.

And then he made his way through a flurry of other way-too-obvious guesses, words he knew wouldn't work but that he had to try, anyway, just to eliminate them:

ELLIETOPPOING

TYLERTOPPING

BRETT

BRETTTOPPING

TYLERBRETT

BRETTTYLER

Nothing, nothing, nothing, nothing. And nothing.

"Okay. Let me think," Tyler said. "I remember getting this dog when

I was seven. Only had him a year, though, before he died. We really loved that dog. So maybe . . ."

He typed in the dog's name: WINIFRED

Another try: WINNIE

Nothing.

Now he was officially out of ideas.

He reached up to close the lid, slowly running his thumb along the top edge of the screen. Reluctant to give up. "I keep thinking of all the things he loved," Tyler said. "It's like this long, long chain. If you start with me—the most recent thing he loved—you can work your way back."

"What do you mean?"

"Well, like I said, first there's me. Before that, there was Mom." He took a deep breath. "My God—he loved her so much."

Bell sensed that he was letting his thoughts unspool a little more, the thread traveling back and back and back. "My mom told me once about going to a doctor for this knee pain she was having," he said. "The orthopedist explained to her that when the cartilage wears away, it leaves one bone rubbing against another bone. That's what creates the pain. But my mom didn't see it that way. 'You know, Tyler,' she said when she got home, 'to me that sounds like family. Bone on bone. It's like the very core of us, the essence, is rubbing up next to the people who matter most. Who are as close to us as our own bones. And sometimes that can be painful. Painful *and* wonderful, both.'"

"Your mom came from a big family, right?"

"Oh, yeah. Back in Briney Hollow. After her mom died, she helped take care of her brothers and sisters. It was total chaos, all the time. A real circus. But she loved it, too. Loved the craziness. All of them packed inside this little house." Tyler grinned. "Man, the stories she used to tell me about those days!" He looked at the laptop screen, and then he looked at Bell. "You know what? There was one person she loved way before I was born. And way before she even met my dad. A long time before. And my dad knew that. Because he loved us, he paid attention to what we loved. That's how he knew about *My Side of the Mountain*. And that's how he knew how much she loved her brother."

Bell remembered the thought she'd had at Rhonda's wedding. *If you love someone, you know what they love best in all the world.*

"Then maybe . . ." she said.

"Yeah." His eyes were bright. "Maybe."

He typed in: HENRY

The file leaped to life.